# THE DIAMOND GAME

Dennis T. Cosgrove

DELENOVA
PUBLISHING

Library of Congress Control Number 2025590846


Paperback First Edition 2025


ISBN (print)   979-8-9985676-3-6
ISBN (ebook) 979-8-9985676-4-3
ISBN (audio)  979-8-9985676-1-2


Published by Delenova Publishing, Fort Myers, Florida, United States of America

*Acknowledgements*

My family and friends' support and encouragement made this book possible. I appreciate every one of you. I sincerely thank John Kuchta and Jaime Camacho for their indispensable help in creating this book. Huge thanks to my brilliant editor, Annie Jenkinson, for her guidance and wisdom.

*To Lenore*

# Prologue

FBI Headquarters, Washington, D.C.

"I'm done here. You're free to go but I don't know what awaits you out there. Do you?" the examiner asks as he reaches across, detaching the constricting belt from my torso, then deflating and releasing the blood pressure cuff on my upper right arm.

Finally, he removes the finger clamp.

"My destiny," I say almost nonchalantly, looking up at him but seeing only the top of his head. He's still busying himself, probably thinking of the next appointment as he positions the items neatly back into his case, everything in its rightful place.

"Huh? What was that?"

Just as I surmised, he clearly wasn't listening, leaving me to ponder the value of asking anything in the first place. Why even bother?

The final piece of equipment now back in his case, he snaps shut its twin latches.

"Nothing," I say, now standing to put on my sport coat, then I walk over to the lock box outside the examination room to retrieve my weapon—a semi-automatic Glock pistol—as well as my handcuffs and FBI credentials. As I open the main entrance door, I emerge into brilliant sunlight, automatically delving into a coat pocket for my sunglasses.

It's already late afternoon by now, but the sun is still beating down harshly on the concrete sidewalk, the hot humid air hitting me upon turning the corner away from that cold granite building. It's one of those unbearably hot and breezeless summer days in Washington, D.C., but I don't care. In fact, I sort of like the oppressiveness, the intensity of it all.

Anything is better than the relentless cold and darkness of winter.

I stop and glance back once clear of the building, reading the inscription carved into the granite facade above the entrance: 'Federal Bureau of Investigation Headquarters.'

I have survived the day, and I'm still an agent, an FBI Special Agent to be exact.

There is a lot more work waiting for me out there, but it can continue to wait until tomorrow. For today, one thing is certain: the polygraph exam is over, and it has cleared me.

The thought brings the slightest hint of a smile as I gradually leave the building behind me, my pace quickening, stepping swiftly along the crowded sidewalk on the approach to the Metro entrance. There, I will board the train to carry me far away from FBIHQ, away from the district and toward my hotel in Pentagon City, to whatever fates may greet me there.

# Chapter 1

New York Police Department Archives, 1992

"Ms. Jennifer, did you find what you were looking for?" asks the elderly well-dressed gentleman attired in a suit and tie that could date from the 1930s or 40s.

The young lady doesn't look up. Instead, she continues to fixate on a microfiche reel of 1930s New York City newspaper articles.

"Yes, I think so. But if I may ask, how did you know him? My grandfather, Thomas Cosgrove. Did you work with him? What was he like as a detective? I need ..."

The young lady finally looks up from the screen to find the man has gone, as if he were never there. She narrows her eyes as if momentarily confused, evaluating.

The desk in the NYPD archives where she sits is littered with papers, energy bars, and water bottles. She appears to have been there for some time, perhaps all day since it opened.

Another voice startles her. "Ms., you do understand we are closing in a few minutes? You can come back tomorrow," the woman tells her.

"What? But the gentleman who knew my grandfather said there was no rush, that I could stay and should feel free to continue my work, my research. I don't know when I can come back here again," she says politely, but not pleading despite her slightly urgent tone.

"Huh, what gentleman are you talking about?" the woman says, glaring. "There's me, and that's it. There is no gentleman working here."

The young lady looks back to the screen, frantically copying and compiling what she has gathered. "OK. Well, I will leave as soon as I can put my things together. Thank you for the access. I would like to come back sometime, and I ..."

The woman employee has already turned and is walking away, her purposeful stride making it all too apparent she wants to close up the place and head home.

Jennifer quickly gathers up her papers and belongings and runs toward a waiting taxi. The driver checks out the young woman, athletic and sharply dressed, as she enters his cab.

Like all drivers, he at first attempts small talk with his attractive fare.

She shuts him down immediately. No, she is having none of that.

She puts her reading glasses on, looking intently at one of the printed-out news articles, focusing on a grainy black-and-white photo which looks to be some sort of beach scene.

New York City, August 1937

A search party has been scouring every inch of the beach for evidence of little four-year-old Joan Kuleba, vacationing with her aunt.

It has been a grueling day with nothing to show but a small pair of shoes and a neatly folded beach jacket reposing on the sand, the only trace that little Joan was even here earlier in the day. Her aunt was making lunch when Joan ventured out onto the sandy beach to play, and no one has seen the girl since.

The search party, exhausted, and drenched in sweat from their heavy wool uniforms and the heat of another New York summer day, accept no other conclusion than that Joan must have wandered into the rough surf and drowned; her small body will almost certainly wash up along the shore in a few days' time, so goes the consensus.

"There is just nothing here to pursue. We've exhausted our search," is the short statement of defeat given by the police to Joan's aunt and the news thirsty press.

Off in the distance, Detective Thomas Cosgrove, a tall, and stern-looking Irishman in his mid-thirties, is trudging through high marsh and swampy waters toward an abandoned looking dilapidated plank board bungalow.

The search party has already left, with the sun slowly setting.

Cosgrove finds himself alone. He slowly draws his service revolver from underneath his suit jacket as he is nearly at the door of the abandoned bungalow. With one powerful kick, the paper-thin door flies open, and he forcefully charges into the darkening room.

Something isn't right. Suddenly, there is a flash of movement in the shadowy and broken-down bungalow, movement from another room. A figure emerges out of the darkness.

Cosgrove doesn't wait. He lunges at the figure, throwing him to the ground, and quickly cuffing him, all over in seconds. The killer, a fifty-seven-year-old painter, grabbed the four-year-old from the beach where she was playing alone, immediately silencing her screams by strangling her before taking her body to the basement of the bungalow.

This is what the perpetrator, Simon Elmore—now in custody —has confessed to Lt. Cosgrove, according to the newspaper accounts.

Little Joan Kuleba isn't the only young girl to have been killed in New York this summer. Yet, no one even considered the possibility that there was a serial killer on the loose, preying on young, innocent children. No one except Detective Cosgrove.

# Chapter 2

Monterey Beach, California, 1992

The magic of the beach is an illusion, its secrets never revealed. I am the lone runner left on the sand there, cassette player in my grip, listening to a Russian language tape. I quicken my pace to finish the long but exhilarating run. The sun is setting; I need to get off this beach.

My attention shifts from the cassette player, my eyes abruptly caught by the motion of someone in the distance in the empty beach parking lot.

There is one vehicle with someone familiar, someone dressed in suit and tie, standing next to it; his arms are folded, and both the driver and passenger doors are fully open.

It's FBI Special Agent Paul Campo, a seasoned veteran agent assigned to the Monterey Bay Field Office. He says nothing upon my approach.

There are no words at my side either; we both know how it is. Simply, I remove my headphones and enter the vehicle.

The driver and I, his only passenger, remain silent as if understanding one another instinctively, despite the unexpected nature of the veteran agent and his vehicle appearing in the beach parking lot. He waits there for me to finish my run, or so it appears.

I am an FBI Special Agent, temporarily assigned to Monterey Language School, studying Russian. After a few minutes, I break the silence to ask, "Paul, what is it?"

"Kidnapping. Last night in Mountain View; it's all hands on deck for this one. You won't be back in language class until this is over. The director's called the boss, and he's mobilized everyone, no exceptions. When we arrive at our command post in Palo Alto, they'll brief us; there's more than one already set up."

Upon arrival at the Bureau's office in Palo Alto, over thirty agents and support personnel are busy setting up phones, computers, whiteboards. Campo and I enter the room almost unnoticed. Finally, a senior agent approaches us, giving us the background of the case and that of the kidnapped victim. "Strap in," he tells us at the end of the briefing. "I don't think we'll be getting any sleep until this is over."

Campo turns to me. "Your handcuffs, keep them with you."

Though my head nods, there's nothing to say. More than a hundred agents have been assigned to this case, and Campo knows what he wants.

But why will I need handcuffs? For what?

It's better to say nothing, out of respect for the veteran agent.

Charles Geschke, owner and founder of Adobe Systems, vanished without a trace from his Mountain View, California residence a couple of days prior, with no leads, no suspects, no information as to his whereabouts, or even if he's still alive.

Some unknown suspect has been making phone calls to Geschke's only daughter from random telephone booths throughout the San Francisco Bay area.

The suspect is demanding the daughter delivers $675,000 in unmarked banknotes to a location he'll soon relay. The kidnappers are not allowing the daughter to hear her father's voice as proof of life, something that's always troublesome; why hand over such a hefty sum when the victim may be dead already for all we know? But there's no delicate way to deliver this view to Geschke's family, of course. A small team of agents is now working out of the Geschke home, trying to keep the wife and daughter calm. While the family is very wealthy, they drive modest vehicles, also living in an unassuming home in Mountain View.

One thing is for certain: they were not expecting any of this.

The Bureau has assigned Campo, me, and three other agents to cover the southern reaches of its San Francisco Field Office territory. So, we receive orders to go to the town of Santa Cruz and wait for further instructions. We have already raced in unmarked Bureau vehicles to several phone booths from which our suspects made calls in the previous days, but the kidnappers were long gone by the time we arrived. We are always too late, and meanwhile, the clock is still ticking.

Day Four begins with the agents growing weary. Exhaustion, frustration, and boredom set in. We need a break, and more than a modicum of luck.

With each day, the chances of finding Geschke alive grow dimmer.

Finally, on this fourth day, Campo receives a call from the Command Post.

He briefs our small team, explaining that the SF Office, and its head Special Agent in Charge Richard Held, are under intense pressure to find Geschke alive.

A kidnapping of Exxon executives on the East Coast, New Jersey, took a bad turn, the Bureau arriving too late and finding the victims buried alive, suffocated to death.

There can be no repeat of that abysmal occurrence; no matter what it takes, Geschke must be found and rescued, breathing. We cannot have a second failure, and another dead victim.

Unexpectedly, as the sun sets over Monterey Bay on Day Four, the Bureau radio comes to life, informing us to race as quickly as possible toward the Monterey area where the ransom drop will occur. With an agent hidden in the vehicle's trunk and a surveillance team in hot pursuit, the victim's daughter races to the assigned location in her car, transporting the requested bag of banknotes. There are stacks of them to be exact, all $675,000 drawn from a simple check written by the daughter out of her own bank account.

Predictably, hidden inside the bag are tracking devices.

Campo tells me he'll drive his Bureau vehicle, a meticulously clean and well-maintained Pontiac Trans-am. He watches me closely as I enter the passenger side.

I already know he detests dirt and grime, bearing a reputation of being a bit OCD. No one dares comment to him or to anyone else about this quirk out of respect for the older agent.

As we listen to the chatter on the Bureau car radios, Campo and I realize we're heading to Marina Beach where three days earlier, I commented to Campo that Geschke was probably being held in our area. In a half-joking manner, I'd said to him, "We'll be back here in a few days dealing with this shit. Mark my words. We'll be seeing this place again soon."

Campo says nothing, seeing my head shake in disbelief as the news comes over the radio. "A beach, it just had to be a beach," I say, sighing under my breath.

"Doesn't matter. Just be ready," he tells me.

It is now dark, a typical cold, foggy night along the Monterey Bay coast but this time, there's extreme tension as the most critical phase of the kidnapping is about to begin.

The suspects have given precise instructions for the money drop, and the SWAT and surveillance teams must carry out their jobs with extreme caution to prevent arousing suspicion and scaring away the perpetrators. Geschke's life is on the line.

This is the time to get it right.

Campo and I stay on the perimeter, parked along a quiet service road close to the highway which runs along the coastline, toward the city of Monterey.

"What now Paul?" My voice breaks the silence of our vehicle as we stare out, pensive.

"What now?" He pauses. "We wait, and hope," he finally responds.

As all good plans go, this one is no different. But good plans don't necessarily lead to successful outcomes, do they? Good plans often do go awry, unfortunately.

Who could have predicted this? From the radio chatter, the money drop has been made, but there's been a massive hitch; the surveillance teams weren't in position.

So, the bag of money is gone, vanished, our best chance of pursuing the kidnappers already lost because of the surveillance team's poor execution of what we all agreed.

There are no signs of the suspects, and even worse, the small tracking devices concealed inside the bag are not functioning. Even a malfunction of the trackers would have been better than this, but these devices appear wholly flat, perhaps as if they haven't been charged.

The radio chatter is frantically reporting on the missing bag.

No suspects, no bag, no money and worst of all, no victim.

Campo remains strangely calm in spite of it all, and I can only look at him, perplexed at his demeanor, yet simultaneously impressed. This guy just doesn't get rattled.

While we could sit mulling over how this could have gone so badly wrong—and filling the air with blame and expletives—we have no time or inclination to give to such thoughts.

"Time to get to work," I say to Campo. "This is our area, so let's get the Sheriff's Office guys out here with their tracking dogs and find this guy. He, or they, are out there somewhere in those dunes. Or they've already made their escape by water, which is unlikely."

Minutes later, now nearly midnight, Monterey County Sheriff's Deputy Sgt. Vance Stevens shows up with his tracking dog. I set off immediately with them.

On our own, Sgt. Stevens and I scour the vast expanses of the dunes, a sand factory and several adjoining abandoned structures requiring thorough checking and clearing.

Stevens, a former Army Ranger, is soft-spoken and not easily unsettled; and I like him immediately. Although he's a bit of a loner in his department, and an outcast of sorts, I've already heard he's competent and cool under pressure, exactly how I find him to be.

Meanwhile, the SWAT Team, kitted out with all their latest equipment, is low crawling along the dunes. Though there's no sign of our stealthy fugitive(s), we manage to spot these SWAT guys with no trouble at all, bringing a wry smile and an inward groan. In the distance, they look almost comical as they move across the sand in unison, with their inching bug-like movements as they follow each other so closely. The moonlight silhouettes me and Stevens from our high vantage point, allowing us to survey the area from the top of the largest dune.

The SWAT Team is a well-trained group accustomed to working as a team.

Despite this, however, they are clearly out of their element in the vastness of the expansive beach and sand dunes, all moving too slowly and cautiously for my liking. As for me, I feel comfortable working like this, and alone. Here, it's only me, Stevens, and Argo, his obedient Belgian Shepherd. I glance over at Stevens, his facial expression showing a cool, confident, but not arrogant operator. There is something familiar about the entire scene.

I shake it off as déjà vu, thinking, SWAT will find this kidnapper or the ones who picked up the ransom package. I hope. I turn to Stevens and remark, "Vance, it's the first time we've worked together but it's not our last. I can feel it."

He looks back at me, trying to process my words, and only shrugs. We need to focus on the mission for now and clear the sand factory and its adjacent buildings.

Stevens, his tracking dog, and I continue searching alone, heading through the vast dunes through the night which offers us no break, no time to rest, no letup.

God knows, losing $675,000 of the family's money is bad enough; if we also let our victim slip through our grasp, that will not be good.

Geschke's life is on the line. We are his only chance.

# Chapter 3

After the all-night exhausting search, the sun is finally rising, illuminating Monterey Bay and its spectacular coastline with the City of Monterey off in the distance, several miles from the sand dunes. Out among those dunes, agents and several sheriff deputies are still working.

Campo and I return to his vehicle, unsure about the next step. We are both exhausted, as are all the law enforcement officers, having spent the night in what seems to have been a fruitless exercise. Still, we have no one in custody, and the victim's whereabouts are unknown. To say things are not looking good would be a grievous understatement.

Several Bureau vehicles are scattered around the area, with agents talking among themselves; their primary supposition is along the lines that our suspect(s) may have hunkered down somewhere in the dunes, perhaps waiting for us to leave.

Finally, the radio crackles to life. There is hope.

A SWAT agent has found a guy hiding in a tree, clinging to its limbs.

The guy is exhausted, disoriented, and shaking from enduring so many hours in the damp night. It doesn't take much to get a confession out of a person in such a state.

So, he soon tells the agent that his name is Mohammed Albulkari.

He admits, along with one accomplice, to having kidnapped Geschke.

With agents and vehicles scattered across many miles, there's no time for meetings; the race is on. As soon as Campo and I hear the news on the radio, we jump into his vehicle and race toward the small town outside of Gilroy, a quiet bedroom community. The town of Hollister, mostly Hispanic, is but a short drive south of San José. There, the SWAT team will make the entry to the house where Geschke is being held, and we're told we should stay well clear, several blocks away on the perimeter. We must wait, told not to move.

Campo surveys his vehicle as he drives, finding it not as clean as he likes, but at least the sand and rough terrain didn't inflict any damage, something for which he is thankful.

He adjusts the windows, opening them slightly, then closing them a bit, before opening them some more. Up, down, up, down, the fragmented and jolting dance of panes of glass tries to soothe his OCD but is unsuccessful; they are electric windows, so they move too fast and too suddenly for his precise requirements, leaving him sighing. Achieving the correct fractional opening is impossible, especially as he is also the one doing the driving.

Luckily for me, I am able to doze off in the passenger seat and feign ignorance of it all, resting in a sort of semi-unconscious mode from the lack of sleep over the past days and from the extreme physical exertion in those wretched dunes. Resting my elbow on the now open window, my scream pierces the night, abruptly awoken by a long stab of excruciating pain.

That goddamn glass has just closed, taking my hand with it!

Campo realizes, frantically searching and fumbling for the window control, sending our car swerving erratically across lanes of traffic. My eyes are wide as the vehicle careens hard, seeking to avoid colliding with an oncoming agriculture truck.

Finally, Campo regains control, somehow setting us back on the right side of the road.

He doesn't say a word to me as if it's not happened, and in return, there's nothing I can really say to it either, except for, "Well, at least I'm awake now."

And he just carries on driving as my heartbeat resettles to its normal pace.

Soon, Campo finds a quiet residential street a few blocks away from the house which is thought to be where Geschke is being held. Campo seems at ease, almost as if he's on a pleasurable road trip. "Get your popcorn. SWAT will finish this thing," he casually remarks. I feel my hand still throbbing a bit. I'm not so sure about SWAT for some reason ...

"You think so? This is how it ends? With us just sitting in this car, not even bystanders. I suppose it's all right as long as they get him out in one piece," I remark.

It's the only fragment of hope remaining.

In a fashion not unlike most so-called "tactical" teams that in theory are supposed to react quickly, effectively, and in a stealth mode, the operation gets bogged down in the planning phase, all while the clock is ticking. Campo and I, both veterans of SWAT teams from prior assignments, figure as much as there's an eerie silence on the radio.

Akin to how the jungle falls silent when a predator creeps through the dense trees, all radio chatter has stopped. Something is telling me the planning side of things could be better. The greater the stark silence, the higher the likelihood of a mess-up.

Call it intuition, a sixth sense if you like. Or simply borne of experience.

"Experienced street agents could have done this on the fly without this BS," I tell Campo, finally needing to let it out. He just nods and says nothing, but we both know something is wrong, even though we're no longer exchanging words.

Well, what can we do? What will more talk achieve?

Finally, the radio crackles to life, shattering the silence. The SWAT team has finally made entry. The on-scene Bureau commander, frustrated at the SWAT team's delay in acting, sends the suspect into the house alone, to convince his accomplice to surrender.

It's a high-risk and unwise decision and sure enough, the SWAT team leader, furious and screaming over the radio, now realizes one suspect has already fled, vanished.

The description over the Bureau radio is vague and unhelpful. A bodybuilder type, white male, twenties, wearing a dark jacket. Not much to go on in this mostly Hispanic town of thirty thousand population, in a neighborhood clustered with small single-family homes, residents going about their business, walking on the sidewalks, children playing.

"Paul, who is that guy?" I point to a lone white male walking down the street at a normal stride; catching his appearance, he doesn't look Hispanic, nor is he particularly athletic looking. He just looks out of place, shining to me like a beacon in the dark.

Campo spots him. "Yeah, I see him."

I look at Campo. "Well? Shall we?"

Campo's OCD kicks in. His vehicle is parallel parked tightly on the narrow street. A sudden acceleration out of the carefully placed vehicle could cause bumper damage, and that would mean endless Bureau paperwork, something that would greatly complicate his life.

"Paul!" I scream at him. "We need to go, now!"

By the time he maneuvers the vehicle out of the tight space in a several-point maneuver, the figure is gone, vanished. A hundred yards from where we first saw him, we spot a parked Bureau car with two agents who seem oblivious and offer no help.

But Campo and I both know the territory and we're sure that guy just doesn't fit.

Seconds later, there's the same figure again. "Paul, there he is!"

Campo guns the vehicle, racing toward the unsuspecting individual.

Time slows and I bail out although we've barely stopped, drawing my weapon, a Smith and Wesson 357 revolver. Campo also bails but now, there are many bystanders. We're not alone on these busy streets and we're wearing civilian clothes.

No raid jackets, nothing to identify ourselves as law enforcement.

My torn jeans and a frayed, dirty shirt, don't go far toward making me convincing as an FBI Special Agent. The unknown individual continues walking, not sparing us a glance.

"FBI, put your hands in the air!" I scream at him.

Tunnel vision. Campo's gone. I don't see him!

He is outside of my narrowing vision, my focus on the threat while Campo is fully occupied keeping shocked bystanders away.

His voice is there, but where is he?

A few bystanders encircle us, our vehicle having stopped in the middle of a busy intersection. The people in this close-knit community take care of one another.

We are outsiders. They don't want the likes of us around this place. And they need to know every small thing we're intent on doing, despite the fact that our perpetrator is getting away. Why did they not encircle him instead? Is he known to them?

Did they just not see him?

Campo confronts the bystanders to stop them from moving closer but he's only audible to me, screaming at them to stand back and stay away.

The individual, now the suspect, isn't complying with my commands either.

By now, he has slowed his stride but continues to walk away.

I yell the command again, focusing my weapon's sights on the suspect's body mass. It will be two shots, and I'm ready despite being oddly calm. But the adrenaline rush has given me tunnel vision, the threat the only thing I can see. There is no one else in my world right now.

At any moment, the suspect—who has his back to me, his hands now on his front waistline—will likely reach for a weapon. He will turn and fire at me.

There's no cover, no opportunity to conceal myself. No, it's one on one here, in the open street. Slowly, I take the slack out of the trigger. This will be over quickly.

I will kill the suspect as he turns with his weapon.

What takes maybe a few seconds appears much longer, the suspect raising his hands slowly above his head in surrender, so it appears. I secure my weapon in its holster, now about ten yards from the suspect. The gap closes as I sprint, bringing him forcefully face down on the ground. Campo, too, is right there beside me, appearing out of nowhere.

Reaching behind, there they are, just as Campo ordained. My handcuffs.

Soon, the suspect lies cuffed on the ground and it's over, the handcuffs clicked into place.

Campo, for reasons I don't understand, verbally gives the suspect his Miranda rights right there, the suspect prone and face down in the middle of the street.

My head shakes, nonplussed. It's not Bureau protocol …

But what the heck, who even cares at this point? We have him.

Pulling the wallet from the man's front pocket, my eyes squint to read the California Driver's License name: Jack Sayed. My mind is whirring.

"Jack, what are you doing here?" I ask.

"I am living here. I am studying at the local community college. Why have you arrested me?" he answers in perfect, unaccented English.

"Sayed, you are Palestinian?"

"No, Jordanian," he responds.

"Sure, and you live in Hollister," I comment with more than a hint of sarcasm.

Campo radios in the arrest. The Command Post acts incredulous. "No, you don't have the right guy. We told you, he's a bodybuilder, and your clothing and physical description are all wrong. You've arrested an innocent bystander. Let him go immediately."

Campo's response travels back over the Bureau car radio. "Fat chance on that. We will bring him to you. Let Geschke decide whether this is his kidnapper or not."

Geschke has been freed in the interim, so we can hear it from his own mouth.

We transport Sayed in the vehicle, handcuffed, and present him to Geschke, who is currently standing in front of the house where he's been held as a prisoner for five grueling days, chained in a closet. Bureau agents, police officers, vehicles, and SWAT are everywhere, plentiful news crews also descending on this small, generally quiet town which has probably never seen as much action all at one time.

Geschke, looking surprisingly fresh and well, positively IDs Sayed as one of the two kidnappers. We feel vindicated, though not smugly triumphant; there's no place for being self-satisfied in this job. Regardless, our agents' intuition and street sense have paid off.

The kidnapping is over and our man Geschke is alive, which is all we wanted. My thoughts drift to his family, to the reunion they will shortly enjoy, hugs and tears. The small matter of the $675,000 is something we will need to look at in due course, retrieving what we can for them, if it has not already been funneled away someplace.

Both kidnappers are now in Bureau custody.

My attention fades momentarily, my mind floating away, back to a sudden realization that I need to return to language school. The Russian language course is beyond intense and losing time from it far from ideal since catching up will be difficult, if not impossible.

No matter. My handcuffs were there when I needed them, and now they are clasped around the wrists of a kidnapper. It's over.

For now at least.

# Chapter 4

Monterey, California

Campo drives me back to my bureau vehicle still parked on the beach, and I somehow stay awake long enough to drive back to my residence.

On arrival, I can barely step out of the vehicle, so exhausted and flat am I.

My clothing is in a torn and tattered state. I am finally home but at times like this, the body has an uncanny ability to keep on and stay on its feet while the brain seems to have shut down long ago, dwelling in the strange twilight zone of neither sleep nor waking.

My shoulders slump, my lower back aching, my neck stiff, and my mind lost in a haze.

"Well, you've got them now. I have to get to work, and I'm already late," screams my wife from the bedroom as she hears me enter the house. There is no interest in what we have just done, the stress and the pressure of it. In her head, it's a job, like any other. She is thinking of her need to leave and to hand over the responsibilities of childcare to Dad.

And why should she think any differently? She doesn't know, can't know. But sometimes, it would be nice to return to peace and calm, to a welcome and a 'put up your feet.'

Not today. No chance. There's not even an ounce of strength in me to argue back, a sense of acquiescence and resignation overtaking everything, my body ready to fall.

There's a plaintive murmuring in the air; I realize it's my own voice.

"I need to sleep a little. I can't do it. Can you wait, just give me an hour?" I plead with her. "The kidnapping's over. Campo and I arrested one kidnapper. Did you see it on TV?"

"No, no time for TV. You got him. Good, but now you have the kids to take care of. And what the heck did you do to your shoes? I just threw them in the trash. They were ripped, wet, and dirty. Where have you been?"

I don't answer, can't answer, can't give more. My body collapses onto the bed, the alarm set for one hour, asleep before my head manages to hit the pillow.

***

"Dad, Daddy!" cries the mischievous little girl's voice right in my ear, waking me, tugging me from the arms of much-needed sleep, from the comforting REM phase in which I dream and nurture myself into a form of renewal. My eyes open slowly, begrudgingly, seeing my four-year-old daughter, Kristin, tugging at me, laughing and squealing, ignorant of the fact that her father appears awake but still lost in a slumber state, somehow.

What the hell is that?

Something sticky adheres to the side of my face.

A note from my wife, something I'll read when my eyes can focus again.

I call my sister. "Hey. Thanks for the heads up. Sometimes, you scare me. But you were right again." A few days earlier, she told me the kidnapping was going to take me to a beach.

"Do you know where I've been and what's happened? No, never mind. Why were you in New York? You saw Mom and Dad?" I ask. It sometimes seems odd and alienating that while I am searching for perpetrators of crime, enmeshed in a world my family don't know and are not a part of, they are continuing their normal lives, doing everyday things.

For a while, my mind dwells in a headspace between two lives, so it seems. It takes time to return to this reality and to be a useful part of the family, to be truly back with them.

Jennifer cuts me off. "I was right, huh? Actually, I was in the NYPD archives. You won't believe what I found; it fits perfectly in my thesis. I need to discuss this with my professor but I don't know where to begin. She's really awesome, you know. The Bureau—you—could use her. Oh, and I'm going to the lake tomorrow."

"Jennifer, I'm exhausted, and I don't want to talk about the past. Leave it be and stay away from the lake. Focus on your future, your career. You've just moved to Florida, and you're already back in New York? I don't understand. And the Bureau's going to solicit the advice of some wacko psychologist professor? Are you kidding me?"

Irritated and aggrieved by our conversation, I hang up the phone.

Sometimes, I wonder why I bother to make these calls.


Cranberry Lake, New Jersey


The vehicle comes to a halt in the tight gravel parking area, and Jennifer steps out. She knows the place but stops to survey her surroundings before walking toward a path leading to a cluster of modest homes in the small lake cove. She has been here before. As opposed to her intensity and pace exhibited at the NYPD Archives just days before, she is pensive, reflective, not sure of herself as she walks up the stairs and steps leading to a house.

She freezes on the steps, her head throbbing with intense pain. The flashback is coming, and what's worse, there is no way to stop it.

A young girl of perhaps five or six is playing on the steps, rising to pull open the entry door of the lake house where she sees her mother Linda with Aunt Debby in the kitchen.

Linda looks to be in her late twenties or early thirties, thin, attractive, but with an edginess to her today. Jennifer can hear her mother speaking to Aunt Debby. Linda turns to her sister, saying in a raised voice, "They took everything. The place is cleaned out, Debby. Not a single decent pan left. I know for a fact there were cast iron skillets but now — gone. Who does that?"

Aunt Debby's softer voice tries to calm the tension. "Linda, maybe we're just not seeing everything. It's possible they didn't take anything…we don't know for sure."

She's trying to diffuse the situation, smiling at her as she speaks.

Jennifer walks through the kitchen, sort of skip-walking into the living room where she spots an enormous book, picking it up from its resting place on the end table of the couch.

She sits on the couch and looks at the cover, turning pages, trying to sound out the words.

The book she holds is the family Bible. Still happily seated, she stays engrossed in the meaty tome, slowly and deliberately turning the pages until she stops on one, handwritten.

She sounds out the words, pleased that she can make sense of the words in this weighty book.

A minute into her reading aloud, Linda enters the living room.

"What are you doing? What do you have there, Jennifer?"

"A book. I'm reading it. This was Grandma's?" she asks her mother.

"No, it wasn't and it doesn't belong to you." Linda takes the book out of her daughter's hands forcefully, placing it high on a shelf out of her daughter's reach.

"Can't I have it? It was Grandma's. I want it. I can read the words, and there were lots of names, and I can read them!" she pleads with her mother, but it is not the kind of whining most children would do. She somehow identifies with the book, feeling it belongs with her.

"No. It's not yours. It's not a book for children anyway."

As Linda walks back toward the kitchen, Jennifer's eyes linger on the book. She wants to ask her mother why it matters so much to her. A little sadly, Jennifer leaves the living room, heading outside toward the lake.

Her aunt's soft voice says, "Jen, please don't go near the lake, will you? And I've said before, stay away from the dock. I'll come with you in a minute, OK?"

"OK, Aunt Debby, I'll wait outside." Jennifer smiles, a little sad, and hugs her aunt as the door behind her closes.

***

And with this, Jennifer is back from her flashback which hit her without warning.

How long was she standing there?

A few minutes perhaps, but now she has returned to the present.

Jennifer has reached the house where she almost knocks on the door but doesn't want to alarm the strangers who may be living there. Instead, she walks down to the dock, smiling and recalling when she was just a small child, her older brothers fishing from this spot and jumping into the water, also her cousins playing in the yard. Lost, she feels, gazing out to the swimming raft in the cove, the place which seemed so far away when she was small.

A voice startles her. "Ms., can we help you? What are you doing? Are you OK?"

The woman appears to be in her late sixties, with an older looking husband standing next to her. They are well-dressed, the man attired in a weathered sports coat, with a tie.

It looks as though they've never updated their wardrobes, typical of older people who live modestly or feel themselves too old to bother renewing their clothing. Perhaps they are spendthrifts, seeing their garments as non-essentials, saving and making do when they can.

"I'm OK! Sorry! I didn't think anyone was home. When I was a child, I used to come here, you know," she says, her voice full of enthusiasm and excitement. "You see, it was my grandparents' home. So, my brothers and I, my cousins, we came here. But we stopped when I was quite young, when my grandmother passed away. It was a long time ago."

"You are a Cosgrove?" the woman asks in a New York accent, but closer to a New England one. It seems familiar to Jennifer, but from another time long ago, perhaps.

Jennifer begins, "I'm a Cosgrove. My father ..."

The woman interrupts her, lifting her hand in a stopping motion.

"I know who you are. In fact, I knew your family, your grandfather, everyone. Stay as long as you like, as long as you need to."

The woman, not waiting for a reply, walks away with the man, her husband.

Jennifer turns her gaze abruptly back to the lake where some geese have landed near the dock, making an enormous splash. She turns back to respond to the elderly woman and man.

But they have disappeared from view.

She takes her camera out of the handbag, putting it up to her face, intending to take photos. Instead, she stops and puts it slowly away, then meanders back, this time all the way past the house, down the steps, and toward her parked vehicle.

A woman, perhaps forty years old and dressed in business attire, now heads toward her.

"Ms., are you interested in the house? In seeing it? You might like it as a vacation house, perhaps?"

Jennifer looks at her, perplexed.

"Huh? The house is for sale? I didn't see any signs, and just spoke with the people living here. They said nothing about wanting to sell it. I've only just come from them ..."

The woman cuts her off, her face caught in a frown as if she's confused too.

"Excuse me. What people? They can't have come from this house because it's been unoccupied for some time. There was a couple here, but they moved out years ago. Well, the woman did. Her husband died, and she had to go into a nursing home. Anyway, I'm the listing agent, trying to sell the place for the family. So, are you interested? It's been on the market for a while. Needs work, but it's a very pleasant location on this quiet cove."

"I don't know. Let me think about it."

Jennifer appears distracted and off balance, processing what's happened, wondering who she earlier spoke with, and how they could have known her grandparents and cousins.

The agent hands her a business card and Jennifer departs in her vehicle, gazing into the rear-view mirror as the small gravel parking area and house fade away.

She wipes away a tear as she turns onto the main road.

***

San José, California 1992

Campo and I are sitting in the State Prosecutor's office in San José.

The powers that be have decided to try the kidnappers in State Court, and if convicted, they could face a severe sentence ranging from twenty years to life. The prosecutor, a youthful but seemingly competent and experienced sort, goes over the arrest of the suspect.

"So, you guys had the clothing description, physical description, etc., and based on that information, you arrested Sayed. Is that how it went?"

I look at Campo, unsure how to respond.

Campo speaks up. "Well, sort of. He didn't fit."

The prosecutor stares, says nothing until finally, he manages, "Huh?"

Campo continues on, "You see, we both know Hollister, we know the streets, we know who belongs and who doesn't. And Sayed, well, he just didn't fit in. He wasn't Hispanic, walked a bit too fast for our liking too. He wasn't a Caucasian either."

The prosecutor stops him. "OK, agents. Enough of this. One of you is going to have to testify in the preliminary hearing; it's a sort of mini trial before the actual one, an oddity of the State of California, but not so unique. One of you needs to testify that Sayed fit the description you had, and that you stopped him based on that. Your voodoo, intuition, street-smart shit won't hold up, so you can't possibly testify to that. The judge, and then if we make it to trial, the jury, will think you're reckless cowboys. You do understand this, right?"

We say nothing, looking at one another briefly.

He continues, "I get it. I appreciate your gypsy or tracker dog instincts, sixth sense, intuition, whatever you want to call it. But this is a court of law. We have laws, we have procedures, and just because an individual doesn't 'fit' according to your standards, that doesn't mean you can draw down on him, pile on, handcuff and arrest him. Jesus, you almost shot him as I understand. Were you guys fucking losing it?"

Campo has had enough, about to boil over, barely able to contain himself. I find myself sort of amused by the whole thing, but say nothing, eyeing them both.

Campo stands up, as if about to leave. He turns to the prosecutor. "OK. This is how it will go. Cosgrove will testify that Sayed fit the description of a bodybuilder, etc., and that is why we stopped him. We cuffed him for safety reasons, his and ours."

The prosecutor nods.

Campo turns to me. "Is that OK with you?"

I nod too; yes, it makes sense. "Fine, and what about this Miranda warning problem?"

The prosecutor looks down at his file. "Yeah, the interviewing agents never mirandized Sayed. Not sure why, but I understand that you, Campo, verbally did so during the arrest. Is that accurate?"

"Yes, I did," Campo responds.

"Well, it's a damn good thing since Sayed's confession would likely be inadmissible without it. I am so glad you guys did that. That is all for now. Oh, no, one more thing. What if you were wrong? What if you arrested an innocent bystander on the street; what would you have done then?"

Campo is quick in response.

"If we'd been wrong? Probably buy him a steak dinner. But we don't make mistakes like that. We are Special Agents of the Federal Bureau of Investigation. Have a nice day, prosecutor."

With that, Campo ends the meeting, and we walk out of the office.

# Chapter 5

San José, California, 1993

The Bureau car radio crackles and comes to life as the dispatcher summons me back to the office. There is no reason given. Just, "Get back here." I don't allow my mind to wander, speculating why the sudden need to return. There could be a thousand reasons, though most of them not good. Best to just get back there and deal with whatever's waiting for me.

I pass through the doorway into the reception area, finding a young, attractive, well-dressed woman sitting there alone.

Buzzed through into the Bureau's inner offices, I head to the office of the agent on duty.

He says, "That woman out there, the one you just walked by, she wants to speak with a Russian-speaking agent. You're it. Good luck."

"Did she say what she wants? Did you run a background check on her?"

"Nothing came up. You're experienced and the only Russian speaker in this office. She doesn't look too dangerous to me."

He seems preoccupied with other matters, either that or he's downright disinterested.

"OK. Then I'll talk to her in the interview room. Shouldn't take long. I've got plenty of other things to deal with and really don't need this. She could be a nut, but I'll talk to her."

The agent on duty just stares as if he has no time for this preamble. Or for anything.

But I carry on making my views known, regardless.

"When I walked by, she was sitting quietly, sort of staring or meditating. Not sure." I head back to the reception room to meet the young lady and pay heed to her story or her complaint.

"You speak Russian?" are her first words when she sees me entering the reception room.

She looks at me with an intensity and stare I haven't experienced in a while.

"Yes."

"Good," she says, intensifying her hard gaze. "Can you protect me?"

With this question, her piercing amber eyes seem to brighten, forbidding me to look away.

Escorting her past the metal detectors, I lead her into the interview room.

"Protect you from what?" I ask her. As soon as the words are out of my mouth, I realize this is no way to start an interview. I am already losing control and she, the woman calling herself Annie Nazari is now interviewing me. I need to regain control of this right away.

"From powerful and dangerous people," is all she adds as if she has released me from her hypnotic, superpower stare, turning to look out of the office window.

Yet, she still seems the one firmly in control of the room, and of me.

My mind races. Haven't I traveled down this road before in another time and place?

Yes, my first office of assignment, Kansas City, on the case that nearly broke me. Two confidential sources murdered, police corruption, a serial killer, and a violent drug trafficking ring at the center of it all. So, this is a déjà vu moment, but the kind of déjà vu that brings only stress and regret, nothing more. This woman, perhaps Afghan, Tajik or Uzbek, judging from her appearance, is mysterious and cunning. She is in no rush. Not desperate, not needy. Assertive.

She exudes independence and sophistication.

And she knows men, that much is apparent to me. Control of this interview still eludes me.

"So, Ms. Nazari, why exactly are you here? Why come to an FBI office, asking to speak with a Russian-speaking agent?" My words seek to wrestle back control of our exchange.

She is sizing me up. I am certain of that. But Nazari is going to reveal nothing until she has a sense of my character, or at least until she feels comfortable enough to reveal to me what she knows. For her, the information she possesses has value; it is a commodity so she isn't simply going to hand it over as she would a piece of chocolate or a slice of cake.

"What do you know about diamonds?" she asks, reengaging me with those piercing amber eyes, also swiveling her chair back to me. It is now my turn. She is playing a game, determined to stay in the lead, unwilling to allow me to control the interview. She has the knowledge after all, having voluntarily come to the office. She is in charge, not me.

This will not be easy, nor will it be a quick interview. That much I can figure with her question, and the sense I'm already developing about her. On the brink of pausing the interview to summon another agent to the room with me, another thought comes.

No, I can deal with this woman alone. Besides, there aren't many agents in the office on this sunny afternoon. They're out on the street. So, I'm on my own, just Ms. Nazari and me.

"I know nothing about diamonds. So, tell me, Ms. Nazari, tell me your story. You're taking my time while there are other cases and other things to do. But you have my attention for now. Go ahead, or please go on your way. You have come here voluntarily, asking to speak with a Russian-speaking agent. Here I am. Now, tell me what brings you to me."

Honestly, I've had enough already. With a heavy caseload weighing on me, I am wasting valuable time. The days are long enough in the Bureau, seemingly endless.

There has been a hiring freeze for the past few years, with the obvious result that we have far fewer agents to handle an ever-growing workload.

Agents experience burnout and remain in a constant state of exhaustion.

"OK. I will tell you. Only you. But you need to listen. Are you listening?"

This Annie Nazari—Nazari as I think of her—is no ordinary woman, that much I am fast coming to realize. The story this mysterious woman reveals seems incredulous, a tale involving the looting of the Russian treasury.

Diamonds, gold, priceless art, and other valuables.

If what she is saying is true, it will not be easy to investigate or to prove.

Nazari tells me she has access to individuals running a company called Golden ADA in San Francisco, the company receiving and selling these purportedly looted treasures.

Two Armenians founded Golden ADA, their names Ashot and David Shagirian.

She explains they are brothers who immigrated a few years earlier from Yerevan, entering the country along with a third person, a Russian national. Nazari only knows him as Andrey.

It turns out that Andrey is involved too.

Hailing from Moscow, Andrey's intent was to move to the United States to oversee the operation. Nazari tells me the Russian mafia and corrupt government officials from the Kremlin are behind the whole thing. She knows a lot about it all, so it appears.

But I also know she is holding back, not surprising. Whatever her game or intent, it will take time for it to play out, and for Nazari to reveal more of what she knows. So, as I mentioned earlier, I have been down this road before, back in Kansas City. Due to certain events there, it's imperative to avoid repeating mistakes in dealing with female sources.

That's if I can avoid it. If even half of what Nazari is telling me is true, then this investigation is set to be complex, consuming, challenging, and dangerous.

I later write up the interview into an FD-302 format, the standard report form for the FBI, filing it away in a locked drawer in my desk, the details too sensitive to upload into the Bureau's case file system for now. If this woman is eventually going to work with me, her identity and information will need to be protected just as she requested.

I also need to know more about this Ms. Nazari. Who is she exactly, what does she do for a living, and what is her motivation in coming to the Bureau's San José office?

The Golden ADA company is based in San Francisco, with their offices at the prestigious Transamerica Pyramid building. So, why wouldn't Nazari go to the Bureau's offices in San Francisco instead? Why make the effort to come to San José office?

No matter, I have plenty of work before meeting with her again.

The next time, I will be ready for her, also better able to stay in control. Hopefully.

Nazari's last words as she is leaving are still playing on my mind, troubling me more than they should as I pull into the garage of my home in the Monterey area.

"Can you keep this between us? I will work for you, no one else," she says as she rolls up the window of her vehicle and spins out of the office parking lot.

It causes a flashback to my experiences with such sources in Kansas City.

There, two young, attractive female sources, both with drug addictions and working the streets, ended up brutally murdered. Several weeks later, authorities discovered their bodies in a park but I would soon find out that no one cared much about their fate.

Not Quantico, not the Bureau, no one.

I am determined not to have Nazari meet the same gruesome and untimely fate, although she seems capable of taking care of herself. Yet so did those women, and it's not my place to consider how capable they are of looking after themselves. Nobody knows for sure.

As I close the Bureau vehicle door, my two young children already come to greet me, happy to see their father. Work fades away instantaneously at their bright faces and incessant lively chatter, filled with enthusiasm at me having finally escaped from work.

My wife is in the backyard, tending to our garden.

Bureau wives are accustomed to not asking their husbands about their day and what they've been up to, an unspoken rule. Besides, with the classified nature of some of the work, there is nothing much to share, not even with my spouse. The rare exception is if the case has made it into the media, in case of an arrest, search warrant or trial.

Even then, they do not share the details, the spouse being an outsider.

The Bureau is everything, and the organization demands unconditional loyalty, acting as a "jealous mistress" as one of my FBI Academy instructors at Quantico used to tell the class.

"You can keep secrets from your spouse or family, but never can you do it to the Bureau. The Bureau never forgets and never forgives."

These words stay with me, a warning to all of us and not to be taken lightly.

At the kitchen table on this evening, I stare out the window in thought. My wife Lenore has seen this kind of behavior before from me, so she knows what it means.

Something has happened today at work. "So, what's up? You have a fresh case and you're thinking about it, aren't you?" she asks, trying to elicit a reaction.

"Yeah. It's getting overwhelming. I sort of wish I were back in Russian language school. It's just that I'm juggling a lot. Drug trafficking cases, money laundering, frauds, sources, helping other agents, surveillances, and today, a new person came into the office with a story. Well, I really don't know what to make of it. With this hiring freeze going on nearly two years, and no new agents coming on board, we're all suffocating. It's oppressive, you know? Sixty plus hours a week plus commuting time, I don't know how much longer I can do this. But we're all in the same situation. No matter. One day at a time, I suppose."

"So, this person who came to your office … A female, right?"

My wife had a sense or intuition, something like that, not much different from my sister. Maybe that was why they got along so well.

"Yeah. She was or is."

"And she's pretty but mysterious. You're intrigued by her. She probably has you all figured out. You better never meet her alone, and please don't give her any of my clothing this time," Lenore says with an icy stare.

Women.

They will all drive me crazy, eventually—my sister, wife, mother, even my daughter and my past and present female sources. I'm better off staying away from the lot of them.

"I have no intention of doing that, never again. Look, that woman, that source, Lenore, we talked about it, didn't we? I'm sorry. She had nothing left, nothing, and I already had two murdered sources. I didn't want a third. We had to move her away as quickly as possible for her safety. Let's drop this discussion, please. Enough, it's in the past. It's over, gone."

I want my wife to drop it forever, but even now, she periodically raises it.

This time, I should have seen it coming, needing to accept the fact she'll never let it go. The only way to understand it is to tell myself it must hold a deeper significance for her, deeper than I can fathom or recognize.

# Chapter 6

The typical workday in the Bureau office begins early, agents beginning to arrive from six o'clock in the morning, while eight o'clock is considered late.

There is plenty of paperwork to catch up on, plus squad meetings, informal chats between agents, case strategy discussions, a lot going on. It seems to never let up.

Yet, there are compartments. The Bureau compartmentalizes information, people, and squad areas, limiting access, and sometimes completely closing it off unless you have business being there. Not everything, or everyone, is privy and fair game for display or discussion, or for sharing in the office.

There's always something going on behind the scenes.

As an agent, you accept that fact. We work the entire socio-economic spectrum in our cases, just as I was told in my first office. You can meet with a street-level drug dealer, and in the next moment, can be in the office of an elected official, sometimes in a highly confrontational and imposing setting. You have to hold your own, regardless of the environment. It's that kind of job, one in which you have to maneuver, work, and move along this wide spectrum, seamlessly. Otherwise, you will never be successful as an investigator in the FBI, it's that simple. You have to be capable of handling all kinds of people. Subjects, witnesses and sources from diverse backgrounds, cultures, and life experiences.

This is a day-in, day-out challenge, and some agents are good at it, others, not so good.

I believe I am good. Not claiming to be the best, but far from the worst.

As a midshipman, then naval officer, eventually ending up with the Bureau as a Special Agent, I have traveled extensively on top of having grown up in a tough New York City neighborhood. I have seen a lot, maybe too much in certain ways.

My commute to the San José office turns out to be longer than most.

My wife and I have stayed in the Monterey area after Russian language school, and I manage the commute, with my wife working nights at the local hospital. It's not an easy arrangement, but still, it's one that will benefit our son and daughter for the next few years.

I arrive in the office that morning before seven, remove my weapon from the holster and place it in a locked desk drawer and begin work. My work inbox is nearly full. Most agents have routine leads and a few unusual tasks in theirs. The challenge for us is to juggle everything and not become overwhelmed, particularly at the start of the workday.

The nature of the work as an agent also varies; it depends upon your squad assignment, your seniority, and the level of your ambition. Some agents happily sit back and wait for work to come to their inbox while others are more aggressive, getting out on the streets, developing informants and sources. But sometimes, in the pursuit of good contacts and cases, it's easy to forget a couple of important popular sayings.

Early in my career, a seasoned agent used to tell me, "Big cases bring big problems, little cases bring little problems, and no cases bring no problems."

The second saying was, "Be careful what you wish for."

So, some agents hustle for cases, preferring the presence of at least some problems over the chance of staying idle, i.e., picking up no cases. However, on occasions, a hustled large case will turn out to bring more than its fair share of those aforementioned problems.

"Hey Sharon, can you come over to my desk when you're free?" I ask Sharon Austin, an intelligence analyst supporting the work of street agents. Everyone in the office knows her as one of our best analysts. Sharon worked under Director Hoover, the Bureau's longest serving director with forty-seven years of service under his belt by the time he died in 1972.

Her loyalty and fidelity to the Bureau and its mission are legendary and unquestioned, and there is little doubt her experience of working with J. Edgar Hoover has much to do with her ethos. Even a decade after his passing, many in the

Bureau still revere or even idolize him, and there is no doubt that working for Director Hoover has created its own brand of loyalty to the Bureau. Sharon will carry that brand till the end. I enjoy working with her; she cares and knows what she's doing, as well as being unafraid to disagree or to question things.

I need her help, but Nazari has instructed me not to share her information with anyone.

Yet my mind is telling me I can trust Sharon, and that she really doesn't count when it comes to the "don't tell anyone" warning. Besides, I possess neither the time nor the energy to go it alone. An analyst has access to databases on which I haven't been trained, as well as resources and a network of contacts with other agencies and police departments.

So, I decide to bypass the advice and ask Sharon for her assistance.

"What's up? You're talking about that attractive Afghan woman from yesterday?" she asks.

"Yeah. You saw her?"

I'm forgetting that not much goes on in that office that the support staff don't see, and they've seen a lot. Agents come and go, transferring to the various Bureau offices after a few years while the support personnel stay put in one office for the entirety of their careers.

They become the all-seeing eye, the oracle of what goes on.

"You were with her for a long time yesterday. She must have had a story to tell, otherwise you wouldn't have been with her for so long. Well, she was pretty but looked edgy to me. She's trouble." Sharon is conveying a warning, yet expressing her interest at the same time.

I hand my FD-302 to her to review and develop backgrounds on the individuals and on the company Nazari mentioned. So, now it begins. Sharon will do a deep dive with the company, the Shagirian brothers, and try to identify this mysterious Andrey from Moscow.

She is in, hooked. Sharon loves this sort of stuff and why not? This case could be big.

But something takes me back to the warning lurking there in the back of my mind, the veteran agent's words that big cases inevitably bring big problems. Still, I forge ahead with it.

It's late afternoon when Sharon reaches out to me, already having lots to share despite the fact that her research and analysis have barely begun.

She says, "First, you couldn't pick a more secretive industry and trade than the business of diamonds. And this mix—diamonds, Russia, mafia … You realize the chances of this case going anywhere are highly remote. Oh, and let's not forget the possibility that this is some sort of Russian intelligence operation, or provocation of some sort from their side. That said, let me give you an overview of what I've already found. Let's start with De Beers."

As Sharon begins her briefing, I get up from my desk and close the office door, not wanting agents or anyone in the office to overhear talk of diamonds, De Beers, and the Russian mafia. Not yet, anyway. Sharon explains all she's learned about De

Beers, their global reach, and their control of the worldwide distribution of diamonds.

They are essentially a monopoly and prohibited from conducting business in the United States, not directly, anyway. They established their principal offices in London where they were known as the Central Selling Organization, distributing and mailing out stones both cut and uncut from their principal offices in London.

It was all rather murky and mysterious. De Beers had cornered the market in the late nineteenth century, with their mines in South Africa.

The United States market was the largest diamond consumer market, with Japan a close second, followed by the European market and the rest of the world.

There were several hubs for cutting, polishing and distributing diamonds: Antwerp; Tel Aviv; and New York. Also, there were a few other smaller operations around the globe.

San Francisco was not a significant player in the diamond market.

"And here's the most interesting aspect to De Beers and Russia. I found De Beers has an arrangement with Russia—well, with the Soviet Union—for the distribution of Russian diamonds to the outside world. The Soviet Union, now Russia, can only sell them through the channels provided by De Beers. But this 'contract' or arrangement itself is murky.

"Obviously, I don't have access to the actual contracts and could only find general references in trade publications and other papers about this so-called 'arrangement' between De

Beers and Russia. But if this company—Golden ADA—is a genuine new player in the diamond business, then De Beers would definitely know something. It would only make sense. It would be in their interest to keep tabs on such things, right?"

"Yep, you're right, Sharon. So, our first move will be to ask the FBI legal attaché office in London to reach out to De Beers. Then, maybe we'll have clarity about what the heck is going on. Maybe not. But it's worth a try," I respond, pleased that Sharon seems interested and has achieved good work in a relatively short period.

"I know you have lots of other cases to assist with, Sharon, but I need you to get me as much background as you can about those Shagirian brothers, and about this Annie Nazari. But please don't let anyone else in the office know what you're doing, no one. If anyone catches wind of what you're up to, or wants to know, refer them to me.

"I don't want to sound paranoid, but something's off here. Call it intuition but I feel I'm being played. By whom, I have no clue and for whatever reason … Well, I don't know that either," I tell her with a sinking feeling as my thoughts wander back to Kansas City and to that case, the one I can't seem to shake off. I have been on surveillances before, in vehicles and on foot. Other than practical exercises at the Academy, I haven't ever experienced being the target of surveillance. It seems I pick it up a few stop lights from the office.

Something seems off. A pickup truck and a late model Mustang.

They stay with me even when I deliberately make a wrong turn into a neighborhood outside of San José. A young woman with short brown hair is the Mustang's driver, and the pickup truck has an older guy behind the wheel, his face partially covered by a ball cap and sunglasses. This makes little sense. Two vehicles following me? Is the Bureau behind this? I wonder. Is it one of their SOG teams? It would be a rookie mistake to follow me into a neighborhood like that, though.

Why didn't they break off the surveillance when I turned into here? What are they after?

Or is it all a coincidence, my mind playing tricks on me?

I get back on the highway, and the vehicles vanish.

I tell myself that if the Bureau were following me, there could be several reasons. Perhaps for internal training, or possibly to test me but these reasons seem too far-fetched.

Is it connected to a case of mine? A prior case? Or are they looking for someone else and following me only in error? Perhaps it was the local police or another agency. Or maybe there was a connection between this mysterious woman, Annie Nazari, and the vehicles.

Regardless, in the absence of answers, it was clear I needed to be alert now, certainly not wanting to lead them to my home with my family there.

I get an early start on the workday, out the door before six o'clock.

There are other cases to deal with, and the Bureau expected agents to juggle and handle a multitude of tasks and cases simultaneously. I am assigned to an understaffed Organized

Crime and Drug Squad. The investigation of Mexican Drug Trafficking Organizations—MDTO in Bureau parlance—comprises much of the work. But there are other criminal "organizations" on the rise, everything from Asian street gangs to sophisticated international theft rings, intent on stealing technology and equipment on a large scale.

After all, this is Silicon Valley and the biggest companies in the growing tech market have their headquarters in the area from Google to Apple, along with many others. Silicon Valley attracts and needs a wide assortment of expertise from around the globe to meet the ever-increasing global demand for new technologies.

Work visas are easy to get for foreign nationals with a skill.

Sometimes, there is fraud and criminality, however, the visa process being far from perfect, allowing many fraudulent cases to slip through as is to be expected.

Visa fraud is hard to detect and agencies have other priorities to deal with.

So, a lot slip through these cracks, Russians included.

The San José PD is seeing an uptick in organized crime activities in the Russian-speaking community and has reached out to me for help and guidance. Of course, I help as much as I can, while also dealing with my own cases. It's a challenge to balance it all.

However, the job requires the Bureau to assist local and state law enforcement agencies and work closely with other agencies too, the days of the Bureau going it alone long gone.

Everyone knows there weren't enough personnel and resources; besides, outside agencies have a plethora of talented and well-trained personnel to offer us, particularly in California where they are often better paid than Bureau agents.

The Bureau needs these agencies perhaps even more than the agencies need the Bureau.

So, when the phone call comes in this morning from the IRS agent—the Internal Revenue Service—it's not unusual at all. The agent, a criminal investigator named Jason Whitley, knows me from a few months earlier when he called the office asking for help with interviews of Russian-speaking individuals on a tax fraud case.

I stepped in and helped him then, also feeling grateful for the opportunity.

Speaking Russian well, this offered an opportunity to use it on the street and keep up my proficiency. Speaking and understanding Russian is a highly perishable skill, something I didn't and still don't want to lose.

Learning Russian in the school in Monterey has been both grueling and intense, but I've somehow managed to get through several courses, staying for over two years.

The Bureau has made an enormous investment in me and others like me, allowing us as selected agents to remain "off the books" and become full-time students, an earned privilege.

One day, however, the Bureau will expect to take its pound of flesh.

There will be payback; the Bureau will make sure of it. The Defense Language Institute, the DLI, carries a formidable reputation for chewing up and spitting out even the most talented. You don't just walk into that place. First, you have to score highly on the Defense Language Proficiency Test or DLPT. Then, you need to survive the first critical weeks.

***

The Institute was first established during World War II to train military personnel in foreign languages where the need was critical and immediate. Most students would have arrived just out of high school, enlisted personnel who'd scored high on the DLPT. For those from the interior of the United States, and from small-town America, this would have been the first time they'd ever set their eyes on a large body of water in the form of the Pacific Ocean; the Defense Language Institute situated on a hill right next to Monterey Bay.

Regardless of the stunning locale, it used to be and still is a high-stress environment.

The failure rate for the forty-seven-week basic Russian language course is nearly 50 percent, the Institute sending students packing without hesitation if their test scores are low.

There's no recycling of military personnel; they serve out their enlistment period regardless.

In terms of the FBI sending agents to study Russian along with other languages including Mandarin Chinese, Arabic, Italian, and Spanish, the drop rate is not much different.

Agents may continue their careers if unable to manage language school, but never again will they receive the highly desirable opportunity to become language-trained Special Agents. I already spoke Spanish at a level close to fluency on arrival, Russian was a hard language to master with its Cyrillic alphabet, and the complicated grammar structure with case endings. At the end of the first week of class, I admitted to my wife that I wasn't sure if I would last more than a few weeks, it was that tough.

Of course, she just told me to gut it out; after all, we had made no small sacrifice for me to receive this one-time opportunity, having relocated our family across the country! So, she was not about to let me opt out of it. No, she made it quite plain that I just had to push through it, and she was right. I had done so before, when we were newly married, and I was in law school.

Back then, she'd even worked two jobs to support us. So, it was more than just a case of us having relocated; the whole family had made considerable efforts to support me in the Bureau, and it was down to me to take full advantage of the training on offer, achieving a good outcome. With hindsight, I am so glad my wife believed in my abilities so much that she knew a positive result was achievable; I had to just push for it. Sometimes, when you are exhausted, the psyche comes up with all manner of excuses for why succeeding is too long a shot. Now, I was aware that success in the Russian language training was a non-negotiable.

The instructors for our Russian language courses were mostly from the former Soviet Union. They were tough, but fair. The training materials comprised workbooks and language tapes, also daily quizzes along with periodic exams. After a few weeks, English was barely, if ever, spoken in the classroom; it was full immersion, and utterly exhausting.

When classes ended at three p.m., there was only time for a few hours of exercise or to catch up with family, but afterwards, it was study time. On average, there were almost four hours of study a night, and I got accustomed to it after a while. It never came easy, but my capacity to keep what I was learning was improving. My brain was absorbing more and more.

In the early days, I would substitute Spanish words subconsciously, but that slowly ended as Spanish receded deeper into the brain, the Russian language evidently replacing it.

Eventually, over many months, words and expressions came faster.

No, not easier necessarily, but far more expediently. It was during the advanced Russian language course, when no English was allowed and the topics for conversation got more and more complicated, that the unimaginable happened. It was a typical summer afternoon in Monterey, neither warm nor cold, and a bit overcast, with a fog set to roll in from farther out in Monterey Bay as would often occur late afternoons into the evening hours.

I turned on CNN to catch up on the news for a few minutes before heading out for a run along the nearby beach. My wife and children would be arriving a bit later.

Sitting on the couch, I couldn't tear my eyes from the TV set on which CNN had breaking news. Many East German tourists on summer holiday in Communist Hungary were fleeing, mostly on foot, through openings in the border fences near the town of Sopron, along the Austrian Hungarian border. What's more, no one was stopping them.

The Hungarian border guards were letting them through, and the Austrians were welcoming them. There were thousands fleeing daily on foot, as well as by bicycle and car.

They consisted of both nuclear families and extended families, none of whom had any intention of returning soon—well, anytime—to East Germany despite their love for their homes and possessions they had abandoned there. Their need to be free was visceral.

The CNN commentators weren't sure what to make of the whole thing. No one was talking about this signaling the end of the Cold War, the beginning of the end, but as I was sitting there, I knew it meant something and that this incident was significant.

It would be difficult—in fact, impossible—to put the genie back into the bottle.

The only nation capable of stopping this refugee flow from the East was the Soviet Union but they had their own internal issues to contend with, such as a collapsed economy with a discontented population that had had enough of the communist experiment with its state control over every aspect of their work and lives. If the Soviets didn't send in their tanks soon, it could crescendo to other border crossings opening between the East and West.

The Iron Curtain was showing its age, exhibiting serious signs of weakness.

As my wife entered the apartment, she intensely watched the televised reporting.

She asked, "So, is this the end? Will we have to leave Monterey?"

She had processed and analyzed the entire event, not through a global or political or foreign policy perspective, but as the mother of two young children, a woman who was acutely aware of being responsible for their welfare and that of the entire family.

Her question made sense, although I laughed at how she'd boiled things down to the local level, to our family microcosm.

"Yep. It could be the beginning of the end of the Cold War," I began. "But a lot more has yet to happen. And an actual war has to be avoided at all costs by the major players, between our country and Russia most important of all. I don't think the Bureau will kick me, and therefore, all of us, out of language school just because a bunch of East German tourists are fleeing to the West without getting themselves shot. Russia's a big player on the world stage, and the Bureau will probably need Russian language speakers in the form of agents regardless of the outcome of this frenzied free for all on the border.

"But something's happening, you're right. You know, I didn't think we'd live to see this day. But people everywhere just want to be free; it's human nature. Today is a good day for humanity, I think."

It was a long answer to a short question, and I'm not sure what she made of it.

By the time I finished Russian language training many months after that summer, the Cold War was indeed ending. In November 1989, the Berlin Wall fell, and by late 1991, the Soviet Union had ceased to exist. In its place were fifteen separate, independent countries, with Russia the largest and most powerful of fifteen republics stretching from the Baltic and Black Seas all the way to the western Pacific Ocean.

It was during my teen years that I had my first interactions with these peoples and the various nationalities of the vast and expansive Soviet Union, the SSSR or CCCP, the Cyrillic language abbreviation for the Union of Soviet Socialist Republics, the USSR.

There was a grain shortage that year in the USSR.

Richard Nixon was President of the United States and Leonid Brezhnev the Soviet Premier. For whatever reason, Nixon and Brezhnev agreed the United States would help ease the suffering caused by the grain shortages. As part of the agreement, the United States would load American grain onto Soviet merchant vessels in U.S. ports and transport it to the ports of the Soviet Union to feed the starving masses.

As my father worked for a company responsible for organizing the arrival, departure, and loading of the Soviet merchant ships berthed in New York, I sometimes went with him to visit Soviet vessels. He once turned to me as we walked the pier with the longshoremen engaged in the loading operations and told me, "Don't look at them. Just walk. They aren't happy doing this, loading Russian ships. They may think we're communist sympathizers. Just ignore them if they say anything as we walk by."

Once on board the ship, the captain and his senior officers greeted us.

My father whispered to me, "The second in command will be from the KGB, their intelligence service. He's there to make sure no one defects while the ship is in New York."

Some looked Russian while others had darker features with brown eyes, dark hair, olive skin. There was a real mixture among the crew, with light hair, dark hair, olive skin, fair skin.

My father explained, "The Soviet Union isn't just Russia. There are many nationalities in the country, reflected in the different physical appearances of the crew of the ship."

As a fifteen-year-old, I sat around the table in the captain's stateroom, drinking vodka, and found myself amused and sort of liking these peoples even though they were "communists" and opposed to democracy and freedom, adversaries of the United States.

They seemed normal and likable.

It was my first exposure to the peoples of the vast Soviet Empire. And I heard my first Russian words: на здровье or "na zdrowie"; рюмка or "roum-ka"; and До свидания or "dos vidaniya." These words would stay with me, for whatever strange reason I couldn't yet fathom. Maybe the vodka, even the small amount I had sipped that afternoon, made those words and expressions stick inside my head.

It was a few years later, as a midshipman traveling to remote parts of the globe—to Africa, South America, and the Mediterranean Sea—when I would next encounter these diverse peoples of the Soviet Union. This time, the encounters were not so pleasant.

I eventually found myself on the bridge of a U.S. naval warship, playing cat and mouse with Soviet vessels and trawlers—spy ships—in the open seas. The close and potentially deadly encounters were unsettling, with collisions barely avoided. A seafarers' old saying warned, "A collision at sea could ruin your whole day."

The Soviets were global adversaries not to be taken lightly. I had now experienced this reality firsthand from the bridge of a U.S. Navy warship.

As a midshipman and later as a naval officer, I had also seen their tanks, vehicles, and heavy equipment being unloaded from their ships at ports and in unexpected remote locations in parts of West Africa, each vessel bearing the hammer and sickle insignia. The Soviets' reach and influence extended beyond their adjacent border regions.

The Soviet Empire was a global presence, actively taking part on the world stage and commanding a formidable force at sea. This much was certain to me.

***

"Cosgrove," is all I say into the receiver when the phone rings at my desk.

Some things haven't changed over the years in the Bureau, all the agents answering using their last names. No one knows why.

It's just that way and will probably stay that way as long as there's an FBI.

"Hey, it's Jason, from IRS. Thank you again for your help a few weeks back. Now it's my turn to return your favor, so we'll be even, I suppose. There's someone you might find interesting to speak with about Russia and the mafia. But I won't get into the details on the phone. I can bring the person by your office today, or tomorrow? What works for you?"

I consider the recent visit of Nazari to my office. No, this cannot have any connection to it. "OK, later today is fine with me. It won't take too long, right?"

"No. Look, she's in a jam with us, and with the California State tax authorities. So, she's looking to barter. You know how that goes."

Hmm, it's a she, he tells me. Could it be this Ms. Nazari?

"OK, Jason, see you later; just tell the receptionist to buzz me when you arrive."

# Chapter 7

It's late afternoon when Jason and the woman arrive at the Bureau's office. I've thought ahead and asked Sharon to sit in on the interview. As the only analyst I'm aware of who can write in shorthand, she'll be able to take notes and write up the report.

Just as I suspect, the woman turns out to be this mysterious Nazari. I can tell by Jason's body language and introductions that he has no clue she's already dropped by the office. Sharon keeps quiet and follows my lead. I don't know what sort of game Nazari is playing or why, but to disclose the previous visit would be awkward and could backfire.

There may well be a logical explanation, but it's not the priority at this moment.

Jason has brought this Nazari to my office in return for a favor, and now I have to conduct the interview as though we haven't yet met, without giving the slightest hint to Jason that Nazari actually visited the office days earlier. The question in my mind is not only the "why" but also, who tipped off Nazari about a Russian-speaking agent working in the San José office? There is, in fact, only one, and that's me.

And, more importantly, what is her reason for coming to see me?

Is this really some sort of orchestrated provocation, or is it Nazari playing a kind of game with which I am not familiar? Does she know something about my past?

No matter. We proceed with the interview, and I let Sharon ask preliminary questions, background stuff. Jason adds details from the IRS side.

"Ms. Nazari is here voluntarily and has information she thinks might interest you. To be transparent, Ms. Nazari is the subject of an IRS criminal tax evasion investigation, relating to her gas stations operations, and the California Tax State Authorities are also investigating her for criminal tax evasion, but that is separate from the IRS investigation.

"I can't share the details of this investigation with you, but it's serious as Ms. Nazari knows. So, go ahead with your questions as she has information regarding a matter not connected with the current tax fraud cases," explains Jason, wanting to get things moving.

It's already late afternoon, and the workday is winding down.

"Thanks, Jason. OK, Ms. Nazari, go ahead. What is it you wish to share with us today?"

As soon as the words are out of my mouth, I regret asking her such an open-ended question. I should have begun the interview with something easier, narrower.

In short, I have just made a rookie mistake.

It is no surprise to me when she immediately pivots, turning the open question to her advantage. "I have information about diamonds. Diamonds being stolen from Russia and brought here, to San Francisco. It involves serious people from that country who have set up a company to import the diamonds; it's being run by two Armenian brothers, David and Ashot Shagirian. I've known them both for a while, and I know their cousin very well.

"In fact, their cousin has done business with me in the past, but we've gone our separate ways. I run several gas stations and was in the same sort of business with that cousin as well. His sister, Lara, is married to David. David Shagirian."

"Why do you think someone stole the diamonds from Russia?" I ask, trying to assess her access and reach to the potential subjects.

"They told me so," she says smugly and simply.

"Why would they admit such a thing to you, even if it were true?" I respond. She is likely, after all, exaggerating, recognizing that cooperation with the FBI on such a case might help her own situation, what with the serious criminal tax evasion charges looming, and the implications for the survival of her businesses, income, and livelihood.

But before she can answer, I follow up with my next questions.

"So, tell me about these two brothers. What's their story? What's their background?"

I figure it makes more sense to shift back to more measurable and basic questions. After all, if diamonds are being looted and smuggled from Russia to the United States, the more I understand and know about the backgrounds of the principal players in the U.S., the better the chance of any investigation actually succeeding, so I figure.

"They sell flowers," Nazari responds, matter-of-factly.

"Huh? What do you mean?" I don't understand her response.

"Well, they were selling flowers on the streets of San Francisco. Not so long ago. Now, they have plush offices in the Transamerica Pyramid building and are buying their own building for diamond cutting," Nazari adds a hint of jealousy and a smirk.

She probably knows the response will trigger a reaction from me.

She looks confident that she's gained my attention, to her advantage. She also appears pleased that I do not mention or reveal our prior encounter with Jason sitting there in the room. I see it in her eyes; I have passed her "confidentiality" test; well, so far at least.

"OK, let's back up a bit. How can you be selling flowers on the street one day, then suddenly, you are an executive working in the Transamerica Pyramid building? There must be more to it?"

Nazari is stringing me along, but she has hooked me.

I am intrigued, hearing this new information from her, but I have to let the interview play out to extract as much information as she will share in this first "official" meeting.

I already figure there will be more such meetings, at least I hope so.

In my mind, Nazari's information seems firsthand, and not through a third party. But it is difficult to judge much of anything with such a person as Ms. Nazari.

She is a survivor, and as a young Afghan woman in a man's world, owning and operating gas stations, men do not intimidate her. She probably enjoys playing with them, and with me.

Well, whether it is a game to her or not, her direct access to the potential subjects is important if she is going to work with me against these brothers and perhaps others who could be involved in this potential criminal case, from the U.S. side anyway.

Jason remains quiet, not seeming at all impressed by Nazari's story as I can see from his body language, slouched in his chair with his back turned to Nazari as she speaks.

By this stage in our first "official" meeting, I am satisfied, having accomplished much of what I set out to do in this interview. I now have a good sense of Nazari's access to the principals, the subjects of this potential case, and to a lesser extent, an understanding of the depth of her knowledge about the theft scheme.

But it still isn't clear if she is getting her information from more than one person.

No matter.

It is better not to probe too much in that direction, not in this first official interview, with an IRS Special Agent sitting in the room. I will first have to deal with the pending charges Nazari is facing. She cannot work with the Bureau if she is close to being indicted or arrested. An indicted person will have little to no credibility with the subjects. They will stay clear of her. Nor will she have much credibility with a jury at trial if things progress that far.

"Ms. Nazari, before you leave today, there is something I need to know from you. You can think about it and let me know later, but you will have to decide in the coming days.

"Are you willing to work with the Bureau? To possibly meet with these individuals involved in this matter, and to record those conversations, and perhaps, eventually, to testify in court against them? I don't need an answer now; just think it over and let me know. We have little time, however."

I have to raise this one question, the central question at hand.

No doubt this Ms. Nazari will not be the easiest person to deal with as a source, a confidential source, but I've handled complicated and vulnerable young women before, and not always with the desired outcome. 'Running' sources is an essential part of the job as an investigator. There are no other viable options available to me at this early stage.

In my mind, Nazari's information, although singular and without independent corroboration, provides a sufficient basis to open a preliminary inquiry.

Now, the actual work to corroborate her information and story will soon begin.

Walking back to our offices, I turn to Sharon.

"Strap in. This is going to be one hell of a ride. I can feel it already," I venture.

She says nothing in response, only nodding in agreement.

When my cell phone rings on the drive home, I just know it is her, my sister. She starts straight away, skipping, "How are you doing?"

"So, you still not interested in my work, my research? You need to listen to me. Our grandfather was a pioneer in using behavioral analysis. You probably didn't know that. I'm uncovering more and more."

"Jen, I can't talk right now. I'm buried in work and had a tough day. Let's talk later."

"But I'm onto something. I just know it. I'm having episodes again, and flashbacks, worse than before. I don't know why; maybe my research is triggering something. Anyway, I went to Cranberry Lake. Something happened to me there."

"Look, you need to live in the present time, Jen. Heck, I can barely get through my day, and you're focusing on the past. It's gone, Jennifer. The past is the past. Let it go."

"But you once told me you got flashbacks and saw things. Isn't it true? Did you forget that? I'm telling you … You need to listen; are you listening? He's still out there. The killings haven't stopped. You're in California doing whatever you're doing, but he's out there, stalking and killing. It won't stop just because you saved one of his potential victims."

I am silent. Just a few days ago, Nazari also asked me if I was listening.

Women. They're all driving me crazy.

My sister's call throws me back to that time, to my first office, Kansas City, with crack cocaine rampant. It was the new rage on the streets, highly addictive and readily available everywhere. I had developed sources close to a violent Cuban emigrant drug trafficking group dealing in this deadly poison. Three of the four sources I'd developed were females, young prostitutes and drug users working the Kansas City streets.

They were young, vulnerable, but somehow relatable.

I was comfortable around these street savvy women, though not even understanding why I could relate to and talk to them in a language they understood.

Two of my sources would end up being murdered, three months apart, and my Bureau partner and I somehow managed to grab the one remaining female source off the streets before she had time to meet the same gruesome fate.

She would eventually testify to the Federal Grand Jury and enter the witness protection program, leaving Kansas City forever for a better life, or so I hoped.

I suspected a serial killer, possibly associated with the Cuban drug trafficking ring, was behind these killings. The two young women, Nikki and Carmen, had been close friends, and they'd almost died together too, just as they'd lived their lives, close to one another.

It was sad to think of it in this way, yet also oddly reassuring they were now not alone in that next plane, wherever they had gone to after their respective killings. They were not actually murdered together, but ended up in the same place, not that far apart time-wise either.

Their bodies turned up in Kansas City's Gillham Park, a mere three months apart; someone had strangled them to death.

During those days, unknown assailants were violently murdering not only those two friends, but also many other women in Kansas City.

In fact, there were dozens of young women, mostly prostitutes, being violently murdered around the city, week after week, month after month, year after year. The Kansas City Homicide Detectives felt frustrated and exhausted.

They were making little progress, and also had no solid suspects.

***

Now, as I arrive back at my residence, I force myself to return to the present and put the thoughts and feelings from those times out of my mind, at least as much as I can manage.

There is no point in revisiting the past with its multitude of unsolved murders.

Not yet at least.

# Chapter 8

New York City, 1937

"Detective Cosgrove, what made you suspect the deceased, Joan Kuleba, was in that bungalow on the day in question?" asks the prosecuting attorney in front of the jury sitting to decide the fate of the accused. Simon Elmore, a fifty-seven-year-old unemployed painter, has been charged with the young girl's brutal murder.

"I heard noises coming from the bungalow, the sound of someone moaning, or in pain. I realized the noises could have been the little girl, and the bungalow looked abandoned and in disrepair. I immediately suspected she'd been abducted, so I swiftly took action and found the accused inside. In the basement, I came across little Joan. She was dead."

The jury becomes fixated on the detective's testimony, which goes on for nearly three hours as he explains his detailed and methodical questioning of the suspect, and the admissions he has made, including the confession of having killed "little Joan Kuleba" as the newspapers call her. She was only four years old.

The prosecutor asks, "Explain to the jury why you decided to break away from the rest of the search party, which had been looking in the beach's shallow waters for many hours, suspecting she'd drowned while playing on the beach that day. While the search was winding down, you went off in a completely different direction, on your own. Why did you do that?

"What evidence or information did you have that made you walk away from the search party, through the high reeds and through such a swampy area, to the isolated bungalow?"

The prosecutor seems perplexed about why Cosgrove broke away from the search party, when the consensus was that the little girl had drowned, and they would find her body in the coming days, washed up on the beach. Cosgrove has some explaining to do.

Everyone is eager to hear what he has to say.

"Her clothes," he answers, and pauses. "Her shoes and jacket were neatly folded, arranged and laid on the sand, near where she'd last been seen by her relatives. A four-year-old child would never act in such a deliberate manner. That sort of behavior would be exceptional for such a young girl but not for an adult. In analyzing the scene, I realized this was no drowning, and it was more probable that someone older had abducted her.

"A stranger most likely," he concludes.

"And regarding your 'analysis' as you call it, did you learn about this technique in training or from your fellow detectives?"

"No. I have been studying and researching the pathology and behavior patterns of criminals, their habits, their traits, and tendencies. I believe this knowledge, and using analysis, scene analysis, can help me and my department solve such murders."

"Well, in this case, your so called 'analysis' proved right, Detective Cosgrove. My questioning is over for today. Thank you for your testimony. You are dismissed."

Two days later, the jury returns a guilty verdict, sentencing the accused to death.

This summer, several other young girls will be found murdered in New York City. In fact, young women are being found dead in alarming numbers around New York City, and this has been the case going back several years. Most of the homicides remain unsolved.

New York City, in these times—the darkest days of the Great Depression—is experiencing serious crimes of all sorts. Families, children, fathers and mothers are struggling to survive, unable to put bread onto the table or to heat their meager rooms.

Many are losing their accommodation, as dire as it was anyway, being turned out onto the streets by desperate landlords who say, "I don't give charity. I also need to eat."

Work is scarce and unemployment is high and rising fast.

There are missing children, orphans, starving people, homeless people—growing exponentially in numbers due to all the missed rent payments—camped out all over the city.

The New York Police Department faces a shortage of resources and personnel to handle all the crimes. Detective Cosgrove's fellow detectives do not embrace his "analysis" approach and ideas, nor the leadership of the department.

To them, it makes more sense to rely upon the more traditional and long-used approaches in dealing with the investigation of such heinous and violent crimes.

Suspects' confessions often only come as a result of beatings and intimidation.

"Analysis" and a different approach to interviews are seldom, if ever, used. It is a fact, a sad reality that no one seems to question or even to mind in these dark and desperate days.

# Chapter 9

San José, California, 1993

"Don, do you have a few minutes to talk?" I ask from the doorway to the Bureau office of Donald Pierce, supervising Special Agent of the San José Organized Crime and Drug Squad.

"Sure, Cos, but make it quick. What's up, dude?"

Pierce has a relaxed demeanor but knows his stuff after years of working the streets. We first met during the kidnapping of Charles Geschke, and Pierce later used his pull with the boss of the San Francisco Division to get me assigned to his squad in San José.

I say, "I want to open a new case; it relates to diamonds stolen from Russia and brought to California. The Russian mafia's likely involved. Think I might need a subpoena for some records. Do you have any ideas which AUSA—the term used for a federal prosecutor or Assistant United States Attorney—I can work with?"

"Aren't you busy enough? We have plenty going on already, and you want to open a new case? You have some solid evidence about the theft?"

Pierce's points are valid, but I want to avoid an in-depth discussion with my boss at this early stage. My plan is to alert Pierce to the case, and get a recommendation regarding a prosecutor, nothing more.

Donald Pierce has a reputation among the office staff for being a straight shooter, quiet and direct, but a competent agent. He is also a gifted athlete, an accomplished windsurfer.

He traveled the world competing on the amateur and pro circuit, years back.

"I just need subpoenas for documents, but don't know which AUSA would handle Russian stuff," I respond, trying to keep the response short and to the point.

Pierce turns his head and looks out of his office window.

"There is someone in San Francisco. He's an AUSA on the Organized Crime Strike Force in the U.S. Attorney's Office; his name's Terry Miller. Tell him I referred you and get up there to see him, pronto. Let me know how it goes and keep me posted about this case. But don't neglect your other stuff. Stolen diamonds? You do know everyone's corrupt there in Russia. So, you'll not get any help from the Russian side, and don't be naïve thinking otherwise. And the Bureau has no legal attaché office in Russia; that will never happen. Well, good luck. Later, dude."

It is Pierce's customary way of ending a meeting.

"Thanks. I'll keep you posted," I answer, heading back down the hall to my office.

At least my boss has now been informed. Heck, he's even given me the name of an AUSA, so that box is now ticked.

Now, I have to get up to San Francisco and meet this Terry Miller.

AUSAs can be fickle and difficult to work with; at least this one comes via a strong recommendation from my boss. Pierce has also told me that Miller is a veteran prosecutor, and he's prosecuted organized crime figures in Cleveland, Ohio.

It seems unlikely that Miller will be at all familiar with the Russian mafia, however.

I've been in the San Francisco U.S. Attorney's Office a few times, but never met Miller before. However, I've interacted with Organized Crime Strike Force attorneys while working in Kansas City, so I have a sense of what to expect and what's required of me.

As I knock on the office door of AUSA Miller, he is behind his desk.

He stands up to greet me.

"Don called and told me you're working on a case with connections to Russia. Sounds interesting. Tell me about it," Miller says.

He motions for me to sit in the chair facing his desk.

"It's a new case, and there may be connections to the Russian mafia and to corrupt officials in Moscow. They are transporting stolen diamonds from Russia to San Francisco. I am still identifying the players, but the dominant entity involved on this side is a company called Golden ADA." I tell Miller I have a new source, but it has some serious issues with the IRS and with the California State Tax Authorities.

"Well, if the diamonds are stolen, let's see, what could be our violation?"

Miller surprises me with the comment; I assumed Miller would immediately recite the federal criminal statute upon which the case would be based.

Next, he reaches for the thick Federal Criminal Code and Rules book, the bible for any federal prosecutor, sitting on the desk and shelves of most FBI Special Agents.

Miller says, "Well, let's say someone stole the diamonds from Russia and is transporting them to the United States. Yep, those acts fall under Title 18, Chapter 113, Stolen Property. Proving this won't be easy, but let's not get ahead of ourselves for now. What will be your next move? What is it you need from my side?"

"My source tells me the principals in Golden ADA—the Shagirian brothers David and Ashot, and a third guy who's sort of a mystery, Andrey, a Russian national—have applied via Shell Oil Company for franchises to operate Shell Oil gas stations. I understand they have to provide a lot of background information as part of the detailed application and vetting process. My intention is to serve Shell with a subpoena for this information."

"OK. Well, I need to open a Federal Grand Jury investigation from my side, so I can issue subpoenas, and start things rolling from the U.S. Attorney's Office. Send me the details regarding Shell Oil. Their address, what sort of documents you want, etc., and I'll get you the subpoena. You can serve it yourself and retrieve the documents. How does that sound?"

"Great. Thanks, Terry. I have a question for you about my source. With criminal tax evasion charges looming over her head, I need to get those charges suspended or set aside. The source cannot work with us when there's stuff like that pending. And, besides, if one day the source were to testify, we would have to deal with that, right?"

"Yeah. Better to talk to the IRS, and I'm not sure who to speak with on the California side for the State tax violations. It's always something with sources. At least … it's a she, right?"

"Yeah, she."

"Well, at least she isn't the subject of a murder investigation."

That would complicate things much further.

"Terry, can I ask you something?"

"Sure."

"Don tells me you've prosecuted organized crime cases in your previous assignment in Cleveland. Did you work with agents there?"

I'm simply curious but also trying to get a sense of who Miller is, and his prior relations with the Bureau.

My agent colleagues from another FBI Field Office would probably share something with me about this Miller. Heck, they might vouch for him or at least give me some insight into Miller such as what it would be like to work with this prosecutor, the dos and don'ts.

Miller sits up in his chair and shifts to a serious tone.

"I worked with several FBI agents there and prosecuted two, relating to their dealings with sources, and the deliberate nondisclosure of information. It wasn't a pretty case, and I didn't enjoy it, but they left me no choice,"

I am not expecting this sort of response, trying not to act surprised, though I'm wondering why my supervisor didn't clue me in about Miller's past work in Cleveland.

Prosecuting FBI agents for misdeeds is a serious matter and won't make a prosecutor very popular with FBI Field Office agents. No matter. I am too far down the road now with Miller to find another prosecutor. Besides, he seems interested in working with me too.

He comes across as a competent and experienced prosecutor. I will need someone with OC experience, and a willingness to think and act outside the box. The past is the past as I told my sister a few days earlier. It's best to let it go. Miller is the guy for now, and at least he didn't hesitate or question my strategy of getting information from Shell Oil.

"Hey, before you leave," Miller asks. "I forgot to ask you something. Who do you intend to work with from the Russian side? Did someone tell you, or will someone from their government come forward to say the diamonds are stolen?"

It is a logical question.

"Well, I'm working on that. We have no FBI representation in Russia. No legal attaché office, not like in London or Paris. But I have other ideas."

"Well, OK. Let's stay in touch. Oh, and Don tells me you speak Russian. That's good. Might just come in handy. He also mentions you have OC experience from Kansas City. The KC Mob was pretty strong back in the day; did you see the Scorsese film? Not Goodfellas, but the most recent one, Casino. Same principal actors but they've added Sharon Stone to the mix. Interesting how he portrays the KC mob. Well, that's all in the past, right?"

"Yeah. I suppose so. OK, Terry, I've taken enough of your time. Thanks for the support, and I look forward to working with you."

"Oh, another thing. Geschke—you met him? During the kidnapping case, I mean. And you testified, so I've heard. He and his company, Adobe Systems, basically invented computer scanning. It's a game changer for business, and for ours. You'll see; we'll be scanning stuff all over the place; the fax machine will be nothing more than a paperweight one day."

Miller's comments about the Geschke case surprise me, but they are enlightening.

Miller has done some checking on me.

I can't decide whether that is a good or a bad thing. No matter. We all have pasts, particularly in this business.

I leave the office and return to San José, mission accomplished for this day. But there is plenty to deal with and the case is now officially opened in the U.S. Attorney's Office as a Federal Grand Jury investigation. One day at a time, one day at a time.

"Welcome back, Special Agent Cosgrove!" says Sharon Austin in a slightly sarcastic tone. "Are you ready for your briefing on De Beers and the diamond business?"

"Sure. Guess I need to understand this stuff if we're going to be digging into this business, right?"

"Yeah. And digging is what this diamond stuff is all about. At least that's where it all begins, in the diamond mines. The ones concerning us are in Russia, mostly Siberia."

Sharon explains what she's learned in her research and the outreach to her own Bureau connections in Washington, and elsewhere.

The Bureau has experts in every subject and field, even in the diamond trade.

"De Beers has been a big player in the diamond trade since the late 1800s with their mines in South Africa. The Oppenheimer family eventually took over the business, focusing on the distribution of rough, uncut stones. Ernest Oppenheimer transformed the company into an empire, the 'Central Selling Organization' establishing exclusive contracts with both suppliers and buyers, everyone benefiting. Yet everyone recognized the diamond market was artificial. The flooding of diamonds onto the market, without controls, could collapse it.

"The valuation of stones had collapsed years back in the 1930s, so no one wanted a repeat of that. But the real genius of De Beers was in their marketing and advertising. You've heard the phrase, 'A Diamond is Forever'?"

"Of course. Who hasn't?"

"Yep. Well, things really took off with that campaign, not just in the United States, but in Japan. In fact, I found articles stating only 5 percent of Japanese brides wore diamond engagement rings in the late 1960s. By 1981, some 60 percent of all Japanese brides had these rings. All from De Beers' marketing and reach into a market not in existence before."

"OK, Sharon, so what does this have to do with our situation?"

I feel myself getting restless and impatient.

"I'm getting to that. Now to Russia. Well, the Soviet Union and De Beers. The Soviet Union began mining diamonds in the 1950s. Their government agreed to sell its production only through De Beers. I suppose it made sense, since the Soviet Union needed hard currency, and they couldn't sell diamonds directly to the West, to diamond distributors, because it was too complicated and wouldn't work for them.

"De Beers already had an established and successful global distribution network. Here's where things get really interesting. My research and contacts tell me De Beers executives were dealing with the United States and with the USSR. Apparently, the U.S. government permitted De Beers executives to travel unimpeded in and out of the U.S., despite monopoly restrictions which severely limited their U.S. operations."

"Oh boy. I see your point. This may be a sort of intelligence operation. We could wind up in a real mess. I can think of a bunch of reasons Golden ADA and the Russians are now setting up a diamond cutting and distribution company in California. But my gut tells me that based upon everything we know so far, this is a criminal conspiracy. Yeah, it's possible certain U.S. government entities sanction or support this operation. No matter. I'm working the criminal angle and in the meantime, in reality, if this whole thing is nothing more than an intelligence operation … the nature of which I do not know …"

I am rambling, and she cuts me off.

"Dennis, those are our choices as I see it, for now anyway."

Sharon appears to have embraced the investigation fully. "Our" choices, she tells me.

"OK, Sharon. Thanks for the background. So, we can continue to work this case as a criminal investigation, and if we get pushed aside or pushed around by the higher ups in the Bureau, or by another U.S. government entity, we can react, and deal with that issue when and if it happens. Or we can stop right now before we get in too deep and wind up in a real mess from which we cannot extricate ourselves. No one has directed us to open this case and if we close it, no one will care or object."

I am waiting for her response.

"It's your call. You're the case agent. As long as we aren't naïve about the possibility of an intelligence angle, maybe that's enough for now. We just march on, and let things develop as they may."

I say, "What about seeking legat office help in London, to have them reach out to De Beers, to their Central Selling Organization? I think we need to check that box. De Beers may already know about this Golden ADA operation. I don't see how they'd be pleased about it either, assuming they do know of it. If De Beers is involved behind the scenes for whatever reason, the risk is we'll show our cards by revealing our investigative interest."

She meets my eyes, then I ask, "So, the risk is minimal, right?"

"I'm ahead of you," she responds. "I drafted a lead for the legat office in London to speak with De Beers. Look at the lead; you'll need to run it by Pierce and get him to sign off on the request."

She is really on top of things.

"OK. I'll get Don to sign off on the help request. Maybe he knows someone in our London office to push this along so we don't have to wait for months for them to speak with De Beers. They're super busy there, I understand. The FBI's London office is the biggest we have overseas."

***

The telephone rings in the early morning at my desk the next day.

"Dennis, it's Jason. There's a U.S. customs agent I've worked with in the past. We were just catching up with one another and he's mentioned an interesting importation he's examining regarding diamonds from Russia. Wants to know if I can think of anyone in the Bureau he can reach out to. I think you should meet with him if you've decided to pursue this thing. His name is Rich Marino. I'll send him your way if it's OK with you."

"Sure, just give him my telephone number so we can meet. The sooner the better. Thanks for the heads up," I tell him.

I have worked with the U.S. Customs Service before and should have been expecting this stuff to come up. It will be interesting to see what Marino has going on. I can simply ignore the Customs Service and continue the case, but the importation of goods into the United States also falls within their jurisdiction. It is worth exploring the possibility of working with this Customs Service special agent. We schedule a meeting for the next day.

U.S. Customs Service Special Agent Rich Marino arrives in the office, exactly at the agreed upon time. He wastes no time in laying out what he's discovered. There are several declared importations of diamond, cut and uncut rough stones. The import documents all appear in order, but Marino suspects there is something going on behind the scenes.

He is a seasoned investigator, and relies on his experience, also his intuition.

There are no other Bureau agents to work with. They are all occupied with other cases, and this Rich Marino, with his New York roots, seems to be someone I can team up with, besides Sharon, the intelligence analyst.

I ask, "Rich, do you think your management will allow you to work this case? With the Bureau? With me, that is. It's going to take time to figure things out. We know very little about the players, the scope and nature of this criminal enterprise. That's assuming it is criminal, but I've already got a subpoena served on Shell Oil for their records and met with an AUSA in San Francisco. Are you game?"

I don't want to waste valuable time with the lengthy process involved to enter a formal interagency cooperation arrangement.

"OK. Let's try it. I'll inform my boss that the Bureau is committed to the investigation and inquire if we can collaborate. I think he'll green light me to work with you."

"Rich, we'll be partners. Let's keep each other informed, and no proactive moves without clearing with one another. I've got a new source but need to get through a few hurdles before we can actively engage her. She seems to have access to some players."

Marino says in a somber tone, "Dennis, one other thing. There looks to be SFPD involvement, yeah, the San Francisco Police Department. I'm not sure about the department's role. Some of their sworn officers are providing security for the operation, off duty. Just something to keep in mind. This could get ugly."

"OK, Rich. I didn't know that, but we need to be mindful of our moves and conducting any discreet surveillance of Golden ADA operations and personnel could be tricky if SFPD officers, off duty or not, are providing security."

# Chapter 10

The documents from the subpoena I've served on Shell Oil are ready sooner than I expect. I place the large box on the passenger seat and head back to my office. As soon as I am at my desk, I remove the lid and pull out copies of the application packet for a Shell Oil franchise.

The application consists of many pages. It looks to contain plenty of background information about the applicants. I call Sharon into my office, and we begin to methodically review the documents page by page, paragraph by paragraph. A fuller but not complete picture is emerging about Golden ADA, and about the individuals running the company.

Among the subpoenaed documents is information about David and Ashot Shagirian, corroborating some of the story told to me by Ms. Nazari. Andrey Kozlenok's full name is also there, listing him as one of the applicants for the franchise. His employment history from Russia includes mention of prior work with a joint venture, Sovkuwait-Engineering.

One reference catches my attention, a Russian named Eugeniy Bychkov, head of a Russian government entity known as ROSKOMDRAGMET, the Russian Committee for Precious Gems and Metals. The application packet includes several other character references in Russia and the United States, with whose names I am not familiar.

Among the character references are several individuals with Armenian sounding names, all listed as living in California. These include Grigor Azarian, and Artiom Kevorkian.

I recognize the Kevorkian name, since he is a former business partner of Ms. Nazari's, and the brother-in-law of David Shagirian.

It will take time to analyze and understand the information in the subpoenaed documents, but it is a good start and importantly, a discreet or covert way to begin the investigation. Yet many questions remain unanswered. It is not clear why the individuals from Russia are working with Armenians from California. There has to be a reason for this, and it is important to understand the nature of the relationship between these individuals.

If this is indeed an international criminal conspiracy, there has to be a structure. Someone has to be in charge at the top of this structure, particularly since the amount of money involved seems substantial. And the smuggling of diamonds from Russia, well, that is a mystery with many layers to peel away and understand.

To unravel such a conspiracy will take time and patience, and maybe a little luck.

"Cosgrove," I answer as I pick up the desk phone.

"Meet me at twelve at Khyber Afghan Grill. You probably haven't been there before."

"OK, Annie. See you then," I respond, not allowing myself to ponder why the sudden request for a meeting from Ms. Nazari.

The restaurant looks authentic Afghan. The Afghan diaspora has settled in a handful of cities around the United States, including San José, most arriving after fleeing the Soviet invasion, including refugees from Kabul, like Annie Nazari.

At a secluded table in the corner of the restaurant, Nazari is there waiting.

I spot her easily.

She stands to greet me, looking stunning in a traditional Afghan dress with intricate embroidery. "I have a dinner tonight, formal," she says. "That's why I'm dressed like this. I already ordered for us. You like kebabs?"

"Yes, of course. So, what's up, Annie?" I ask, wanting to focus on the case, and her cooperation or potential cooperation.

"I want to let you know I will work with you. Just tell me what you need from me, and I will do it. I don't want to deal with anyone else, just you," she tells me.

"OK. Good to know. There will be times you may have to work with other agents besides me. That's the Bureau, Annie. You understand that."

The waitress brings a large tray of food, an impressive array of dishes with which I am not familiar.

"This is the food of my homeland, the food from my home, where I was born, grew up, and had to flee from as a young girl. You heard of 'Afghan refugees,' right? My family and I were part of that wave," she says, with a sad look on her expressive and delicate featured face. "Look at me now. I am a successful businesswoman working with the FBI. No one would believe this back home."

She sounds so enthusiastic.

"Annie, please don't reveal, ever, that you are working with us or with me. Not with anyone. Not your family, your friends, your work associates. No good will come of it."

Her smile is instantly gone, my words hitting like a slap across her face. This is not the first time someone has slapped her. The smile that evaporated with my words is already back.

"I need to resolve some issues before you can actively work with me," I begin. "I will need to deal with the pending state criminal tax evasion charges filed against you. As far as the IRS, they have agreed to put their investigation on hold, considering your cooperation.

"But Annie, you need to pay your taxes in full, and don't play games with the IRS or with the California tax authorities. And whatever you do, don't let any of your business associates steer you in another direction or convince you otherwise. You will wind up in jail, and they will seize your property, your bank accounts, your businesses. You will face ruin. There will be nothing I can do to help you. From here on, you need to do everything by the book. You understand me, Annie?" I tell her in a definitive and serious tone, figuring I need to be direct so she understands how high the stakes are.

I have somehow persuaded the IRS to hold off and not pursue their investigation against her. But I still have to deal with her pending state charges.

"I understand, and will do a good job for you. I promise. Now, let's have lunch. This is the best Afghan restaurant in the city. None better. Oh, my first name is actually Roxanne, but here people call me Annie."

"Roxanne? OK, I will call you as you wish, Annie."

I figure it is enough business talk for today, so the conversation shifts to small talk. If I am going to direct Nazari and put her in harm's way against the conspirators, I need to get to know her as a person, not just a confidential source. I consider myself capable of dealing with sources and for whatever reason, most of my sources—from my present assignment to my past assignment in Kansas City—are women, young and attractive.

I long since promised myself to never cross the line with any of them and never have done. Strictly business. Most sources, informants, are highly manipulative and streetwise creatures who can turn on you in an instant. But they are also the bread and butter, a necessity to have if you are going to be a successful investigator in the Bureau. All good agents run multiple sources. The tricky part is to not allow the sources to run you.

As we depart the restaurant, Nazari turns and faces me, placing her hand for the briefest moment on my arm as if to make her point.

"I think I am being followed in my car. I am not sure, but have this feeling. I just want you to know. I am not afraid, and it could be nothing, but it started a few days ago."

My mind races, also thinking I am being followed. So, this revelation could be Nazari's imagination, or her wanting to see my reaction to the threat, or several other possibilities.

"Annie, just keep your eyes open. If you get a license plate or vehicle description, call me. Don't approach or play games with any following vehicle or vehicles if you think you're being followed. If you're on the road and feel someone is following you, call me right away. Don't go directly home, just drive, and don't try, whatever you do, to outmaneuver or evade the vehicle. You could get hurt. It's likely your imagination. But you never know. Just use your head, OK?"

"OK. I will," she promises. "Goodbye for now."

On the drive home, I find myself back in Kansas City, back in that case.

The newspaper accounts presented it as a highly successful investigation, with me as lead investigator for the Bureau, targeting a violent drug trafficking ring run by Cuban immigrants who had settled in the area. They had come to the United States from the infamous Mariel boat-lift in 1980. The drug ring, composed of eight individuals, had been supplying twenty "crack" cocaine houses in the Kansas City area.

Drug users frequented the crack cocaine houses, and so did female prostitutes addicted to the powerful new drug on the street, "crack," a derivative of cocaine which was usually smoked, giving the user an immediate and intense euphoric high.

I discovered several murdered prostitutes associated with the drug trafficking group even before opening the investigation. The murders would continue during my investigation, however, with the 1987 murders of Nikki and Carmen within three months of each other.

The case took a toll on me. The intensity of working a drug case with multiple subjects and sources, executing search warrants, and making "controlled buys" of cocaine through undercover Kansas City, Missouri police officers, and also with the use of sources, required exacting and detailed planning and execution. It was physically and emotionally draining on me. To make matters more complicated and challenging, I learned that a Kansas City, Kansas detective, had been providing so-called "protection" to the drug ring during the investigation.

They eventually charged him with corruption for his activities with the criminal group, ultimately summoning me back to Kansas City from Russian language school in California, to testify in Federal Court against the detective.

After they found Nikki's body in that park during the summer of 1987, I met with the KC Homicide Unit detectives and offered to assist in the murder investigation.

The detectives reminded me of our grandfather, I told my sister.

Something about their demeanor was so reminiscent and familiar; though never able to explain exactly what it was, I felt something. Their group had a magnetic pull, and they may have also perceived something that day, when they unexpectedly closed their office door to show me the many boxes containing case files of the unsolved murders they were actively investigating. I felt shocked. After all, they had shared none of this information with the press and told me so. Most victims were young prostitutes working the streets in the Kansas City area. They had become addicted to the powerful, new and highly addictive drug.

The detectives told me they'd exhausted all leads and interviewed many witnesses along with potential suspects, but with no success; they were back at square one.

I thought of Quantico and the Behavioral Analysis Unit, the BAU.

I vaguely knew of the work of the unit, but only from my training days at the Academy.

Their offices were remote, in a windowless basement room of the main building. Surely, they would assist. The detectives suspected there could be a serial killer, possibly more than one, on the loose in their city. Someone had murdered a shocking total of seventy-two women, eighteen of whom were not, in fact, prostitutes, from the mid-1980s until 1990.

The killer(s) murdered most of the victims by strangling them, then left their partially clothed or naked bodies in parks or empty and abandoned city lots. I asked around my office in Kansas City to see who had reliable contacts with the unit, the so-called BAU.

I called the Quantico-based unit, thinking that surely, they would be interested and enthusiastic to provide their unique support and guidance as there were already many victims, the count also continuing to climb, and no suspect had been identified or placed in custody.

The agent on the phone told me that BAU didn't profile cases like mine, since the murdered victims were mostly "high risk" victims working as prostitutes, so their lifestyles exposed them to a much greater risk of death or bodily harm than so called "normal" people.

I felt deflated by it all.

The declension of BAU help left me stunned and off guard.

I asked the BAU agent why they couldn't profile cases like mine regardless of the nature or lifestyle of the victims. After all, the killer or killers could change MO and target so-called, "normal people," couldn't they?

The response from him was weak and underwhelming.

It left me feeling maybe this unit wasn't as competent as it claimed, and if they didn't want to profile such cases, there was no chance of me pressuring them to do so.

I was still a relatively new agent, and these BAU agents were supposed to be veterans, highly skilled. So, instead of attempting to find another agent at BAU, I accepted the agent's statements and the declension of BAU help at face value and as their ultimate word.

I turned away from the murder investigations and refocused on the case's original priority, the investigation and prosecution of the drug trafficking ring members. My primary mission was to dismantle this violent group and take it off of the streets of the city forever.

In the end, the authorities indicted, prosecuted, and convicted all eight members of the group in Federal Court. They were behind bars. The community was safe, or safer than it had been when the group was running around the city.

In the meantime, my sister had kept up with the local newspaper articles reporting on the murders; these had continued after I left Kansas City for Russian language school in Monterey, California.

"I can't go back there, Jen," I told her more than once. "If I could do things over, I would never have taken that BAU agent's word as final, as gospel. I regret it, I really do, but I need to move on. There are very competent detectives there in Kansas City. I met them and worked with them. They will find the killer; I am sure of it."

I tried to persuade my sister that the killings would stop. They never did.

"You need to get back there." My sister wouldn't let it go. She continued, "Let me read something from one of the newspaper articles, and I quote, 'The slayings stopped in December 1987, possibly coinciding with the prosecution of the Cuban drug dealers in state and federal courts in 1988. There have been no further slayings of Main Street prostitutes since late 1987.' This is your case the article is referring to. So don't tell me you moved on."

# Chapter 11

San José, CA, 1993

"I need to talk to you. When can you get here?" Don Pierce sounds hurried, a bit distracted.

"Give me an hour, OK?"

I'm down on the beach in Monterey, finishing a long run. By now, it is midafternoon and I figured I would go for a run near home, having finished up covering leads in the area.

There is no reason to return to San José, or at least not until that telephone call comes in, from my supervisor. "What's up, Don?" I ask shortly, as I enter his office.

It is nearly six p.m. now, but most of the office staff are still here, working, processing evidence, writing reports, and talking on the phone. The job isn't 9 to 5, and the volume of work needing to be dealt with daily can crush.

"The boss wants to speak with you about Russian organized crime. Apparently, you're now the expert in the division since you have several active cases. I'm not sure if he wants a briefing or just general background information about Russian O-C. Get up there to the 'city' tomorrow. Rebecca will get you on his schedule." Don Pierce can be a tough read, and I decide not to ask for further details if there are any to be had.

"OK. Will do, Don. I will let you know how it goes," I add.

"Just keep it simple and short. Oh, and my sources inform me the boss' interest might have a connection to Chief Ken Burda, the SF Police Chief. He and Burda are pals," Pierce adds, offering a hint of caution to read between the lines.

Don Pierce has been working in the San Francisco Division of the FBI for several years and knows a lot of the key people. Agents and staff confide in him, viewing him as a competent and trustworthy agent. I can only speculate who this source of Pierce's may be.

It doesn't matter. I will have to be on my toes for this meeting, and Pierce dropping the SFPD chief's name is no coincidence, I figure.

The drive to San Francisco from Monterey takes over two hours in the best of traffic conditions. I park my Bureau vehicle in the basement of the Federal Building and head directly to the boss' office. Rebecca is sitting outside of it, at her desk.

She is a sophisticated forty-something-year-old woman, married to an agent, and she knows pretty much everything going on in the office.

"He's ready for you. Go on in," Rebecca tells me. "He asked me when you were coming, and has other meetings lined up, but he wants to speak with you first."

Rebecca's comments are helpful and give me a sense of what I will walk into, since Rick Webb is the Special Agent in Charge of the entire FBI SF Division.

It is a good bit of intel. She knows precisely what to share and what not to share.

Her heads up and advice can be helpful but only if she likes you. And if she doesn't, you better stay away from her and then do your best to regain her favor.

"Thanks, Rebecca. I just hope I can keep my badge and credentials when this is over," I tell her, in a half-joking manner.

Rick Webb is seated behind his large cherrywood desk. He stands to greet me as I enter, motioning for me to sit in the chair near the coffee table in the room's corner.

"Dennis, thanks for coming in. I have only a few minutes. According to Don, you are the Division's expert on Russian OC. I got a telephone call a couple of days ago, from my good friend, Ken Burda, the SF Chief of Police as you probably have heard mention of, or maybe even dealt with some of his officers. He asked me about Russian organized crime and wanted a briefing from the Bureau about Russian organized crime activities and specifically, what's going on in this area, the City of San Francisco and the Bay. I would like you to meet with him and give him an overview. Be as helpful as you can. He's a friend of the Bureau's, and a good friend of mine. His department works closely with us, and we'd like to keep our relationship that way, open and friendly."

Webb glances for a fleeting moment out of his office window as if he is about to add something but decides not to. It is only a momentary glance, but I pick up on it.

There is something more, but I certainly will not open the door, question the boss, or make any attempt to elicit more details from the head of the division.

That could be considered rude and out of bounds. I let it go.

"OK, boss. I'll reach out to the chief's office and meet with him. Did he say if he had any specific concerns or areas he wanted information about?"

I ask it yet already know the boss is likely to tell me he's aware of nothing more.

Regardless, I cannot resist the urge to test Webb to see if he does, in fact, know more—more than he will share, that is.

"No. He didn't say." Webb breaks eye contact with me for only an instant, but it's long enough for me to conclude that yes, he knows more, just as I thought.

I've conducted enough interviews over the years and have been working as a street agent for over seven years by this time. Even if this interview or meeting is with a Bureau senior official, it doesn't matter on some level. Agents just can't help themselves sometimes.

It's not possible for agents to switch off their intuition and instinct. It is always there for most street agents, at least, who rely on instinct and intuition every day.

Sometimes, it is a matter of life and death.

So, my gut is telling me there's more at play here than Webb is revealing.

I depart from the office after a few minutes of small talk with the boss, about family, food, and sports. Webb is head of the office, but he's been a solid street agent, and a good one.

With no exception, agents respect one another regardless of tenure, position, and rank.

I walk out to the parking garage, find my bureau vehicle, and head back to San José.

I'll have to meet this Ken Burda eventually but let a couple of days pass before calling the chief's office for an appointment. If it's related to Golden ADA, I suspect the meeting with Chief Ken Burda, the "good friend" of Rick Webb, won't be a walk in the park.

There is something about running on sand on a beach. Whatever it is—perhaps the combination of sand, sea, salt air, and the solitude of a long run—I am not sure, but for me, it always, or nearly always, proves to be a mood shifter. My beach runs rarely have anything but a positive effect on the psyche, often helping me to reframe challenges and obstacles, sometimes providing a solution that simply pops into my head during or immediately after finishing a run. There is no logical explanation for the effects on the psyche, none I know of, anyway. Yet, sometimes, a run does not have such a positive effect on me.

In fact, on occasions, it can instead draw me far back into the past, the distant past of my childhood growing up in New York City. And back to that one beach, on that one day.

This is one of those days, one of those runs destined to trigger memories. I feel it coming. Perhaps the meeting with Webb has triggered it, or the anticipation of having to meet with the SFPD chief; I am not sure but I feel it, anyway.

New York City, 1967

"Dennis, where's your brother?" my mother calls out from under those huge framed "Jackie O" 1960s sunglasses, covering most of her face.

"I, I don't know. He was getting me some water for our sand fort, and I think he headed down the beach. He's around somewhere."

I scream the words back to her, yet continue to dig with the plastic shovel to finish the deep moat around the sandcastle; we've built it a few yards in from the destructive reach of the waves breaking on the semi-deserted stretch of beach.

It is midmorning, and at this time of day, the beach is always empty.

The same beach that our detective grandfather would repeatedly lecture us to stay away from. He never explained why. Our mother liked this beach and would take me and my brother with her on occasion whenever she felt like it.

There is a line of trees and brush after the sand, and some bungalows nearby, but nothing more. No facilities or lifeguard towers, none close by at least.

"Well, find him. Stop that digging right now and find him!" my mother screams again as she sits up from the beach blanket, now scanning up and down the deserted sands.

Tucker is gone, vanished, and he is not responding to our calls.

But he can be like that, focused, and in his own imaginary world. With the passage of time, a few minutes at most, panic sets in.

Where is my brother? Has he ventured into the surf and got caught in the undertow?

I am older, nearly ten, while he is just seven years old, a mischievous sort with an endless curiosity about all the things around him. Perhaps he is playing hide and seek to see how long it will take for me to find him. He has done something similar in the past, but never quite like this. This time, it is over ten minutes of frantically calling and running up and down the nearly deserted stretch of beach in search of him.

I am quickly exhausted as the sand is loose, shifting, and heavy.

It takes a lot of effort to run fast, more effort than my mother can imagine.

"I'm going up to the parking lot. I think there's a pay phone there somewhere, or I'll try to find a lifeguard. Don't leave the area and keep looking. Bring him back to the blanket once you find him." My mother seems genuinely panicked, and her panic is visceral. I have never seen her in this sort of state before. Nothing ever seems to rattle her, but this is … different.

Now it is only me. I am alone, no one else.

My mother has left the beach, and my brother is gone, but gone where, we don't know and only wish we did. We dearly, desperately wish it, my mother and I.

I am alone running up and down the beach, calling, screaming out for my brother. He can swim a bit, mostly doggy paddle, but the undertow can be treacherous and take you out to sea if you aren't careful. I can't imagine him venturing into the surf; there's no reason to do that.

He always fills his bucket with water at the end of each wave as it breaks ashore.

Yet his water bucket is gone … and so is my brother.

I spot a line of trees in the distance and run toward them, where there are a few modest and older bungalows scattered about, some abandoned and some with seasonal occupants during hot summer months. The area around the beach looks run down and is not very inviting, but it is good for sunbathing and for kids to play in the soft sand, building sandcastles and running around with balls and kites if they are fortunate enough to have such things. I run fast, fueled by adrenaline and panic, toward the bungalows.

It is nearly thirty minutes since I last saw my brother and twenty minutes since our mother took off toward the parking lot. To get help, I can only assume.

There doesn't seem to be anyone in or around the first bungalow, but I think I hear voices as I approach the second. The place looks run down and abandoned. Perhaps my brother headed there, looking for something, scraps of wood for the sandcastle, or something else. I spot footprints in the sand but can't be sure how fresh they are.

They look small but there are other prints too, larger, maybe adult sized. I call out to him again, screaming his name. I am about to knock on the door when suddenly, there is a firm hand on my shoulder, an enormous hand pulling me back, away from the front door.

I look up. It is my uncle John.

He has his weapon in hand, pointed at the door.

It's a revolver I have seen once before, one he always keeps holstered near his chest.

My uncle being there leaves me speechless and shocked.

I try to speak, but nothing comes out. I am so focused on the bungalow, not noticing him approaching from behind.

Seeing it's my uncle, I figure my mother must have called the police, and my uncle, an NYPD detective, must have heard the call over the police radio, or something like that.

"Step back, stay outside, Dennis," he tells me as he kicks in the door.

It swings open, my uncle moving inside quickly.

I follow out of curiosity, wanting to help but unsure how, or why my uncle hasn't bothered to first knock before kicking the door open.

Seconds later, I hear loud shots, four shots making my ears ring.

My uncle is shooting at a man standing there, inside the bungalow. My brother is there too, sobbing, but alive. It all happens so fast, in a split second.

The man seems to raise his hands in the air, but my uncle shoots at him anyway.

It is too much for me to process in that fleeting and intense moment.

The man falls backwards, hits the floor hard, then slumps over in the dark corner of the room. He is struggling to breathe, clutching at his chest.

Suddenly, his arms go limp as they fall to his sides. He soon stops breathing; he is dead.

My uncle slowly holsters his weapon and picks up my brother who keeps sobbing as my uncle secures him in his arms; my brother's small frame hugs Uncle tightly as they walk outside. It is over. For a moment, I think about asking my uncle why he shot the man.

He was raising his hands in the air, wasn't he?

But I decide against it. My brother is safe, and my uncle has saved him.

It's all that matters now.

Once again, I find myself on the beach in Monterey. I have covered more than a mile on the sandy beach by the time the flashback ends. I haven't thought about that day for a long, long time. Considering calling my wife, brother, or sister crosses my mind, but I choose not to. Better to let go of the past and of that dramatic day.

It seems so long ago now, and no one in the family has ever talked about it again.

I once told my wife, and even she said to leave it be.

She was right, of course. And right now, I have plenty to deal with in the present; my sister might tell me otherwise, but for now, I just can't bear to reach out to her.

# Chapter 12

San Francisco, California

Chief Ken Burda rises from the large office chair behind his desk as soon as I enter his spacious office at San Francisco PD Headquarters. The chief is welcoming and friendly.

I mirror his openness as we shake hands but immediately sense the chief has his own agenda. No doubt he wants information from the FBI.

Burda is a veteran law enforcement officer, former street cop, and accustomed to dealing with rank-and-file officers, detectives, investigators, and senior officials from other agencies, including the Federal Bureau of Investigation.

"Thanks for coming in to talk to me, Dennis. Rick tells me you are the Bureau's expert on Russian organized crime. I know little about this topic, only that the threat posed by Russian criminals is growing, and not just in the Bay area, but all around our country. Isn't that so?"

The chief has dropped his friend's name sooner than I expect.

From this, I know it is going to be that kind of meeting. The chief is a politically savvy guy. He has to be, to rise in the ranks of the police department, to the lofty position of Chief of Police in a city like San Francisco.

"You're right, Chief, the threat is on the rise for sure, and most agencies aren't aware of it, frankly. Most agencies are not au fait with the linkages between Russian organized crime members here in the States and in Russia, and there are few Russian speakers. In the Bureau, we have been investigating the LCN or La Costa Nostra for many years and have a fairly good sense of its structure and activities. Just not the case with Russian OC. We have sources, but the Bureau has a long way to go in trying to understand, let alone successfully investigate and prosecute Russian OC members. We'll get there, eventually."

I want to give the chief something, but don't want to disclose too much, too soon. After all, Rich Marino has told me that SFPD is providing security to Golden ADA, and the chief hasn't yet mentioned anything about that. Gradually, I realize I'm in a chess match of sorts with this chief. It is a fine line to navigate, to be helpful enough to him, but not to reveal too much. I certainly don't want him to pick up the phone and complain to his good friend, Rick Webb, that I haven't been helpful and held back information.

No good can come out of that.

"Well, I don't know if you are aware or not, but several of my officers are providing security to a company based in the city. I understand they are involved in the diamond import and distribution business. The business is called, Gold ... something, and they recently bought a building on Brannan Street, a pretty sizable building. Diamonds are high-value items, so I can understand the need for security. I don't mind my officers working there off duty, but considering the business' connections to Russia, I am concerned about the involvement of Russian organized crime. Have you heard anything?"

Bad-a-bing, just like that, the chief confirms the real reason for our meeting.

This is what I suspect, at least.

Now, I have to weigh my comments and each word I speak to him carefully, without him suspecting or having any reason to think I know more than I'm sharing.

"Yes, I've heard about the business, Chief. There was something in the papers about it recently. Chief, I don't know the diamond business, but I grew up in New York and there was —or is—a vibrant diamond trade there, and in a few other places, like Antwerp. What do your officers do for this company? To provide security, I mean," I ask, in an easy, matter-of-fact tone, and to keep the conversation flowing.

"Their diamonds are from Russia, and the officers provide security to the building and protect the shipments when they arrive by plane. Heck, they offered my department the use of their helicopter, no charge. When they're not using it, at least. They have some sort of landing pad on top of their building."

This is news to me, the offer of a helicopter at no charge. I try not to react or overreact. Is this a quid pro quo? Is the chief providing something in return for this "gift?"

My head races. Is this a kind of red flag signal?

Should I be careful in what I say to Chief Burda from here on out?

"Chief, I suppose they want to make sure the city and your department won't raise objections to a helicopter landing on top of their building. Would your department make use of the chopper?" I decide to extend the chief a lifeline, to see how he reacts.

"Yeah, sometimes. But we would need approvals; bureaucrats, you know. This may take some time." The chief suddenly seems distracted and hurried as he checks his watch.

Burda asks,"Well, what is your take on this company? Do I need to worry? Are they connected to Russian organized crime? They seem legit. It's a pretty big operation, and they appear serious about their business. They invited me to one of the networking events at their offices, part of their marketing strategy, I guess. Well, this sort of business may be good for the city, and heck, might help the city's economy. People rarely associate this city with the diamond business."

The chief only wants to "check the box" it seems to me, to tell the SF City Council, or Mayor's Office, or whoever, that he has met with the Bureau, receiving a clean bill of health from them concerning his department's dealing with this company.

This is trickier than I have been imagining.

I now wonder if the chief might have a personal stake or interest in this venture.

After all, I know little about the chief, almost nothing about his background, interests, hobbies, or if he has any "baggage," or potential conflicts.

I have encountered police corruption in the past, once coming at me unexpectedly during a drug trafficking investigation.

"Chief, I don't see any problems or cause for concern at the moment. The company looks legit based upon what you're telling me. Frankly, I also don't know and understand nothing about the diamond business. If we learn anything of relevance, I will let you know."

My assertions are a surprise to even myself.

The words come out of my mouth, but without my brain, my conscious brain, having much to do with it. There is something off about the chief, his manner of speaking, what he says or doesn't say, that troubles me. I can't quite put my finger on it, but he is the one holding back. For what reason, it is difficult, not impossible, to determine. It might be nothing. He could be a completely honest player, perhaps just naïve—but that naïve?

The next statement from the chief seals it for me.

It's usually that last point or statement in this type of interview that gives everything away.

Often, it's the last comment or question that bears the most relevance and is at the core.

An investigator just has to be patient, to wait for and to recognize that final statement, question, comment where everything is revealed, the great denouement.

It's all in the art of the interview. It takes time, patience and experience.

But the reward is worth the wait. It is there, I am certain. It's coming at any moment. The chief shifts his gaze toward his desk drawer as he begins to speak.

"Dennis, let me give you the business card of the head of the Detective Bureau. He's also head of security for Golden ADA."

With that one statement, the chief has revealed the real reason for wanting to meet with the Bureau. Bingo, we have a winner! He is in deep in this company, in over his head, perhaps, or is concerned about the blowback in case things go south.

He has sanctioned his officers to work security for the company, sanctioning his own head of detectives to work as security chief.

Chief Burda, naïve or not, certainly understands the potential repercussions; a member of his own, handpicked inner circle, the head of the Detective Bureau for SFPD, is now intimately involved with this company, and in a leadership position.

And he does in fact know the full name of the company which he pretends not to recall when he speaks with me. I am close to anger over the apparent charade but need to maintain my composure. There is much more at stake.

"Chief, can I meet with your head of detectives?"

I can't let the door close unaddressed when the opportunity presents itself.

"Sure. You have his card. Tell him we spoke, and I suggested he speak with you."

"Shane Sullivan," I read the name on the card aloud. "OK, Chief. It was good to meet with you today."

"Likewise. Let's stay in touch. Give Shane a call. I am sure he will be more than happy to meet with you."

"Definitely, Chief. Have a great day. I'll let Mr. Webb know we spoke."

I know it won't be necessary since Chief Burda will be on the phone with my boss the moment I leave the office.

Something I haven't disclosed is the fact there's an ongoing investigation, a Federal Grand Jury investigation. Hopefully, the Special Agent in Charge of the FBI office for Northern California won't contradict my previous statement to the chief.

I put the thought out of my head for the time being.

I have no intention of reporting back to Mr. Webb.

Besides, what would I say to him? That I lied to his good friend, a friend of the Bureau? And that I don't trust Mr. Webb's good friend?

It could be disastrous for the case, and for me as Special Agent working under Rick Webb.

No matter. The plot thickens. "This tale, my friends," I whisper under my breath, strolling down the busy sidewalk back to my bureau vehicle parked a few blocks away, "has yet to play out. So much to do, so little time."

I allow myself to laugh louder, mostly out of relief at the meeting finally being over, and I have learned more from this chief than he's learned from me.

This is not my first rodeo after all, far from it. Yet, it is no time and no place for overconfidence or smugness. I have survived the meeting, nothing more.

"The game, Doctor Watson, is afoot." I am recalling a classic line from a Sherlock Holmes detective novel. Indeed, it is, Mr. Holmes, indeed it is.

***

New York City, 1971

As I watch the NYPD officer's testimony being broadcast on the local TV station, it all makes sense now. The Knapp Commission is everywhere, in the newspapers and now on TV, exposing corruption in the New York Police Department on a grand and unimaginable scale.

Everyone is on the take, so it seems.

I watch the broadcast, unable to turn away or change channel.

Officer Frank Serpico is testifying, saying things that seem outrageous and far-fetched. I am mesmerized by what Serpico is telling the Knapp Commission.

He is a marked man, saying such things about his fellow NYPD officers.

He's a rat, a tattletale, but to me, Serpico reminds me of my uncles, perhaps a combination of both of my uncles in a way. The story is all over the newspapers, and on TV talk shows.

My brother and I deliver newspapers each and every day on the paper route to over one hundred houses and apartments, day in, day out. We listen to the TV, and we read the papers, all the time saying nothing between us. After all, this is not just news, it is intensely personal.

There is family involved, our own uncle John, perhaps.

Supposedly, he has gotten caught up in the mess. The same uncle who rescued my younger brother on that fateful day on the desolate beach a few years earlier …

Our grandfather died years before, a renowned detective, a homicide detective from a different era. It was a colorful era, but still a very different one.

Uncle John, corrupt or not, is also colorful, also entertaining and approachable, and fun to be around. The clues have always been there that he could be "on the take."

He has been known to carry cash, humongous wads of bills, also working narcotics in the gritty parts of the city. I recall hearing the term "dirty money" for the first time as a boy.

***

I cannot be over ten years old. My grandmother hurls the stack of bills back across the table when we are vacationing at her Cranberry Lake home in the summer.

She says she doesn't want any of that "dirty money" from our uncle.

To me, the money looks clean, not dirty at all, not the way Grandmother is asserting. Compared to the bills I receive when doing my weekly collection on the paper route, they appear quite normal. In fact, they even seem cleaner than my own bills, and definitely they are much larger denominations. But later, I come to realize the reason for her disgust.

She knows. She knows where that money came from.

My brother and I are also no angels, for sure.

But we have never thought of ourselves as corrupt or dishonest, having had enough encounters with the so-called corrupt police. We run from the police cars chasing us, often escaping by bike or on foot into the woods to avoid being caught.

We run after busting neighborhood streetlights with rocks, stealing candies from the local grocery stores, and after hocking, the term we use for stealing, carting away building materials from home construction sites to build our forts in the nearby woodland.

It's just a game for us, almost taunting the police, daring them to give us chase. The police are mostly lazy in our minds, rarely bothering to leave the comfort of their vehicles to come after us on foot. It's that kind of childhood, and that kind of neighborhood.

All the kids do it, more or less.

Some get caught, but nothing much ever happens to them either. Others, caught for more serious offenses, became known as JDs, juvenile delinquents. They show off their JD cards and demand respect since in a way, it's seen as a badge of honor to carry a JD card.

There is violence, in homes and on the streets. Daily street fights occur, most people using their fists but sometimes throwing rocks, leading to visits to the hospital for stitches.

For me, my brother, and our friends, this is all normal, everyday stuff.

It is what we know, and it's mostly fun until someone gets injured.

Our Uncle John knows what we get up to on the streets; his NYPD friends report back to him about us, but he never makes a big deal out of it with me or my brother, and never rats us out to our parents, either. Uncle John doesn't encourage us, but never admonishes or scolds us, either. Heck, he was much worse as a kid growing up in the city.

At least that's what I've heard.

Our other uncle, Uncle Bill, our grandmother's favorite, is also in the NYPD for a time, then suddenly has to resign for reasons unknown to my brother and me.

But Uncle Bill seems honest, and he's a role model to us.

Not an angel, but we are certain he's never taken money, never, according to our cousins. Anyway, for some reason, this uncle has a falling out with members of the family for reasons I will never quite understand, but that doesn't matter to us either.

Uncle Bill is a good guy, though perhaps not as entertaining or colorful as our Uncle John.

My cousins, my brother, and I all admire and respect Uncle Bill; he served in the navy during World War II, yet no one really talks about that either.

It's all too far in the past. Something like that, I guess.

* * *

"Dennis, I am going to share something with you and your brother, something I haven't shown to anyone else in the family. Not one of your cousins, no one. It will be our secret."

Uncle Bill leads me and my brother to a room in his modest house on the lake and closes the door. Inside the room, a large map has been unfolded on the table, covering most of it, small colored pins everywhere. "Do you know what this is?" he asks us.

"Yeah, it's a map of New York, New Jersey," I respond.

"Yes, you're right. But something more, much more. These are UFO sites, boys; each pin represents a sighting or landing. You have heard of UFOs, right?"

Our uncle isn't joking or exaggerating.

He is serious, confiding in his two young nephews. For what reason, I can't fathom.

"Have you seen them or met them?" my brother, Tucker asks.

It is a logical question. UFOs aren't in the news every day, but we've both seen sci-fi movies, and as newspaper delivery boys, we often get to flip through the local candy store's magazine racks while waiting for the newspaper truck to bring the stacks of papers to deliver.

Sometimes, the magazines tell sensational stories about UFO landings and witness encounters. For my brother and me, our uncle is simply confirming what we have been reading about on a nearly daily basis.

Uncle Bill explains to us that he is a member of an organized but secretive group of UFO watchers who track this sort of stuff in their respective regions.

Well, he says, the group has been noticing an increase in witness sightings of UFOs over the past couple of years. He tells us to keep what he's shown us to ourselves, not to share it with anyone, not with friends, or with anyone at school, and not with any family.

Certainly not with our parents.

We promise we will keep our word. And that is what we do, never sharing what he has shown us, not even with our younger baby sister. Not for many, many years, in any case.

For me, keeping secrets is normal. I and my friends pride ourselves on our ability to keep secrets, and there are many secrets to keep. For us, secrets are a commodity, a gift of sorts but not for exchange or trade. Disclosure of such information is disrespectful and beneath someone. You just don't do that. Besides, you'll lose respect among your peers if you rat out your friends, or if you're a tattletale or a gossip.

Beatings for revealing secrets are therefore common, even for revealing minor ones.

You can also face a permanent ban from building forts or entering someone else's fort.

This is our creed, our code. It has always been that way, so it seems to us.

Sure, not everyone believes in things like UFOs, but if our own uncle believes in such things, that's proof enough for me. They are real, then.

Our uncle has confirmed it to us, and I am sure on some future day, I will encounter UFOs myself, and maybe even investigate, track, and find them, as my uncle does!

It's all a matter of destiny, of fate, and of luck; if something is meant to be, it will happen in its own time. I just have to be patient and wait for it.

# Chapter 13

San Francisco, California

It isn't often that a cop, or a detective, invites another law enforcement official, let alone someone from the Bureau, the FBI, to a restaurant for a meeting.

So, I already know this will be no ordinary meeting.

The meeting with Chief Ken Burda has been challenging enough, and I somehow got through it without tripping over myself or stepping over the line.

Heck, I've learned more from Burda than Burda's learned from me, at least in my estimation. Meeting with the Chief of Detectives for the San Francisco Police Department in so-called normal conditions can be pretty cool, and even informative.

I have grown up around NYPD detectives, my own relatives, working with detectives in Kansas City too, but also testifying against a corrupt one.

So, there are good and bad cops, good and bad detectives. But I have to shed all that to go into this meeting with an open mind. I have never heard of this Shane Sullivan, only knowing he is a thirty-year veteran of the force who has risen through the ranks to head the detective bureau for his department. He is also close to Chief Ken Burda.

I would prefer not to meet Sullivan at such an early phase in this complicated investigation, but there isn't much choice. Or no choice to be precise.

The chief has given me the business card and suggested I meet with him.

The tricky part now is to get through the meeting without tripping up and revealing more than I need to. Besides, Sullivan could well be a useful source of information.

He is the head of security for Golden ADA operations in California, not just some security guard or doorman. How he might have come to be Head of Security and Chief of Detectives at the same time is, however, a complete mystery to me.

Needless to say, Chief Burda didn't reveal it, and I didn't want to pose the question to him either. No good can come of that sort of line of inquiry, to appear too inquisitive.

I am barely seated at the corner table in the nearly empty restaurant when Sullivan speaks.

"Dennis, the chief told me about your meeting with him and suggested we meet. I hope you like Italian food. It's the best in the city. Well, all the good Italian restaurants are in North Beach." He stops and waits for my response.

"I don't know the restaurants in the city, and I've only been to North Beach twice. But I'm originally from New York, so I know good pizza, that's for sure."

Sullivan is already sizing me up and it seems he's decided to start with small talk.

He appears uptight, borderline nervous.

I consider it odd, my prior experiences with detectives having been very different.

I usually find detectives exceptionally good at dealing with people from all walks of life, being calm, poised, and supremely confident, never nervous.

But there could be countless reasons for Sullivan's odd demeanor.

Now it is my turn to get the conversation going in the right direction, to take the lead if Shane Sullivan is going to be passive and nonassertive.

I decide to address Sullivan by his first name.

"Shane, the chief tells me you're heading up security for this company called Golden ADA. How can you juggle both jobs? For me and for most agents, we have a hard enough time doing Bureau work, and you seem have two serious roles. Got to be exhausting, no?"

"Yeah, but it's not too bad. I supervise detectives, but they're all professionals and highly competent at what they do. I support them when they need my help, and I have direct access to the chief if needed. As far as my job with Golden ADA, it's sort of the same. I meet with the folks managing the company, and make sure they have enough security in place for what they do." Sullivan doesn't appear to be minimizing his roles or responsibilities, nor is he trying to impress me with the stature of the senior positions he simultaneously occupies.

"Get the veal. It's the best in the city," Sullivan suggests.

The recommendation immediately brings to my mind the scene of Michael Corleone sitting in the restaurant in the Godfather movie where he shoots the corrupt NYPD Captain, the first bullet in the neck, the next one in the head.

I can't believe what Sullivan has just said.

Is he playing with me? Or is he that clueless?

It doesn't matter. I take the recommendation and nod to the waiter. "I will take the veal."

"So, Shane, this company is importing diamonds from Russia, as I understand. Sounds interesting, but serious in a way as we're talking about a big operation. I know nothing about diamonds, or the diamond business, but it's fascinating to me."

I decide it will be a better tactic to stay away from direct and probing questions. Sullivan is a seasoned detective, and corrupt or not, he will not appreciate being questioned or challenged by an FBI agent. If Sullivan wants to share anything, it is his call. I will not elicit information from such a person by asking clever cross examination style questions.

It would only be rude, and Sullivan could become defensive, even suspicious.

That will serve no purpose and bring me nothing.

He goes on, "As a matter of fact, I know a thing or two about diamonds and jewelry. I am quite interested in this field. I make my own jewelry, rings, and necklaces. This stuff has completely captured my heart; you see, I made this ring."

He extends his hand across the table to show me his work. The ring has several precious stones, all set in yellow gold. Not something I would wear; it's flashy, and seemingly out of character for a detective to wear such a ring. My mind flashes back to my uncle John.

Yes, my uncle might wear such a ring, my corrupt detective uncle.

"Nice ring. I wish I had such a skill. So, Golden ADA is a perfect fit for you, and for them, I suppose. You ever been over there? To Russia?"

I don't know exactly how the diamonds are being transported from Russia to California.

My U.S. Customs Service partner, Rich Marino told me the company uses a private jet, and Chief Burda has told me they also have a helicopter to transport precious stones from the airport directly to the building—and they offer it free to SFPD.

How much Sullivan is involved in the transport, and how much he will admit about his involvement can be revealing about both his character and Golden ADA operations.

"Actually, I have been to Russia. Well, sort of, if you count the airport tarmac in Moscow as visiting a country. I'll tell you about my Russian adventure. You were there ever?"

Sullivan, for whatever reason, wants to share his story with me. Perhaps it's to validate himself, or his involvement; it is hard for me to judge.

I remain quiet and lean in, interested in what Sullivan is about to tell me, and pretending not to know anything about Golden ADA and its operations.

This is not the time or place for probing questions. I need to be a listener, nothing more.

"A few months back, I flew on the corporate jet from San Francisco, all the way to Moscow and back. There were a few folks from Golden ADA on the jet, and I was there for security reasons. Now, we land at a smaller airport in Moscow, not the main international one. It is an impressive operation. We are on the ground only long enough to refuel and are airborne again in one hour or less. As soon as we land, armed personnel in uniform quickly surround the plane. I estimate there are over twenty of them, with a few military looking vehicles close by. I am not sure if they are police, KGB, or military. No one tells me exactly who they are, but they look like official Russian government types, for sure.

"Someone carries a small briefcase onto the plane. None of us deplane, not even to stretch our legs. Our only task is to take possession of the briefcase, which contains cut and uncut diamonds in small envelopes with markings, and bring it and its contents back to California, to the Golden ADA office. We place the diamonds into the vault for temporary storage, until they are removed for sorting, cutting, polishing, and eventual sale.

"The business looks pretty legit to me from all angles, very official and well organized. I notice nothing strange. All legitimate. Golden ADA has solid government connections with the Russian authorities, no doubt about that. There is an official government committee responsible for the care and custody of precious gems and metals, and its senior leadership has sanctioned and supported this operation."

Sullivan seems almost relieved to unload the story on me, not stopping to draw breath.

Now, he is awaiting my reaction.

I am not biting. Many questions come to mind, but again, this isn't the time or place. Sullivan has his own agenda. In fact, Sullivan thinks he has won the lottery in a big way.

He is likely close to retirement from SFPD and can wind up making serious money working for Golden ADA. It is better to let Sullivan think I am not that sharp or ambitious, maybe even dumb or slow. I have to let go of my ego to give Sullivan that impression; it has to be this way. A good investigator has no place for ego.

It's not a simple thing to do, but it just has to be like this, sometimes.

"So, you couldn't even get off the plane and had to fly right back with no break? That's over twenty hours on a small jet. I would have gone crazy, sitting on the plane that long. Suppose you must really like flying, huh?"

There is no point in asking Sullivan his opinion whether he thinks this operation is involved in theft, or connected to the Russian mafia, or to corrupt high-ranking officials from Russia. He already told me it all appears legit to him. Sullivan could have asked me for my take on things, my opinion, analysis, but he didn't. That speaks volumes to me. And what strikes me as odd is how Sullivan isn't even trying hard to justify the legitimacy of the operation either. He certainly isn't seeking approval or validation from me.

To me, this means Sullivan is driven all right and perhaps blinded by his love of money and his greed, nothing more.

It all seems crazy on some level, but my gut is telling me that for Sullivan, this is all about the money. Is Sullivan a corrupt cop on the take?

Perhaps, but one thing's for sure: he is greedy.

He loves jewelry, diamonds, and thinks he's hit the jackpot.

He is head of security for a major diamond distribution operation, right in his own backyard and flying across the world on a private jet to faraway Russia.

He could have reached out to the Bureau many weeks prior, and Police Chief Burda could also have done the same. Yet, neither one did. They certainly knew that the Bureau, the FBI, possessed extensive experience and knowledge in all matters concerning Russia, and formerly the Soviet Union. So, was there not reaching out to anyone in the Bureau's office for so many weeks from their ignorance, or lack of knowing who to turn to for insight or guidance? It is difficult for me to judge. I conclude it is likely a combination of those factors.

The chief eventually calls his good friend, Rick Webb, likely after realizing he can get himself in a serious jam, if the "helicopter for free" deal goes south, or if his own Chief of Detectives, Shane Sullivan, somehow gets in over his head. It is then, and only then, that the chief reaches out to his good old pal, Rick Webb, head of the Bureau's SF Division Office, asking for the meeting. For me, the bottom line is that Ken Burda and Shane Sullivan are only using the Bureau, or trying to. They are not friends of the FBI, that much is certain.

The rest of the lunch conversation with Sullivan is unremarkable and consists mostly of standard cop banter. I stay away from any probing questions about Golden ADA, the people involved, what Sullivan knows or doesn't know. I don't want to give Sullivan the impression I am interested in recruiting him as a Bureau source, a potential confidential source of inside information about the company and its dealings.

My gut tells me this Sullivan is likely cut from the same cloth as my uncle, the corrupt NYPD one. It is better to let Sullivan think I am in over my head, or perhaps naïve, clueless, or both, than for him to suspect I am playing with him. I figure we may meet again one day, but Sullivan is no knight in shining armor who will help me with the investigation. Sullivan has only met with me because his chief ordered him to do so. When Sullivan insists on paying for the lunch and grabs the check from the waiter, he seals the deal.

Yes, Sullivan is indeed corrupt. I tell Sullivan the next lunch will be on me.

To me, Sullivan wants to get me on his side, to show me he is one of the good guys, approachable and trustworthy. Perhaps he intends to use me as a potential source of information for his personal benefit, and to advance his own agenda.

Why not? It makes sense in a way.

We depart on good terms, exchange business cards, but I know it's unlikely I'll meet with Sullivan again, or that Sullivan will reach out to me.

Not soon, anyway. There is nothing in it for Sullivan, not at this stage.

I leave the restaurant on foot, walking several blocks to my vehicle, checking for surveillance in the reflections of the store windows along the street.

My instinct tells me a chief of detectives, this one in particular, may have a surveillance team at his disposal for "security" reasons.

For whatever reason, a phrase pops into my head, and I murmur quietly, speaking to no one but myself. "The tales we weave, and the lies we tell. Yes, the game, Dr. Watson, is definitely afoot, and it has only begun."

# Chapter 14

Judge George Sprizzo is a senior judge, having been a California State Court judge for over twenty years. I don't wait long in the reception area of the judge's chambers when the secretary tells me he is ready to see me. I have no sense of—or insight into—how he will react to my request today. In short, I want him to agree to the state prosecutor's request to drop the criminal tax evasion charges against Ms. Nazari. If Judge Sprizzo says no, it is no.

But in that case, it will mean Nazari cannot actively work with me, with the Bureau. The case won't be over, but it will be difficult to identify and develop another source like Nazari, with her access to some of the main players in Golden ADA.

"Thank you, Judge, for seeing me. I understand the prosecutor has spoken with you about the situation, and the Bureau would appreciate it if you could allow the charges against Ms. Nazari to be dropped, for the time being, at least.

She is particularly important, your Honor, for this case and her active cooperation at this investigation stage is critical. I can't get into the case details, or the exact nature of what Ms. Nazari knows or can provide, but—"

The judge raises his hand to interrupt me.

"Look, Special Agent, I don't need to know about your case, the nature of what you are investigating, Ms. Nazari's role, etc. You've come into my chambers to ask me to agree to dropping the pending charges against her. That's enough justification for me. If the Bureau needs her to assist in its mission, then it must be a matter of national security. I agree with the dismissal of the charges. I wish you all the best in your investigation. Have a nice day."

"Thank you, Judge. On behalf of the FBI, I appreciate your support and confidence."

I am taken aback. I came into Judge Sprizzo's chambers thinking it would be difficult, close to impossible, to get the judge to agree to the dismissal of the charges.

He has been more than accommodating and supportive.

There is no point in over analyzing why the judge has turned out to be so agreeable. It's just one of those lucky breaks that this judge apparently likes the Bureau for reasons he chooses not to reveal, and I am certainly not going to question him or probe further.

Now the hard part comes; this is to figure out exactly how to deal with Annie Nazari, and how to "work" or "run" her as a confidential source without getting her in over her head, or leading her to be exposed, or even worse, killed.

My meetings with Police Chief Ken Burda, and the one with his Chief of Detectives, Shane Sullivan, only confirm to me that the investigation and uncovering of the inner workings of this conspiracy is going to be challenging, and possibly dangerous, particularly if trained and observant law enforcement officers are providing "security" to Golden ADA and its operations. No matter, one step at a time. The meeting with Judge Sprizzo has gone better than expected. This doesn't mean the investigation is going to succeed, but it is a necessary and important step. Things look to be moving in a positive direction.

Now, it is time to sit down with Ms. Nazari and develop a strategy and plan to guide her. She is a strong willed, intelligent, and clever woman. She is motivated.

But she also has her own agenda, and I have to be mindful of that. Dealing with such a personality is going to have its own set of challenges, no doubt about it.

But first things first; I need to meet with Rich Marino, my one and only partner in the case. Earlier, we promised each other to stay in close contact and to coordinate any investigative steps we may undertake closely. Marino needs to be informed about the SFPD meetings, and Nazari is now ready to actively work with me.

"Your sister called, looking to talk with you. I told her you'd call her back when you got home," my wife calls out to me from the bedroom as she hears the door open.

"OK. Did she say what she wanted?" I ask.

"Does she ever? I'm not blood. She said she needs to talk with you, and to tell you it has something to do with Kansas

City. What the heck? What are you two up to?" Lenore isn't upset judging by her tone, so it sounds to me, but perhaps she's a little tired of such calls.

My wife continues, "She just never stops, never asks about the kids or me. It's always 'Where's my brother? I need to speak with him.' What is with your family?"

Lenore is now getting herself worked up, close to anger, but more frustrated than anything by the sound of her voice.

"I'll call her later. I know what you're saying, but can't control her. She's my sister, so what do you want? For me to not talk to her anymore?"

"Please. You won't do that. Your family has so many secrets and issues. The Bureau is perfect for you, with its secrets. I don't even know what the heck it is you do every day,"

"I don't want to relive my workday when I get home, Lenore, you understand that by now. And I do share things with you. You remember the kidnapping case? I told you about that, and you weren't even interested until you saw it on TV."

After dinner, when things quieten down and the children are asleep, I call my sister.

She starts in right away, as is her nature. "I'm thinking about going to Kansas City. You left a serial killer out there on the streets. He's still killing, and no one seems capable of finding him. I know where to start. Heck, the newspaper articles alone give plenty of information with names, places, dates..." Jennifer says as her voice trails off.

"Please don't go there. You are not law enforcement, and I can't protect you. You could wind up dead, like those women.

And I am not about to travel there either. The Bureau would not appreciate that, believe me. I know you know the murders stopped once we made the arrests, but they only stopped for a brief time. Jen, I never had evidence or information linking any of those subjects to the murders. Not directly, at least. Do I regret not devoting more time and effort to solving them? Of course, but Jen, you need to understand, I had so much on my plate in those days, running informants, making drug buys, conducting surveillances, dealing with police corruption, and handling paperwork.

"The case was pushing me to my limits, physically and emotionally. Besides, Quantico, the Behavioral Analysis Unit which I called and pled with for help, turned me down.

"Yeah, maybe I should have found another agent there to talk with. But I didn't, and I regret that. Who knows, perhaps the second guy would have said the same, that they couldn't work up a profile or help because of the 'high risk' lifestyle of the victims. They were mostly prostitutes and drug users. I'm not justifying Quantico, but I couldn't convince them to help me and I tried. So, give me a break and stop this insanity. It's way too dangerous for you to go to Kansas City and wander around in those neighborhoods. You won't last a week."

I lay out the argument and reasoning to my sister, and not for the first time.

My sister still isn't budging.

"What about that priest? That Santero priest? You told me the guy was creepy but respected in their community. Heck, they checked in with him before picking up their drugs and making any major decisions. They believed in his powers. Is he in prison still? He might know something or could be involved himself. You once told me he was a sort of mind reader, and you thought he had 'the gift' even though you said he was evil."

"I've no desire to speak with him, never. Santeria is scary stuff. I'll tell you, he read my mind once, and that was enough to freak me out. Maybe it was all in my head, and he doesn't have the 'gift' like you, but no matter. I'm done with that guy, forever. Let it go. The KCPD Homicide Unit folks are good; they will catch the killer. I don't want my sister winding up dead out there."

"And what do you make of what I told you from my visit to Cranberry Lake? Remember the elderly couple living next to our grandparents? I saw them, Dennis, I really did. And I spoke with them. They seemed very much alive, and real to me. I think they wanted to share something with me ..."

I cut her off. "Enough, let it go."

I am now getting agitated, and this conversation is going nowhere.

"Who is this informant you're working with? She's young, but manipulative, and oh, beautiful, huh?" She laughs slightly.

"Where did you hear this? From Lenore?"

"No. I felt it. I am right, huh?" she adds, sounding confident in her assertion.

"Yeah. You freak me out sometimes with your so-called 'powers.' Please stop doing that. And don't go to Kansas City. It's all in the past. Leave it be," I say sternly, finishing the call with her.

# Chapter 15

New York City, 1937

"Hey, Detective Cosgrove, the captain wants to speak with you, now." The desk sergeant on duty tonight can be gruff, but he's the messenger, nothing more.

"What's up, JB?" Cosgrove asks the captain who goes by his initials, JB, for Julian Branigan. JB is a tough Irish cop from Hell's Kitchen.

He's seen a lot in his thirty years of service in the NYPD.

"You need to get to NYPD HQ tomorrow, first thing. They won't give me details, only that someone high up wants to discuss the Kuleba case with you. Be there at 09:00 and don't be late."

The captain returns to reading the papers scattered on his office desk and dismisses Cosgrove. The detective decides not to allow his mind to ponder why he is being summoned to NYPD

HQ, but it doesn't sound good. No matter. He will deal with it tomorrow.

***

On arrival at NYPD HQ early next morning, Cosgrove identifies himself. The desk sergeant escorts him down the long corridor, then up the stairs to the fourth floor.

Cosgrove has never been on this floor, but he knows it is where the senior management of the NYPD work, to include the Police Commissioner himself, Lewis Joseph Valentine.

Mayor Fiorello H. LaGuardia chose Valentine for this position because of his anti-corruption crusading in the department.

Cosgrove stands at attention upon entering the expansive corner office. He still can't fathom what the Commissioner wants from him this morning.

"Sit down. The mayor's all over me about the little girl slayings around the city that are still unsolved and have been going on for a few years. The newspapers are writing all about it. Guess there isn't enough fresh news for them these days. I've been following your recent case, the murder of that little girl on the beach on Staten Island. I hear you testified about some sort of case or scene analysis, and it led you to the perp. Is that so?"

"Yes, Commissioner. But I'm not the only officer to have been on the beach that day. Commissioner, I suspected the girl was abducted, not drowned."

"Look, I want you to look at the case files for the girls. They are over there on the table, over twenty of them. The press only report nine, so thank God they didn't get their numbers right; LaGuardia would go nuts. He isn't happy as it is. Review the files, do your analysis, interview whoever you need to, and then report back to me, and only me.

"Here is a letter, signed by me, giving you the authorization to work on this. No one will get in your way; or if they do, let me know immediately. Don't take your time with this. I need you to get out there and deal with this pronto."

Cosgrove boxes up the files, takes the letter, and leaves the office, unsure what to make of the tasking from the Commissioner. He's been a veteran detective and former police officer for several years already and has never heard of anyone receiving a tasking directly from the Commissioner. There isn't much choice, however; the Commissioner has ordered him to review the files and do what is necessary to find the killer or killers. This will not be easy, that much he knows. He also figures the detectives assigned to the murders will not be pleased or willing to assist. Where this assignment will take him, he has no idea.

He is alone in it; that much he does know.

# Chapter 16

"Hey, where are you?" Sharon asks, walking right into my office minutes after my arrival.

"What? I'm here and so are you," I respond, anticipating Sharon is about to unload something on me. Women. They are all driving me crazy, this sisterhood.

"I can tell by your face. What are you thinking about? Some past case? Let it go. We've enough to deal with in terms of the mess you've dragged me into. We need to focus on getting your Ms. Nazari into the mix. Do you bother reading the papers anymore?"

Sharon sounds annoyed, but she's committed, and that is certain.

It's a good thing.

"Nope. I'm juggling a lot, Sharon, drug cases, covering routine leads, meeting with sources besides Ms. Nazari, and I'm about to step into two other potentially enormous cases, besides our Golden ADA adventure. I know it sounds crazy, but sometimes, you just have to go with it and strap in for the ride."

"If you're trying to impress me, you're not. Look at me. No, look at this article!"

Sharon has the clipped newspaper article in her hand, waving it inches from my face. "Golden ADA is hosting a huge gala at their brand new premises next week. We need to cover this event; it will be a who's who of San Francisco high society."

After reading the article, I motion for Sharon to sit in the empty chair next to my desk.

"OK. Yeah, I admit, I didn't know about this gala. It's the official opening of their new building on Brannan Street, and you're right. We need to cover this event, but there are risks, risks to the integrity of the investigation. We need to weigh them.

"Let's think this through. Here are our options. Option one, do nothing, no surveillance of the event, stay far away. The downside of this is that we won't have a clue as to the players, associates, and connections the company's made, and the folks involved in the business from the buyers to the city officials, or the politicians who could be involved. That is a huge downside, right?"

"Yeah, but don't forget you've got lots of security involved from the San Francisco Police Department itself. If they sense or catch on to the fact that outside law enforcement—the Bureau—is watching, that could be a problem."

"Sharon, let me bring the US Customs Service special agent Rich Marino into our discussion. We have so little time. The only person who can possibly get inside, and perhaps get an invitation to this gala is our Ms. Nazari. It's a risk, but what the heck?

"We won't task her to do anything specific, and I'm not sure if I'd have her wear a wire to record anything. It would be a sort of test to see what she what she can do, and who she can speak with. It's a marketing event for their company. Besides, there will probably be Champagne and vodka flowing, and lots of excitement with a building full of movers and shakers and all those diamonds. Nazari can mingle and collect business cards.

"She's more than capable of that. I wish I could get in there myself, but that's a non-starter. Or, put an undercover inside, but there's not enough time to get authorizations. And with the likelihood of elected officials in attendance at the gala, the Bureau will be cautious, perhaps hesitant. Besides, it would take weeks to get the authorizations, and there's no time."

"You better reach out to Marino, get his take on this, and then we'll have to deal with your Ms. Nazari."

"You mean our Ms. Nazari," I remind her.

"You need to brief Don Pierce about this gala, and Dennis, at some point, you're going to have to deal with the OC squad in the city. They're going to go nuts when they find out you've been working in their territory and haven't informed them.

"You also may have Russian officials at this gala; the Bureau's counterintelligence folks in San Francisco may already be involved. How will you deal with that? Oh, and let's not forget about De Beers. The London legat hasn't responded to our request yet. Who knows what De Beers will have to say? Heck, it will be funny if they show up at the gala! If I were De Beers, there's no way I wouldn't be there, at least surreptitiously."

"OK, Sharon. I hear you. One step at a time."

My head spins, thinking of the complications and obstacles Sharon has raised. It's enough to make me consider, for the briefest of moments, about closing the investigation.

I already have plenty of work unrelated to this Golden ADA affair.

I set the thoughts aside.

According to my wife, I am fairly good at compartmentalizing things in my head. But there is no point in dwelling on things offering no solution for the time being.

"Let me get a hold of Marino, and we'll go from there," I tell Sharon.

She stands up and returns to her office. The issues she's raised are relevant and will have to be addressed at some point, but it seems better not to look too far over the horizon. If we can somehow keep the investigation discreet, and quietly gather more information about Golden ADA, the players, its activities —financial activities in particular—that is the better route. We need to try to get a sense of who the players are in the wider orbit around the company; this intel will help inform a future investigative strategy, and more importantly, help plan proactive steps we might take in this increasingly complicated, tangled puzzle.

I pick up the phone to call Marino. We agree to meet later in the afternoon at a local recently opened café.

Sharon is good, but she's an intelligence analyst. I need to bounce things off of a streetwise investigator. Rich Marino is my only partner now, and we've promised one another to work closely and coordinate everything.

Promises have to be kept and respected.

"Rich, I see little downside in Nazari attending this gala. She can use her connections with the Shagirians to get her in there," I tell him, taking the non-fat latte off the counter as we find an empty table outside.

"OK, Dennis. I agree to a certain extent. But, let me play devil's advocate here for a minute. You haven't used her operationally at all yet, and her first go-round is to send her to this gala? Are you nuts? True, she will talk to a lot of interesting people, but she could stumble, say the wrong things, ask too many questions, and be challenged.

"Then it will be game over for using her. She will be finished as a source if that happens. If we stay on the fringes, do the surveillance from a distance with cameras, we'll be risking nothing, and at least we can see who is there and mixing it up with Golden ADA. I don't trust this Annie Nazari. She has her own agenda, and the only reason she isn't in jail is because of you. You have rescued her from both the IRS and the state tax authorities."

"Exactly, Rich. Exactly. But she is aware of this and motivated. What source doesn't have their own agenda, and isn't difficult to deal with? Name one good one. You can't because there aren't any. The risk is minimal. We can even put her on the clock. Allow her to spend, say, one hour, max one-

and-a-half hours inside, then get out. This way, she can observe the crowd, mingle a bit, engage in a few conversations, perhaps get introduced to a few interesting people, exchange business cards, and then leave.

"She can be charming, very charming. Granted, she's manipulative, but so what? We can use it to our advantage, can't we? It will be an excellent test run, and I think it's worth the risk. She has the gas station businesses with the cousin of the Shagirians, so they know her, and, yeah, there will probably be other people there who'll be more interesting for them to talk to—the political figures, and the wealthy elite, potential clients and buyers … But after all, she's a woman, attractive and intriguing. Believe me, she will dress to thrill."

"OK, I agree." He pauses for a moment in thought as he finishes his coffee. "But she needs a strict time limit in that building. The longer she's inside, the more complicated it can get. And no wandering around the building once she's inside. We can't put a wire on her. Not this time. They may check her. Heck, there are diamonds inside, so they'll have ample justification for security checks for everyone entering and leaving the building. Is that agreeable to you?"

"OK, I'll meet with her just before she goes in, and contact her tomorrow, so she can figure out how to get herself invited to this gala. Let's get out of here; that's enough latte for one day. This stuff is addictive." I toss the paper cup into the trash.

We shake hands and head across the parking lot to our separate vehicles.

***

"Annie, did you know about this? This gala?" I ask upon entering her office, and hand her a copy of the news article reporting on the inaugural opening of Golden ADA's new premises at 999 Brannan Street in San Francisco.

"No, but do you want me to check into it? I can ask …"

I interrupt. "Annie, please don't go asking around. If you contact someone for an invitation, who will you reach out to? Artiom Kevorkian? Or one of the Shagirian brothers?"

"I will take care of this, Dennis."

"No, Annie. We need a plan. I need to know who exactly you will contact for the invitation, and what reason you will give."

"I can ask Ashot, or maybe David's wife, Lara. I don't need a reason. They know I am a businesswoman, always looking for opportunities to expand my businesses. You want to go with me?"

"No, Annie. I would love to, believe me, but I can't expose you or me in that way. But if you can, get an invitation without making a big deal out of it. If they decline, just accept it. The important thing is to stay on good terms with the Shagirian brothers and do nothing to raise their suspicions or anger them. Agreed?"

"Yes, Dennis. I will do as you say. You'll see, I will do a good job for you."

"Annie, keep me posted on this. And no pressuring them for the invitation. If you get invited, we will meet again to prepare for your attendance. Annie, you need to understand, you may not only see but also wind up talking to powerful people at that gala. You will need to be careful. Well, we can talk about all that later."

My voice trails off, realizing this is the first time Nazari will act at the direction of the FBI, and while the risk of harm to her is low, her participation can lead her to far more dangerous liaisons.

I call Rich Marino as soon as I leave Nazari's office.

Marino says, "I'm in the area, so let me swing by and we can talk face to face. Be there in twenty minutes." I hang up, and he arrives in the office sooner than expected. The Bureau receptionist is getting to know him and buzzes him right through.

I spot him walking down the hall, motioning for him to step into my office.

"Rich, I just met with Annie Nazari. She's going to try and get an invitation to this gala. I'm fairly certain she'll get one, and on that basis, I think a pole camera set at the entrance to the building is too risky with SFPD providing security to the company. They could find it and freak out, protest, whatever, and besides, I would need our tech agents in San Francisco to install it. That's a non-starter for now."

"What about placing a van with camera equipment a block away from the entrance to the building?" Marino asks.

"Sorry, but I don't think it's worth the risk. If Nazari gets inside, we will have no choice but to depend on her to report on what she sees, who she is introduced to, and who she talks to. I have been thinking about this gala. It would have been ideal to have an undercover inside, but it's just too early in this investigation, and there's so much we don't yet know or understand. So, let's get Nazari, our source, inside, and hope for the best. It will be a wonderful opportunity to get acquainted—for her, and for us—with the players, and with those in the orbit around the key players and this company. There are still a lot of unknowns, Rich. This SFPD angle is bothering me, a lot. But it's a reality."

"She's your source, and I've told you how I feel about her. But I'm on board with your approach to get her into the gala and see what she learns. We may learn a lot, or very little. But worth the risk either way."

"Rich, I've been thinking about this case, well, about strategy. We can't let fear paralyze us from taking proactive actions, but we need to remain aware of what we're up against.

"First, this involves Russia. It's a black hole to us. We don't know the players over there, the politics, practically nothing. And we've got no legal attaché office in Moscow, and no trustworthy connections with law enforcement from their side.

"Second, we're talking about diamonds, with all the intrigue in that secretive business. Third, we have the players based right here in California, and there will be powerful people surrounding this company, no doubt about it. You and I both recognize there's corruption and likely criminal elements involved on the Russian side, but the same goes for the U.S. side. Nazari's alluded to a form of protection Golden ADA has.

"We could unknowingly walk right into that ... that mess. And Rich, another thing we haven't talked about is the national security or intelligence angle. The intelligence services could be involved from their side, or from ours, or both. Who knows?"

"So, what's your point? To close this and walk away?" Marino asks after listening to my litany of concerns. "I understand what you're saying, but what the heck? I'm game, are you?"

"Rich, there is a great quote from Winston Churchill about Russia. I think it was something he said either during or at the start of World War II. Goes something like this: 'Russia is a riddle, wrapped in a mystery, inside an enigma.' But Churchill also said perhaps there was a key to unravel it.

"Rich, I hear you, and if we're going to stick with this case, we can't sit around and wait or hope for things to happen on their own. We may never find the key to unravel this conspiracy, but we also can't be afraid to act, to take affirmative investigative steps, measures, whatever. But we need to be mindful we're in a chess match of sorts.

"If we decide to make a move, and take our hand off of that chess piece, we can't undo the move. We are stuck with it, with that decision. And, to make things even more complicated for us, we don't know what the rules of this chess match actually are. There's no playbook for this kind of case. It reminds me of some things from childhood."

After saying all this, I realize Marino will have no clue what I am driving at with the reference to childhood. I continue hastily, averting his likely question, "Let's go with it. Heck, what's the worst that can happen? Our agencies send us both packing back to New York? So what? We grew up there. We will survive, right, Rich?"

Nazari is indeed dressed to thrill at the gala, looking stunning in her formal gown. The event is a black-tie affair, and she's had a dress made just for the occasion.

She seems genuinely excited at the prospect of going into the metaphorical arena for the first time with the FBI. Somehow, she has convinced the Shagirians to invite her to the event.

"OK, I am ready. I will only stay one hour, and get out of there, like you told me. I will keep my eyes and ears open and try to circulate to meet as many people as I can. Oh, and I will collect, no, sorry, exchange business cards like you said."

"One other thing, Annie, just be yourself, and relax. You belong there. You need to be mysterious, but not aloof or arrogant. It's a social event, remember? You're not there to interrogate anyone or to get incriminating admissions. Let them talk, gossip, whatever. They will do it on their own with little prompting, believe me. When you leave, take a taxi to the Embarcadero, go to Houston's. I will be at a corner table at the back of the restaurant."

Although the risk of physical harm to Nazari, our source, is relatively low, sending any source against the subjects of an investigation, with a view to gathering evidence or information against them is a stressful event, requiring careful planning and execution.

We are far from the days in Kansas City.

Then, I'd send sources with hidden transmitters and recorders to monitor and record conversations during controlled drug buys against dangerous, unpredictable traffickers.

More than once, it was just me and the source out there alone, on the mean streets of Kansas City. No back up, no one to call. Just my semi-automatic pistol, and long-barrel shotgun at the ready in the vehicle. If things became chaotic during the buy, I'd advise the source to promptly drop to the floor and use the code words we had agreed upon.

I'd come in as quickly as possible with guns blazing to rescue him or her. It was far from Bureau protocol and I knew it, prepared to accept the consequences if things went south.

The Kansas City OC and Drug Squad had lots on its plate in those days, and agents weren't always available to assist. The drugs wouldn't wait, so there would be no postponing of the operation. I had survived the mean streets of the city as a kid, in a pretty tough neighborhood. Surely, I could manage myself as a trained FBI Special Agent.

"Who needs back up?" I would tell my fellow squad agents after I returned to the office alone to process the drug evidence after one of my successful controlled buys.

They just looked at me as if I came from another planet, no one objecting or commenting.

They were probably relieved they didn't have to be out there on the street with me since buying drugs through sources was a high-stress operation to manage.

A lot could go wrong and sometimes did. You had to be quick on your feet, be decisive, and be ready to engage with deadly force if that was what the situation demanded.

I feel like having a beer to calm my nerves while sitting and waiting for Nazari to arrive from the gala, but I hear my voice tell the waiter that bottled water with lemon is fine.

Nazari is right on time, every head in the restaurant turning to look at her as she strolls through the place to the corner table, stunning and mesmerizing in her evening gown. I forgot she would be formally dressed, and for a discreet post-operation rendezvous, this venue isn't the best. But so what? It's unlikely anyone from Golden ADA will be here this evening.

Nazari is keyed up, full of animation as she speaks.

"I did it. Everything you wanted. I met so many people, and we exchanged cards, well, I exchanged cards with the ones who had any. I even met Andrey Kozlenok and his wife, Nina. She's charming, and we got along. I think we will become friends! She doesn't have many friends in the U.S., did you know?"

Nazari opens her purse and removes the cards she has collected. There have to be a dozen or more, and she seems pleased with what she has done. "You know, I don't drink, but it was all right. I told the waiter at one bar that I didn't drink alcohol, and he told me it didn't matter, he would make me special cocktails without the alcohol. They were so good!"

"OK, Annie, let's begin with Andrey and Nina."

"So, I introduced myself to Nina. She was getting a drink at one bar that had been set up. She's very elegant and speaks four languages, did you know that? And she enjoyed talking to me.

Like I said, I don't think she has many friends here in California. Andrey dragged her and their son here; they bought a place in Orinda. She is not aloof or arrogant. I didn't push things with her but told her about my gas stations. She seemed interested and commented about their company needing to diversify beyond diamonds."

"OK, and Andrey?" I ask impatiently.

"Oh, he's very ambitious, I think, and they were with some people from Moscow, maybe from the Russian Consulate, but I am not sure. There were lots of people around him all evening. I think there were police officers there. I saw a badge when a gentleman opened his wallet to leave a tip at one of the bars. He was talking to Andrey, but I couldn't tell what they were saying. Maybe he was security. I am not sure."

"Who else, Annie? Who else did you meet?"

"I spoke with David and Ashot. They were so excited. A long way from when they used to sell flowers on the street. There were speeches. Andrey spoke, then a few city officials, I think … Mayor Jordan and some elected officials, even; I am not sure. There were many people there. The Chief of Police was there, I am pretty sure of that.

"He said a few things, welcoming the company to the city, and said he was thankful for the offer of a helicopter to his department. There was some sort of senator there, Mr. Lemke, I think that was his name, and a big fat guy. Oh, I have his card. He was nice, friendly."

She shows me the card.

"Art Roggenbuck, Security Consultant," I say, reading the name on the card aloud. "OK, so who else? Just give me the cards, I will copy them and give them back to you later."

Nazari hands over the stack of business cards. There have to be at least a dozen.

"I did a good job, right?" Nazari says, wanting to hear positive feedback and assurances from me that her first operation as a Bureau source went well.

"Annie, you did fine. We'll talk later about follow-up for some people you met. Do you think you could reach out to Nina in the future? Not right away, but in a few days, perhaps?"

"Yes. She likes me. She loves art, you know. She decorates their offices. I told her I can help with finding good paintings and art for their offices and for their home. Her French is pretty good."

"Huh? You spoke French together? Interesting," I say, surprised at the revelation. "Annie, did anyone mention De Beers?"

"No, I didn't hear De Beers mentioned at all, only that they would try to do business with different jewelry stores in the U.S., and elsewhere, I think I heard Antwerp, but I am not sure." Nazari seems to tire as it's getting late, and the restaurant will soon close.

"Annie. Let's get out of here. I will drive you back to your San José office to get your car, and you can go home. Enough for tonight," I tell her as I ask the waiter for the check.

Soon after, we leave the restaurant. It is nearly empty as we walk out together.

As Nazari opens the passenger door of the Bureau vehicle to walk back to her car, she suddenly turns as if she has forgotten something. "Were there other agents in vehicles around the building? If there were, please tell them not to follow me as closely in the future."

"Annie, what are you talking about? It wasn't us. Are you sure about this? What vehicles were there? And did you catch …"

Nazari cuts me off in mid-sentence. "Don't worry. It's probably just me. I don't know why anyone would be interested in me. They were probably working as security for Golden ADA or were security for those officials inside. Maybe they were just watching the building, you know? They need to be careful with all of those diamonds."

The comment sends my head spinning. There are so many players involved, and the gala has brought them all together for this one special evening, from SFPD, to Russian officials, city officials, local politicians, and I can't exclude the intelligence services; they could have been there all right, under aliases. The press will probably report on the opening, giving free marketing for the company. After all, it was a dazzling and dizzying affair, putting San Francisco on the map as a new diamond distribution hub.

Where the investigation is going, I am not sure.

As I drive home, I have doubts. Am I in over my head?

And what if the entire operation is legit and sanctioned by the Russian government, with the help of factions within the U.S. government itself?

No, it can't be legit. There's something here. I feel it. No matter, one day at a time, and one move at a time. This chess game is just beginning.

The game, Dr. Watson, is afoot. No mistake about that, no mistake.

"Rich, here, look at all the cards Nazari's collected," I say, pulling the small stack of business cards from my desk drawer and handing them to Marino. "She collected quite a few, some players we already know, but one or two new interesting names as well."

"Dennis, this is interesting, and it's good she can clearly move in those circles, but we're a long way from understanding what is going on behind the scenes and who is who."

I nod and continue, "We need to be patient. This is going to take some time, maybe even luck, but that Nazari met a handful of the key players is good. Now, the tricky part is to figure out how to move things forward. We can't have her act too aggressive, otherwise they will get skittish, and cut her out. The best angle is the gasoline stations.

"They are all about diversifying their business. Heck, they went to a lot of trouble to fill out those Shell Oil franchise applications. Between Nazari's info and the information in the applications we got from the subpoena, it's about all we know. I hope the FBI's office in London can shed light on things with De Beers. There is absolutely no way De Beers isn't aware of what's going on here in San Francisco. Heck, they may watch Golden ADA. Nazari thinks she was being followed, more than once."

"You better be careful with her. She's a snake and a manipulative operator. She can be charming, but she is dangerous."

"I hear you, Rich, but she's our only insider for now. We can't just go knocking on doors to recruit other players from Golden ADA. I have an idea I want to run by you …"

But before I can finish, Marino cuts me off. "I need to tell you something. In two days, there will be a shipment arriving for Golden ADA. I got the heads up from my sources at the municipal airport. You know, the one for the corporate and private jets?"

"Yeah," I reply, leaning forward in my chair with intense interest at this unexpected news.

"What about us covering this thing? We can set up a camera and photograph the plane and see who steps off of it. That will be interesting. Heck, we might get a look at what items they bring in. Customs inspectors have every right to examine items entering the country."

"Good idea, Rich. It will tell us a lot. I hope. Back to the idea I want to run by you. Rich, I don't want you to think I'm nuts, but I think we can convince the Russian government to let us know if this stuff has been stolen and is being unlawfully taken from their treasury or storage vaults. Look, without someone from the Russian side stepping forward and providing proof the diamonds and valuables have been stolen or removed without authorizations, we have no case. No federal criminal statute violation. No violation of the ITSP statute, that is. We may have other violations such as criminal tax evasion, money laundering, and maybe some corruption violations here and there, but that is beside the point."

I can see Marino is following, but getting impatient, and wants to interrupt.

"Give me a minute, Rich. I am getting to my point. We can approach the Russian Consulate here in San Francisco. They definitely have an SVR representative, well, the former KGB 'Resident Agent.' I know it's a risk, but we can give them just enough, the minimum, for them to do follow-up work in Moscow. Granted, the risk is that the KGB, now the SVR, is involved in the scheme. It's possible they are, but to what end?

"Look, if they are directing this operation, or involved in some way, they will either string us along, or give us nothing. Or, if there are indeed secretive or separate—let's say, corrupt factions, silos—in Moscow that are responsible for this looting, there may be equal and opposing factions outside, unaware … Or aware and just as opposed to what is going on.

"Then SVR might just help us with identifying those opposing players, and perhaps even put us in direct contact with them. We won't lay out the entire case for them, just tell them we have been following the news reports on this company, Golden ADA, with ties to Russia, and are concerned about the origin of the precious items arriving here in California.

"If we want, we can ask for background information on the Shagirian brothers, on Andrey Kozlenok. Heck, even this Eugeniy Bychkov, head of ROSKOMDRAGMET. So, Rich, what do you think?"

"Sounds OK to me. I know you have other cases going on that are taking lots of time and effort. I get that. Let me play devil's advocate for a minute with you. Say the KGB, or SVR as you call them, is involved. We'll expose our interest, but so what?

"Golden ADA isn't hiding in the shadows like some drug trafficking organization; they just held a huge gala, marketing themselves as big-time diamond cutters and distributors, with their diamonds from Russia. This isn't a secret; it's in the newspapers.

"They have the SFPD chief and political heavyweights involved, as also reported in the papers. That we are interested would be normal. We asked the Russian government about the company and its operations, through the only official communication channels we have with them at present. It's true the KGB is an adversary, but this is a criminal case. You're assigned to an organized crime squad, and we are interested in this matter from a criminal violation aspect. Let's do it," Marino says as he shrugs. "What's the worst they can do to us? Close the case and ship us both to New York City? So what? At least we tried, right?"

"OK, agreed. I'll reach out to one of my Bureau contacts in San Francisco who knows the consulate folks to give me the name and telephone number for the resident agent, the residentura. But think this over, Rich. Once we make a move like this on our chessboard, we can't undo it. We'll have to own it, whether it turns out to be a good move or not."

# Chapter 17

It is nearly midnight by the time we receive word from Marino's customs inspectors that the Gulfstream jet will soon be landing at the municipal airport. Marino and I set up the camera in a discreet location close to the designated parking spot for the jet. It is a clear, starry night and we can see the jet as it approaches the runway to land. The immigration and customs inspectors are first to board, as a normal protocol for an international flight arriving to the United States. One by one, the passengers exit the plane and walk to the processing office.

"Rich, take as many photos as you can," I say, looking through the binoculars. "Oh, there's Ashot, with David, his brother, and a woman. I think it's Nina, Andrey's wife. Oh, and yeah, there's SFPD Detective Shane Sullivan. Thanks for the heads up, Shane, on this."

My tone is decidedly sarcastic.

Rich's radio crackles; it's the customs inspectors.

"Hey, they want to know if you'd like to have a look at the contents of the briefcase, the one carried by David. Are you game?" Marino asks.

"Really?" I am surprised.

"They may inspect this import separately. They won't hold or seize the valuables, since all the paperwork is in order and the freight forwarders filed everything, but they can bring us the briefcase, to have a look if we want, OK?"

The customs inspector brings the briefcase to Marino and opens it. The inspector tells us there are over sixty thousand carats in diamonds inside.

I notice the small paper envelopes and open several.

"Rich, they're diamonds? They look like quartz stones, cloudy, just pieces of rock like my rock collection from childhood. How can they be diamonds? Rough and uncut, I suppose?"

Marino looks. Neither of us has ever seen rough, uncut stones before.

The customs inspector tells us we are looking at over sixty million dollars' worth of diamonds in this one briefcase.

"Rich, let's photograph one or two envelopes and their contents, just for us. Don't forget this is not the first shipment, either," I say, shaking my head in disbelief.

Upon the examination of this one briefcase, the immense scale of what we are dealing with has suddenly become real and tangible. Until tonight, there has only been talk of the diamonds and valuables due to come in from Russia. Now, it is a reality. It feels intoxicating to me, to look at the stones, even in their primitive and unaltered state. They are not glittery or shiny. It doesn't matter. These are diamonds, right from the mines of Russia, so it seems.

Someone from the Russia side put the stones, rough uncut stones, into that briefcase and handed it over to them to bring to the United States.

To me, it speaks volumes. I will never forget tonight.

"Imagine, Rich. Shane Sullivan meets with me, tells me all about his little sortie to Moscow a few weeks back. Then he does the same freaking thing. Does he mention any of this to me? That he is heading back to Moscow for more diamonds? A phone call? Nope, not a word. Nothing. He definitely takes me for a fool. Or is he so mesmerized or spellbound by diamonds and money that he's lost his way, even lost his soul perhaps?"

I'm shaking my head in disbelief.

"This is strictly business, just business, that's all, and you're taking this personally! It's not about you. You ever been to a jewelry store? With your wife, perhaps? You ever noticed how girls, women, come under the trance of those shiny little stones? I'm not making excuses for Sullivan, but you have to understand he's under a spell of sorts. You've worked drug cases and seen and dealt with many addicts and dealers. In a way, these people are diamond jewelry addicts. We need to be mindful of the intensity of that 'addiction' or 'trance.' It's only a matter of time, and one future day, we will have to confront them.

"That day will come, Grasshopper, believe me. But not today, not today."

I reply, "I get it, Rich, I do. It's greed, nothing more. One of the seven deadly sins, and it's evil. I can understand what you're saying, but this is evil, the whole operation.

"Anyway, let's get out of here. We've got the photos, and now we've also seen what these diamonds look like, these stones, 'almaz' in their natural and unaltered state, before they become 'brillante.' Our job is done, mission accomplished, for tonight at least."

Although I am still managing other cases unrelated to Golden ADA, the case requires my attention on nearly a daily basis.

It isn't the sort you can set aside for a week and pick up where you left off. There is a lot going on, many moving parts. Subpoenaed financial records are revealing more and more about the company's money flows. Yet, there are many unanswered questions.

I decide to see if Nazari can shed light on what the subpoenaed records are revealing.

"Annie, I need a better understanding of the finances of Golden ADA, including how they are using the money they currently receive, as well as the funds they received from diamond sales since the company's establishment."

"Let's start with Kevorkian. I know you and Artiom Kevorkian were one-time business partners. The Armenian connection with Kozlenok is interesting and I need to understand this more. Heck, Kevorkian sold his own home to Kozlenok. Annie, you need to come clean with me on Kevorkian, no holding back, OK?"

I say it to her in a serious tone, as serious as I can muster.

"OK, I understand. Kevorkian was a wealthy businessman at one time. When David, his brother-in-law, became involved in Golden ADA, he seized the opportunity. David was the one suggesting to Andrey they get into the gasoline business. They eventually formed subsidiaries to deal with the gasoline stations, with Kevorkian in charge of managing them."

"Annie, you know this how?"

I would not normally ask a confidential informant to reveal the source of their information unless there is a compelling reason. I figure since Nazari is my most reliable source and has unique access to the principals of Golden ADA, at least in the United States, this is justification enough for asking her to reveal her sources.

"Kevorkian has mostly burned his bridges with Andrey. He was apparently skimming profits from the gas stations. Andrey found out. I am not sure how, but he did. There is something else I believe may be interesting. I can't reveal how I know this, but I do."

"OK, Annie. Go ahead, tell me."

"In early '93, Andrey needed cash, a lot, and quickly. Fifty thousand dollars to take back to Moscow, supposedly to pay Golden ADA employees there. David asked their bank, Bank of America, for cash from their accounts, but was told it would take nearly two weeks.

"So, he turned to Kevorkian, who had plenty of cash on hand from his gas station operations. David provided Kevorkian with cashier checks from Golden ADA, in exchange for the cash. This happened more than once, I think."

"Annie, so Andrey flew back to Moscow with the cash more than once?" I ask.

What she asserts makes sense. Cash was king in Russia, and if the cash was used to pay off corrupt officials or to keep the diamonds flowing, it all added up. And Kozlenok was bribing the officials with the money earned from the sales of the looted diamonds.

"Annie, what I don't get is how do the Shagirian brothers know Andrey? This is important."

"I am not sure, but I can ask them," she responds as if what she is suggesting will be easy.

I am surprised to hear after all the various talks we've had about the subject of subtlety and discretion, she again says she will ask them something like this. I have to stop her before she puts herself or the Bureau into a difficult position, even jeopardizing our investigation.

"Annie, please don't do that. They will freak, and it will be the end of your relationship with them. But what about Lara, Annie? I mean, can you casually probe this?"

I stress the word casually. That it's not to sound as though she is desperate to know it.

Then I continue, "It's not something I need to know right now, but at some point, it would be good to understand. Someone has to have introduced and vouched for them. As you pointed out to me, it's not been long since the Shagirian brothers were selling flowers on the streets of San Francisco. Now, they are moving in the same circles as the Russian elites and the elites of San Francisco."

"OK, I will try to ask about this in a lighthearted, woman-to-woman way. I am sure Lara will know, and she and I get along fine."

Something about her confidence and attitude slightly troubles me; while I applaud her enthusiasm and willingness to do all she can to assist us, at the same time, we need all of the information to come out in a natural way. She is new to this, needing help to grasp subtleties.

Suspicions are aroused far too easily by certain styles of questioning.

"Annie, listen to me. Don't push this stuff. Let them talk. I have been meaning to ask you, you would be OK with using a hidden recording device, right? We have to figure out how to hide it so there is no risk of discovery. Could you wear a wire?"

Her brow furrows slightly. It doesn't mean she senses trouble, only that she is thinking. If I can say one thing for Nazari, it is that she is bright and keen, and she wants to be proactive.

So, as over-enthusiastic as a few of her responses may come across, I value her input.

"Can you hide it somehow in my pocketbook?"

"Hmm. We just might do that. I will talk to our technical folks and get back to you. Can you let me borrow your pocketbook for a few days?"

"Sure. I have many others." She empties the contents into a smaller purse and hands me the bag. I am not sure if the Special Agent techies will be able to embed a device with microphones in secret, but it is worth a try. They are the best and will love the challenge.

The disappointed expression on Sharon's face gives it all away as she walks into my office with a document. "What's that in your hand? Something not good, I suppose?" I ask.

"The London legat office has responded to our request," Sharon answers.

"Oh. Good news, I guess not?"

"Read this," Sharon says as she hands me the document.

"Seriously? They didn't even get into the front door? De Beers has nothing to say? Nothing?" I comment, not hiding my disappointment. "Well, we can check that block for now, I suppose. There's no way De Beers don't know or don't care. They just don't want to share or discuss this with U.S. law enforcement. Heck, the U.S. Department of Justice banned them from doing business in our country because of their monopoly, I think. So, I can understand why they aren't keen to cooperate with us. Unless it's something else. Something personal. They don't like our office there, or the agent, or they didn't find the right person in De Beers to talk to. No matter. That avenue is closed, for now."

"So, what's next?" Sharon asks.

"Next? Keep moving forward in this chess match. Frankly, I am struggling lately, Sharon, to manage my other cases, and deal with this one. I can't get sloppy. Pierce has already cautioned me about devoting too much time to this case. What did he say to you when he handed you the response from London?"

"You know Don. He said little, only that I should give this to you. I never know what he's thinking, but at least he wasn't negative. I guess he'll talk to you soon."

"Sharon, I'm going to reach out to the Russian San Francisco Consulate. I already sat down with Marino. We think it's worth the risk."

"Are you crazy?" Sharon seems both incensed and animated in her reaction to this unexpected news. "You'll be stepping into a world you should stay away from. Tell me how this advances the investigation, and how you calculated the risks."

I say, "I already reached out to the guy, the resident agent from SVR. I got the name and contact info from a friend of mine who works in our San Francisco office. Look, we don't intend to say much, only that we've read several news articles about the company and its connections to Russia. We'll ask them to do some checking, just to make sure it isn't a mafia operation or that the stuff is being stolen. It's widely reported there's been a lot of looting of resources in Russia since the breakup of the Soviet Union. Everyone knows about it.

"So, I will explain that our interest is from the criminal investigative side, that's all."

I realize I should have run the idea by Sharon, and that her powerful reaction comes partially because of her feeling that she's been left out of the discussion.

"I'm sorry, Sharon. I should have discussed this with you first. I haven't told Pierce either, and nor do I intend to, at least not yet. I'll have the meeting, and if nothing comes of it, I'll let it go. It's doubtful this is some sort of intelligence operation."

"Oh. And you're an expert on this? I know the Bureau's counterintelligence folks will find out, and they won't like this. They may protest formally, to Pierce, even to Rick Webb.

"But yes, I get it, on some level. You want to find someone, a kind of faction in Russia, perhaps, that can provide clarity or proof the diamonds are stolen, but it's a long shot."

"Sharon, I can't keep this case going around and around. We need to find someone we can work with in Russia. I know corruption is endemic there, but there must be an honest cop out there, right?"

"You just said it—a cop! SVR and FSB; they are not law enforcement, not cops; they are an intelligence service. Well, let it play out as you like to say, and see what happens. But you need to tell Pierce, and soon. Dennis, sometimes, I wonder why you're so aggressive as an agent. My psychologist's brain tells me it comes from your childhood. Don't go there, please. Just a thought I had. I've been in the Bureau for a while. You're right there on that razor's edge and you better watch your balance."

***

Dmitry is right on time, waiting on the agreed upon corner two blocks from the Russian Consulate on Green Street, one of the most upscale and prestigious neighborhoods in the entire city. He jumps into the passenger seat of the Bureau vehicle.

Marino is already waiting in the restaurant close to the consulate, at a corner table.

Dmitry's English language skills are nearly perfect. I speak in Russian, but Dmitry responds in English, preferring to practice, or perhaps show off a bit.

It is midafternoon, and the restaurant is nearly empty.

I open the conversation. "Dmitry, thanks for meeting with us today. We won't take much of your time. Rich is with the U.S. Customs Service, and I am with the Bureau, as you know from our phone call, assigned to the San José office where I work on an organized crime and drug violations squad. We've read the news articles about a company called Golden ADA, based here in San Francisco, which claims to be a diamond importing and distribution firm sourcing its diamonds in Russia. Have you heard about this company?"

"I read something in the local papers, but I can't say I am familiar with this company. It's a joint venture or something? Who are the owners?"

Dmitry is probing, not surprising for an intelligence officer. He wants to gain information by disclosing nothing. Whether Dmitry actually knows anything is an open question.

I continue. "The company is owned by two Armenian brothers and a Russian foreign national. We have no way of determining whether the items they are importing are stolen from your country, your government."

Marino jumps in, saying, "And I reviewed some of the import documents they filed with my agency. Nothing stands out. But as Dennis says, we have no way of determining if this stuff is in fact looted or being stolen from your government or from an agency within your government responsible for these gems."

Dmitry looks at us, thinking and finally says, "I can check through my channels in Moscow. I really don't know about this company. There are plenty of new joint ventures with foreign firms doing business in Russia these days. Don't know how long it will take, but I'll try to get back to you as soon as I can."

The three of us sit there in the restaurant for another thirty minutes, talking about the changing landscape in Russia and what life is like now there's no Soviet Union, and now the Russian economy is struggling so badly.

I find Dmitry pleasant enough, and engaging, but not overly probing of my and Marino's work. It isn't surprising; after all, he's a veteran and a highly skilled Russian intelligence officer. In any case, there is no need to pose any probing and possibly chilling questions during this first meeting; it might even be the first time Dmitry is meeting an FBI agent engaged in the investigation of criminal matters, so I will take it easy with him at first.

I'm aware he has contact with FBI agents from the counterintelligence side of my agency, however, since he is his government's official liaison representative from his intelligence service. So, why doesn't he ask where I studied Russian? To me, it's a natural and logical question, given his background. Then I consider … It is possible he already knows, perhaps through his own channels. Or he simply isn't that interested in such things.

"Rich, did you catch that striking looking woman sitting alone at the bar?" I ask, after dropping Dmitry off near the consulate.

"Huh? What woman?"

"Rich, you're kidding, right? The one dressed like she was from another time and place. The beehive hairstyle and her outfit were late sixties, and she left shortly after I arrived with Dmitry. I got a fairly good look at her face but couldn't say whether she was Slavic looking or not. She was attractive and walked, well, like she was a former dancer or athlete, perhaps."

"You think they sent her to watch us or Dmitry?"

"Not sure, Rich. Maybe I'm just getting paranoid. Heck, she could be from the agency, or from the Bureau, or from SFPD, Golden ADA, De Beers, SVR. Take your pick. Or she could be a time traveler, visible only to me!"

Marino offers, "If you're asking me, I like the time traveler choice. I honestly didn't see her, but maybe I missed her by being so fixated on the entrance door, so I'd see you guys when you arrived." He seems confused about how he could have missed someone like that, a person who could have been there to surveil us, or to eavesdrop on our conversation.

"No matter Rich. I don't want us getting paranoid. Well, not more paranoid than we already are, but we, me included, need to be alert and aware more than usual, that's for sure."

***

When the telephone rings two days later, I am not that surprised. On the line is an irate FBI counterintelligence agent, Special Agent Ed Abel. I met him once, but only briefly. "Who the fuck do you think you are?" the agent screams so loudly I have to move the telephone receiver away from my ear. "You can't just go meeting with the SVR resident. You are out of bounds, and now I have to fix things."

I have never encountered another agent behaving or talking in such a manner. This is something agents rarely do to one another since we are generally polite and respectful by nature, a necessity to be able to speak with and gain the confidence of just about anyone.

There are disagreements during the course of our work, naturally, but an agent calling out of the blue, and screaming obscenities at another agent? Well, that just isn't done and isn't called for either. I have been yelled at before, of course—who hasn't? That part isn't a big deal to me. What strikes me most is this agent claiming he alone has access to the Russian diplomat; he almost reminds me of how some guys behave when you talk to their girlfriend. Possessive and off the rails, for no reason at all. This is probably the kind of guy who throws punches in a bar when you cross paths with his missus and say hello.

I think, heck, the guy doesn't work criminal matters; he deals with counterintelligence related issues. Why would he even care? He could at least be civil and talk it through.

"I am investigating a criminal matter involving Russia. It has nothing to do with counterintelligence," I say in a deliberately calm, hushed voice, hoping to diffuse the tension.

"I don't care," Abel says. At least he's stopped screaming into the receiver. "You can't meet this guy directly, only through me."

"OK, so you want me to add you to the Federal Grand Jury 6E List?"

"Huh? No, you just need to understand you can't contact Dmitry ever again, never," he tells me.

"OK. Got it," I respond, to end the conversation.

I will have to come up with another solution.

This agent can make things difficult for me. He can file a complaint to senior management, protesting my actions.

But I still need to find someone on the Russian side who can confirm whether the diamonds are stolen. There is no Bureau office in Moscow. If there were one, I could send a request to the office to reach out to their law enforcement counterparts for help.

Without a legal attaché or "legat" office in Bureau parlance, there is only the San Francisco Russian Consulate and the SVR, at least that is how I perceive it.

And that is how I came across Dmitry.

But it's clear: Dmitry no longer exists for me. At least not until he makes contact—and luckily, he decides to do just that. At least two weeks have passed since the meeting with him, when he next makes contact. So, to schedule a meeting, he gets in touch with Marino.

Part of me is relieved Dmitry has not chosen to call me directly; I never tell him not to, but for whatever reasons, it is Marino to whom he reaches out, not me.

"Rich, I can't call Dmitry or use the Bureau vehicle to pick him up. The counterintelligence side of the house will have my head. But Rich, there is nothing preventing you from arranging this meeting, is there? And I can just happen to be there when you both arrive at the restaurant. How does this sound to you?"

I am expecting Marino to express reservations or concerns over this new arrangement, in which he would be justified. He replies, "Sure. If this helps you, no big deal. However, I have to ask, can I get in any trouble doing this? From your agency? Or even from mine?"

Dmitry is a declared Russian intelligence officer, and the Bureau's C-I side has now restricted me from dealing directly with him. So, his questioning makes sense.

"Rich, for me, it's a no go. But you don't work for the Bureau. Yeah, I suppose we could both get in trouble, but the worst that could happen would be suspensions for us. I don't see us getting prosecuted or fired."

"Oh, that's a relief," Marino says sarcastically. "What the heck, I'll do it. So what if we both wind up back in New York, with the best pizza, bagels, and pastrami in the world? We'll survive."

The next meeting with Dmitry goes better than expected.

I determine he's followed through with Moscow, now telling us they are discreetly working to determine ROSKOMDRAGMET's role in the Golden ADA diamond affair, and the nature of the relationship between the government agency and Golden ADA.

He also tells us they are working on finding a reliable source of information from inside that agency to shed light on what is going on. He just needs more time.

I am pleased to know SVR is being cooperative and hasn't ignored our request.

It isn't an ideal arrangement, far from it as things could go south, particularly if the Bureau's counterintelligence folks learn I am continuing to engage with Dmitry, contrary to their insistence I stay away. But it is worth the risk. To agree to the contact terms set by the counterintelligence side of the Bureau will be counterproductive to the investigation and potentially compromise its integrity. I don't intend to show weakness to them, considering many of them arrogant and aloof. They aren't working in the trenches, in the line of fire in a high-risk environment on the criminal side of the agency.

I am a criminal investigator in the trenches and have already seen and done plenty.

The last thing I want is to have counterintelligence types snooping around a criminal investigation, my investigation. They will have entirely different objectives, along with their own secret agenda. They don't share information with the criminal side of the agency, and I have no intention of caving in and letting them dictate anything to me.

The involvement of SFPD complicates things enough, which the counterintelligence folks likely have no clue about. I will take my chances.

"Brick time" is a possibility, but it isn't about to distract or deter me, not for this case.

# Chapter 18

Sitting at my desk, I pick up the receiver on the first ring. The caller starts even before I speak. "Dennis, I need to meet with you. When can you come over to my office?" Nazari asks, almost sounding out of breath.

"Annie, I will come over in a couple of hours. Are you OK?"

"I learned things I need to share with you."

When I arrive at her office, she is on the telephone but ends the conversation quickly and hangs up.

"Last night, I ran into Lara. I think she is having problems with David, and perhaps she just wants someone to listen to her so she can vent. I didn't have my special pocketbook with me to record anything, but I listened to what she had to say."

"It's OK, Annie. There will be times when you can't record conversations, but it's good you called me so we can discuss your conversation or meeting afterwards."

She needs guidance, and as a person with close contacts to some of the inner circle of Golden ADA, she is bound to have such chance encounters, planned or not.

That is normal and expected.

"So, you know about Fabergé eggs, right? The Russian imperial family's bejeweled eggs?"

"Not much, only that the Russian Tsar used to give them as Easter gifts to his wife or children, something like that."

"There is much more than just history. Do you like art or antiquities?"

"Frankly, Annie, I don't know that much about art or antiquities, although I like history—mostly ancient history, the Greeks and Romans. So, what's your point, Annie?"

I am getting impatient. Nazari sometimes has a tendency to speak indirectly or around topics. It is her nature, I have concluded.

"Andrey got his hands on one of those eggs. It's not clear how, but Lara thinks he keeps it at his home in Orinda."

"So, has she actually seen it?"

"Not sure. But I think I can get more information, perhaps from Ashot or David."

"Annie, just don't be too aggressive with this. If Andrey has an egg, a Russian Imperial Fabergé egg, he could be holding it as insurance, or even for someone else. Who knows? I will do some checking through the Bureau to see if any eggs have been reported stolen or missing. Perhaps Interpol knows. But I have to be careful, for obvious reasons. Maybe the Russian government doesn't even know it's gone."

"You know Andrey and his wife Nina are big art collectors, right?"

"No, I didn't know that. But I'm not surprised. Are they buying art here in the U.S.?"

"I am not sure, but word is that Andrey has bought a few serious paintings. A Renoir, and a Picasso, maybe more."

"Really?"

I have never encountered art or antiquities in any of my cases, but it makes sense. With all the money and Andrey fixated on projecting a certain image for himself and his company, possessing valuable artwork and showing it off makes business sense.

Russia has lots of art from the days of the Tsar, housed in museums and taken as reparations from the Nazis at the end of the Second World War. With their economy struggling in the transition to a free market model, everything not nailed down has been up for grabs and at risk of disappearing or being stolen. The Russian mafia is getting stronger, and no one seems positioned or capable to stop it.

"What else, Annie? Is there something else you want to share with me?" I ask.

It seems there is a daily new twist in this saga, but it fits. I think of Churchill's timeless quote about Russia. Yep, a riddle, an enigma, whatever, but finding a "key" to unlock it all as Churchill suggested? Doubtful. Things are getting more complicated and challenging. This enigma is becoming harder and harder to penetrate, not easier.

My caseload is ever increasing, making it difficult to devote the time and attention the case is demanding. Commuting to San Francisco is taking its toll as well, on me, my wife and children. To make matters worse, the Bureau hasn't hired one new agent in over three years.

The work for most agents and staff is crushing and exhausting.

But it could be worse. At least there's no one throwing rocks at you, like when I was a kid in New York. Not yet at least.

Nazari's voice cuts into my thoughts.

"They got their hands on a bunch of gold coins. Well, they received them. David was complaining to Lara months ago about it. He showed her a coin once, from the Russian Tsar, Tsar Nikolai II. They received boxes of them, and do you know what they did with them?"

"No. But you're going to tell me," I respond, shaking my head in disbelief.

"They had them melted down into gold bullion. They are all gone. Andrey then instructed the Shagirian brothers to sell the bullion to finance some ventures Golden ADA was involved with. Lara thinks the coins came from that Russian Committee. The Shagirians had them transported to Los Angeles, to a company there, called Elite Metals, something like that; well, that's what Lara said. I didn't want to press her about it. She was just venting. I don't even know why she told me that. Maybe it's a test, or perhaps it's not even true. David and Ashot's cousin, Ed Nazarian, supposedly found the company in Los Angeles."

"Annie, if Lara or anyone ever mentions the gold again, just try to remember everything. Do not bring up this topic yourself. Agreed? It could be a sort of trap. I just don't know. Or it could be entirely true, and as you say, Lara was just venting."

I am stunned by the story.

If true, it means Andrey and this Russian Committee of Precious Gems have far greater access than I imagine. It is shocking to have access enough to take diamonds out of Russia, and sell them abroad, but gold? And gold coins from the time of the Tsars?

And now, a Fabergé egg is in the mix too?

These people seem to have the keys to everything "in the kingdom." Who has given them these "keys" and what was the price for them? Nothing is free. Someone always pays. My corrupt NYPD uncle thought he had it all until suddenly, he didn't.

And does this small group—Andrey, David, Ashot, and maybe this Eugeniy Bychkov—have the power, influence and ability to just take things, valuable things, when Russia's economy is a complete train wreck, and most of its population is suffering?

On some level, it makes little sense, and it is difficult to get my mind wrapped around it.

Someone has to be sanctioning this operation, someone extremely high in the food chain, perhaps. And who else knows about these gold coins? Not just in faraway Russia, but who on the U.S. side in California? Shane Sullivan? The Chief of Police?

And where are the intelligence services in all of this mess? Asleep, or themselves involved? Perhaps even in a nefarious way. Anything and everything is possible. I head back to my office to find Sharon. She needs to do some research—and fast.

Diamonds, gold coins from the Russian Empire, a mysterious Fabergé egg, priceless artwork … Where does this stop, or does it?

I have almost forgotten about the gas stations and the possibility of using them for money laundering. It is overwhelming. Enough. One day at a time.

I suddenly feel a melancholy depression washing over me. Maybe I am in over my head, and simply don't recognize it, or my ego won't allow me to admit it. Regardless, I am on the razor's edge. Even if I want to step away, how can I do it? No, to back down now, and admit defeat? No way. Time to go for a run or do laps in the pool to clear my head.

My thoughts race back to Kansas City, to the unsolved murders, the murders of my sources. To the serial killer still out there, somewhere, lurking in the shadows.

It suddenly hits me: my sister.

I haven't reached out to my sister in a while, and she hasn't contacted me either.

God only knows where she is, and what she's dug up since we last spoke.

"Sharon, can you—?" I ask. She is already on her way before I can finish.

Most of the agents in the office rely on her for research and analysis. She is thorough and willing to work long hours, with no complaining. Sharon is at the office door in seconds.

"Go ahead, hit me. Well, figuratively, OK?" She's in a good mood. "I told Don Pierce, you know. Don't freak out. He smirked, and Don never, ever smirks. Something is up. And please don't think I did it to get you in trouble. I regretted it as soon I told him, but I'm concerned about you. You're way out there; you need someone like Don to have your back. Having our agency's C-I side lined up against you will bring trouble."

"It's OK, Sharon. I was going to tell him soon, anyway. Look, there are new twists in this saga, this odyssey it is turning into. Nazari says they've got their hands on a Fabergé egg, and on a bunch of gold coins from the Russian Imperial Empire days, which they've had melted down to bullion. You can't make this stuff up, Sharon."

"I'm on it. I know a little about Fabergé eggs so I'll see what I can find. Did she say what it looked like? And the coins, not sure about that. They were from a museum or what?"

"Nazari hasn't seen the egg, but I have a feeling it's true, and Andrey has it. I don't doubt it for a second. As far as the coins are concerned, there's a company in Los Angeles that's melted everything down, called Elite Metals, something like that.

"Oh, and Andrey is collecting and displaying art, buying serious stuff—supposedly, a Renoir, Picasso, not sure what else. The guy is out of control. Somebody's going to get whacked soon, Sharon, I can almost feel it. Too much money, greed, and intrigue wrapped up in one case." I trail off, barely able to finish the sentence.

Fatigue and exhaustion are overwhelming me.

"Get out of here. Go for a run on the beach in Monterey. Play rugby, or swim with your kids. Take your wife to dinner. Just go, it will all be waiting for you tomorrow, or the day after."

****

She is right, of course, and I find "it" still waiting for me the next day, just as she promised. I am becoming more and more dependent on her for research and analysis, perhaps too much.

"So, where do you want to begin? Well, let me start," she says, answering her own question as we sit together in the empty conference room. "There's a company in Los Angeles called Elite Imperial Metals. Looks legit, and they certainly would have the ability and capacity to melt down gold coins. As far as the Fabergé egg, that's a scrambled mess if you don't mind the pun. There are interesting papers and publications about these bejeweled eggs, and several are, in fact, missing. After the Russian revolution, the Bolsheviks sold some of them for hard currency, which the regime needed. A few went missing, and some are in museums and private collections. I'm not sure about the price for one of these eggs, likely in the millions. I prepared a report for the file, and for you to clear. You realize Don has to approve and sign off on everything before it gets filed, right? You should get in and talk to him. His support may be necessary for you, and soon."

"I know. I intend to speak with him when the time is right. Despite the risks at this stage, I'd like to go to Los Angeles to check out this Elite Imperial Metals company. If they're still doing business with Golden ADA, they may not be so cooperative. On second thoughts, my visit might have other unforeseen and grave consequences. Perhaps a chilling effect, and they could somehow link it back to Nazari. I just don't know, Sharon. Probably better to make a note of this stuff, for later, much later."

Sharon tells me, "Stop your over-analysis. I'm the analyst, not you. Leave that part to me. You're the investigator, so you'll know what to do once you're there in LA. I have no doubt you'll manage."

"Thanks for the confidence boost, Sharon. Yeah, I've been thinking, perhaps overthinking, about the nature of this conspiracy. You know, this operation isn't some sort of 'bust-out' scheme, where the subjects make a bunch of money, then suddenly fold up shop and disappear. I have a feeling they're in it for the long haul. They think they're untouchable, with SFPD and politicians in their pockets. We'll see about that in due time."

I feel as if we're back in the game after my momentary bout of depression and that melancholy feeling washing over me yesterday.

"I need to talk to Terry Miller. Haven't spoken with him in a while. He needs to be updated since he's the prosecutor, and after all, he was kind enough to open a Federal Grand Jury case from his side. Eventually, he's going to have to brief his own chain of command.

"But maybe I'll head down to LA just to get a look at this business and check in with the Bureau's LA office to see if they have any reliable contacts there. Given the nature of that business, the Bureau in LA just might already know or deal with that company.

"It's worth a shot. And I need to do a bit of digging around Glendale, since there are more Armenians living there than in any other area across the globe, except in Armenia itself. Think I'll take Marino with me. It's about time we hit the road, anyway."

"Go see Don Pierce, now," is what Sharon has to say. "You're going to need him, and you can't cut him out, not on a case like this."

"OK, will do," I respond, pushing back from the conference table and heading down the hall to Pierce's corner office.

"Don, got a minute?" I ask, approaching the chair in front of Pierce's desk, where he has a pile of case files stacked for his review. This is the unglamorous part of the squad supervisor's job, to stay informed of all investigations being handled by the agents, and to make sure nothing is going off track. The "front office" in San Francisco doesn't want to be blindsided, never. FBIHQ wouldn't take kindly to that either.

"Sure, Cos, what's up?" Pierce asks.

I explain my rationale for reaching out to the SVR representative in San Francisco, and the reaction of the counterintelligence agent with the ruffled feathers, claiming I was crossing into his territory. Pierce says nothing in response. Not anger, shock, laughter, nothing. Maybe he's just a hard guy to read. I inform him about the update on Nazari, the gold coins, the Fabergé egg, and the latest shipment of stones from Moscow.

I include a bit on the SFPD and the gala in a low-key manner, not wanting him to get cold feet and direct me to close the case. He has every right to do so. I have plenty of other work to do, and the case is full of landmines, with SFPD and politically connected figures not just on the fringes, but also in close orbit in and around the company.

The case is technically outside of the San José office's regional jurisdiction.

Pierce will eventually have to explain or justify why an agent from his squad in San José is running around the streets of San Francisco.

He looks up, calmly places his pen down on the desk, and speaks.

"Cos, I understand you reaching out to SVR. I do. But this won't play out well. The counterintelligence side of the house may make things exceedingly difficult for us. We may win the battle, but we'll lose the war. I have an idea and will get back to you in a day or so. Hopefully, with a solution. Just sit tight. If you need to go to Los Angeles, go. And keep Miller in the loop. Later, dude."

That is it. The meeting is over. Pierce has a habit of getting to the heart of a matter, no fanfare, no small talk, directly to the point, no mincing of words. And when he speaks, he is clear and articulate, never wastes time, not his or anyone else's. But you need to listen carefully when he speaks. It is an interesting and unusual personality trait, but I like it, and like Pierce as my boss, although he too has blown up at me a few times in the past.

Anyway, I mostly deserved it.

After saying what he has to say, even if his tone is gruff, when it's over, it's over.

Nothing is left lingering in the air, nor are relationships altered or fractured.

Once you understand it is simply Pierce's style and personality, it's a sort of pleasant experience, strangely. As long as you do what he asks, follow his direction, and avoid repeating the mistake, nothing changes.

He will not treat you any differently or hesitate to trust you in future.

On this occasion, it's about as positive a meeting and outcome as I've ever had with Don Pierce. If he wanted me to close the case, he would simply tell me that. Yet, he says nothing of the sort, not even a hint. Heck, he's even telling me he may have a solution to this SVR question. That is promising. I have no inkling what sort of solution Pierce has in mind, but it doesn't matter. If Pierce can solve it, it will be a tremendous relief.

I leave his office, feeling surprisingly good about the meeting.

The Geschke kidnapping case pops into my head since that was my first time of dealing with Don Pierce. I wonder if those hectic and stressful days left a good impression on him, about me, my character, and my capabilities. No matter. The case is long since over, in the past as I now work for him on his organized crime and drug squad, something else entirely.

It is time to see Terry Miller and give him an update.

AUSA Miller is in his office when I arrive. Rich Marino is already there, and there's also another person at the small office table. Miller introduces him as Special Agent George King from the IRS, the Internal Revenue Service. Miller speaks first.

"I've given this some thought, and we, the Organized Crime Strike Force, feel we need more resources to manage this case. It's time we formed a mini task force of sorts, and I've invited George to join us." Miller turns toward George King as he continues. "As a Special Agent with the IRS, George will have direct access to tax records, which he may not share with us directly, but it will help guide us in some ways. After all, one of the best ways to gain cooperation of subjects in a case like this is through federal tax violation charges."

I say, "Terry, I am not opposed to expanding our operational group, but we have to pledge to each other that we'll continue to cooperate and share information as much as the law permits. Most important of all, we can't do anything proactive or operational without full consensus. There's too much at stake, and I don't want to put sources in harm's way."

I've never worked with King before, but Miller obviously knows him from prior cases.

"We need to retrieve the tax filings for the corporation and assess their structure and financial flows," says King. "I understand Golden ADA has set up several subsidiaries as they're intending to diversify their business activities, running gasoline stations, and other enterprises." George King strikes me as a no-nonsense agent.

He is a seasoned investigator for the IRS, and FBI-led task forces usually have at least one Special Agent from the Criminal Division of the IRS taking part.

Miller is right about the potential of discovering criminal tax evasion charges. After all, Nazari has been caught in such a web, and she is cooperating with the FBI because of the serious tax charges she was facing from the IRS and the California State Tax Authorities.

"Only George has the authority to look at the tax returns. He can't share that information with us. As an Assistant U.S. Attorney, I will have to apply to the U.S. District Court for an ex parte order to allow me access to the tax filings," Miller explains. "But they can be very helpful and provide guidance to us."

"So, we've got a mini task force of sorts: the U.S. Customs Service, IRS, FBI, the U.S. Attorney's Office Strike Force. Anyone else need to be added?" Marino asks.

"Rich, let's keep it like this for a while. I need to brief you all on the latest developments in the case."

I turn to address King and Miller. "Rich and I surveilled the Golden ADA jet a few days ago when it arrived from Moscow with about 66,000 carats of diamonds. And with none other than SFPD Lieutenant Shane Sullivan on board. Yeah, George, it's that kind of case. I can't state unequivocally that Sullivan is dirty, but I can tell you he's not cooperating, and he could do that more than once. For whatever reason, he's out there doing his own thing. Oh, and we're still trying to figure out how to identify and contact someone from the Russian government who can confirm the diamonds have been looted, stolen, unlawfully removed, and transported here. It's difficult, George. But we're working on it."

I'm hoping King will recognize this case is far from ordinary.

"Welcome to the three-dimensional chess match where the rules … Well, there aren't any, and heck, it won't matter anyway, since the rules seem to be classified, so it appears."

The rest of the meeting focuses on bringing Miller and King up to date on the latest intel and discussing the potential next steps.

"Terry, you have a minute?" I ask as Marino and King move to leave the office.

"Sure, what's up?" Miller asks.

"Has Washington, well DOJ, asked about this case or shown any interest at all?"

"Funny you should mention that. So far, nothing. But you never know. They will wake up eventually and we need to be ready. We don't want them to run or control this case from Washington. So, at some point, we're going to have to provide them with something. But just enough to keep them off of our backs. Of course, if we decide to pursue a Title III, electronic intercepts, we'll have to work with them for the approvals, but that is down the road a bit."

"Yep. And we can subpoena phone records to see who they're calling. But I suspect they may be calling people in Russia, and we won't have any way of identifying who they're talking to, so it could be problematic to meet the probable cause threshold. Who the heck would I go to for subscriber information, the KGB? Oh well, we'll deal with that later. One day at a time, right, Terry? See you later."

I rise from the chair to leave the office.

"Oh, one last thing. Don Pierce is working on something for me. A solution, he says. The Bureau's counterintelligence folks aren't happy with me. Actually, they're pretty pissed off, but who cares? I'll keep you posted about what Don comes up with. Now, I need to get back to San José. I still have a lot of stuff unrelated to Golden ADA to deal with. Later, Terry."

# Chapter 19

Over two weeks pass with no significant fresh developments in the investigation. I am busy with other pressing matters and lose track of time. It's not all that unusual to have to set things aside in one case to address another one. An agent's caseload varies, and the routine leads and follow-ups still have to be dealt with. Sometimes, all other pending matters have to be dropped when there's a kidnapping or child abduction, but those are relatively rare.

I find a small opening in my schedule, convincing Marino to travel with me to Los Angeles for a few days. There is a large Armenian community there, and it will be good to establish face-to-face contacts with agents working cases related to Armenian organized crime. It will be worth the two or three days away from San José and San Francisco.

The meetings at the Bureau's Los Angeles office go well.

The agents assigned to LA's organized crime squad are open to future communication and seem to appreciate our visit. I may need their help in future, so establishing personal connections with them may pay off. I also learn they have reliable sources inside the criminal world within LA's Armenian diaspora community.

"Rich, let's go to Elite Imperial Metals while we're here. It will be good to get eyes on the place and conduct discreet surveillance for just a few hours to get an idea who's going in and out of the place. I don't think we should cold call and try to speak with anyone though.

"It's too risky they'll reach out to the Shagirians as soon as we leave. But as we're right here, I do think it's worth a few hours to conduct surveillance, just to see if there are any interesting characters entering and leaving."

"Sure. Sometimes, it's good to get a visual on a place like this. If it's true about the gold coins, we're going to have to follow up one day and get business records, interviews, etc. The place is so tempting, I just want to walk right in. In fact, I have my undercover ID. I can pretend I want to have them melt down some old jewelry or something. What do you think?"

"You wouldn't gain much, frankly. And there's the risk they'll get spooked. You don't look like a cop, well, maybe a little, but better to leave things alone until we can go in officially, with subpoenas, or search warrants."

"OK. I suppose you're right, but it's so tempting. We're here, but in this chess match, such a move would mean taking our hands off of the chess piece. We're stuck, and if things go south … Well, I agree, no point. Yep. Let's pass on it for now."

He rambles on as if working through a train of thought but finally, he's decided, and I am glad he's not going to follow up on his initial idea.

The few days away from the office allow me to clear my head, and speaking with agents from another FBI Field Office, away from the investigation, is invigorating. It makes me think about requesting a transfer to Los Angeles, but that is out of the question for now.

Marino extends his stay in Los Angeles for a couple of days to visit extended family, so I head to LAX for the flight back to my home in Monterey.

The airport is large and has many international flights but also boasts a separate terminal for flights to the smaller cities of California, destinations including Santa Barbara, San Luis Obispo, Sacramento, and Monterey.

I somehow get turned around in the terminal, and wind up walking in the wrong direction; before I realize it, I'm heading away from the gate for the Monterey flight, when I spot my sister in the distance. To my astonishment, Jennifer walks right past me, despite my decision not to react or overreact to why she's here in LA.

I stop and turn. She just keeps walking down the corridor.

But it is Jennifer, has to be. Same hair color, eyes, body type, face structure, age, I think.

I certainly know my sister, yet she just walks right by me, not acknowledging me!

Is she lost in thought as she walks through the airport, unaware of her surroundings? Is this a sort of game to her? So many questions go darting through my head.

Or is she in danger, and can't reveal the nature of it by approaching me?

My mind is racing.

I turn to see if I can catch up with her, but she continues at a brisk pace, typical of her.

As I finally close in on her, I think, perhaps it's not her, only someone bearing a striking resemblance. But they could be twins if so, and someone so similar is highly unlikely.

Her height appears slightly off, but it's always difficult to judge height with precision, especially with women wearing heels. For a moment, I think I am losing it. Even if this woman isn't my sister, how can someone bear such a striking resemblance to another human being? Her body type is the same, hair color, even hairstyle, facial structure, eyes, skin tone.

I decide to let it go. No, this can't be my sister, only someone who looks shockingly like her. I have heard of such stories before but never experienced it or considered it could be so accurate. I turn away from following her, find my departure gate to Monterey and walk into the seating area there. As an armed "LEO," the term the airline staff call us, I will be discreetly allowed to board first, to introduce myself to the captain and display my credentials. I shake off the whole "Jen" incident as just my mind playing devious tricks.

My sister has been on my mind lately, so perhaps this is just my subconscious reminding me I need to reach out to her.

I find an open seat in the waiting area. In typical "cop" or law enforcement custom, it is a seat permitting observation of most of the passengers as they enter the seating zone for the departure gate. This seating area includes the gates for several regional flights, mostly for coastal towns in California, to include my destination, Monterey.

My gaze shifts back to reading a magazine when my mind snaps back to Jennifer suddenly; now, I hear her unmistakable voice close by, sounding as if she is speaking with someone on the telephone.

Yes. I realize it is, in fact, my sister.

I know her voice, have known it my whole life!

So, somewhat irked at how she strode by me and what she might be doing here, I look up from the magazine, and no; it's the lookalike. I study her features discreetly. Same age, mid-twenties … check. Hair color … check. Face structure … check. Body type … check. Mannerisms … check. Height … Hmm, not so sure.

Admittedly, this young woman seems slightly taller than Jennifer, but the body type is identical, lean and athletic. I listen to her as she is speaking on her call.

Since she is standing so close to me, I can't avoid hearing her.

In the end, I have to conclude it isn't my sister after all, though this woman bears a striking physical resemblance to her. Her voice, its pitch and tone, even her mannerisms, are also nearly identical. If someone is playing a game with my psyche, who is it, and what is their aim? To rattle me, to send me some sort of message? Do they want me to react?

The loudspeaker announcement notifies passengers that boarding for the Monterey flight will begin in ten minutes. I stand up from the seat and decide to approach the lookalike.

I have never used my FBI credentials, other than for official Bureau business, so in my hand, I hold them closed. It isn't just out of curiosity that I decide to approach the woman, but it is her voice, that same unmistakable tone as my sister, that compels me. I have to talk to her but must make the approach natural, to not alarm her or make her feel uncomfortable.

Maybe she will not react well; after all, doesn't it sound lame, the kind of thing a misguided or stalkerish man might say to a woman as a sort of cheesy chat-up line?

Does any woman really appreciate being thus "accosted" in the airport?

But I decide she looks approachable based on my limited observations and what I overhear, essentially eavesdropping until her phone call draws to a close.

"Excuse me, I don't want to alarm you, but before I ask you—and believe me, I would normally never do this—but I am with the FBI," I quietly say, discreetly showing my credentials to the young woman.

"Oh?" she says, a bit surprised.

She doesn't appear upset, but wears a "well, what do you want from me" expression.

"You bear a striking resemblance to my sister. When I saw you in the corridor, I was shocked when you walked right by because I had convinced myself you were her."

Yes, it does sound lame; why would a stranger be at all interested in how my sister looks?

She says, "Really? Well, they do say everyone has a double, right?"

I nod, feeling a little awkward.

"Look, I'd never have approached you as I realize you aren't her, but when I heard you speaking on the telephone, just now, frankly, it freaked me out a bit. Your voice is identical to hers as well. Can I ask you where you're from? We grew up in New York, in the city."

"I'm from the Santa Barbara area. My husband attends language school in Monterey. He is on active duty."

"Oh. I went there a few years back and studied Russian. Pretty intense environment. I hope he gets through it. Well, I'm sorry to have bothered you. It was just, well, like I said, it was too difficult not to speak to you."

She smiles. "Oh, I get it; I'd be the same," she says.

And I can't help what I blurt out next. "It would be funny if you two were to meet one day. You never know, right? The world is small. Have a pleasant flight."

If they were to meet? What the hell?

I walk away and head to the departure gate counter, identifying myself to the airline representative at the gate as an armed LEO to board the flight early.

It strikes me as ironic that the most interesting part of my travel to Los Angeles is this somewhat bizarre chance encounter with my sister's double, her doppelgänger.

You just can't make this stuff up. But it fits in a way.

After all, the Golden ADA case is full of surprises, in so many ways.

As I sit on the small propeller plane on the flight back to Monterey, with my sister's double a few rows ahead of me, I ponder, could she possibly be a blood relative?

A long-lost niece or cousin?

But the woman tells me she's from Santa Barbara, and I can't probe any further with her, can I? She could freak out, and that would be wholly justified.

Well, anything is possible. I shrug it off and begin to doze, resting my head against the fuselage bulkhead. It feels good to be going home.

It is the sudden impact of the plane's wheels hitting the runway that wakes me. I have fallen into a deep sleep and instinctively reach for my sidearm.

It is still there, to my relief.

When flying armed as a LEO, it isn't a clever idea to nod off, not even for a moment. After all, if the flight attendants need help for whatever reason, perhaps with an unruly passenger or in an emergency, they are aware of the seating location of the LEOs and may request assistance. I always keep handcuffs and zip ties at the ready, just in case.

I have also been dreaming. It's been a long time since I had dreams of Uncle Bill; perhaps it's the strange encounter with my sister's double at LAX that has triggered it.

The official story of my uncle's disappearance, the family version, is that my uncle was a tortured soul, having mental issues going back to the war and that he simply left, or ventured deep into the nearby forest and something unspeakable happened.

I never believed those versions, even though I was in my early teens when he unexpectedly vanished. My uncle had left the NYPD years earlier but was no doubt still investigating UFO sightings. As far as I was aware, only my brother and I knew of our uncle's work in tracking UFOs. My sister, much younger at the time of the disappearance, didn't understand it at all. Due to her young age, she was never that close to our uncle.

Yet, strangely enough, several years earlier, she had experienced what she described as a "visitation" from Uncle Bill. I wasn't sure what to make of this, whether Jennifer had actually experienced something, or had made it up for whatever reason.

Yet, it was possible, since my sister, even as a young child, seemed to possess gypsy-like clairvoyant powers and intuition beyond my comprehension, especially given her early age.

Maybe Jennifer had glimpsed him somewhere. If that were true, it would mean he was still very much alive, perhaps in hiding, or he had simply moved far away to begin a new life.

Yet, there was another possibility. Remote, yet possible.

Alien visitors had abducted my uncle.

Sure, this sounded bizarre and unlikely, but I would rule nothing out. If UFOs were real, why wouldn't there be abductions? It wasn't such a stretch in a way.

There were an increasing number of reported UFO sightings in the region at the time my uncle went missing, and my brother and I, both newspaper delivery boys, would read the periodicals and newspapers while waiting for the delivery truck with its stacks of freshly printed newspapers to be tossed onto the sidewalk in front of our local grocery store.

We would sometimes read sensational UFO stories, having far too long to digest them since the truck was often late. The adults, of course, told us not to believe any of the articles about UFOs, but we knew otherwise.

We told none of our friends or family about our secret and kept our word to our uncle.

It was our secret, and we didn't reveal secrets, never.

For a time, NYPD suspected foul play in our uncle's disappearance, figuring someone he had investigated years earlier may have taken revenge and killed him, hiding his remains.

There were many theories and endless possibilities.

As an adult, I came to realize people did go missing for many reasons; some went missing deliberately, some didn't. It was futile to speculate on the many possibilities.

However, I thought as a young teen that one day, I would conduct my investigation and find Uncle Bill. As the years passed, the chances of finding him alive became increasingly unlikely. If my uncle didn't want to be found, he wouldn't be. It was that simple.

I eventually came to understand that my uncle had his own demons to deal with and had tried to keep them at bay. Perhaps my uncle's fascination with and investigation of UFOs helped to distract him from those demons. It was just my theory or feeling, nothing more.

My wife is waiting for me at the airport when I arrive on the flight from LAX. Monterey airport is small, with a couple of buildings, nothing like a full-fledged modern international airport. And nothing like LAX, with its multiple terminals, and countless gates and jetways.

Landing in Monterey, you walk down the stairs onto the tarmac itself, then take a short walk into the main building, taking a couple of minutes. Even if you wait for your checked luggage, you are still likely to be in your vehicle on your way home in a matter of minutes.

The airport has a homey feel, and after a few flights in and out of there, you come to recognize the airport staff, and they also recognize and acknowledge you.

I look for my sister's double in the luggage area, and don't spot her.

She has likely traveled with only a carry-on bag and is long gone.

Later, I tell my wife the story of Jennifer's lookalike, finding her reaction less than enthusiastic. "So, you talked to this woman? That's an interesting line you used; never heard that one. She looked like your sister, so she was beautiful, huh?"

"Yes, but that's not the point. She not only looked like Jennifer, but she sounded exactly like her. It freaked me out."

"So, what are you going to do about it? Drop everything and search Monterey for her? Forget about it. The kids are waiting for you at home. We have a swim meet tomorrow, a big one. Tomorrow's Saturday, incidentally. Do you even know that? You better not be working again this weekend."

# Chapter 20

Don Pierce is sitting in my office when I arrive there early Monday morning. A couple of weeks have passed since we last spoke. I am perplexed, yet slightly amused, with my boss sitting in my office, waiting for me. Something must be up. A supervisor waiting in your office isn't normally a good sign, and it has to mean he has news or information to pass.

About what exactly, I'm soon to discover. Obviously, Pierce needs to get something off of his chest right at the start of our workday—or maybe he just wants it off of his desk.

"You're cleared to deal with the Russians in San Francisco and to go to the consulate," he says, almost matter-of-factly.

"Huh?" I look at him in utter disbelief, waiting for the punchline of the joke. But Pierce isn't the joking type. "I am cleared? You serious?"

"I called my contact in FBIHQ last night. He talked to Louie and granted you permission to deal with whoever you need to for your case. You have also been given approval for overnight stays in San Francisco, as required."

"Don, I still don't understand. You pick up the phone, call someone in Washington, and bad-a-bing, just like that, like a random magic trick, it's done?"

"Look, I've known Bryant, the deputy director, for many years, and he gave you the green light after speaking with Louie. Cos, just don't mess this up, OK?"

"You mean Louie Freeh, the director, right? And what about our counterintelligence friends in San Francisco? They're going to be infuriated when they hear this news."

"Yep, the director himself. As far as the counterintelligence folks, they already know, I told them," Pierce adds. "Oh, and they want to sit down with you, so they told me. Not sure why, but they do have equity in this since the Russian Consulate is their territory and responsibility. Sit down with them, see what they want, and you'll figure it out."

Pierce checks his watch. He stands up and heads back to his office. I immediately pull Sharon into mine as she walks past my door, heading down the hall.

"Sharon. It's game on. I've been cleared to deal directly with the folks at the consulate. And get this, Louie himself cleared it. Don knows the deputy director well enough to pick up the phone. Just like that, can you believe it?" I tell her, still trying to process and get my head around what Pierce has told me.

"Congratulations. What about the C-I side? They've got to be furious, no?"

"Well, I don't think they will call to congratulate us, but I don't care. Don told me I have to meet with them. Soon, they will reach out to either you or me. I'll let Marino know the cat-and-mouse game is over. I think he'll be more than relieved."

The C-I folks call two days later, just as I predicted. But it isn't the same agent who was screaming like a banshee at me over the telephone weeks earlier.

No, it's another agent whose name I have never heard before, a female special agent by the name of Marcia Benton. She sounds formal, all business on the telephone.

She asks me to come to San Francisco for the meeting. Sharon tells me to be wary and on guard. They aren't meeting with me to extend an olive branch, that's for sure. They obviously want something. What that something is, Sharon and I don't know, not yet.

When I enter the meeting room in the San Francisco office that afternoon, they are already there waiting for me. I am glad to be wearing a sport coat and tie for the meeting since they are all dressed in business attire. Marcia leads the introductions.

"Let me introduce you to Kyle Brown and Megan Little," she says as she stands up from her chair. There's an awkward chill in the air.

No one shows their credentials, which isn't that unusual.

However, Marcia omits to mention where the agents are working, or which particular squad they are assigned to, providing no reference at all.

That does strike me as odd, so I make a mental note of it. They might not be FBI Special Agents after all but perhaps attached to another U.S. government agency. It doesn't matter which one; they're not here for a friendly chat or to make small talk with me.

Megan speaks first. She is an icy blonde with a pretty face but has a fake smile which immediately evaporates as soon as she speaks.

"I heard about your case and contacts with the Russian Consulate. Sounds interesting. The Russian government needs hard currency to get through this tough economic transition period and selling resources—their natural resources, like diamonds—makes sense. Who from the Russian side informed you the diamonds were stolen?" she asks.

I don't like her. In fact, I don't like any of them.

This Megan is all business.

No charisma, no winning personality, and no charm. Her comments and questions aren't out of line, but I have no intention of sitting there passively, allowing myself to be interrogated by individuals who are not collegial colleagues. That much is already clear.

"This is a criminal investigation, a Federal Grand Jury investigation, with an AUSA from the Strike Force assigned. You want to know the basis for the Bureau and the U.S. Attorney's Office opening this case? I don't understand. You are from the counterintelligence side of the Bureau, right?"

I have been through more than one rodeo.

They want information from me, but I do not know with whom I am really speaking.

They are making no effort to develop rapport, to disarm me, or earn my trust. It is insulting on some level, but I decide to let it go, trying not to allow my ego to influence my responses and show any attitude toward them. That said, I certainly will not reveal information concerning a sensitive and ongoing criminal investigation to these virtual strangers. If this is the extent of their interviewing skills and techniques, heck, they don't deserve answers, none.

I am tempted to stand up and just walk out of the room, but curiosity stops me.

"So, who are you guys exactly? Which squads are you assigned to, and can you please show me your Bureau credentials?" I ask, already expecting their response.

"Although we are with another agency, we closely collaborate with your C-I agents. We would appreciate your cooperation. We've heard you are an experienced investigator and speak Russian. You studied in college?" Marcia asks.

Megan is suddenly silent, and now Marcia has stepped in to play good cop, but it is a feeble attempt, even more pathetic in view of the lack of interview skills.

"Since you aren't familiar with Federal Grand Jury rules and procedures, I should at least make you aware of some of the legal requirements and restrictions for these sorts of cases.

"First, information is restricted, and the sharing of it is forbidden for those not included on what is called a 6-E list. The case was opened based on the reasonable suspicion of an ongoing criminal violation of federal law. I am working closely with an AUSA, with an IRS Special Agent, and with a U.S.

Customs Service Special Agent. We are all bound by the rules of the Federal Grand Jury."

Kyle jumps in. "OK. Understood. But if you would be willing, if you have contact with Russian foreign nationals or diplomats, can you please reach out to us? It would be immensely helpful. For obvious reasons."

It is now his turn to give it a crack with me, apparently.

"Sure thing. I'll let the C-I folks know, and they can reach out to you. What obvious reasons do you mean? Sorry, but I'm just a criminal investigator," I tell them.

I assert control of the interview, seizing the opportunity to go on the offensive with the borderline insulting comment from Brown.

Megan says, "Look, we don't know if this is an intelligence operation, or what role their intelligence services are playing, or exactly who is involved. This operation appears quite significant, and the Russians are fully committed to it. You certainly understand there are many layers, like the layers of an onion. We have bona fide interests in this sort of operation and there are U.S. foreign policy considerations that have to be clear to you, don't they?"

I come close to breaking into a smile as it becomes apparent these three haven't prepared for this interview.

No gaming out their approach in interviewing me, no preparation beforehand, nothing.

"Sure. I understand. It was a genuine pleasure," I announce, standing.

For me, the meeting is over, and I have no intention of interacting with these three again, ever. There is no point in remaining in the room any longer either, not for one more minute.

There is nothing to gain or to learn, and they're not in my corner supporting the investigation. They seem to have their own secret agenda, and want to use me, or to see if I am amenable to being used and directed. It is a grievous miscalculation on their part, and I am not about to reward them for their sloppy prep work, nor for their arrogance, and their attitude of entitlement and superiority.

As I drive back to my office in San José, I reflect on the meeting, and on what impact the interest of that "agency" can have on the investigation going forward.

There's no point in over-analyzing it. It's not surprising that the "agency" is interested and wants to learn more, but I'm not about to share information or confide in such individuals.

What logical or legal reason would there be to do so?

This chess match is complicated and challenging enough without including individuals whose motivation is questionable at best. Don Pierce tells me the director has green lighted my interaction with the Russian Consulate.

In the end, that is all that matters, for now at least.

I hope the agency will eventually lose interest and focus elsewhere.

If they really want to dig around the case and the players on their own, there isn't much I can do to prevent it. They have their own interests and no doubt already have developed—or can develop—their own sources to direct or to use for information.

There is no point in worrying about what the agency might or might not do.

I simply need to stay focused on the investigation, keep it moving forward as best I can. Importantly, for now, I have FBIHQ's support, and they neither interfere nor try to direct me.

# Chapter 21

Time for me to meet Ms. Nazari. She called a couple of days ago. We are speaking almost daily now, which isn't unusual given her access and ability to get information from several key players working in and around Golden ADA.

"I talked to Ashot the other day. It was a chance encounter when I was socializing with Lara. He was in a talkative mood. I think he likes me," Nazari says playfully. "Ashot and David have gone on several buying sprees with Andrey. They try to act like it's no big deal to them, but I know where they come from. They're not from the Russian ruling elite class."

"We both know that, Annie. But act like you are impressed. Feed their ego, let them talk."

She says, "Yes, I know, and this sounds crazy, but when they told me what they've been buying, I didn't know how to react or what to say. I am not sure why they tell me such things sometimes. They just need someone to talk to. It must feel, well, surreal, the gold, the diamonds, all that money, even for them, right?"

Nazari tells me the Shagirians and Kozlenok, over the course of the past few months, have traveled together on several buying sprees, the likes of which she cannot grasp.

One Rolls Royce, two Aston Martins, three yachts, luxury condos at Lake Tahoe, another in Bermuda, a brand-new Gulfstream jet, a Picasso, a Rembrandt, a Monet, and much more.

It is dizzying to listen to all they have bought.

For me, the lavish, unhinged spending is in stark contrast to the low-profile lifestyle and behavior of most mobsters from the United States, the ones I have dealt with at least. Kozlenok is a mobster of sorts, but he is different. I attribute it to him having grown up in the Soviet Union. There was a ruling Soviet elite, and perhaps Kozlenok was part of it.

Whatever the reason for such lavish and high-profile spending, Kozlenok must feel comfortable and confident in what he is doing. It is understandable.

I have to admit to myself that I am impressed at the speed and sophistication of it all.

In a matter of months since Kozlenok first arrived in San Francisco, in a land completely unknown to him, he has positioned himself and his company as significant players in the diamond business, spending many millions. Even more impressive, he has surrounded himself with influential and powerful people with little effort, and in a brief span of time.

He has carved out his own space with the elites of San Francisco society, despite their closed and cloistered ways. The high-profile gala is a brilliant maneuver. Near genius.

Andrey Kozlenok is truly the ringmaster for the moment; that much I can't deny him.

Yet, at his core, he is nothing more than a crook, a narcissist, a charismatic, but manipulative conman. In Kozlenok's mind, he is untouchable. No one can come near him, and he believes no one would dare.

Not the FBI, not anyone from law enforcement, so he probably figures.

He's at the top of his game. The company he established a few years earlier is now in a favorable position to grow and expand its business activities and footprint in the United States. Surrounding himself with influential and powerful people, he has also shielded himself and his company from potential missteps or outside threats.

The diamonds are continuing to flow into coffers of Golden ADA, thousands of carats' worth of the precious stones arriving regularly by private jet from Moscow, all under the protection and watchful eyes of Shane Sullivan and the SFPD.

There is no reason to suspect the flow of diamonds will ever stop, not for a while, anyway. I make a mental note to ask Sharon to prioritize tracking the assets and valuables that Kozlenok and his conspirators are gaining at a dizzying pace, to prepare ourselves for their eventual seizure and forfeiture one future day.

# Chapter 22

"It's your sister," my wife says as she hands me the receiver and lets out a sigh.

It is barely seven on Saturday morning.

"Jen, what's up? You're calling early. You OK?"

"I'm on to something. Despite your disapproval, I visited Kansas City. I walked those neighborhoods and tried to talk to the girls working the streets."

"Are you nuts? You're lucky to be alive. You don't know what you'll encounter, and believe me, you'll never see it coming. I told you not to go there."

"I was careful. I had my knife with me, strapped to my leg, and I can handle myself. A few of the girls talked to me. They suspect a killer may still be on the streets, stalking, waiting. It hasn't stopped them from doing what they do, unfortunately."

"You could have been the next victim, and if it becomes known you are my sister, the odds get worse, much worse," I tell her.

Aware she can hang up the phone, I try to remain calm.

"Oh, and I made more progress in looking into our grandfather. He had a few tough assignments in the NYPD. I can't imagine what it must have been like to catch killers, child killers, during that era before the war. No behavioral profile unit, no criminal analysis, nothing. He was really on his own, chasing a serial killer or killers around the city, with only his instinct and intuition to guide him. When I read those articles, I feel somehow close to him. I know he died before I was born but he was still my grandfather."

"Jen, try not to get too absorbed in that stuff. It was a long time ago, and a vastly different era. I agree, it's fascinating in a way to research those times, but policing and the manner of investigation were hugely different back then. We have evolved since those times. Although there were skilled and capable investigators back then, no doubt, including our grandfather and uncles," I say, hoping my words will somehow sink in, that my sister will take my advice. But I know it's unlikely.

She's just too determined and too stubborn, a family trait, I assume.

"OK. Oh, and what is 'Santeria'? You said something to me a while ago about this stuff."

"It's a religion of sorts, a blend of Catholicism and pagan practices brought to Cuba from Africa. Why are you asking me?" I am hoping to hear it's something she has simply read about and not learned during her ill-advised visit to Kansas City.

"Two women mentioned it to me. They said the Cubans in the area are into that in a big way and believe in it. They turn to Santeria priests whenever they need help or guidance or advice about anything."

"Jennifer, you need to stay away from this Santeria stuff. It's dangerous, and you're out of your league," I tell her, instantly regretting my choice of words. My sister has never taken well to anyone, particularly a sibling, telling her what she can or can't do or think.

"Look, it won't help you. I know where you're going with it. You think a priest might give you insight or have information about a killer in that community, one who could be still on the loose. But their world is closed to outsiders, and while your Spanish isn't bad, it just won't work. KCPD will catch this guy. They're capable, as I told you, and committed."

The memories flood back into my head.

Santeria and its mystical belief system have become deeply ingrained in the fabric of the Cuban community in Kansas City. I closely dealt with a Santero, a priest, during the drug case in Kansas City; I eventually wound up arresting him, along with the other subjects. The Cuban drug traffickers would seek advice from this Santero before engaging in drug deals, or before traveling to pick up drugs from their main suppliers in Los Angeles.

The priest became an important Bureau source of mine until I discovered he was directly involved in the drug trade himself. It took several months for me and my Bureau partner to uncover that fact.

After the call with my sister, I am not sure she will take any of my advice, no matter how strongly I phrase it. There isn't much I can do; my sister is determined, and I realize in some ways, she is more like our grandfather than anyone else in the family.

Not a poor trait, but it could wind up getting her killed. I have told her more than once that I wish I could have devoted more time and effort to finding that serial killer.

She's right, of course. She's right that he is still out there, somewhere, lurking in the shadows. So many women have already been killed, and where was the Bureau when they were being slain? I can't toss the entire blame back to Quantico either.

I am also to blame for not following up more aggressively.

This morning, as I finish breakfast with my wife and children, I realize I've forgotten to tell my sister the strange story of the LAX airport lookalike encounter.

In a way, it seems better to leave it be, but I still feel a compulsion to convey the story.

So, I tell her. In the end, she is appreciative and curious in learning about my encounter, also wondering who exactly this stranger is, the woman bearing the striking resemblance.

Could she be a blood relative of some sort? There's no way of telling.

Our family doesn't have relatives in California, as far as we know. I inform her I will keep an eye out for the lookalike in

Monterey; the woman told me her husband is stationed in the Army there and studying at the language school.

Could our uncle, the one who vanished years ago, have fathered a child in California? Could this woman be a cousin? Anything is possible. The girl herself might know nothing of her true past, or perhaps she's not been told the true story by her family members.

Another thought comes. Is this encounter in any way related to Golden ADA? The thought crosses my mind, but I quickly dismiss it, thinking this could be paranoia creeping into my psyche, not a healthy sign of my mental state. I convince myself the LAX encounter is nothing more than an unconnected side show, and I write it off as such, for now.

Time to refocus on the challenge at hand, Golden ADA.

Just as I decide it's best to let it all go, my wife calls me inside from the garage. "The Bureau called and wants you to call back as soon as you can. Saturday? Seriously?"

That's all my disgruntled wife says as she walks away from the telephone.

She is not pleased, but for agents, this is our life in the FBI. The Bureau can call us at their choosing, whenever they need us. Daytime, nighttime, weekends, holidays, it doesn't matter.

We better be ready to drop everything and respond. That is the job.

The agent on duty this weekend answers the phone on the first ring. "You need to call Dmitry. He says it's important and you know how to reach him," the agent tells me.

I immediately reach out to Rich Marino. It's better to stick with the arrangement we've made, despite the green light for direct contact allowed by FBIHQ, and the director.

"Rich, I know it's Saturday, but Dmitry called. He left a message with my office in San Francisco, and said it was important," I explain to Marino.

"I'm on it," is all Marino says in response. He is that kind of investigator, not complaining it's the weekend, or that he's busy with personal stuff.

It is only a matter of minutes when the phone rings again. It is Marino again; he tells me Dmitry wants to meet and discuss something face to face.

***

We—I, Marino and Dmitry—meet at our usual place, the cozy restaurant near the Russian Consulate. Dmitry seems excited to talk.

Dmitry begins speaking as soon as we are seated. "I have news from Moscow. The Committee is sending representatives here. They're looking into this matter and have concerns. From what I understand, it is their deputy chairman; his name is Boris Poznikov. I know nothing beyond that, but it's a good development, right? They arrive in San Francisco in a day or so."

I say, "It sure is, Dmitry. I guess we'll have to wait and see what the deputy chairman has to say. I'll get back to you and let you know where we'll meet when he arrives."

"He'll be alone, or will there be others from Moscow?" Marino asks.

"It will be Mr. Poznikov, and perhaps a couple of others from the Committee, along with myself," Dmitry says.

"Will he bring any documentation with him?" Marino asks.

It is a logical question and will give us a sense as to the purpose of the visit. This will be our first contact with anyone from Moscow.

If this Boris Poznikov is the second in charge at ROSKOMDRAGMET, after Bychkov, the visit raises many questions.

Does he have any involvement in the "conspiracy"?

Is he coming to find out what the FBI is doing and what we know?

Is this an internal power play to wrestle control of the committee from Bychkov?

Or is Poznikov coming to San Francisco to close the company's operations and return the valuables to Russia?

Marino and I will have to be patient and wait until the meeting with Poznikov to find out.

Now, it is time to reach out to Terry Miller, to inform him and possibly include him in the meeting. After all, Miller will be interested in talking to officials from the Russian side who could possibly shed light on the ownership of the stones and other valuables.

And to potentially answer the pivotal question: are the valuables being removed from Russia lawfully or not? The entire case can hinge upon what Poznikov might reveal, and what documents he might have and be willing to share with us.

"Rich, we need to keep an open mind for this meeting, and be careful not to show our hands. Don't forget, this is still a complicated chess match, and one in which we really don't know the rules. I'll let Miller know, and I'll inform my boss. My gut tells me the Russians won't reveal more than they absolutely need to unless they feel compelled to do so.

"We are in the dark, Rich. But it's not our move on this chessboard. This next move is from the Russian side. We just need to be mindful of how we respond to it when it comes."

"But we shouldn't be frozen or afraid to act, right? As you told me, more than once," Marino says. He is a solid and reliable partner for me, but this will be the first time we will be operational together and will have to trust one another in managing such a delicate and important meeting. The case, and its success or failure outcome, can depend on it.

At our strategy discussion to prepare for the Poznikov meeting, Miller, Marino, King, and I review the dos and don'ts. There will be questions from the Russian side about our investigation and what the U.S. side knows and is prepared to share.

I say, "Guys, we need to be open and frank, otherwise, they will sense our reluctance to engage with them. But we can't cross the line. They don't need to know the sensitive details gleaned from our sources, or details revealed through subpoenaed documents. It is best to stay with the same approach we've used with Dmitry, along the lines that this

Golden ADA company has come to our attention and there may be criminal violations, and we're in the initial stages of our investigation.

"Oh, and express our gratitude to them for meeting with us, etc.," I add.

Terry Miller steps in. "Look, I think we will be in react mode. This guy, Boris Poznikov, is a senior official in their government, and he's going to want our help to get the diamonds back, or he's going to tell us they can manage it on their own, in their own way."

"We'll have to wait and see what he says," he ventures. "He's not from their intelligence service or law enforcement structures; he's a bureaucrat, and may have a political agenda, or motivations of an unknown nature."

"I agree. It's one of those meetings where the unspoken is as important as the spoken. What do I mean by that?" I ask them, then proceed to answer my own question.

"For example, if he doesn't mention Bychkov by name, or speaks about him in less than glowing terms, it will tell us something. What is most important is for us to seize the opportunity to open this new channel of communication with Moscow, so we can talk with one another directly. If Poznikov finds it's beneficial to be in dialogue with us, then the meeting is a success. It's like that first undercover meeting with the targets of a case. When an undercover agent has that first encounter or meets the targets of the investigation, the most important take away isn't necessarily to gain incriminating evidence. No, it's the bad guys agreeing or willing to meet again, that second time."

"I'm no expert in international affairs, and have never dealt with Russians before, but perhaps they're just feeling us out? To get a sense if they can work with us? We are just as much a mystery and as unknown to them as they are to us," King says.

Miller offers, "Good point, George. Well, we'll find out soon enough. See you all in a couple of days. They've agreed to meet in the U.S. Attorney's Office. A good sign, I suppose?"

***

The delegation arrives at the U.S. Attorney's Office precisely at the scheduled time. Dmitry is there with Poznikov and two others from his staff. Poznikov doesn't appear to speak any English and Dmitry makes all the introductions.

I earlier pulled Miller aside before their arrival to discuss who would be in the lead for questions. Miller defers to me as case agent for the FBI. At the start of the meeting, I introduce the task force members, and Dmitry introduces his side, all in English. Dmitry interprets the English into Russian as Poznikov doesn't speak or understand the language.

The small talk about their travel, jet lag, and San Francisco tourist sites takes several minutes; I realize this introductory meeting is the first time we are talking to someone in authority from the Russian government. Yet, someone has to take that first step, or move, to show goodwill genuinely openly, without putting the Russians on the spot or in an awkward position. I figure if Poznikov's mission to San Francisco is to explore or weigh options for his government to recover the diamonds and other valuables, he will need to provide something concrete to his own superiors, whoever they are, back in Moscow.

I switch into Russian. "Thanks for coming here today, Deputy Minister. We appreciate you taking this time and making the long trip here to discuss this matter. We obviously have concerns from a law enforcement perspective concerning Golden ADA and its activities. It isn't clear whether your government sanctioned their work. The timing of your visit is excellent, and we are hoping to gain a better understanding of things and how we can help you from our side," I explain. For an opening, I think our offer of help—and admission about the lack of understanding concerning Golden ADA—is as far as I can go.

Now, it is Poznikov's turn to respond. Dmitry interprets, oddly enough, into English so Miller can keep up. I realize I've lost awareness that Miller isn't following since the conversation shifted into Russian. I decide to stay in Russian as any chance of developing even the slightest bit of rapport with Poznikov depends in part on my communicating with him in his native tongue.

"Thanks, Dennis. We appreciate your candor and openness with us. We have just begun our review of Golden ADA and its operations here in the United States. As Deputy Minister, I have allowed my staff to examine documents and contracts giving Golden ADA and its Moscow branch, Star of the Urals, the right to cut and polish stones within the authorizations and parameters provided by ROSKOMDRAGMET. We have already found irregularities, but our internal review is ongoing. I'm not in a position to discuss our interim findings in any detail. Not for the time being, at least."

For me, what Poznikov says in those few sentences tracks fairly close to what I expect him to say and to reveal. For starters, he confirms ROSKOMDRAGMET is conducting its own internal review. They have already found irregularities, which I also anticipated.

Does it mean Poznikov is at odds or acting in opposition to his boss, Eugeniy Bychkov?

It is certainly possible, but Poznikov not mentioning his own boss by inference or by name is noteworthy. Yet, it can be that Poznikov remains loyal to his boss, and that his mission is to portray ROSKOMDRAGMET as the victim of a scheme to deceive or defraud it, with Andrey Kozlenok as the guilty party, the principal culprit and deceiver.

I can't ask about Bychkov, since Poznikov hasn't opened the door for such a sensitive line of inquiry. I know better than to even try as it can embarrass—or worse—particularly with Poznikov's associates and Dmitry sitting in the room. When Poznikov returns home, he can be held accountable in the harshest manner as he lives and works in Russia.

I hope no one else from the U.S. side will raise such delicate issues.

The best way to keep the conversation flowing with Poznikov, I think, is to stay in the Russian language as I don't want to give space to my colleagues to ask questions that are too probative or sensitive. It will have a chilling effect and possibly shut things down.

There is no telling what forces are at work in Moscow behind the scenes.

For all I know, Poznikov may be operating out there completely alone, trying to rein things in, perhaps for the noblest of reasons. Or perhaps not.

It could be that Poznikov is in San Francisco to clean up the growing mess, or at least to clean up the mess Andrey Kozlenok and Eugeniy Bychkov created through their lavish and unhinged spending. The Russian government could have sent Poznikov to the U.S. as an assurance to U.S. law enforcement that they have things under control, are fully aware, and are in the process of cleaning up their own internal mess with no intervention by the likes of the FBI, with its intrusive and probative ways.

After all, the potential for the Russian state to earn massive revenue—hard currency, through the sale of diamonds and valuable resources abroad—is enormous. The sales can provide significant stimulus and support to Russia's fledging free market economy, which remains mostly stagnant following the collapse of the Soviet Union several years prior.

The meeting ends after what seems like one hour, one long hour, with me having to speak entirely in Russian. In reality, we've been talking for much longer.

Poznikov assures us he will keep us apprised of any future developments.

We exchange contact information, and that is the end of the meeting.

It is over. On the positive side, we have now established a new line of communication, directly with the deputy head of ROSKOMDRAGMET.

On the negative side, Poznikov has failed to mention or suggest the diamonds have been stolen or that corrupt Russian officials are involved in the scheme.

No, this case has too many twists and turns to be that easy. No matter; at least there are still sufficient justifications to keep the investigation going.

Both red flags and unanswered questions abound.

Importantly, what Poznikov has not told us is that everything is fine, that Golden ADA is doing precisely as allowed by the Russian government.

In fact, he's admitted there's an ongoing internal inquiry of an undisclosed nature, and they've already found what they term irregularities.

The game is afoot, Dr. Watson.

Definitely, the game is on. So, what is the next move, Dr. Watson? Our next move?

After the delegation departs, Miller asks to meet separately, appearing most displeased if I am to go by the look on his face. I suspect he may be unhappy with the way I conducted the meeting, speaking Russian directly to the delegation.

I say, "Terry, before you unload on me, I can understand your frustration or disappointment, but we all knew it might go like this with Poznikov revealing very little, and keeping his cards close to his chest."

In anticipation of Miller's ensuing reproach, I broach the topic, looking him confidently in the eye. He surprises me, however, responding, "Actually, I thought it went very well. We have—or at least I think we now have—a line of communication directly with a high-ranking official from Russia. We've revealed little from our side, which is good, and from their side, they have at least told us there are 'irregularities.' It's something, right?"

Somehow, I keep the look of surprise off my demeanor.

I answer, "Yes, I agree, Terry. We've both played it smart, I think. Well, what I mean is that the Russian side—Poznikov—will never unload everything at a meeting like that with us, and he knows we won't either. But we have at least started, let's say, a dialogue of sorts with one another, showing each other the requisite amount of respect while also giving one another space to operate."

I smile slightly, only in a businesslike manner. Yet he does not return it.

So, I go on, "But something tells me you're not happy, or what? You're OK with what went on there, from my side at least, I hope?"

"Yeah. But I can't get my head around you speaking Russian with him, and then we have Dmitry, a KGB officer, translating for you ... well, for me ... into English. Sorry, but I never thought I would be a witness to this sort of exchange. It's a long way from the Cold War days. I am not sure what to make of this. I guess it's a good thing?" Miller says as he laughs. My vague smile returns, trying to keep this conversation somewhat convivial.

He hasn't finished yet.

"It's got to be a first of sorts, no?" he adds. "I mean, how crazy is this? An FBI agent speaking in Russian at an official meeting, and the KGB guy sitting next to me, interpreting into English." He is still shaking his head in disbelief.

Going through his mind may also be the question of authenticity; is the translation true to the intentions of the speaker? He will never know and has to trust me that it is.

"It's OK, Terry. You better get used to this sort of stuff. I have a feeling far stranger things are in store for us in this odyssey. Welcome to the chess match, Terry, in which no one really knows the rules if there are any," I say to him, shaking Miller's hand as I leave the U.S. Attorney's Office to head back to mine in San José.

# Chapter 23

"Annie, anything new with our Golden ADA friends lately? Any shipments scheduled to arrive?" I ask her a few days after Poznikov returns to Russia.

I decide not to reveal the recent visit of the ROSKOMDRAGMET delegation, to gauge Nazari's access to the targets.

While it is possible Poznikov has never visited the Golden ADA premises, it is highly unlikely he has no contact with Andrey, or someone working for Golden ADA.

So, they have to have known that a delegation from Moscow has been in town.

It seems conceivable for Andrey to host the delegation and, as a master manipulator, even to wine and dine them. Why not? In his own mind, he'll simply be doing his job, taking care of everyone, and all those who matter will merely be profiting from his "generosity."

It is unfortunate that the Bureau has no Title III or undercover inside the organization. The information gleaned from a wiretap or undercover operative might shed enormous light on things, providing clarity on why Poznikov came to San Francisco, and more importantly, what he was doing. For now, I only have subpoenaed documents and bank records, as well as information from Nazari. It is just too risky to even consider approaching anyone else, including anyone from SFPD.

"I heard something," she responded. "Yes, the Shagirians were pretty wound up a few days ago about a visitor from Moscow but didn't elaborate. They just said Andrey was keyed up, but he assured them everything was under control."

She looks at me, wide eyed. Then she continues, asking, "Is it true? Have you heard anything about visitors from Russia?" She asks it in a coy manner.

Nazari is charming, possessing a way of disarming people, but she's no fool, and a highly intelligent woman. She likely senses I am testing her, checking on her continued accessibility to the subjects of the investigation, trying to see if she's holding back information.

"Yes, Annie, it's true. Just keep your eyes and ears open. Don't probe them about the visit. Do nothing to make them suspicious. If they say anything else, please reach out to me as soon as you can. OK?"

"Sure. I need to tell you something else," she says, leaning in and lowering her voice.

"What is it, Annie?"

She says, "I'm being followed. Not all the time, but sometimes, after a few of my meetings with the Shagirians, and with Lara. Maybe it's nothing. Do you think the police department is behind this? Ashot tells me they provide excellent security to their company, and they know everyone in the city, and everything that is going on. It's all reported via their head of security, Shane Sullivan, and this Art Roggenbuck guy. You think I'm in danger?"

This is something I would prefer not to have to deal with, but Nazari could, in fact, have someone surveilling or watching her. There could even be a wiretap on her phone, placed by who knows, but definitely not the Bureau. Not the Bureau in San Francisco, at least. There are several possibilities who, or what agency, could be tracking her movements.

It could be Golden ADA's security, or SFPD, or the Bureau's counterintelligence "friends," or even one of Golden ADA's competitors such as De Beers. Or it could be Nazari just playing with me, keeping me on a string in her specific way.

Regardless, she and I need to be more cautious in how we meet up and communicate, particularly when meeting after her consensually recorded meetings and telephone calls, when I rendezvous with her for the post-meeting brief, and to retrieve meeting recordings.

The thought occurs to me that Nazari could introduce an undercover agent to the subjects of the case, but if we go that route, it will take time to clear the bureaucratic hurdles and get the required clearances and authorizations to open a special undercover operation.

To find the right undercover agent, someone familiar with the diamond business—perhaps a Russian speaker too—will certainly not be easy. I set aside the thought for a future time.

For now, the volume of subpoenaed bank records and other documents demand close study and analysis. Wire transfers of significant amounts are going back and forth between companies in the United States and in Europe. Golden ADA's purchase of the 999 Brannan Street building also needs to be reviewed and analyzed.

A reliable Bureau source informs me the company paid more to the sellers than the building was worth at the time, for inexplicable reasons.

There might be a connection between the company's payment to the sellers, which surpassed the building's value, and money laundering or some sort of kickback scheme. The financial and banking irregularities also seem to be piling up. There is a new twist in the case on a near daily basis, leaving me struggling to manage my other cases.

I will soon need to speak with my boss, Don Pierce, to ask for support from my squad-mates, or at least to convince Pierce to reassign some of my work to other agents.

Either way, it will be a hard sell. Pierce can decide upon another course of action entirely, and reassign the Golden ADA matter to another agent, or direct me to put the case into "inactive status" for a few weeks—or even months—until my other cases close and my caseload situation improves. I figure I'd better speak with Pierce, the sooner the better, before things have a chance to go completely off the rails.

***

I brief Pierce later in the week about the Moscow delegation.

He just sits there passively and listens. It has always been difficult to discern whether Pierce likes what he's hearing, or whether he is listening.

As a supervisor of an active criminal investigative squad, he has to track many cases, and so it is unsurprising that things sometimes fall through the cracks.

He says, "I got a call from Jake Stirrup, the OC squad supervisor in San Francisco, last night. He mentioned he's been reading the reporting on your case. It's a good thing you've been keeping him updated with reports as he's technically the SF Division's OC coordinator and should be informed about this stuff, especially since the case is in his own backyard.

"But we'll talk about that issue later. For now, you need to know the Russian Tax Police are sending a delegation here. They reached out to the Bureau in San Francisco and want to meet. I'm not sure whether their visit is connected to your case or not.

"Regardless, you need to drop everything else and get up there. And as far as Golden ADA, it's still your case, but the OC squad is very curious. Play nice with them. Oh, and you and I have been invited to attend Jake's thirty-year Bureau anniversary dinner, scheduled in a couple of days. Everyone will be there from the law enforcement community. You can bring your wife if you want. Just make sure you're there."

"OK, I'll get up there and talk to them, and meet with the Tax Police. I've never heard of the Russian Tax Police though; must be a new agency?" I ask.

This could be a significant development in the case, to meet with a Russian law enforcement agency, but there is no telling what may come of it.

"One other thing, Cos. You probably know already, but the legal attaché office finally opened in Russia. I never thought it would happen. Apparently, Louie is big on this international cop-to-cop stuff and has orchestrated the whole thing behind the scenes with the Russians. Lawrence or Robert may reach out to you. If they don't, you might call them and introduce yourself. Who knows, you may need their help one day. By the way, the two agents are from the San Francisco Division. I don't know if you know them. The legal attaché is Lawrence Poinier. Don't call him Larry. And his assistant legal attaché is Robert Backus—he goes by Bob. They're both counterintelligence agents or were in their past assignments.

"Lawrence has been in the legat program for a few years. He was in Hong Kong. And Bob was here for a while. You probably don't know him but I understand from Jake Stirrup that Bob arranged for the visit of the Tax Police to San Francisco. Maybe this visit results from their office's liaison efforts. We can't assume their visit has anything to do with Golden ADA. Let's not make any assumptions for now."

This is stunning news to me.

I have been hearing rumblings about a legal attaché office possibly opening in Moscow, but those have only been rumors. It is hard to fathom it's actually happened.

In case things happened to go sideways and negotiations broke down, it has all been kept hush-hush, so I figure. It is a plus that both Moscow-based agents have previously worked in SF Division, but both being C-I, counterintelligence agents could be problematic for me.

Yet, it isn't at all surprising since the Bureau has almost always assigned its pool of Russian speakers to C-I matters. I, a Russian-speaking agent, am a bit of an anomaly with my criminal investigative background and experience. In a strange twist, it makes me an outsider of sorts. I am not a member of the "C-I club," something bringing negative consequences if I make a mistake. No one will be around to watch my back or cover for me.

Do I care? On some level, no; I have a job to do, and that's all that matters.

The meeting with Pierce ends with his usual "later, dude" manner of closing things.

Considering the significant recent developments he's shared with me, there is now no point in asking for help or for my other cases to be reassigned.

It would not go well with Pierce to complain about too much work, which is precisely how he would perceive my request. Besides, the Bureau has now opened a brand-new office in Russia itself, and the agents there are likely fully occupied in working to develop reliable liaison contacts within the Russian law enforcement and security sectors.

This will take time, perhaps many months, even.

And, a relatively new player, the Russian Tax Police are on their way to San Francisco.

For what reason, it isn't clear, but it also doesn't much matter. The OC squad in San Francisco will host them, and they have asked me to assist them.

So much for taking leave with the family; that will have to wait.

It will be an excellent opportunity for me to engage with the agents from that SF OC squad, as I don't know them very well.

And they will engage to get to know me, even to test me in some way.

Dr. Watson, the game is once more afoot, and the chessboard is getting crowded with fresh players and pieces, so it appears. "Game on, Dr. Watson, game on," I repeat to myself.

"Just deal with it, and don't be a baby," my wife sometimes says to me.

Yeah, don't be a baby, Cos.

It is a good thing I don't unload or whine about being over assigned or make requests for help to Pierce when I step into his office. That would only break badly.

"Note to self: always let Don Pierce speak first."

I repeat this mantra several times, so I'll never forget the "ukas", the edict from Tsarist Russia days. No, I must never forget it; I'll need Don Pierce in my corner as he's my only and most important supporter and backer in the entire Bureau.

# Chapter 24

San Francisco's FBI OC and Drug Squad comprises a mixture of seasoned veterans and younger agents. I have no real sense of the squad's focus, but I've heard they have several Title III cases ongoing, mostly drug trafficking related.

I also know that their supervisor, Pierce's counterpart in San Francisco, Jake Stirrup, is getting close to retirement. Stirrup is a veteran agent with nearly thirty years in the Bureau, admired and respected by agents, and by his law enforcement counterparts in other federal, state, and local agencies including the SFPD. They all know him as a straight shooter.

I head straight to Stirrup's office on arrival at the San Francisco premises, figuring it is best to introduce myself first to the supervisor, since he's asked for me to assist the squad in hosting the delegation soon to arrive from Moscow.

"Cos, good to meet you," Stirrup says, extending his hand. "I don't know if you knew Backus when he was here as he worked

C-I, but he wants us to take care of the Russian Tax Police delegation while they're in attendance. They're a new agency, and Bob has already developed good contacts with them. He says to introduce the delegation around the city, give them some general briefings, and just be friendly hosts. I'd like you to take part in the meetings as much as you can. Look, I've read your reporting on Golden ADA.

"We'll talk later about the case, but for now, let's leave it be. I don't know whether the tax authorities are looking into this matter or not, so we won't open the door for them. If they raise it, take the lead in responding however you see fit. Does this all sound OK to you?"

He asks it matter-of-factly, and to my mind, this appears to be a good opening salvo with Jake Stirrup. He seems genuine and approachable. If Stirrup has his own agenda, or is holding back, I don't sense it. He seems a likable guy, and I immediately understand why the agents on his squad respect and admire him. That is his reputation, at least.

"OK, Jake. So, as far as we know, they are coming here on their own dime as I understand, and for no particular reason? Or that is what Backus said, right?"

"Yeah. That's Bob," he replies. "He is a C-I agent at his core, and good at building relationships. He's the right agent at the right time there for that new office. Poinier, the legat is more reserved, but Bob will spend hours out with his contacts, and wine and dine them. It was his idea for them to come to the U.S. to learn about our system. We will introduce them to our contacts at the IRS, and at the U.S. Attorney's Office. Bob says some of their staff are former KGB. Not surprising, they have to be from somewhere, right?

"It's good for us to get in on the ground floor with this agency just as they're getting established. It'll be worth the time and effort; it's only a few days, then we put them back on the plane to Moscow, and you can go back to your work in San José. How does that sound?"

"All good, Jake. And from your squad, who will I be working with on this?"

"It will be Breelove. Peter, who you already know, I think, and Joe Doherty. All things Russian intrigue and fascinate Joe. He's a wonderful agent and experienced in OC stuff, although he's never dealt with Russians. So, get a hold of them, and you guys go from there."

I walk over to the "bullpen" where the rank-and-file agents and staff desks are located.

There are rows of desks with office dividers, but no one has their own private office except for senior management and squad supervisors.

I spot Peter Breelove working at his desk computer.

"Welcome to our squad, Cos! At least for the next few days. Jake tells me you'll be helping us out with this delegation from Moscow. Frankly, I've got a thousand more important things to deal with, and Joe Doherty is in the wind. He's away for the next few days. I've got help from a couple of interpreters from the CI side of the house," he explains.

Breelove is sounding weary. He is always working on a Title III, so it seems, reviewing transcripts or writing a new affidavit.

Title IIIs are labor intensive, and most agents try to avoid them, but they are an invaluable investigative tool, particularly for complex cases, drug and OC cases, mostly. Don Pierce knows Peter Breelove well, having worked with him in the past, and he's always spoken highly of him and his work ethic.

"OK, Peter. We'll manage this. You have a notional agenda for them? I guess they'll need to be accompanied to all their meetings?" I ask.

"Yep. This is a Bob Backus deal, but we can't turn off the visit. Not the best timing, but it never is. Oh, and we have Jake's party in a couple of days. You're invited. You'll go, right?"

"Yeah, and I may bring my wife, Lenore. If she's not working that night."

"Between us, you can float in and out of these meetings and attend whichever ones you want to. I don't care. But I'm stuck with them for the entirety of their visit because of Jake assigning me to oversee everything. I really don't mind. I've actually never met anyone from Russian law enforcement before. Hey, I've heard you're working on some interesting stuff in San José, Russian OC related. Jake tells me this delegation may be interested in hearing about your cases. If you want to give them a briefing or meet them separately, just let me know."

"Sure, Peter. I don't envision briefing them since the cases are ongoing, and I don't know what their interest would be. I'm not paranoid about sharing with them, but I don't intend to say much unless they have specific questions. Is that OK with you?"

"Heck, I don't care. So, I will see you tomorrow morning, then; we will bring them here around ten, then head over to

SFPD and to a bunch of meetings—the U.S. Attorney's Office, IRS, DEA, etc." Breelove hands me a copy of the agenda for their visit.

There it is, in black and white. The meeting with SFPD is with none other than Chief Ken Burda himself. One part of me feels it will be good to attend, but there is also a downside.

The chief could put me on the spot by bringing up Golden ADA and even ask the delegation about their take on things or ask for their help. Anything is possible.

The question for me is whether it's better to opt out of the meeting or attend it.

I will have to think about it, at least sleep on it and decide in the morning.

***

"Rich, can you talk right now?" I call Marino from home in the evening, telling him about the visit of the Russian Tax Police, along with their planned meetings including the one with the SFPD Chief of Police, Ken Burda.

Marino wastes no time in telling me exactly what he thinks of the idea.

"I wouldn't go into any meeting involving SFPD unless you are in control. You've reminded me more than once that we are in a complicated chess match, and if you were to take part in that meeting with the chief, you would not be in control. You will sit there among adversaries, not friends or supporters. And by your presence, that's a chess move in my rule book. Once it's done, you can't undo that move. Put your piece back into its original position. So, what will you gain by your presence? Let me put it another way: what is the benefit of participating? And what's the downside? Can you tell me?"

"Well, I can tell you the downside," I begin. "There's the possibility the chief puts me on the spot. He might say something unexpected or inaccurate about Golden ADA. He is a skilled politician to a degree. Heck, the current mayor, Mayor Jordan, was once the Chief of Police, and Burda may have political aspirations. I'm small fry to him, an inconsequential, possibly even inconvenient player. I mean nothing to Burda. He may even suspect I played with him back when we had that meeting."

"Yep. And don't forget you also haven't heard a beep from either him or Shane Sullivan since. That should tell you something. They are not to be trusted."

"Thanks, Rich. I think I'll tell Peter Breelove I have something going on that I have to deal with tomorrow morning, will skip some meetings, and catch up with them later. He won't really care either way. You're right, no good can come of out that meeting for me, or for the case. Goodnight, Rich," I say as I hang up the phone.

I spend the next morning working in the San José office, catching up on other pending work and cases. I meet with Sharon, who by now has reviewed more of the recently subpoenaed financial records and bank transactions involving Golden ADA.

"So, you think this delegation's visit relates to Golden ADA, or is it a red herring?" Sharon asks.

"Not sure. You'd think our new office in Moscow would give us some details or advance notice. But this visit could have absolutely nothing to do with Golden ADA, and the timing's purely a coincidence. Yeah, there may be tax violations in Russia which involve Golden ADA and associated individuals, but if so, you would think my new friend, Dmitry, would have given me a heads up about that. He hasn't reached out to me or Marino at all.

"I could be wrong, but I believe this delegation is here to see the sights of the city and get some generalized briefings. They're a new agency, and their first visit could be related to their attempt to establish themselves on the international scene. Well, I hope to catch them later this afternoon in the SF office, when they return from their briefings around town."

"What? You're not taking part?" Sharon sounds incredulous. "They may unload intel about Golden ADA operations in Moscow, or perhaps they're looking to talk to someone in the Bureau, and share information? Isn't that possible? And you're the agent they should talk to, not the OC Squad in San Francisco," she emphasizes, sounding a bit agitated.

Sharon's points are valid, but the "chess match" rules take precedence. Don't make the move and take your hand off the chess piece unless you are prepared to deal with the outcome. That matters most, so it seems, for this situation. I explain to her that I intend to meet the delegation eventually but decide to steer clear of certain "briefings" the OC Squad in San Francisco has arranged for them, including the one with the SFPD chief.

Sharon shows she understands, raising her hand as if to ask for my permission to continue. "So, say you meet them, and they unload on you about Golden ADA, or tell you they are investigating the company. What will you do next?"

"I don't know, Sharon. I honestly don't. There is no way for me to predict things that far in advance. As it unfolds, I will handle it. I just hope whatever I say or do is correct."

"Seriously? This is nuts. I'm so glad I'm not an agent."

"Sharon, honestly, for most of my time in the Bureau, it's how I roll. Moment to moment. Governed by, well, I'm not sure what I am governed by anymore. Instinct, hunches, intuition, serendipity?"

"Just don't go arresting anyone using that voodoo stuff," she says. "Oh, I forgot … You already do, or did. I remember the kidnapping case a few years back. You and Paul Campo were out there, just doing your own thing. But you arrested the right guy, I give you that much. I just hope you don't wind up … Well, let's not go there. As long as your motive is righteous, I suppose it will all turn out OK in the end."

She returns to her office, shaking her head and muttering something.

I quietly laugh and grab my keys, then head to the parking lot to drive the Bureau vehicle to SF, needing to meet up with that delegation.

By the time I arrive in San Francisco, evening rush hour has already started with the exodus from the city, but the delegation is there in one of the office's smaller conference rooms, talking with some SF OC squad agents. I am introduced to the three-man, one-woman delegation. There is no mention of Golden ADA.

Through one of the office's Russian interpreters, Peter Breelove summarizes their meetings earlier in the day and goes over the plans for tomorrow.

Surprisingly, all four speak and understand English.

They seem relaxed and approachable. Katerina, the only woman of the group, is an attractive blonde who looks to be in her late twenties; she is dressed conservatively, but judging by her figure and posture could have been a ballet dancer or gymnast previously.

There are very few women in the law enforcement and security services in Russia. I have heard most become assigned to administrative and clerical duties, yet Katerina works as an operational and investigative officer. I make a mental note about introducing her to some of the female special agents with whom I work in San José.

At the start of the presentation, I present the group with an overview of the Bureau's involvement in addressing the OC and drug trafficking challenges in the San José area. I underscore the Bureau's interactions with other federal, state, and local agencies, including the Internal Revenue Service, and U.S. Customs Service.

Breelove asks me if I will join them for dinner in San Francisco this evening, at one of the nicer seafood restaurants in the city with its famous crab cakes and clam chowder.

I nearly decline but now having an option to stay overnight in the city with the authorization granted by FBIHQ, I accept the invite.

The restaurant has an amazing view of San Francisco Bay with its floor-to-ceiling windows. Igor is head of the delegation and sits next to Jake Stirrup, the squad supervisor.

Ivan and Boris sit with the other agents, and Katerina motions for me to sit in the empty chair next to her.

I say, turning to her, "I can imagine you are all tired after the long flight, and with the time change. You'll sleep well tonight, I am sure. The time difference between Moscow and San Francisco is ten hours, I think?"

"Yes, but we slept for a few hours on the flight. None of us has ever been to the United States, and the only person in the FBI we knew, until today, was Bob," she says in English.

Her accent is there, but it is apparent she's studied the language for some time in Russia. Her accent reminds me of my Russian language instructors in the Monterey school.

Most of those instructors were from Saint Petersburg.

"Katerina, how were your meetings today? I understand you met with Chief Ken Burda from the San Francisco Police Department? Anything in particular you found useful or surprising from today's meetings?"

I don't mean it as a provocative question but it will be interesting to hear what she says. In a strange irony, as a foreign visitor, she is more of a neutral, non-aligned player than agents from the SF OC squad who could have close relations with SFPD officers and investigators.

"Everyone was very nice to us, and speaking for myself, we learned a lot about your agency and how you interact with other agencies and departments. We are a relatively new agency, and it is important for us to establish ourselves not only in Russia, but also abroad.

"We have investigative and seizure authorities, not as developed as in your country, but we are still working on that."

I nod. "I imagine it would be hard to establish a brand-new agency in your country. People aren't accustomed to paying taxes, and won't see your agency in a positive light unless you reach out to the public somehow. You'd need public relations specialists to do that."

"So interesting you mention public relations. I am extremely interested in this area, but not sure if my managers understand the importance of such things."

"Katerina, when you go back to Russia, sit down with Bob. I will let him know we've spoken about this, and there are Department of State-sponsored programs that can help you and your agency to develop this capacity," I tell her, trying to be helpful, also keeping the conversation light while avoiding drifting into aimless small talk.

"Thanks, Dennis. Oh, and you mentioned Chief Ken Burda. He understands public relations very well. He was a genuinely nice host when we met him. Some of his senior staff were present, and he didn't hurry us out either. He really likes the Bureau and told us he is a friend of your boss in San Francisco, the head of your office. I forget his name."

"Rick. Rick Webb."

"Yes. And he says he is not rank conscious. He tells us he regularly interacts with his rank-and-file officers to get a sense of what's going on in his city."

"Oh? And did he mention anything in particular that is going on?"

"No. When we asked him about any Russian organized crime activities, he said that it was minimal and referred us to the FBI. That's all I can recall."

"Interesting. And nothing about …?" I pause.

"Diamonds?" she asks, quietly.

"Yeah, diamonds," I say, slightly lowering my voice in response.

"It's your case?" she asks as her gaze shifts away from her plate. She puts down her fork and looks directly at me.

"Yes, Katerina. But I would appreciate it if it stays with us—I mean, you and me."

"It's fine with me. I can't share how I know about this, but you can guess. Good luck. If you ever need something, I will be there and try to help," she says, smiling for the first time.

"Spasiba, Katerina," I tell her as I switch into Russian to talk to her. "Will I see you tomorrow evening at Jake Stirrup's party? They have invited all of you, I hear."

"Yes. Definitely," she tells me in Russian, the dinner now ending.

The agents drive the delegation back to their hotel rooms for a well-deserved rest. It is apparent that jet lag is catching up with them as they are all yawning and seem to fade, red-eyed and all eager to get some sleep.

***

"So, who invited me to this gathering tonight?" my wife asks as she checks out her look in the passenger sun visor mirror, a bit perplexed.

It's a logical question since I wasn't assigned to Jake Stirrup's squad in San Francisco, and I didn't engage with Stirrup and the agents on his squad very often either.

"Pierce told me we were both invited and should attend. It might be fun, and we don't attend many gatherings like this, not since Kansas City at least," I explain to her.

My wife looks stunning in her clingy black evening dress and somehow has the same slim figure as when we married almost fifteen years ago. Must be the Eastern European genes, I figure. People often mistake Lenore for a woman ten years younger than her biological age.

As I approach the restaurant's ballroom, especially reserved for the event, the number of guests strikes me. There are easily three hundred here, sharply dressed, some in formal police uniforms. There are politicians, heads of agencies, county sheriffs, senior prosecutors; it's a virtual who's who of the law enforcement community in the San Francisco Bay Area.

I spot the Russian Tax Police delegation, looking slightly out of place.

They are pleased to see me as I walk toward them and introduce my wife. Katerina looks almost as stunning as Lenore, having changed into an evening dress for the occasion.

It isn't long before Jake Stirrup takes the podium to welcome everyone.

His family is there with him, and it soon transpires that Stirrup will retire in the next few months, and this is his retirement party, not just his thirtieth anniversary event.

Stirrup's departure from the Bureau will be a tremendous loss for the office and for his squad, but after thirty years/ service, he has undoubtedly had enough. It is his time to go.

He notices the delegation sitting among the guests and introduces each delegate separately.

As he introduces Katerina, she stands up and politely waves.

The audience lets out a collective, audible gasp, finding her so stunning. I am not sure if it registers with her; she doesn't act as if it does.

As the evening draws to a close, Katerina asks to speak with me and my wife away from everyone else. "I have something for both of you; I want to present it to you, a small gift. This is a collection of special photographs of the most famous sites in Moscow." She explains each one, showing us the Kremlin, Red Square, Bolshoi Opera House, St Basil's Cathedral, among others. "You will come to Russia and work there one day. You both will."

She says it politely yet firmly, with conviction, as if it is a certainty.

I smile. "I am not sure about that, Katerina," I say firmly but with warmth. "We live and work here in California with our children. I don't see us moving there, although the photographs are amazing. Thank you for your gift. It is very thoughtful of you."

Katerina insists yet again that we will move to Russia and work there, which seems farfetched, yet she says it a second time with such conviction, as if it is ordained.

What should I make of her assertion?

What does she know? Well, if it is our destiny, then why not?

Katerina pulls me aside and asks to speak with me in Russian as we are leaving.

"If you ever need to speak with someone, or to check on something or someone, you can reach out to me. I will help you. You can rely on me. Russia is a complicated and sometimes dangerous place, and things are in a state of flux and constant transition. You need someone on your side, and someone you can trust. Someone who knows and understands Russia, and Russians. I know we only just met, but I am an honest person. Although I love my country, there are certain things happening there that I don't agree with. I hope you can understand that. Taking on the powerful and the corrupt does not intimidate me. I don't think I am particularly brave or anything like that. You have to believe in something, right?"

She pauses, looks at me, and continues. "Well, think about it. You know how to contact me. Dennis, I don't know where your case will take you but be careful. There are powerful and dangerous people involved, but you understand that already. And not all of them are in Russia; some are right here in San Francisco, and some were even in that room, tonight."

She motions with her arm to the building we have just left, switching back for the last sentence into the English language, perhaps to emphasize her point.

"They were in that room, Dennis."

"Thank you, Katerina. I appreciate you talking to me like that and being upfront and honest. It's more refreshing than you can imagine," I say as I extend my hand to shake hers.

She leans in and kisses me on the cheeks, three times, in the Russian Orthodox tradition. As I head to my vehicle with my wife already waiting in the car, I open the driver's side door, turn and wave goodbye to Katerina, muttering quietly under my breath, "Welcome to our chess match, Ms. Katerina. The game is on. Oh yes, the game is definitely on."

***

It is several days after the Russian Tax Police delegation's departure when I receive a call from Terry Miller. He thinks it is a good idea for the task force to meet, to catch up on things, and to discuss strategy going forward. I agree and head up to San Francisco for the meeting.

I open the discussion, briefing the group on the recent visit of the Russian Tax Police, which turns out to be a red herring of sorts; the purpose of their visit appears to have been unrelated to Golden ADA after all.

I decide not to share or mention Katerina's comments to me. Her offer to assist in the case is personal, not meant to be shared with anyone, not even with my wife.

I say, "So, we have had a delegation from ROSKOMDRAGMET, and now one from the Russian Tax Police. Unfortunately, neither visit was very … let's say, enlightening as far as what is going on behind that curtain. Well, inside 999 Brannan Street. We've got our hands on a lot of documents, thousands of them. Tax, business, and financial papers.

"Guys, it doesn't look hopeful we'll uncover a smoking gun in this investigation. Perhaps there is just too much money, intrigue and greed involved, both on the Russian and on the U.S. side. I just don't know. And we still have SFPD in the middle, along with a host of other players, politicians, city officials, etc."

Miller steps in. "What's your point? And let's not forget there's still no one from the Russian government who can provide the clarity needed, definitive proof the valuables have been stolen and unlawfully removed from Russia and taken to the United States."

"Terry," I respond. "I understand your frustration, but let's step back for a moment and look at the big picture here. Do we have a prosecutable case now for the International Transportation of Stolen Property? No, probably not. What about using the Racketeer Influenced and Corrupt Organization Act? Nope. Maybe one day, you never know, but I think we can all agree it's a no at this point in time.

"Do we have a victim? Yes, I would argue, we do. But it depends on how you define 'victim'—the victim or victims are the people of Russia, I would submit. In the final analysis, the valuables belong to them, not to a handful of corrupt and greedy officials. This is a chess match, let's not forget that. Remember? No need to lose faith or panic, or rush."

I continue, taking a long, drawn-out inhalation.

"To remind ourselves of what we're facing," I say, "let me list some pieces on this ever-expanding chess board … Not only the targets of this investigation as we've identified so far, and in no particular order, but everyone on the board as it now appears. It's a suitable time to pause and take stock as it will help us put this whole thing into some sort of perspective.

"So, here goes. We have Golden ADA, Andrey, David, Ashot, all these along with U.S.-based company management and employees, including Art Roggenbuck and Simon Lemke, SFPD, Chief Ken Burda, Lt. Shane Sullivan … And a host of city officials, politicians, and political parties also deserve a mention as Golden ADA is contributing to several.

"Then there's ROSKOMDRAGMET and Eugeniy Bychkov, its head, along with his yet-to-be-identified co-conspirators. After that, we also have the deputy head Boris Poznikov, and all those who may be aligned with him—the Russian Tax Police, legal attaché offices in London and Moscow in particular, the Russian Consulate in San Francisco, and an unnamed intel agency or agencies, both U.S. and Russian. Oh, and we can't forget about De Beers.

"I think that's about all, or all we know about so far. Of course, there are probably other players and chess pieces we haven't yet identified, and don't even know about yet."

Now, it's Miller's turn. He says, "OK. I get it. We haven't exactly unraveled this conspiracy, and that's a fact. And we don't know all the players either, nor do we have a solid understanding of their roles. The chain of command structure of the conspiracy is still a mystery too. But what's our next move? Or better yet, is there a next move? Perhaps there's someone we can approach? Has your source identified anyone who seems approachable?"

"Terry, we have to stay the course," I respond. "We can't go approaching any of the players inside the conspiracy and try to flip them, not at this point. It could backfire and we'll show our hand if the person decides not to cooperate. We may eventually find tax or customs violations being committed by some of the lesser players that we can then use as leverage to gain their cooperation. But we are far from that, right?"

I am posing the question to the group. They nod in agreement. So I continue.

"I don't enjoy investigating in a wait-and-see style, believe me. But I don't see any other alternative now. My source is doing what she can, and she's in good standing with several of the principal players. As far as a Title III or undercover operation, we're just not there yet.

"We need a break, maybe not a miracle, but a modicum of luck. Most cases don't unfold on their own accord via 'wait and see,' hoping for a break, evidence falling into our laps, stuff like that. It doesn't happen that way, or hardly ever. From my side, I don't know if Pierce will let this go on, well, if he'll let me go on indefinitely. But FBIHQ gave me the green light and there's support from the director himself. So, I think we're OK for now. I am OK."

I become aware I'm rambling a bit, caught up in an unusually lengthy monologue.

Miller looks thoughtful, just nodding, his lips slightly pursed as if he is contemplating.

Since nobody wants to say anything, I go on, "Pierce won't order me to shut down the case, or at least I can't see that happening, not in the coming days, or even weeks. Heck, the guy went out on a limb and called HQ to lobby for me, for us. I don't want to let him down.

"We just can't make stupid moves, and I'm not suggesting we've made any either, not with the stakes so high. Besides, none of us wants to raise the white flag and admit defeat.

"We'd be admitting to being out of our depth. It's not a matter of hurt egos either; it's just that we—and I don't want to sound ridiculous or self-righteous—but we have committed ourselves to a life of service, service to the American people, and we've all sworn our allegiance to the Constitution. So, we know damn well that more than the players I've just listed are violating and breaking our laws. We can't throw in the towel, not yet anyway."

# Chapter 25

The time spent dealing with the visiting delegations from Russia has taken a toll on me.

While I'm so wrapped up in this, my other pending cases are not being addressed.

It's also a continuing struggle to keep up with other more routine work, such as covering leads from other field offices, lending periodic support for the cases of the other agents on the squad, and helping in search warrants, surveillances, and arrests.

It certainly does not help that there's still a hiring freeze in the Bureau, and in most of the federal government. In a strange twist, agents seem to be adjusting to the frantic pace. They just have to, or risk burnout, from which it will take weeks, if not months, to recover.

I am doing my best to avoid burnout myself, having seen other agents succumb to it.

My solution is to continue to exercise, and to practice with the local rugby team whenever I can. I've been playing the sport for many years, going back to Academy days at Kings Point. In those days, my wife used to call it, "kill the man with the ball," and in some ways, I believe she was accurate with her description. It seems somehow ironic that if we are not trying to kill ourselves through rugby, we are trying to do it through work instead.

The frenetic and pressured life of the FBI Special Agent means we have no downtime.

Because of this, agents tend to carry their entire lives inside their Bureau vehicles.

In there, you will find sports equipment, a change of clothes, extra shoes, papers, weapons, ammunition, spare everything. There is also a certain amount of risk involved because of carrying so much around all the time; there is the risk of a vehicle break-in or outright vehicle theft, but at least the vehicle trunks have special locks and chains. While not a foolproof system, it certainly helps a great deal to live in a state of permanent preparedness.

As for me, I always carry gym clothes, swim gear, rugby cleats, and running shoes in the trunk. If there happens to be a spare moment during the day, I try to squeeze in a quick workout or swim which helps in managing stress, and it also aids me to reset and refresh my mind as the Bureau workdays are long, stretching nine or ten hours, even beyond.

I also try to make periodic appearances at our children's practices and sporting events, particularly swim club meets.

Swimming is a big deal on the Monterey Peninsula, something that makes sense with the vast Pacific Ocean right there. California and its coastal towns have earned a reputation as incubators for the U.S. Olympic swim teams, and it's been that way for many years.

I am in nearly daily contact with most of my sources, Nazari being no exception.

So, when she next calls to tell me we should meet, it isn't surprising as we haven't been face to face for several weeks. We decide to meet at Nazari's favorite Afghan restaurant, in one of the quieter sections of San José.

"I have so much to tell you," she says excitedly as soon as I sit down at the corner table.

She passes me a handful of tapes of recorded conversations she has had.

I discreetly take them from her, handing her a new set, and I can already sense she is raring to spill everything about every meeting and every conversation. I'll need to slow her before she can start and get carried away by all the exuberant momentum she generates.

"Annie, let's go one by one. You know the drill. I'll need the dates, times, who was there, and for you to tell me exactly what happened. OK?"

She has a habit of speaking in a disorganized and fragmented fashion, jumping from one topic to another, leaving my mind buzzing. If this were anything but work topics, it would hardly matter but it's vital I go away with a firm handle on everything she has talked about. There cannot be a sense of chaos as that is when mistakes will be made. But her enthusiasm and eagerness to please does not go unnoticed, and it is not unappreciated. It can't have been easy for her, and she's remained committed and motivated, so it appears.

"Did you know that Bychkov and President Yeltsin are close friends?" she asks.

"No, Annie. Who told you this?" I ask, quite taken by surprise by the assertion.

"Ashot Shagirian. He says they go back a long way, to Yekaterinburg, well, to Sverdlovsk, as the city used to be called. They were both high-ranking officials in the communist party during Soviet times, according to Kozlenok. Well, that's what Ashot says."

"How'd this come up, Annie?" I want the context surrounding this shocking claim.

"Ashot and David have been having enormous problems with Andrey lately. Ashot says Andrey is a mess, you know. He's drinking a lot, rambling on and on about how they are going to expand their business into many other areas, and he wants them to sell more diamonds, hire more diamond cutters, stuff like that. They are even considering complaining to Bychkov! But they are hesitant to do that, since they know Andrey is a long-time and very close protégé of Bychkov's, and they are still outsiders in a way."

"Annie, so they complain directly to you about this stuff?"

"Yes, and I've also managed to talk more to Nina, Andrey's wife. Unfortunately, I did not have my audio recorder with me, but she was sharing a lot more this time. It sounds like she and Andrey have not been getting along lately."

"She's confiding in you?"

"Oh, yes. She confides. She doesn't have many friends, you know. But I think she feels comfortable around me, says I am a businesswoman, a minority, operating in a man's world, and she can relate to that. She says she values me, our discussions, that we are on a level with each other. She is super smart, you know."

"Well, try to give me a heads up on these meetings, and if you can, record them. I will listen to the tapes, Annie, and may have questions for you in the coming days."

The lunch with Nazari has turned out to be far more enlightening than I envisaged.

Things are becoming more complicated, but this is not entirely unexpected.

If Bychkov is a close friend of President Yeltsin, I wonder if this scheme, this operation, is being sanctioned at the highest level?

Is Bychkov protected by Yeltsin? Or is he operating out there on his own, unhinged and unchecked? Anything is possible. But the alleged close connection could help explain Andrey's reckless and brazen actions. Andrey could be operating under the assumption he is "protected" in Russia at the highest level, and that this "protection" or krysha—"roof"—bestowed on Andrey by Bychkov, actually comes from the Russian President himself.

It will sure explain a lot if it turns out to be true.

But I'm uncertain. Perhaps it's the Shagirian brothers showing off for whatever reason, or there could be something more to it. It seems plausible, given the scale of the Golden ADA operations, but this is no reason to alter or change the investigation's course, not yet.

Nazari's information about the Shagirian brothers having problems with Kozlenok, and airing their grievances to her, is more interesting to me than the alleged Bychkov-Yeltsin connection. It may mean the conspiracy is unraveling or beginning to show its first signs of fracturing. Does it mean the Shagirians will soon be approachable, to try and gain their cooperation? No. That would probably not be a wise move, not at this stage.

But I need to impress upon Nazari that she must pay closer attention, offering to be a good sounding board for any grievances they might air with her.

Returning to my office in the afternoon, I make a mental note to share the assertion with Sharon. Yes, there's one more piece to add on to this ever-expanding chessboard.

What needs adding is President Boris Yeltsin, if what Nazari has heard is true.

So, Yeltsin is also on the chessboard for now.

# Chapter 26

I should have seen it coming. It's been several weeks in the works, most likely. Don Pierce wears his usual poker face when I walk into his office at his request. There is no small talk today, nothing about the weather or plans for the upcoming weekend. Well, I guess there never is time for that sort of stuff with Pierce. Besides, no one, not on the squad, would dare waste his time or their own on mindless chatter. He begins as soon as I sit down.

"I know you'll not be happy with what I'm about to tell you, but please let me finish before you speak, agreed?" Pierce says.

Whatever he's about to say has clearly been forced upon him.

He begins, "Jake Stirrup's been pestering me for days, no, several weeks, about your case. He wants it. He says our squad has no business being involved in a matter in the city. I pushed back as best I could. I worked out a sort of compromise with him."

I feel a slight frown of questioning cross my face.

Before I can speak, he says, "Before you say anything. Let me finish. This case of yours is consuming a lot of your time, most of your time. It's an excellent case, but one like this, eventually, demands more resources, more personnel and attention. I am sure you're thinking of—or even already working toward—a Title III, or how to introduce an undercover into the mix. And where would you find the resources and agents essential for this?

"Not from the San José squad. There is only one squad, that's Jake's OC squad in San Francisco. Now, hear me out. This is what I'm proposing. You would not give up the case but would become a co-case agent. Jake wants Joe Doherty from his squad to work with you as the other co-case agent, and Doherty's seen the files. He's now badgering Jake about the case, and how there needs to be a wire, wiretap. In principle, he may be right.

"But I can imagine this news doesn't sit well with you. You developed the case, and you are the one who's been dealing with it for more than a year, right?"

Stunned and in disbelief, I sit there, thinking I should have seen it coming.

It all makes sense. I knew Jake Stirrup was aware of the case. The visit of the ROSKOMDRAGMET deputy chief, then the visit of the Russian Tax Police, has affected him, perhaps. Or is it his ambition, making him want to grab hold of something new and interesting? It could even be embarrassment that Golden ADA is operating right there in San Francisco, and the agents on his squad have basically been oblivious to what was going on right in their backyard. It doesn't much matter. The fact is, Jake

Stirrup and Joe Doherty will not let up, behaving like predatory sharks and there's already a lot of blood in the water.

I take a deep breath, about to speak when Pierce raises his hand to stop me.

"Look, think about it, sleep on it. If you feel strongly about it, then we can push back. I can lobby the boss, even see what HQ says—but I doubt they'll understand. They see us as one division out here, San Francisco Division, that's all. They want the matter addressed.

"It doesn't matter how or by whom. You will still be case agent, but co-case agent with Joe Doherty, and you will certainly remain in the mix with a leading role. True, you won't be solely in charge, but in the end, it's the Bureau's case; no case ever belongs to any one of us, although we'd all like to believe each one is our own. In the end, we're agents, but also employees working for the Bureau; it's not the Bureau working for us.

"You do understand no one can take away all you've done, mostly on your own initiative. The task force, the sources, the intel you've developed, that's all on record. Your name is in the files, in our case management system, for good.

"Besides, Doherty and Stirrup know virtually nothing about Russians, or about Russia itself. They don't speak the language like you do. On the positive side, let Doherty develop and write the Title III affidavit. It will take the bulk of his time drafting and clearing all those bureaucratic hurdles. You can stay focused on strategy, working with sources, which are far more interesting for you, I would submit. You will have another agent in the Bureau to bounce things off of. For now, yes, you have

Sharon, but she is an analyst, a good one, but she's not an agent. And yes, you will still have Miller, Marino, and King to work with. But you do need more resources from inside the Bureau. Jake Stirrup isn't a bad guy. He's close to retirement, true. But he cares and always looks out for his squad, and for the Bureau.

"Between us, your case has really taken him aback; he's impressed by your work and proactive nature. I'm not saying this to stroke your ego. I'm not like that, and you know me well enough to understand that," Pierce says as he finishes.

Then, he just sits there, looking at me, waiting for me to respond.

This is the longest I have ever heard Don Pierce speak to anyone. I thought he might never finish, in fact, that I'd still be sitting here when the sun came up.

"Don, I don't need to sleep on this," I tell him, sucking in a deep breath. "I get it. I was about to lobby you for agent support, but with this development, I don't see any alternative.

"It's not a one-trick pony, this case, that is. Even with our task force, it's not enough, and you're right, we should work toward a Title III or undercover operation. Those UCOs require personnel, more than one agent, that's for sure. In a strange way, I feel relief.

"And frankly, with all the complexities and challenges of this investigation, I could use a little help. I also understand the SF OC squad in San Francisco will not step aside and simply let me run around in their backyard any longer. Will they try to take the credit if the investigation's successful? Yeah, I'm sure they will. But so what? I, I mean, we know what we did. No one can take that away from us. And as you mentioned, they lack the expertise and knowledge to just take things over, even though they could attempt to do so without our ongoing involvement. I'll reach out to Stirrup and Doherty and meet with them in the coming days. Might as well get this going. The sooner the better."

He nods slowly, appearing relieved, though he's saying nothing for now.

I tell him, "Hey, in the worst-case scenario, I step away. Of course, I'm invested in the case, and quite sure our mini task force will be disappointed, but that's life. I'll give it a fair shot with Stirrup and Doherty. Let's hope for the best."

My remarks seem to resonate well with Pierce. This time, he nearly breaks into a smile, the most relaxed look I've seen from my boss in a long time.

I head back to my office, meeting briefly with Sharon to explain the new dynamics.

She accepts it, although with some reluctance. I next call each of the task force members to inform them too, starting with Rich Marino who doesn't take it well. He and I have worked as close partners for more than a year and we trust one another. In the end, though, what choice is there? It's time to bring Joe Doherty into the task force and meet together.

I can only hope the group dynamic will remain the same, but I have misgivings about that, having heard Doherty's reputation is that he's not a team player.

But we'll need each other and will have to work together regardless.

There are too many moving pieces on this shifting chessboard to manage unilaterally, without closely coordinating and cooperating as one cohesive team.

It will take several days before a meeting with the newest task force member, Special Agent Joe Doherty, can be arranged to accommodate everyone's schedules.

AUSA Miller steps forward, agreeing to host the meeting at his office.

Doherty has previously told me he's read over the files—which make up several volumes—and believes he has a good sense of what the case is about, and where things stand.

However, another agent's boldly assertive comment concerns me; most good Bureau investigators know not all the relevant information will be documented in some file. There is more, much more, to a case than those files can possibly contain.

Is Doherty just acting overconfident, or arrogant? Does this bold assertion reveal some of his true character? I'm not sure. I just hope it's not a harbinger of what is coming from this new and imposed upon "partner," my new co-case agent.

Special Agent Joe Doherty is an accountant, CPA by background.

Sometimes, Special Agent accountants in the Bureau take an approach to investigations that is too sterile, clinical, and methodical to the extreme.

The meeting opens with me providing an outline of the case and its players. I describe a few challenges we are facing, along with the more sensitive aspects, including the involvement of SFPD providing security to Golden ADA, along with the company's expanding political connections Kozlenok and the Shagirian brothers have been nurturing through their campaign and political party financial contributions. When each member of the task force has spoken, it is now Doherty's turn.

I ask him to take the floor.

Doherty begins, "This case needs a Title III. It's the only way we are going to gain a real understanding of the conspiracy, and of the players involved. There is likely corruption on the Russian side, but possibly from the U.S. side as well. We should seek a pen register to cover all the phone lines at the company, and for the phone lines of Kozlenok and the Shagirian brothers. That entire process may take a month or more. The pen register data will show us just who is calling who and help to provide the justification for the Title III application," he says, in a matter-of-fact tone.

I glance around the room for the reaction of the other task force members. From the look on their faces, they don't seem impressed or pleased. They say nothing.

Yet, I have to admit Doherty raises several valid points.

To establish the necessary and compelling justification for a U.S. District Court Judge to approve the use of a wiretap in the case, it will take time and effort, possibly several months. This investigation is nothing like a drug conspiracy case, or even a kidnapping.

It is more of a complex and ongoing financial crimes case with its international linkages, and a wiretap, if approved, could catch foreign nationals talking on the intercepted lines, possibly even diplomats or officials from Russia.

The intercepted calls could include public and elected officials on the U.S. side. This would be interesting and enlightening intelligence, no doubt, but there is a sensitive aspect.

There is no telling who the company's management is talking with regularly. The pen register device will capture and record the numbers being dialed and the subscriber information, providing clues and indications. I wonder, what will it mean if the Golden ADA subjects are communicating with high-level officials in Moscow?

This can get tricky, and FBIHQ could have valid concerns about the resulting implications if politically exposed persons were to find themselves caught or snared on an FBI wiretap.

But that is not the most immediate concern in my estimation.

The most important issue now is for Doherty to transform into a trusted member of the task force as quickly as possible. To accomplish that, he also needs to feel welcomed as a new member of our established team. From the other side, the task force members—Miller, Marino, and King—need to have a level of trust and confidence with this new and unexpected addition. There is no time to waste.

As the meeting ends, Marino motions for me to step into an adjoining empty room. He obviously has something on his mind.

"Dennis, I think you know what I'm going to say," Marino begins.

"OK, Rich. I'm not sure but can guess. But tell me what's on your mind," I respond.

"Did you note what Doherty hasn't said? He hasn't acknowledged the work of the task force, nor that he's appreciative or thankful for all we've done in the past. What, over fifteen months together? Not a peep, no acknowledgement, nothing. He's read your files, which are several volumes, yet he has no questions, none to any of us sitting there.

"That's weird. Hey, I am not saying or suggesting he should kiss our asses and praise us, but seriously, he basically shows up, tells us what we ought to be focused on, what we need to do, and what he intends to do. Not even a 'thanks guys, great work,' nothing. Who knows what nonsense he's pulled behind the scenes to push you out, to make himself 'co-case agent,' seriously?" Marino says, almost shouting.

He seems to be incensed with a growing rage, his face turning red.

I whisper, "Rich, I get it. But please let me try to explain. Hey, it's not my first rodeo. It's not a perfect arrangement, but there isn't much alternative."

I am trying to calm down Marino from his highly agitated state.

"Dennis, the guy obviously has issues. Inflated ego, self-confidence problems; there's something wrong with him. I don't like him. He's not someone I can trust. I can't speak for the other task force members, but I don't think they feel differently. He's clearly ambitious.

"But it's clear. He doesn't care about you, or about any of us, and it's not really about the case and our mission; no, it's all about him, with his own personal agenda. I honestly don't know if I can work with someone like that," he says, finally sitting in the chair at the small conference table, glancing out the window as his voice returns to a normal volume.

"Rich, let's try it. Yeah, he's not from New York like us. I know little about him frankly, other than hearing he's worked on OC cases in the past and is from Boston. But I—rather, we—need the resources and personnel from his squad to support this investigation. If we go up on a wire, we will need personnel and resources, more than we have access to at the moment, a lot more. It's a labor and time intensive undertaking to work toward a wire, let alone to do the prep work to get to that stage. There will be plenty for us to do regardless, wire or no wire. Can you at least give it a chance? If I think it won't work, or if he becomes a burden or problem for the case, I will not hesitate to confront and deal with it—with him, even to raise it with my boss if that's what it takes. Is that acceptable to you, for now?"

Marino lets out a sigh. "OK. Agreed. Hey, sorry for unloading on you like that, but better to air it out sooner rather than later. It's my nature, I suppose."

"All good, Rich. We'll manage this, and nothing has changed between us. We're still partners and friends. Let's get out of here, enough for one day."

We walk out of the U.S. Attorney's Office together.

The drive from San Francisco to my home near Monterey takes over two hours, with no traffic. It gives me time to reflect on that meeting with Joe Doherty.

What did Doherty's involvement really mean for the case? For me, I will have to deal with a new "partner" not of my choosing. Thoughts pop into my head.

Why has Doherty lobbied so hard to get assigned to the Golden ADA case?

In my entire time in the Bureau, I've never experienced or heard of an agent lobbying to take another agent's case, unless he or she is being transferred or retiring.

This behavior is unprecedented in my experience. It will be the first time working on this case, on any case, where I feel I need to watch my back, from inside my agency, no less!

Does Doherty have an agenda beyond his own personal one? He's certainly not new to the SF Division. Why has it taken more than a year for him and Jake Stirrup to awaken from their slumber? Copies of the case file have been available to them for many months.

Does either of them even have a clue what the case is really about?

Perhaps they don't care. Doherty and Stirrup see things differently, and neither of them knows much about the former Soviet Union and Russia, so it seems.

For Doherty, does he have a darker, secret agenda beyond personal ambition, besides making a name for himself? Does he know something? Something he won't share with me and the task force? Is Marino right? Does Doherty have issues?

Maybe problems of self-confidence and an inflated ego?

Physically, he is not a large man, and of slight build. Does that limitation factor into his psyche and character? FBI Special

Agents come in all shapes and sizes, and there's a wide range of abilities, some highly motivated and gifted, and some are just trying to get through the day. Agents are human beings, after all. A person's character isn't solely determined by physical prowess or outer appearance, although there's a degree of correlation.

I think back to childhood, where the bigger kids often picked on and sometimes bullied the undersized kids viciously. To survive, the smaller ones would often react by becoming physically aggressive and scrappy, even picking fights, and sometimes fighting dirty.

The bullied become the bullies commonly; that's just how things are.

Or they can go another way, becoming meek and withdrawn, relying on an older brother for protection on the mean city streets.

But even in adulthood, there's a much joked about phenomenon of which people talk, which is "small man syndrome." Sure, it's the butt of humor, but in essence, it bears truth.

Am I over analyzing the situation? Perhaps this is some sort of paranoia beginning to envelop me like the cold, misty, and damp SF fog obscuring my field of vision as I drive away from the creeping fog bank threatening to engulf the entire city.

Is that fog smothering my logic and reason?

Equally, couldn't it be my gut, intuition, gypsy sense, blinking red, warning me there is much more at play?

Rich Marino doesn't like Joe Doherty; he has told me plainly, and he's been expressing those feelings openly to me after that very first meeting. Marino is a solid guy, a talented investigator with street smarts. Perhaps there is more to it.

As I finally arrive back at my home near Monterey, I realize I shouldn't dwell on things beyond my control and which cannot be resolved in a few days, as it isn't healthy or helpful. Joe Doherty will have to be taken at his word unless he missteps. He's told the task force he is going to work on the pen register application, the first necessary step for a Title III wiretap.

If the coming days and weeks show otherwise, I will deal with it then. For now, Doherty and the SF OC Squad have become part of the task force. There is no changing that reality.

I close my garage door and set the concerns aside, deep into the recesses of my compartmentalized mind. There is no time and no point in thinking about the multiple possibilities any longer. It is hard enough to keep track and manage the many pieces and players on our ever-expanding chess board.

A few days have passed since that first meeting with Doherty and the task force, when Doherty calls, asking to meet separately with me. He wants to discuss the pen register application and his analysis of Golden ADA's financial documents, which the task force has subpoenaed. We agree to meet halfway in the Palo Alto offices of the Bureau.

He starts off by saying something slightly surprising.

"Hey, I apologize if I came across abrupt during that meeting in Miller's office, and I owe you an explanation," he begins. "When I learned Miller was the AUSA assigned to this case, I was surprised, not shocked. You know he prosecuted FBI agents back in Cleveland, right?"

"Yeah, I heard. Joe, I know little about his past, but my feeling is we need to let that go. He may have had his reasons, and it wouldn't be right for you or me to judge him now. I wasn't there. Since I first met him, I have had only positive interaction with him so far at least. He's been helpful, accommodating, and approachable."

"OK. Well then, let's put it in the past. And another thing is, I am not accustomed to working with outside agencies. You probably sense that already. But I will do my best to be a team player, going forward."

I tell him, "Frankly, you didn't come across as a team player at the meeting. At least you recognized and admitted it. Look, I have no issue with the points you raised about the pen register idea and working toward a Title III, but we've been at this for many months; I think it's more than one and one-half years since I first opened this case.

"It's been a roller coaster, Joe. I'm not suggesting you tread lightly, but you're the new guy. It would have been better if you had requested input, thoughts, or just something from the other task force members. You had no questions and expressed no interest in what they knew and had done, as if you don't recognize all that time and effort the task force has put in. See where I'm coming from?"

I recognize it's important to speak frankly, and to seize the opportunity to get things on the right track, particularly since Doherty has opened up with me.

"OK. I agree," he says simply, as if this doesn't warrant a broader and more thoughtful answer—brushing it off again, I feel. He carries on, changing subjects already. "I've been looking at the financials for this company. They have a lot of money moving around by wire transfer and by check. It will take serious time and analysis to unravel things. That's for sure. Their managers and staff are well paid, and everyone is reaching out for money or dipping into the cookie jar. It wouldn't surprise me if the Russian mob is involved in this or at least aware. Certainly, if we were talking about LCN, the Italian mafia, they would be all over this operation. And we'd already have bodies in dumpsters or in landfills."

Again, I am a little concerned he is riding roughshod over— or blatantly ignoring—the work we have already achieved, some of which would surely benefit him.

"Joe, it's good you're looking at the subpoenaed documents, but please coordinate with Sharon. She has a lot of background information and has done a lot of work already. I am sure you are well aware of SFPD providing security, and that the head of security is a high-ranking officer in their ranks, Shane Sullivan. Oh, and he is also a close confidant of the SFPD chief, Ken Burda. We, that is I, decided not to approach anyone in that department, not the chief, not any of their officers we have worked with in the past. I don't know if anyone has co-opted them, but I have my suspicions. You've worked corruption cases before, I suppose?" I am hoping Doherty will tell me he has some experience in that arena.

"Yes. I have, and I get it. We'll stay clear of their department for now. Guess surveillance would be more challenging if the police are in and out of that building."

"Definitely. We might be exposed, and it isn't worth the risk. We could set up cameras to see who goes in and out, but that is labor intensive, and I am not sure we would gain that much. Certain aspects of the Golden ADA business are legitimate. It's better to make use of our human confidential sources and analyze the intel from the sources to gain more of an understanding of this operation. Heck, we still don't have a reliable law enforcement partner on the Russian side. I'm not sure if we ever will. But I'm also not ruling it out, not yet.

"When I opened this case, I told Pierce we'd find some honest cops to work with in Russia. He practically laughed at me. I can't blame him. He's technically still correct, unless we get lucky. Let's hope for a break, Joe. Who knows, someone from inside the conspiracy may eventually crack or misstep and we will then be able to react quickly.

"There are brewing internal conflicts in the conspiracy, one of my sources tells me, and while things haven't gone off the rails, Kozlenok is spending like crazy. I can't imagine his superiors in Moscow, whoever they are, are happy about that. As far as you and me, if there is ever anything on your mind, you can talk to me, straight up, no frills, no BS.

"I grew up in New York City, in a tough neighborhood, and my ego doesn't bruise easily. I would rather you talk to me frankly if you have concerns or questions, rather than going around and around, you know? Just thought to get that on the table, Joe, so there's no misunderstanding later on. This case is a chess match with many movable pieces on the board. But don't ask me about the rules of this game. Those seem to change unexpectedly if there are any rules at all," I say, and shrug.

He simply eyes me confidently, nodding.

I close by saying, "It's Russia after all. You know what Churchill said, right?"

I half figure he'll not pick up on the Churchill reference. I have no sense if Doherty even knows anything about Russia, its people, and its complicated, yet fascinating, history.

"Yeah. A riddle, wrapped in a mystery, inside an enigma," Doherty responds, beaming with schoolboy confidence.

I am impressed, having not expected a response so spot on and immediate. The question isn't meant as a test, but Doherty likely perceives it that way, so it seems.

The correct response also doesn't mean Doherty is a scholar of Russian history and politics, but it signals he at least knows something about Russia.

I take it as a positive sign for my new co-case agent. We will need to trust one another to manage the case and move things forward. There is simply no alternative.

# Chapter 27

"They are still following me," are Nazari's first words as I answer my office phone.

"What?" I respond excitedly. "Tell me exactly what's going on, Annie," I tell her as I reach for my pen to take notes.

Nazari says, barely stopping to take a breath, "The vehicles have changed from the last time. Three cars, maybe four, driving in front of me, perhaps one or two trailing behind. It began as soon as I left my office, and went on for a while, practically all the way until I reached home last night. I turned down a quiet residential street, just to see what they'd do. Well, I caught her, that blonde. It was the same woman as last time, I'm sure about that. She's got an interesting face, sort of pretty. I was that close."

Nazari doesn't sound upset, which she would have every right to be, given the situation. It's odd to me that Nazari's reaction is restrained and relatively mild.

But I have to remind myself she's a real survivor. She escaped Kabul, with only a few possessions, her clothes in tatters. This will be nothing in comparison.

"That blonde you got a look at. Did she look, hmm, icy?"

The woman I'd met from that agency weeks before, the one introducing herself as Megan Little, suddenly pops into my head.

"Yeah, icy! Sure. She had angular features, sort of Slavic looking, high cheekbones, even behind huge sunglasses. She may have realized I got a look at her. I hope not. So, what am I supposed to do? Let them follow me? Try to outmaneuver them? You think they are listening to my phone calls?"

"Annie, I don't know but never play with them. They aren't trying to run you off the road. Driving down a street like that, to catch or outsmart them, is not a good idea. You shouldn't do that, and there's no need to provoke them. My gut tells me they are not out to harm or confront you. They may just be interested in anyone connected to Golden ADA and are curious about you. But it's just my theory. Frankly, I am not sure. Annie, in the future, you need to call me immediately from your cell phone in your car if you notice this again, anytime, day or night. You'll call my mobile number. Understood?"

I am concerned, but revealing too much of that concern will serve no purpose other than to upset or frighten her. If the "agency" is responsible, they may have been attempting to access her, maybe with the intention of eventually approaching her to recruit her to work for them.

Anything is possible. There are so many possibilities for who may have been following her, ranging from Golden ADA, SFPD, De Beers, the "agency," Russians, even the Bureau's counterintelligence side.

"OK. I'll call you right away. I promise," Nazari says, not even rattled. "I actually called you for another reason, to update you. I have been working hard for you. Can we meet?"

"Sure, Annie. I can come to your office first thing in the morning," I tell her.

***

When I arrive at Nazari's office early the next morning, she is her usual pleasant self. She has already settled in and made coffee.

As she pours it, she tells me, "I met with Nina. She told me in confidence the Shagirian brothers may soon be out. Andrey is unhappy with them, she says, and it's about time for them to leave. And she mentioned a consignment agreement with the Russian suppliers, and that the Shagirian brothers are not happy about that either, and they don't understand business."

"Consignment agreement?" I ask. "Annie, has this agreement ever come up before?"

I am perplexed. Is this part of an elaborate cover-up scheme to claim the diamonds and valuables were consigned to Golden ADA by the Russian government?

It wouldn't be the first time crooks tried to use that sort of defense, claiming the actual owners consigned the property to them instead of them having stolen it.

"And there's more," she adds. "I met with Ashot. I think he likes me, and since he knows me to be a successful businesswoman, he likes to bounce ideas off of me. He says Andrey wants him and David to sign nondisclosure agreements and leave the company.

"So, they had a huge fight! About what, he hasn't said. Only that he and his brother have an attorney involved to represent them. They have no intention of simply leaving the company. And he says he and his brother made that company and are part owners.

"They are negotiating the terms of their leaving, but he does not want to tell me more about that. I didn't press him. You told me not to do that, right?"

"Yes. Let him talk. He'll eventually tell you, but you can't press him, Annie."

"Oh, and I forgot something. Nina thinks Andrey has a girlfriend, and they may have recently flown together on the company jet to Bermuda. The company is buying property there, she says. She doesn't know for certain about the girlfriend, but she seems upset and says she is thinking about a divorce but isn't sure. They have a young son, you know."

"Annie, stay in touch with Nina. Again, don't be aggressive with her, just be a sounding board, listen to her, and don't probe or pester her with questions. Let her talk. Did she give you a name of this girlfriend?"

"Helga. I think she works for Andrey at Golden ADA, in what way, or capacity, I am not sure."

The meetings between us are usually short, but informative. This meeting has delivered more than its share of fresh developments. I return to the office to document everything.

A consignment agreement? This news is not so surprising. It could mean Andrey and his conspirators are feeling the pressure, or perhaps they're planning some sort of defense to an eventual claim or charge for theft and misappropriation. With the recent visits of the deputy head of ROSKOMDRAGMET and the Russian Tax Police, it's almost to be expected.

It all makes sense, if true. There's even a possibility they are now being coached by their attorneys, or by someone like Shane Sullivan from SFPD. He certainly understands criminal law well enough to help them plan their defenses in the event of possible criminal charges.

It also makes him a potential co-conspirator, if true.

As I drive back to my office, I reflect on what Nazari has told me about being followed. Should I try to get photos of the "icy" blonde to show to her for identification? Or would that set off too many bells? It will not be easy to get photos of such individuals in any case, and the request alone could trigger a powerful reaction from the Bureau's C-I side.

And what if the "agency" is following Nazari?

What then? I can hardly tell them to knock it off or stay away.

It would only infuriate them, possibly making matters worse. They could file a complaint against me through their own channels. No, better to let things play out.

Nazari will call immediately if she thinks she's being followed in future. Besides, she's a tough woman and not easily intimidated or threatened, and with considerable street smarts.

But there's another side to this puzzle. I can't entirely rule out that Nazari is only playing with me for whatever reason, that in fact, there is no one following her.

Sources always have their own private agendas, and it's certainly the case with Nazari. She's been in serious trouble with the tax authorities and has been looking at jail time.

I decide to keep the information to myself for now, tucked away in my compartmentalized mind, which is nearing its capacity. As I open the door to my office, a new thought suddenly pops into my head. If the Bureau is following her, might it be for other reasons?

Am I the actual target and reason for this surveillance? Do they suspect I've crossed the line and have grown romantically involved with Nazari, my source?

What might be the basis for their suspicion? True, I have far more female sources than male, but that alone isn't sufficient reason for their suspicion. Or is it? Has the C-I side of the Bureau been so infuriated with me that they've complained, and they're looking to entrap me as payback for being pushed aside by FBIHQ and Director Freeh?

I have never crossed that line though, not with any source, male or female, never.

Yes, several of my sources past and present have been female and attractive, but they have all been sources with their own personal agendas and motives.

Most were manipulative and cunning creatures in a way. But I knew that and understood their nature—at least I thought I did.

By the time I close the door to my office and sit at my desk, I have already filed the thought away, deep in the recesses of my mind.

There is plenty enough to deal with on this day, back in the real world.

# Chapter 28

I feel the pace of the events and activities unfolding around the investigation speeding up, a phenomenon I've seen before. Drug trafficking cases have their own unique pace and tempo.

As a case agent, you sometimes feel you are just along for the ride and not really in control. The drug deals just happen.

As a case agent, you don't always have a say when or where they'll occur. If you can't accept that reality, you have no business "working drugs," or so the veteran agents tell me back in Kansas City. The Golden ADA case seems to be similar in that respect, although there's no sign or evidence illegal drugs are involved, not yet anyway.

The commodities being trafficked aren't drugs, but diamonds, precious gems, artwork, and gold. There is money laundering, corruption, and tax evasion, so it seems.

And there are other similarities to drug trafficking cases in which the criminals laundered and invested the proceeds of the illicit drug sales in both legitimate and illegitimate activities.

With Doherty's entry to the case, I now have another Bureau agent to work with. It is not yet clear how this new partnership will work out, or if it even will.

On the positive side, Doherty and I are talking and meeting regularly. He focuses on analyzing the subpoenaed telephone records showing calls around the world to cities, including known diamond trading centers such as Tel Aviv, London, Antwerp, and New York. The frequency of calls made to Moscow particularly interest Doherty.

We both lament the fact it will not be possible to get subscriber information, to know the identities, the "subscribers" to the numbers the Golden ADA subjects are calling.

No one on the Russian side can provide that critical information, and there's no one we can even ask. We desperately need a reliable law enforcement partner in Russia for this sort of information. It looks doubtful we'll find anyone, not in the short term.

It is a rare quiet moment at the office for me, catching up on paperwork, and dealing with routine leads previously set aside when the phone rings. It is an agent from my former office in Kansas City. I know Evan Kelliher and his wife, Jackie, from my time there.

Kelliher still works on a white-collar crime squad, while Jackie is assigned to a violent crimes squad. Jackie, a fluent

Spanish speaker, has sometimes translated recorded drug deal tapes from my drug case as a favor.

I assume Kelliher is just calling to say hi and to catch up on things. Kelliher and his wife Jackie were the last agents my wife and I saw as we drove from Kansas City with our two small children, heading for California and language school.

It turns out Kelliher isn't calling just to say hi, after all.

"Know where I've been lately?" he asks, proceeding to answer his own question. "No, you probably don't. But I got a teaching gig in Russia, in Moscow. It was a one-week course, white-collar crime investigations. We had Russian police and prosecutors in the class."

"Good, Evan. I bet it was interesting. How did you get the invite to go?" I ask him.

"From Quantico, and they got the request from the legal attaché office in Moscow. Did you know the Bureau's just opened their office there? It was an interesting visit, but I don't think I would want to live there. I don't speak Russian, and you really need the language skill. But I am not calling you just to tell you about my experience there. No, I had something happen that I found. Well, the Russians say, 'the world is tight' and I have to agree with them," Kelliher says with a laugh.

"What, Evan? What happened?"

I am getting impatient as Kelliher seems to take his time getting to the point of the call, and I have a pile of work on my desk to catch up on.

"Be patient. I'm getting there. Well, it was a basic 'economic crime 101' type class, but we had senior investigators from their police, their MVD as they call it. One student, this guy named Aleksandr Filippov, I call him Sasha, approaches me after the class and asks me for a favor. I figure, oh no, here we go. He wants me to spy for him or something. Nope.

"He tells me he is investigating a company, some people in Russia, who have established a company in San Francisco. He wants to get incorporation documents, that sort of thing, and he has no clue how to do that. I refer him to the legat office, but he gives me the name of the company anyhow. I think he enjoyed knowing I was an investigator just like him, and we sort of bonded after the one week of training. So, when I fly back home, and I'm in the office, I type the name of the company into the case management system, and wouldn't you know it? Your name pops up as case agent."

"Seriously, Evan?" I ask and nearly fall out of my chair. He has my full attention now. The papers I have been reviewing spill onto the floor as I press the receiver hard against my ear. I do not pick up the scattered documents.

"Yep. Some case with this company called Golden ADA. Aleksandr says he is investigating them for stealing diamonds and other valuables. You are working on this, I suppose? Well, in California, right?"

"Yes!" I respond, practically screaming into the receiver. "Yes, I am. What else did he say? About his investigation."

"He told me it's pretty sensitive, and he has a small team of investigators working with him. But he has no one in the United States he can turn to for information or guidance. He's old school Soviet in a way, but Sasha was one of the best students in the class that week. He's an experienced guy, for sure. I guess you weren't expecting this, huh?"

"I hoped one day, we would find someone on the Russian side, and Evan, I am, well, honestly, I can't express my current feelings to you precisely. I'm completely shocked, attempting to comprehend what you've just told me. To be frank, I am speechless."

He says nothing, so I continue, "Evan, I'll reach out to Moscow, to the legat office, and see what they can do. They must be familiar with this Aleksandr-Sasha guy since they selected him to attend your training class. Give my best to Jackie. And Evan, thanks for following up. A lot of agents wouldn't have bothered to check our system when they returned from such training, but you did, and I am grateful to you for that. I owe you one. I will never forget this. Dos-vee-dan-e-ya, Evan." I hang up the phone.

The world is indeed "tight."

And, yes, Dr. Watson, the game is on. It is surely on now!

I am numb after the telephone call. It is no time for celebration, but still, this is a huge break in the case, potentially. Yet, I can't just pick up the phone and call this Aleksandr Filippov in Moscow, can I? The clock is ticking, and I must take action. There is no way of determining where things actually stand with Filippov and the alleged investigation he says he is working in Russia. First things first. I make a mental note to call Joe Doherty and give him the news. Perhaps Doherty has brought a bit of luck to the investigation after all.

"Joe, are you sitting down?" I begin before telling him about the call from Kansas City.

Doherty seems thrilled and immediately grasps the implications. If we can somehow team up with reliable law enforcement partners in Russia, this could be a game changer.

We agree it is best for Jake Stirrup, the San Francisco OC Squad supervisor, to make the first call to legat Moscow. The request from the supervisor of a squad will probably be better received than one from a case agent investigator; legal attachés tended to be rank conscious.

We will need the Moscow office's support to coordinate things with Aleksandr Filippov and the MVD. Once the legat office is on board, the next step will be for Doherty and me to engage with Filippov directly somehow.

"Joe, we need to get Filippov to the United States," I say emphatically, hoping Doherty will agree and come up with a solution.

I believe arranging a face-to-face meeting among the investigators is far better than making an international telephone call on an unsecured and static line.

We can't hope to build trust through an impersonal international call between parties who have never met. It will take much more than that. It has to be case agent to case agent, or in this instance, Bureau agents to Russian MVD investigators, face to face.

If we can somehow arrange it, that will be something. I have no clue how.

To my surprise, Doherty immediately follows up and comes back with the response the very next day. There is a ten-hour time difference between California and Moscow, so communication with the legal attaché office in Moscow has a limited time window.

To speak with the legat office, San Francisco has to call early morning, by which time Moscow's working day is nearing its end.

Doherty sounds excited and breathless on the phone.

"Stirrup and I just spoke with the legat office. They're supportive, but they don't have a budget line to finance the travel of MVD officers to the United States. The SF Division budget won't support that sort of case expenditure either. However, Lawrence Poinier, the legal attaché, told us there might be another way to arrange for Filippov to travel here.

"There is the Freedom Support Act. Congress passed this legislation after the fall of the Berlin Wall, and the breakup of the Soviet Union, to help the countries of eastern Europe with their transition to democracy, including reform of their law enforcement and criminal justice systems. Poinier, the legal attaché, will reach out to his contacts at the State Department in Washington, and at the U.S. Embassy there to see if they will allow us to use funding from this law, this FSA he calls it, for the travel of Filippov to San Francisco.

"Lawrence mentioned Filippov's travel to San Francisco could be viewed as an extension of the training he received from the Bureau agents, which the FSA sponsored."

I reply, "Sounds good to me, Joe. Whatever it takes. We just need him here as soon as possible. You realize we're in the dark as far as where things stand with Filippov and his investigation? Heck, he could start it only now. Or it could all be a sham, a facade, and Filippov's just following orders from who knows whom, and for some unknown reason.

"We just don't know. We can't know. The only option is to get Filippov here, physically here, and meet him face to face, one on one. Only then will we know. Or I hope we will."

Is this the break I've been hoping for?

Is Filippov that one honest cop I've told my boss, Don Pierce, I will eventually find? In a country facing such serious corruption challenges at every level and at every turn, to include their law enforcement ranks, it seems unlikely, but is worth a shot.

I pick up the phone and reach out to the task force members to tell them of this recent development, and for them to stand by.

It will probably take several days, but I remain hopeful the legal attaché office can make it happen. It is all riding on them in a way. The legal attaché office in Moscow is about to earn its way, as a full-fledged player, to this chess match. "Welcome to the game, legat Moscow," I say under my breath. "You guys better strap in, we've got quite a ride in store."

As soon as I hear the phone ring as I step into my home in the evening, I just know—sense—who it is. My sister. My wife gives me one of those looks as she hands me the receiver. So typical that Jennifer calls the very moment I get in the door; she has that kind of timing, and I have to wonder—in humor—if she doesn't have a tracker on my car! As usual, she doesn't bother with the standard "how are you" stuff but goes right to the core.

"I forgot to tell you something. I found a Santero priest when I was in Kansas City, and she told me I had the gift. And get this, she knew why I was there before I even said anything," she adds.

"No, please don't tell me you did that. I hope you're joking, but I know you're not. You can't go back there, ever. And messing around with Santeria is a bad idea, Jen. It is voodoo stuff, powerful, and dangerous."

She counters immediately, "I know what I'm doing. And I have some new theories about that serial killer. It hit me when I was again in the NYPD archives and researching our grandfather's cases. I think he was chasing a dirty cop. A cop was killing those kids! It made sense as I looked at the news articles. I need to go back there ... And our cousin's told me she's tossed out all the albums with the photos and news clippings from his police career. I could kill her, I swear. It seems there was a flood in the basement that caused damage to everything. Now, I only have the archives." Jennifer is sounding deflated.

"Hey, slow down. You need to stop this nonsense. It's in the past and was a long time ago. It's over Jennifer. Over."

"Really? This is how you think? You're wrong, dead wrong. Oh, and that girl at LAX. You think it was by chance, just someone looking and sounding like me? You think that's over as well? It's not, I'm telling you, it's not. Not sure what your

LAX encounter was all about, and why it occurred, but I'll tell you this; you need to pay attention. This case of yours, with this Afghan woman, and this attractive Russian one, the blonde, there's far more to it than you realize," she says in a hurried, stream-of-consciousness way. She isn't done.

"And what about Cranberry Lake, and those elderly neighbors I met on the boat dock? They were real, as real as me and you. You believe in UFOs, don't you? Yet, you never saw one with your own eyes. You believe in them because of what our uncle told you many years ago. Yes, it's true, I have a gift. Curse or blessing, who knows? But I think you also have that gift. Stop denying it. Allow it to speak to you. It may save your life one day."

She finally stops talking or pauses long enough to take a breath.

"Wait," I cut in. "You mention a blonde Russian woman. Who told you this? I don't recall talking to you about her. Did Lenore speak to you about her?" I ask, hoping that's the reason.

How else can she be aware of Katerina from the Russian Tax Police?

"No, I haven't spoken to her about it. I see things, but not the way you imagine. Things just come to me, and I 'see' them. It's true, though, isn't it? There's a woman, so be careful; I'm just not sure about her, that's all I can say. But now, maybe you believe in my abilities."

"OK. Well, I got to give you credit there, sis. You called it during the kidnapping case, that things would go down on that beach, and you were right. So, I guess I can't dismiss what you're telling me now. Your brother is listening. But do yourself a favor and do it for me as well, and don't go back to Kansas City. No good awaits you there."

"I hear you, but no promises. Later, brother," Jennifer says as she hangs up.

It takes a couple of weeks to navigate the bureaucratic hurdles, but the legat office in Moscow's somehow accomplished the impossible.

They first had to convince the political officer—dealing with FSA funds at the U.S. Embassy—of the compelling and urgent necessity.

The next step could take time and wind up stalled or forgotten in Washington's slow-moving bureaucratic machinery. The approvals from the State Department in Washington could easily have taken several months, not weeks, yet the legat office has somehow done it.

I drop everything when word comes over the phone from Joe Doherty.

Aleksandr Filippov, along with another investigator named Vasily Melnik, will be arriving in San Francisco in several days. The Embassy's Consular Affairs Section has even streamlined the issuing of visas for the two MVD officers.

I call the task force members to let them know, and Terry Miller suggests we all meet at his office to prepare for the visit.

"Guys, we've been hoping for something like this for a long, long time, and it's actually happening. I think we all realize we've still got a long road ahead of us, but this is a huge development. A big thank you to all of you for staying with me.

I have to tell you, Don Pierce was stunned, and believe me, not much rattles him," I tell them, and continue. "I understand they'll be here for a few days. We know nothing about their investigation, and they certainly know nothing about ours." I want to hear what my colleagues will say next.

"Will they have anyone from the Russian Consulate accompanying them?" Marino asks.

Doherty answers, "We aren't sure. It's possible, and we can't keep them out of the room, but it could affect what we say, and more importantly, what Filippov and Melnik have to say to us. Not much we can do if it happens. Let's all just hope they don't show up."

The presence of Russian diplomats could have a chilling effect on the exchange of information. Everyone understands that reality, but we agree there's no sense in worrying about it at this stage.

Miller raises his hand for permission to speak.

"Yes, Terry?" I ask, amused at Miller asking permission to speak like a schoolboy in class.

"If anyone from their consulate shows up, we can tell them it's a closed session, and this is a Federal Grand Jury Investigation. We can keep them out that way," Miller says.

I can't go along with his suggestion.

"Terry, you may technically be correct, but it will put Filippov and Melnik in an awkward situation. We are Americans, they are Russians, and we don't want anyone from their side to think we are trying to co-opt or recruit them. I don't think we can, or should, keep them out of the room. After all, we've discussed this case with Dmitry and with Boris Poznikov already. Who knows, Dmitry may show up, and we can't tell him to sit outside, can we? That could be disastrous for us."

George King from the IRS is the next to speak. He has been quietly sitting there, looking over a number of papers he's brought with him.

"So, let me understand how this will work. They come to the office, we sit down with them, and talk about the case? What exactly can we share? They'll have questions for us, and we have questions for them, right?" King's concerns are valid and need to be addressed.

Miller stands up to speak. "George, this is a Federal Grand Jury investigation, a restricted case. All FGJ materials are protected and accessible only to investigators and staff on the special 6E list. I don't see how we can discuss any information obtained through subpoenas or derived from confidential sources. The Russians haven't submitted a formal request, a letter rogatory request. We have no treaty or agreement with Russia to expedite cooperation on such cases, nothing like a mutual legal assistance agreement, or mutual legal assistance treaty. I already checked, just to make sure. Apparently, the State Department is working on one, but it could take months or even a few years."

Miller sits down as he finishes.

"Terry, no, this can't be," I say, expressing my frustration at his comments. "So, they fly all this way from Moscow, for what? We can't talk about our investigation, yet we expect this Aleksandr Filippov and Vasily Melnik to reveal the details of the investigation from their side? Equally, why would they want to do that? They don't know us, have never met us.

"We are Americans, on opposite sides during the Cold War. This is no way to start a relationship. They'll just think we don't trust them, and with good reason if we behave like you've just indicated. There must be a way. In fact, we have to find a way, or it's already over, done. They will fly back to Moscow, and I promise you, we'll never hear from them again. We'll never get to know what they are doing over there. I couldn't blame them if they went radio silent on us in that case. We absolutely can't expect them to take the first steps in this game of chicken. We've invited them here to San Francisco, and the legat office has gone to a great deal of trouble to make it happen. Heck, everything going on in connection with this case in Russia is nothing but a black hole to us. It will remain that way.

"Filippov and Melnik are the only ones who can enlighten us and shed light on this conspiracy. We are operating in the dark, and it's close to game over for us. For me, I mean. Don Pierce will pull me off of this case, and frankly, I wouldn't blame him. So, I'm looking to you to tell me there's another solution, alternative, something. There has to be."

It is now Doherty's turn to speak.

"Terry, I don't care. We can all leave the room and let them stay there and go through our files, or selected files, or papers," Doherty says.

He waits for the reaction of our colleagues.

Rich Marino next steps in. "Obviously, that one's a no go for me. I can't be a party to that. We can talk to them, face to face, explain the limitations and our law, and hope they take that at face value. Heck, from their side, they probably have restrictions as well in what they can share or tell us, right?"

Miller sits quietly during the exchanges which go back and forth for the next half hour or more. He closes his eyes and appears to be deep in thought.

Finally, he stands up and speaks.

"Right. I have listened to you all, to all sides of your arguments, and I have a solution. There is a way, a legal way. Here goes. If sharing Federal Grand Jury material directly advances the interest and goal of the investigation, we can share such materials.

"So, by us sharing the evidence, documents, information we have compiled and gathered so far with Filippov and Melnik, we remain within the letter of the law. It is by law, in fact, permissible to do this. But it must directly advance the investigation's interests."

He sits down and breathes a noticeable sigh of relief.

Sure enough, he has found a pathway, a legal and permissible one.

"We have those numbers, those telephone numbers dialed from Golden ADA to Moscow. We do not know who the subjects are talking to, who are the subscribers to those numbers. So, that means we can share all this information as well, right, Terry?" Doherty asks.

Miller nods affirmatively.

I say to the group, "Well, we can share the information, and it will be an excellent test to see if they'll provide us what we need. Oh, and when they come into the room, the case files, the several volumes of documents will be in another room, or do we just have everything there, on the table, waiting for them?"

Doherty is quick to respond.

"No. We bring everything, I mean everything, into the room. Lay everything out right there on the conference table. Well, we have to protect sources' identities and sensitive stuff, and we'll need a couple of our Bureau interpreters to help with translation but let's not play games with them. Filippov and Melnik can take notes as they review the documents.

"I don't think we should be making copies of any documents for them to take back, with exception, that is."

Doherty's proposal makes sense. He recognizes the potential psychological impact on Filippov and Melnik. Case files set out on the conference table will show openness, trust, and confidence with our new partners, far more than words alone can do.

When I finally receive word of Filippov and Melnik having arrived at San Francisco International Airport that morning, I assume they will head to their hotel for some rest after the long journey and that the meeting will take place the next day.

Surprisingly, however, they insist the agents attending to greet them at the airport should take them to directly to the Bureau's office, so they can begin work right away.

The conference meeting room is all set, the case files and documentation arranged in meticulously organized stacks at the end of the large table.

Aleksandr Filippov and Vasily Melnik introduce themselves in Russian, with Nick, one of the Bureau's best Russian interpreters translating.

I am in attendance, along with Miller, Marino, King, Doherty, and several agents from the SF HQ Organized Crime Squad. Melnik and Filippov want to get to work right away.

Their gaze naturally turns to the large stack of case files and documents at the far end of the conference table. I provide welcoming remarks and try to make them feel comfortable. It is no doubt their first time in the United States, and their first time in an FBI office.

Melnik appears younger than Filippov; Melnik is a captain in the MVD, likely in his early thirties by appearance. Filippov is a colonel, in his early forties with a stocky build.

He looks as though he knows his way around a gym or boxing ring.

I decide to keep things light on this first day. Having just completed a long and exhausting journey, I figure they will not manage to keep much in memory, and it will make more sense to get into the details of the case the following day, after they have rested.

We are only an hour into the meeting when Doherty picks up one of the case files, which contains details about Golden ADA's incorporation, ownership, and offices.

The MVD officers seem keenly interested, beginning to take notes as Doherty is speaking, through interpretation. They seem interested in every aspect, and in every document relating to the case. They aren't asking questions, just absorbing what they are being shown and what is being told. There are many pages in the case files to review.

And for Filippov and Melnik, it is all new, or so it appears by their reaction to what they are being shown and what is being explained to them by the task force.

The task force discusses and reveals several topics and issues during this first day, meant to be an introductory one. The entire case file has been made available, except for informant or source reporting, and everything is at their disposal, from records and documentation relating to the importation documents for the diamond shipments, to bank records showing wire transfers and cash flows, to the real estate purchases, which include the Golden ADA headquarters office building on Brannan Street.

Before I realize it, several hours have already passed, and we are coasting into the late afternoon. Filippov and Melnik appear exhausted by now, but they still maintain focus.

I find it difficult to gauge whether their expectations are being met and if they are satisfied with what they have seen and heard.

Doherty shows Filippov several pages full of telephone numbers. He points to a listing showing the many calls to Russia. "7-0-9-5," he says to Filippov.

"Yes, Moscow," Filippov responds in English. He looks inquisitively at the pages and pages of telephone numbers.

"We do not know who they are calling in Russia," Doherty tells Filippov. "Can you possibly get that information for us? Subscriber information?"

"Maybe," Filippov responds, switching back to Russian as he writes the numbers, folds the paper and stuffs it into his pocket.

It will be important information for the investigation to proceed on the U.S. side, and to have some notion of with whom the Golden ADA principals, Kozlenok and the Shagirian brothers are in communication in Russia.

Russia is still a black hole for me and the task force. Filippov seems to grasp the significance and importance of the 7-095 numbers.

At that moment, to me, Filippov just feels and looks like a street-smart investigator, a gumshoe, maybe even an NYPD detective. He may be the real deal, at least I hope he is.

"Enough for today, guys," I finally tell them as we need to wrap up for the afternoon. "We can continue tomorrow, first thing. All the files will be here, on the table. We'll review them together, just as we have done today, but it will take place tomorrow."

The task force members all seem to sense it is not yet the time to probe Melnik and Filippov with questions about the status of the investigation from the Russian side.

Not on this first day, at least. Tomorrow, after they have time to rest, things will be different. For today, it is mission accomplished.

We are with them, face to face. I can check that box. We have made our case files accessible to them. Check on that box as well.

It has been a successful first day in my estimation.

The Russian officers aren't guarded and seem relaxed, but it is difficult to judge exactly how they have processed this first ever face-to-face exchange with their law enforcement counterparts from the United States.

I figure our next day will be more revealing as the real discussion will begin. The clock is already ticking. There isn't much time since the Russians will be back on the plane to Moscow in three days. The San Francisco based agents drive Filippov and Melnik to their hotel, the Fairmont, one of the best hotels in the city.

Jake Stirrup asks me to pick them up from their hotel for dinner, hosting our visitors at one of his favorite restaurants in San Francisco. It will be the first opportunity for Bureau agents to socialize with our visiting Russian officers. Maybe the real discussion will begin at dinner.

But it doesn't really matter. Regardless of any dinner table discussion content, the Bureau needs to be friendly hosts to these visitors from the other side, the other side of the world.

# Chapter 29

I arrive at the Fairmont a few minutes past the agreed time to pick up our Russian guests from their hotel. I knock on the door several times before it is finally opened by Melnik. He motions for me to enter the room, despite the fact we are already late for dinner.

"Guys, let's go, they are waiting for us at the restaurant," I tell them in Russian.

I notice Filippov sitting at a small table in the room, chairs arranged around it.

Oddly, they have obviously been eating and drinking, as there are snacks on the table. They have even found some fresh vegetables, cucumbers and tomatoes, artfully arranged on the small round table too. I have to assume they must have been quite hungry and discovered some snacks in the local market. Filippov motions for me to sit with them.

"No time, Aleksandr. We need to go. We're already late," I tell him. But Filippov and Melnik aren't budging. I am confused and repeat the request, this time slower in Russian, so there can be no misunderstanding. Are they too tired to go out?

I couldn't blame them if they prefer to stay in their room tonight. They have been on the move for many hours, and haven't yet slept, not since leaving Russia for California.

"Relax, Dennis," Filippov responds, opening a bottle of vodka and pouring the contents into a large water glass. He then pours vodka for himself and Melnik, but a meager amount compared to the full glass he now places in front of me.

I look at him, confused. I have Bureau car keys with me, and I am responsible for my Russian visitors this evening.

"We will go with you, but first, you are to become one of us, a 'militsionaire'," Filippov tells me, referring to the term traditionally used for a police officer in Tsarist Russia.

"What?" I ask, a bit perplexed. Melnik explains the ritual, telling me when someone becomes a police officer in their country, it is customary to toast in Russian, with the honoree having to drink the entire contents of the glass in one swallow. It is vodka, nothing else.

This is a rite-of-passage custom as Melnik explains it. Filippov only nods.

It suddenly dawns on me, the significance of what is now unfolding in the hotel room at this moment. Filippov and Melnik, for whatever reason, have included me as one of them and seek to bond with me, welcoming me into their special circle of trust.

I figure the circle of trust may not apply only to me, but likely, by extension, to the other members of the task force. All that really doesn't matter at the moment.

The challenge before me is to somehow drink the entire contents of the glass, filled to the brim with pure vodka. I flash back to the times visiting the Soviet merchant ship as a teenager, drinking vodka with the captain and his officers. That was also a rite of passage of sorts. This occasion is more serious, and I realize the time we spent together earlier today may have impacted Filippov and Melnik more than I appreciated.

Perhaps our openness and willingness to share sensitive documents from our files, and to speak openly about the case has had the biggest impact upon these visitors from a place so different, and so far away. But I can't simply jump into the minds of my Russian guests to understand what is taking place.

Whatever it is, they have obviously been impacted by the day's events, maybe even pleased and surprised at the openness we showed to them in that conference room.

So, now comes the hard part. I have to drink that full glass of eighty proof alcohol, somehow, without vomiting or passing out, then keep my wits about me to safely drive them all to the restaurant in the Bureau car. It will be too embarrassing to call my Bureau colleagues and try to explain to them how I've been drinking vodka with our Russian guests and can't drive.

So, I take hold of the full glass, raising it, making the requisite eye contact with my new friends. We clink our glasses, say the traditional "na droviya" to our health, toast, then tilt our heads back as we swallow the entire contents of our glasses in one long gulp.

As I place the now empty glass back on the table, Filippov pours juice into the same glass, and tells me to drink it all, and to eat some of the snacks. We chat back and forth for a few minutes before Filippov stands and motions toward the door. It is time for us to leave.

We arrive at the restaurant only minutes later, or so it seems. I feel surprisingly well despite the full glass of vodka just consumed. Normal in fact. It is definitely vodka I drank, but perhaps the juice and food immediately following dampened the effect of the alcohol on my system. I am not sure, but I decide to never disclose to anyone else what has just taken place with my Russian visitors, now my new and trusted friends.

Something tells me sharing such an experience outside of that hotel room might somehow demean or diminish the significance of the ritual in which I have just taken part.

A few days later, I share the story with my wife.

I laugh heartily, but she is not the least bit amused.

She tells me I am genuinely crazy, that I should not have caved in and downed all of that vodka. No good was ever going to come from such a reckless and immature act.

A small sip would have sufficed, she says. But my wife doesn't understand the Russians and their culture, so I tell her. Not so simple. The Russians were also sending me a message brilliantly. Yes, they were pleased with the turn of events that day and expressed it in their own way, but what took place in their hotel room that evening had a serious side as well.

There is now an expectation from their side, that I will not betray the sacred trust they have placed on me. I am inside their circle of trust, and it will be my obligation and duty going forward not to let them down.

As an honorary Russian police officer, I have no desire or intention to betray that trust ever. I am now one of them. It is not possible to undo that or to break it.

I ponder, for a moment, just what the conditions of this newly anointed trust are.

What are the terms of this trust, this covenant? I suddenly feel melancholy as my memories drift back to my uncles, then to my grandfather, the NYPD detective from another era. What sort of ritual or rituals did they go through when they became detectives in those days? Were there different circles? Yes, there are at least two types, a corrupt circle and an honorable one. I hope I have just entered an honorable one.

The coming days and weeks may reveal the nature of it; at least I hope so.

***

Filippov and Melnik are already waiting at the hotel entrance when I arrive early next morning. They look rested, ready for a full day at the office.

"I want to show you something," I tell them as they enter the car and we drive away. We head over to 999 Brannan Street, the impressive headquarters building of Golden ADA, parking on a side street a block away. "Well, there it is," I tell them, pointing to the building.

"The HQ building for Golden ADA. It's all done there, the cutting and polishing of the diamonds. The executive suites are on the top floors. They receive a lot of visitors, and off-duty San Francisco Police Department officers handle the security."

They look at me, a bit puzzled.

"Yeah, I haven't yet figured out exactly what role the police are playing, besides providing security for the staff and the building. I'm still working on that," I add.

I figure it best not to get into a lengthy and complicated discussion on the sensitive topic, as there are plenty of other issues to deal with on this second day with my Russian guests.

I have given thought to the day's agenda, deciding to pose a scattering of basic questions to my visitors before they become too engrossed in their review of the reports and documents.

"We know little about Kozlenok's background, and most of what we do know comes from his Shell Oil franchise application. Can you give us more of a sense of this guy? What he did before Golden ADA?"

It is a logical place to begin, and the question won't put Filippov in an awkward position. He seems to take it in stride and turns to face the group around the table as he begins.

"Yes, of course. He has political connections, and relatives in high places. A few years ago, he served as the chief accountant at a renowned Moscow eye clinic, eventually becoming a general director of a company called SovKuwait Engineering, supplying vehicles and equipment to the Moscow traffic police."

He takes a breath before he continues.

Then he adds, "Andrey is a protégé of Eugeniy Bychkov, head of ROSKOMDRAGMET. But it was Bychkov who first introduced Andrey to the director of Moscow's 'Kristal Factory,' Yuri Sorokin. Andrey convinced Sorokin to enter into an agreement with him and his new company, Star of the Urals, and to wire more than one million dollars to the United States to help capitalize Andrey's new company in California, Golden ADA."

"Thanks, Aleksandr. Enough for now. We can continue with the document review if you don't mind," I suggest.

There are many questions for our visitors. For now, it is better to show restraint and patience, and to let things unfold gradually and naturally. I saw the names Kristal and Yuri Sorokin among the subpoenaed documents, and hearing Filippov, our Russian law enforcement counterpart, explain things now brings everything to another level.

It also means Filippov and his MVD team are looking at the financial flows from the Russian side, following the money trail. Just how much Filippov and his MVD colleagues know about the mechanisms employed for the removal of the valuables from the vaults of the Russian government is not yet clear to me. I figure it will take time for Filippov and Melnik to share such details of their investigation.

Perhaps they aren't ready to reveal what they already know, or they may not have the authorization to share this information. It can also be that their investigation has not yet reached that point. I remain hopeful they will soon solve the mystery.

The document review continues for the next several hours, Filippov and Melnik taking notes as the Bureau interpreter sits alongside them, translating everything into Russian.

The task force members periodically interject and elaborate on the contents of the documents when asked to do so.

During one break, Filippov pulls me aside. "I need to call the minister tonight, so don't think we can meet for dinner. Is that OK?" he asks.

"Huh? Sorry, Aleksandr. No problem with the dinner, but you said minister. Did I understand you correctly?"

I must have misunderstood him.

He couldn't have meant the actual minister, the minister of the MVD. As a Colonel, Filippov is a midlevel officer but speaking directly with such a high-ranking official, a Russian minister no less, would be highly unusual. In short, an exception to protocol.

"Yes, the minister. He wants to receive a daily briefing directly from me," Filippov says.

I just look at him and nod.

There is no point in challenging or questioning Filippov about why he has to brief someone so senior in the Russian government. But what am I to make of it? I am certainly in no position to ask for details or reasons. Better to accept what's been revealed, and let it be.

"Oh, I almost forgot something else," Filippov adds. "You wanted to know about the subscriber information for the 7-0-9-5 numbers, right?"

"Yes. But don't worry, I know it will take time, even a few weeks perhaps. We can wait, Aleksandr," I assure him.

"No need. I had my team follow up last night," he says with a slight grin. "The numbers all belong to the Kremlin's dacha complex."

"Really? Can you please explain what that means?"

I am mystified about what I've just heard.

"Sure. Certain officials working in the Kremlin have access to dachas, weekend homes in the forest, outside of the city," Filippov explains. "Not like the country, rural cottages, or homes you might think of here in your country. Rather, these 'dachas' are large, elaborate, and ornate. The grounds are secured by the Kremlin's special guard force, accessible only to certain Kremlin officials and their families."

"So, do these officials have exclusive access? For each dacha, is there one official assigned? Or do they share dachas?"

"Not sure," he begins. "I think they each have their own. The perk goes back to Soviet times. Even the President has his own dacha there, on the complex grounds. He has several around the country, but I am talking about the Kremlin dacha complex outside Moscow."

For me, the revelation is stunning. It means several Golden ADA players based in California are in direct and regular contact with high-ranking Russian government officials working at the Kremlin. Does it mean Kremlin-based officials are part of the criminal conspiracy? Or worse, they are directing the entire operation from the Kremlin itself?

No, not necessarily, but it is now a real possibility.

Do Filippov and Melnik understand what they are now facing, or is this dacha connection revelation new for them too?

Prior to us providing them with the 7-095 telephone numbers, did they suspect officials from the Kremlin itself were involved? It is difficult to say with any certainty, but one thing appears certain; the U.S. task force, and our new Russian "partners" have, at the very least, strong indications that powerful actors may be at the center of this unfolding and complicated criminal conspiracy. And more concerning to me, Filippov and Melnik are soon to return to Moscow, armed with this new, and potentially dangerous, knowledge.

On the last day of the visit, Miller pulls me aside to talk.

He asks, "Do you think you can ask them about the violations of Russian law they are investigating and who their targets are?"

"Terry, I can understand why you need this information, but I can't ask them directly. Not at this stage. They've shared a lot already. Off the record, they've informed me about corruption violations, officials exceeding their authorities, tax violations, and theft. They are in the preliminary stages, and MVD is an investigative agency. They may have to turn everything over to the Office of the Prosecutor General for the next phase of search warrants, seizures, arrests, etc. As far as targets, they are looking at some of the same figures, Kozlenok, the Shagirian brothers, Eugeniy Bychkov."

"So you're telling me we can't ask them straight up for more details?"

"Yes, Terry. We—I—can't. It would serve no purpose and possibly have a chilling effect on this new partnership. We are operating in new and uncharted territory, Terry. I am not saying we need to tiptoe around them, but they, Filippov and Melnik, are out on a limb right now. They've spent several days with us in San Francisco. We've opened up to them, opened our files, in a way they didn't expect. It's a lot for them to process. They also need to report back to Moscow, to their minister."

"But ..." Terry interrupts.

"We'll be fine, Terry. The case is solid, and we have Russian law enforcement working with us. These guys seem legit to me. Let them get back on the plane and go home to Russia. We will stay in close contact with them and bring them back when the time is right. OK?"

"OK. But it would be good to communicate with them somehow. Do you guys have a way of doing that? In a secure manner?" Miller asks.

"Hmm. No idea. I'm making this up as I go Terry!" I say, half jokingly. "So, think about this: newsflash, FBI agent arrested for spying, discovered calling Moscow regularly, speaking with a Russian cop on an open line. Yeah, we may all wind up in jail. No, seriously, we'll figure it out. You're right, we need a secure way of communicating with them. We've entered a new phase of this investigation, and now we have partners in Russia, we have to reach out directly to them, to exchange information, discuss strategy and coordinate activities."

I tap Filippov on the shoulder and motion for him to sit down in the room's corner, while Melnik continues to review documents and take notes.

"Aleksandr, you guys are heading back home soon. I am not sure how we will talk to one another when you're back. Of course, you can go to the legal attaché office at the Embassy, but it is probably not the best idea to do that, certainly not regularly, too many eyes watching. If we talk by phone, the world listens in if you know what I mean. We have to develop a way to communicate in a secure, or semi-secure, manner. Do you agree, Aleksandr?"

"Sure. OK. Let me think."

Filippov raises both hands to his face and sits quietly for a moment, in thought.

Finally, he speaks. "I got it. We will talk in Russian, of course, and in code," he tells me, pleased to have come up with a solution.

"In Russian, OK," I respond.

It may work, but if anyone is listening in, this will only serve to make them even more interested in the conversation. "Go ahead, Aleksandr. What about this code?"

"It will be simple. Let's write it all down," he tells me as he hands me a sheet of paper, and Filippov takes a sheet with pen in hand. "Number One, Boris Nikolaevich Yeltsin, yes, number one."

"What? So, we'll be talking about President Yeltsin and referring to him as number one?" I say, incredulous.

"Definitely. And number two, hmm, that will be Viktor, Viktor Chernomyrdin."

"Seriously? OK, so number two, Russian Prime Minister, Viktor Chernomyrdin," I say as I write the name and assigned number. "Who else, Aleksandr? There must be more?"

"Oh, yes. Several. Number three, Eugeniy Bychkov, head of ROSKOMDRAGMET. And the fourth number belongs to Boris Fedorov, Minister of Finance. Number five ..." Filippov says, continuing with his proposed list of the names and their assigned code numbers.

Some names are familiar to me, and some are new.

By the time Filippov has finished, there are nearly twenty names on my sheet of paper, with the accompanying code number assigned to each. My head aches looking down at the handwritten names. Yet, Filippov doesn't appear at all fazed, taking it all in stride.

Perhaps he is simply too good at faking it.

So, this is our secret code. It isn't the most sophisticated system, but better than referring to such individuals by their names on an open and insecure telephone line.

If we are going to be discussing such influential figures as President Yeltsin, though, what does that mean going forward?

I understand some of the individuals on the list are subjects in Filippov's case, but if someone like the President of Russia is a target in it, suspected of playing a role in this criminal conspiracy, that is serious indeed, and potentially dangerous— more so for Filippov and Melnik, soon to be heading home to Russia.

I struggle to process what Filippov has just relayed to me.

I am about to put Filippov and Melnik back on the plane to Russia, and our future "coded" communications will refer to such high-powered political players? The prospect is difficult to grasp. But it all fits and makes sense in a way since this case has had more than its share of intrigue from day one, the day the mysterious and attractive Afghan-American woman first appeared at the San José FBI office asking for a Russian speaking FBI agent.

But the intrigue and twists just never let up; on some level, it's intoxicating and thrilling.

The game is afoot, but what exactly is the game? Things can take a sudden and unexpected deadly turn at any moment, a possibility with which I am familiar from previous cases.

This case reminds me of some of my prior drug trafficking cases, where you really are just along for the ride, reveling in an illusion if you think you are in control of anything.

As an investigator, accept that reality. You can't bend fate to your will. Be willing to accept fate, to embrace the unknown, to hope for the best outcome. The Golden ADA case seems no different, yet the stakes seem higher and are serious, deadly serious.

I force myself to pull away from such thoughts and misgivings.

The drug case in Kansas City bears some striking similarities to this one. And there's been violence and murder, and a serial killer still on the loose in Kansas City.

No, better not to dwell on the past, rather to box it up and leave it alone, along with childhood flashbacks and the warnings from my sister. As I look up from my handwritten list, Doherty quietly signals to me that we need to talk when I'm done speaking with Filippov.

"You need to know something," Doherty begins, motioning for me to move our conversation to an empty corridor. "It happened shortly after I became involved in this investigation." I just look at him. Whatever he's about to tell me, I can only hope it's something manageable, better yet, something solvable.

"OK, Joe, what is it? Just tell me straight up, whatever it is."

He says, "They wanted to meet with me a while ago, and I put them off. Right before Filippov and Melnik came, I sat down with them. Think it was the same group from the agency that met with you. Well, that's what they told me. They pitched me. Can you believe it?" Doherty says, shaking his head. "They told me there was much more going on than I could imagine, throwing around terms like foreign policy and national security implications."

His agitation burgeons as he speaks.

"That woman, that blonde with her aloof demeanor, she got under my skin. She told me this would remain between them and me. Our little secret."

"What did they want from you? Information? Introductions?" I ask.

"They said whatever I felt comfortable sharing with them. They are interested in everything related to the case. The subjects we're looking at in the U.S. and Russia, information about our Russian counterparts, banking documents, telephone records, everything. They basically want me to hand over our case files. I put them off, telling them I'd think about it, and get back to them. I didn't want to close the door completely. They're not going to just walk away if we tell them it's a no go. I suppose they won't stop, not until they've exhausted all options, or if something distracts them and they turn elsewhere."

I say, "Joe, thanks for sharing this with me. I wish they would just stop, but it doesn't look that way. That blonde, the icy blonde, she got under my skin too. I feel like they're out there, hovering over us, watching from the shadows. I don't trust them, so just be careful and stay alert. My source has reported she's been followed several times. I suspect it could be them, or someone from their agency. I don't mind having to deal with the bad guys, but this added layer, I—we—don't need it. It's a distraction, a potentially dangerous one. I suppose it comes with the territory, with this sort of case. No matter, they've shown their hand. If they want to meet with you again, give me a heads up, OK?"

I am relieved Doherty feels comfortable enough to share what's occurred, although it has also taken him several days to talk to me about it.

For what reason does Doherty reveal it to me at this moment? I can only imagine. It certainly isn't something that's simply escaped his mind, that he forgot about it.

I brush it aside for the time being, accepting it as a good sign he appears to be opening up with me. I just hope he's not keeping quiet other secrets or information relating to the case. As a veteran and experienced FBI agent, he has his own sources and can even develop additional ones relative to the investigation. That is perfectly acceptable, as long as he shares any pertinent information provided by such sources with me and the task force.

Doherty continues, "As soon as Filippov and Melnik are wheels up, I'll turn my focus on drafting that affidavit for a Title III. It will take time, but it's important. And what Filippov told us about the 7-095 numbers belonging to this complex, the Kremlin dacha complex, is unsettling. Let's hope the Department of Justice in Washington doesn't freak out when they learn our case has connections to the Kremlin. They have to approve these applications, as you know, before the packet can go to a judge."

# Chapter 30

"You look exhausted," Sharon says, nearly shouting upon seeing me in the office a few days after Filippov and Melnik have returned to Russia. "You can't keep this up much longer."

"I know. But there's not much of a choice, is there?" I shrug.

"Look, things are in pretty good shape as far as Golden ADA goes. Think about it, you've got the Russians on board, and that is huge. You have the task force fully engaged, and now, SF OC squad agents are working on the Title III application. Plus, your source seems to do her job, and is following directions, so far at least."

"OK, Sharon. You're right. I think I need a break. Maybe a few days to decompress."

"I've got a better idea," she says. "There's the annual Gilroy Garlic Festival in a couple of days, and they could use help. My contacts tell me there's an opening for one more volunteer at the tri-tip barbecue grill with the Santa Clara County Sheriff's

Office deputies. You still like to barbecue, right? It's an all-day event. It will help you reset and take your mind off of work and this case. You can talk regular cop stuff all day long. What do you think?"

"Sure. Why not? I'll do it. It will be good to get away from all of this madness for a day," I tell her, waving my hand toward the growing pile of case files and documents covering my desk. "Hopefully, there are no arrests or searches planned with the other agents in our office."

I barely finish talking with Sharon when my phone rings, the display reading 7-095.

Moscow is already calling; it has to be Filippov, I conclude, rifling through my papers for the handwritten code we've agreed upon.

"Prevet, Aleksandr," I say into the receiver.

"Prevet, Dennis. But it's not Aleksandr. It's Katerina. I am calling from Russia," she tells me.

I feel immediately embarrassed to have made such an assumption. What a rookie mistake!

I switch into Russian, so no one in the office will understand what I'm saying. "Kak dela? How are you?" I ask her.

"All good here. I don't have long, but wanted to tell you something," she responds.

Her comment about not staying on the line for long immediately clicks with me. It will lessen the chances of outsiders listening or being able to record our conversation.

"You know, B.N. and Bychkov have known one another a long time. They worked together in Sverdlovsk, during Soviet times. As far as I know, they're still close. You need to be mindful. And, you had visitors from Moscow recently. I don't have reason to suspect they have another agenda beyond what they may have told you but be careful, regardless. If I learn more, I will let you know," she says as the line goes dead. She probably ended it deliberately that way. The entire exchange takes less than thirty seconds.

I sit back in my chair, trying to process what Katerina has just told me. I wasn't able to take notes, but it seems there were two main points, the first being that B.N., which I figure to be the initials for Boris Nikolaevich Yeltsin, and Bychkov, are close.

How is this significant, and why does Katerina convey this information to me?

Is Yeltsin intending to take action to protect his friend?

His friend who is the target of a criminal investigation … Or have they had a falling out? Is there some other meaning embedded within her comment, a warning of sorts?

And for Katerina to refer to her president, the most powerful figure in all of Russia, isn't that dangerous for her, or is she following orders?

And the second point I catch is her mention of the MVD and their visit to California. Does she have inside access to what's going on with MVD and its investigation?

Does Katerina actually work for Russian intelligence, and her cover job is with the Russian Tax Police? There is no point in dwelling on the endless possibilities.

I met Katerina face to face, and even then, she struck me as sincere.

If she represents the Russia of Churchill's riddle and enigma puzzle, so be it. I need to stay in communication with her, regardless. There is no choice. For the time being, I will keep this new line of communication confidential between me and Katerina.

No one else needs to know, no one in the Bureau, and no one in the task force either.

Sharon is right about the barbecue. It is cleansing to be cooking at that grill, focused on turning the large tri-tip beef slabs over the red-hot coals.

I take a turn at slicing the grilled meat for the sandwiches too, the most popular dish.

Glancing around at the other officers, I realize there are more holstered weapons attending this one grill than I've ever seen before, even growing up with NYPD family in New York.

It feels so good to be here, grilling large chunks of raw meat, talking shop, and preparing the sandwiches. For the moment, I am a key part of this pure and primeval ritual, going back millennia. Men standing around a fire, grilling their captured game after the hunt, sharing the nourishment with the community.

It is engrossing and intoxicating, with the heavy smoke you can almost taste, along with the visual of the cooked and seared meat, then serving it to eagerly awaiting multitudes.

The smell of fresh garlic is heavy in the air, enveloping the entire festival, rising from the nearby garlic fields to drift into the festival grounds.

There is the standard garlic bread, of course, but also garlic soup, garlic pasta, garlic sauce of every kind, even garlic ice cream. I forget about work, about the case, about everything.

It is freeing and exhilarating, this grilling of fresh meat over hot coals; there is such simplicity in the task, yet its outcome is immediate, satisfying, and delicious.

"Hey, is that your phone? It's ringing," the nearby officer tells me as I awaken from my garlic-induced trance.

"Oh. Thanks. I didn't hear it," I respond, considering for a moment whether to ignore the call. But the ringing has already broken the trance, so I might as well answer it.

Heck, I am still here at the festival. Maybe it's nothing urgent.

I can deal with it and come back to what I am doing. I step away from the grill and head off to a quiet corner of the tent, pressing the phone to my ear.

"It's Miller. Hey, I need a summary of the case, the Golden ADA case. A few pages will do. Can you get something to me this afternoon, or in the morning at the latest?"

"Huh?" I answer, perplexed. "What are you talking about, Terry? A summary of the case? For DOJ in Washington?"

"Sort of."

"Terry, what does that mean? Sort of," I respond. I am in no mood to play cat and mouse with the prosecutor, my prosecutor. "Terry, I'm not in the office, so just give me the straight scoop on this. Who needs this summary?"

"OK. Well, the U.S. Attorney got a phone call from Deputy Attorney General, Gorilek. Jamie Gorilek. She needs the summary for the Vice President's Office. They asked for one."

"What? Why would they want a summary, and Terry, how would they even know about this case?" I ask him. This is concerning to me.

"Well, there is this Gore-Chernomyrdin commission meeting. They are in regular contact with one another, and apparently, Russian Prime Minister Chernomyrdin asked VP Gore about Golden ADA, and Gore told him he'd look into it, and find out what the DOJ is doing on the matter. Since the request is coming from so high up, I don't think there's much we can do about it. Let's just give them the summary, and that will be the end."

Silence. I take a breath.

There isn't much time to process, or to understand the meaning behind this request, coming from the highest levels of the U.S. government, The White House.

"Dennis? Are you still there?"

"Yeah."

"So?"

I take another deep breath. The smell of the barbecue, combined with the garlic, envelops me like a fog. I need time to think, but Miller can go elsewhere for that summary if he doesn't like what I have to say. This is a Federal Grand Jury case with rules, strict rules.

I had to confront those rules when the Russian MVD delegation came to San Francisco. Now, the Vice President of the United States wants something, and he intends to share this information with his Russian counterpart from the Kremlin itself. I am unmoved.

No keeps blinking like a red light in front of me.

No, don't do it. It comes from somewhere, from my childhood experiences in New York? I'm not sure. The words flow out of my mouth. As if I am a spectator, watching from a distance, I am finally ready, ready for my response to AUSA Terry Miller.

"Terry?"

"Yes?"

"You realize if I write up that case summary, Melnik and Filippov are dead. Dead, Terry," I tell him firmly and seriously.

"No, you don't understand," Miller interrupts.

"Yes. I understand. I do. But you tell Ms. Gorilek that at this very moment, FBI Special Agent Dennis T. Cosgrove is working on the summary and will provide it momentarily. There's only one thing, well, two things, Cosgrove will need from her side."

"OK?" Miller says, sounding a bit confused.

"He needs the full official name of the Vice President, and, more importantly, he needs the VP's social security number."

"What? What are you talking about?" Miller asks, sounding impatient, and now annoyed.

"When the Federal Grand Jury meets, and they ask for the 6E list of individuals who have had access to this case, this restricted access case, the Vice President's name will appear on that list, along with his social security number, just like the numbers of all other individuals, the agents and support personnel. But I need to get it first, from their side."

"They will never agree to this," Miller says, somehow sounding relieved.

"Yep, precisely."

I am not sure where the idea has come from. Is it something woven into the barbecue smoke? Perhaps the heavy garlic mist enveloping me is messing with my senses?

Is it something from my past, my childhood experiences?

My relatives from the grave directing me? Whatever it is, it doesn't matter.

The phrase "Truth to power" pops into my head. "Truth to power."

"OK, Special Agent Cosgrove. Have a good day, wherever you are. Hey, sorry to have bothered you," Miller says as the call ends.

I never hear him mention the request from the Vice President's Office again.

It is a calculated risk for sure. To take on The White House can backfire, and they can retaliate in countless ways. But worth the risk, definitely worth it.

Lives are at stake, the lives of my Russian partners out there alone, working the case on the dangerous streets of Moscow. Filippov and Melnik can disappear, or both wind up dead, their bodies tossed into some deserted alley in Moscow.

It will not be difficult to kill them or to hire someone to kill them. Then, the case will be over, done. So, I have responded, moved my chess piece and taken my hand off it.

That is my move, my response to the request from the Deputy Attorney General and the Vice President's Office.

"Game on, Dr. Watson, game on," I repeat under my breath as I make my way back to the barbecue pit. There is a lot of meat that needs grilling.

An agent I have been working with on several drug trafficking cases, named Oz, approaches. "Who was that pestering you?" he asks.

"Miller."

"What did he want?"

"Information."

"Screw him," Oz says. "You need a break. Tell him to F off."

"Yeah," I smile. "That's pretty much how it went. Well, let's get back to cooking this tri-tip. We've got a lot of hungry customers, Oz, and they don't want to wait."

I turn back to the grill, and to the task at hand. "Man, there is nothing better!" I add, turning to Oz. "Nothing."

# Chapter 31

As soon as I pick up the phone two days after the Garlic Festival, I just know it is Nazari, perhaps because it's been more than a week since we last made contact.

"We need to meet, my office, as soon as you can get here, OK?" she asks impatiently.

I drop everything and head over to her office.

I am barely in the office chair facing her desk when she unloads.

"They're both out," she sighs. "Out." She pauses. "The Shagirians got their 'golden parachute,' five million. Andrey told them to keep their mouths shut forever, or else they would each get a bullet in their heads."

She appears agitated and upset. I have never seen her in such a state, a marked departure from her usually calm and composed demeanor.

"Annie. OK." I take a long breath and pause a moment before continuing. "Let's back up and take this from the beginning. First things first. Who exactly told you this?"

"Nina. I ran into her at the hair salon. I tried to activate my recording device, but just couldn't do it discreetly in front of her. Sorry."

"It's OK, Annie. I am glad you called me. Let's go slowly. It's not your fault," I add. "Stuff like this happens. It's beyond our control."

"Nina told me Andrey was furious with them for a long time. For many things. The deal breaker was when David and Ashot wired the ten million from Switzerland to ROSKOMDRAGMET without prior authorization from Andrey. I think I should try to meet with Ashot. What do you think?"

"Annie. Slow down. Let's first finish talking about Nina and what she told you." I try to calm her down, speaking slowly in a hushed voice. "Nina told you directly about Andrey telling the Shagirians they would each get a bullet in the head if they talked?"

"Yes. That's what she said. She seems to be having enormous problems with Andrey. Remember I told you about his girlfriend, Helga? Nina also told me Andrey is out of control, spending wildly, and the company is having trouble paying its bills. She said even 'those Americans,' Simon Lemke and Art Roggenbuck, cannot rein him in. Something like that."

"OK. What else did she tell you?"

I raise my hand so Nazari doesn't jump in before I finish. "And Annie, try to remember exactly what she said, word for word if you can. It's important."

"She said she is worried about her future and the future of her son. I think she would like to stay in the United States. Nina is very smart. She could run the company herself, you know. She once told me Andrey listens to her advice about investments, and what companies they could set up. Well, he used to listen. I don't think he pays much attention to her anymore."

"This is very interesting. Nina and Andrey are still talking, right? Is she considering leaving him?"

"I'm not sure. He controls their money and the company. I am not sure about her role these days, other than as an informal advisor to her husband. I think with the Shagirian brothers out, Nina may become more active in the company's affairs. But I really don't know. She's sort of all over the place. It seems like she's under a lot of stress, from what is going on inside the company, perhaps."

"Annie, what makes you say this? Did Nina tell you these things, or is it your opinion?"

"She doesn't speak so directly, but she definitely shows signs of stress and the relationship between her and Andrey isn't good. Maybe she is glad the Shagirians are out. You know, I don't think she ever liked them much. I think she may try to step in and take their place. She is educated, sophisticated, part of the Russian elite. They were nowhere near that level. I told you they were selling flowers on the streets of San Francisco before they hit the lottery, and Andrey took them into Golden ADA."

Despite my best efforts, she is still rambling, not making clear which parts Nina has actually said—if any of it at all. Nazari just keeps reiterating, "I think."

"Annie, do you think Nina is an ambitious woman?"

"Definitely. She once told me she was the real brains behind everything, but Andrey kept her in the background. It bothers her a lot that she gets no credit for anything. You know, Bychkov likes her. Well, that's what she once told me."

"Annie, give me your pocketbook, with the recorder. I need to take it to my office, to make sure it works properly. In the future, you need to record everything, Annie. I understand sometimes it isn't possible, but you need to try. You're a smart woman. Go to the bathroom with your pocketbook, turn it on. There is always a discreet way to activate the recorder for these meetings. We showed you how to do that."

Irritated, I try not to lecture her and shift the conversation.

"So, Annie. What's next? Can you meet with the Shagirians? Do you know where they are? They were riding the crest of the wave for quite a while, and now they are suddenly tossed out. Yeah, they got a good chunk of change, five million, but they may be looking over their shoulders for a long time. It would be good if you could talk to them, to give me a sense of where their heads are at, and what their intentions are. They were inside the company and close to Andrey for quite a while. But listen, Annie, and listen carefully to me. You can't push them. If they want to talk, great. Just let them talk."

I lean forward in my chair to emphasize what I'm saying, and to make sure she is paying close attention. For whatever reason, that first encounter with Nazari pops back into my head.

The time when the tables were turned, she said to me, "Listen carefully," asking me to protect her. Now, I am asking if she can continue meeting with the Shagirians although the company has tossed them out and Andrey has allegedly threatened them with bullets to the head if they disclose what they were doing in Golden ADA.

Back in my office, I close the door, needing time to think. If it is in fact true that the Shagirians are out, and Kozlenok's threatened to murder them if they talk, what does it mean for the case? More importantly, what does it mean for Nazari? If I send her back to meet with the Shagirians, will I be putting her in danger? I don't yet have the Title III up and running, which might give me a sense of what's going on in the company, and inside Kozlenok's head.

First things first, I will have to reach out to the task force about this latest development. I inform Doherty first about it, stating the Shagirians are out and allegedly threatened by a bullet to their heads from Kozlenok. After that, I tell the rest of the task force.

The consensus from the task force members is to let things play out and not take any action which could expose the investigation.

It is simply too much of a risk to approach the Shagirians to see if they will cooperate. We still have no leverage over them, and there's no outside motive for them to cooperate. Andrey has provided them with sufficient compensation to ensure their silence, forever.

To approach them at this moment in the investigation, and in this complicated chess match, could backfire and derail everything.

If the Shagirians reject the approach, they could react unpredictably, possibly panic and inform Kozlenok that the Bureau has approached them. That would not be good.

However, with the Shagirians out, I have no reason to believe Golden ADA operations will shift or shut down. Kozlenok's ego is just too big to let go. He only used the Shagirian brothers for as long as they suited his needs. Now, he has tossed them out, granted, with a generous severance package; they won't have to sell flowers on the streets of San Francisco, never. In Kozlenok's mind, he has moved on.

They are in his rear-view mirror. He is done with the two of them.

I decide the better strategy is for Nazari to stay engaged with the two brothers, and with Nina, but only by telephone for now until the situation stabilizes, and a clearer picture emerges. At least I hope things will become clearer.

***

The next few weeks are eerily quiet in the case, the downtime allowing me to focus on my other pending cases, and to catch up on routine leads. Doherty is busy working on finalizing the Title III affidavit, and the rest of the task force is continuing its work, analyzing documents, particularly examining the company's corporate tax filings.

It is one of those rare quiet days in the office when the phone rings early morning. It is 7-0-9-5, and Katerina is calling me from Moscow. I get up from my chair and close the office door. She once again doesn't bother with greetings or small talk.

"I can't talk long. There is a change. It looks like they will try to salvage things here and in California. I am not sure how they are planning to do that, but it could involve replacing Kozlenok, and possibly others. There is talk that he is a liability, and they want to move him out," she says, and the phone line goes dead.

I put the receiver down and stare out of my office window. If what Katerina tells me is true, are the higher ups in Moscow covering their tracks by potentially replacing Kozlenok soon? Yes, the Shagirians are already out, but Kozlenok is still there, running things.

The question in my mind is how do they intend to rein him in?

He has been spending extravagantly for some time. The only person capable of controlling Kozlenok is Eugeniy Bychkov, the head of ROSKOMDRAGMET.

But Kozlenok himself could be in grave danger if the Moscow higher ups view him as a liability for their own futures and want to get rid of him. After all, Kozlenok is a reckless guy, but he's also highly intelligent; he set up Golden ADA as a real player in the diamond trade, with sights set on expanding and diversifying their business and investments, not just in the United States but also in Western Europe. In a relatively brief period, he surrounded himself with influential and powerful people in California, who he figures are genuinely loyal to him and will protect him and his company if needed.

The notion, of course, is naïve.

Kozlenok is likely clueless and in denial at the possibility he could be in imminent physical danger. His ego is simply too big to allow himself to fathom such a possibility.

I have never been good at waiting, even before the Bureau. It is not my nature to sit and wait passively for something to happen; it's a sign of weakness. It is better to strike first, and strike hard, to take the initiative, be the aggressor, and act decisively.

So what if the decision turns out to be wrong?

It is better to act, to do something, than nothing. Otherwise, your opponent can get the upper hand, the drop on you. That was the way to survive growing up in New York, to act first, strike first. But now, many years later, as an experienced FBI Special Agent, I have to overcome this ingrained behavior pattern and my ego, to consider it is sometimes better, when the situation calls for it, to leave things be. Sometimes, the advantage can lie in letting things develop on their own, at their own pace, and not in taking action.

To wait isn't necessarily a sign of weakness or indecision.

But part of me still wants to take action. To do something.

It feels as if it is only a matter of time before someone gets killed. If this were a drug case, like my case back in Kansas City, the body count would already be climbing. But this is no drug case. No matter, my street sense and my gut still tell me something is coming, soon.

There will be violence.

There always is.

# Chapter 32

The U.S. Attorney's Office in San Francisco is in the same building as the FBI office. A few floors separate them, making it convenient for FBI agents to meet with federal prosecutors. I am in the U.S. Attorney's Office this morning, working with Miller, reviewing the case file and discussing the Title III affidavit to which Doherty is putting the finishing touches.

The entire "package" will then need to pass through several layers at DOJ back in Washington. I hope there will not be pay back from the DOJ for having outmaneuvered the Deputy Attorney General weeks prior. Miller and I haven't discussed the incident since that telephone call during the Gilroy Garlic Festival.

I take his not mentioning the conversation as a good sign. There is no point in raising the prior incident now, nor the solution I proposed to him on that day. If it were still on his mind, Miller would certainly have mentioned it by now, after so many weeks have elapsed.

When Miller's office phone rings, I don't react.

The phone rings constantly in his office anyway; today is nothing out of the ordinary.

There are telephone calls from other prosecutors, judges' chambers, and defense counsel, a day-in and day-out occurrence. But this time, the phone call is not for Miller.

"It's for you," is all he says as he passes me the receiver.

"Hey, it's Doherty. You better get over here as soon as you can. Aleksandr is in the hospital," he says, and abruptly hangs up. By the tone of his voice, he sounds shaken. I have never run inside an office before, not in an FBI office, nor in a U.S. Attorney's office, but this time, I decide I need to run, and fast. Hurtling down the long office corridor, past cluttered desks, cubicles, conference rooms, and break areas, I clutch my bag full of papers.

I jump into an elevator just as the door is closing. The three or four people already inside it step back and give me a look as though I'm a wild beast or rabid animal that could strike out at any moment. As soon as the elevator door opens, I jump out and run to the reception area, flashing my FBI credentials so the receptionist can buzz me in.

I reach Doherty's office in a matter of seconds. He is sitting at his desk with his head down and his hands covering his face.

"Joe, it's me. What's going on? What's happened?"

He looks up. His face is red and in that moment, he looks to me like a startled bystander who has just witnessed a horrific accident or seen someone killed.

"It's over. Done. This case is over. The legal attaché office called me. Aleksandr Filippov is in intensive care. Someone severely beat him. He's lucky to be alive."

"What? This just happened? And where is Melnik?"

"I think it happened a couple of days ago. Melnik is OK. For now. But Bob from the legat office called and informed me Melnik had also received threats. It was a pretty direct threat, too. He was on the metro when two thugs approached him, told him to step off the train, onto the platform. They told him to walk away from the Golden ADA investigation, and that they know where he lives, where his wife works, and where his kids go to school.

"Not good, not good." He repeats the phrase several times as his voice trails off.

He continues, "We can't have blood on our hands. Bob thinks Filippov will survive, but he doesn't know the extent of the injuries. It sounds like a severe beating, meant as I warning, I suppose. Bob has little in the way of details himself; probably someone from MVD's called him to let him know as they were planning another trip here to see us. Now, everything is on hold. I think we're done."

Doherty seems deflated and shaken by what he's learned.

I am not so sure. Our Russian colleagues, our trusted partners, and our brothers are suffering. One from a violent altercation, and thugs have threatened the other with the inference they can harm his wife and children if he doesn't walk away from the case.

I am in California, so unfortunately, I cannot jump in my Bureau vehicle and race there to offer help. I feel powerless at the moment, and more than that, I feel anger, a boiling rage stirring inside of me. Not at the prospect that the case could be closed, but anger at whoever has assaulted Aleksandr Filippov and threatened Melnik. I want to find out who is behind this attack and the threats, to make them pay for what they have done. I suppress the raw feelings as Doherty just looks out his office window, stunned, at a loss for words.

"Joe, it's not over. Not yet," I tell him. The words coming out of my mouth sound non-sympathetic, cold, and uncaring. "Filippov's still alive. Melnik is still alive. Yes, blood has been spilled, but we knew this could happen, didn't we? We put them back on that plane to Moscow knowing exactly this could happen, and it did. We should not give up the ship because of it, not yet. Closing the case would be the equivalent of abandoning our colleagues, our brothers, when they need us most. Let's stay in the fight.

"Plus, something tells me Aleksandr won't throw in the towel. No way. I'm no Russia expert, but this is a warning, a shot across the bow, maybe from a faction inside the Russian mafia, or from someone there in Moscow who is feeling the heat. It's a sign we're getting close, Joe. They feel threatened, and now, they're panicking. They will make mistakes."

Doherty looks up at me, silent, looking as if he's processing what I have just said.

Perhaps he sees me as an indifferent person, without empathy.

But on some level, I don't care what he thinks of me as an investigator or as a person. Not that I am cold, devoid of empathy, or too ambitious, but at this moment, I find myself back in New York, back on the streets of my old neighborhood, fighting.

The violence was so normal back then.

Yes, Filippov's beating was horrible and disturbing. But he's a tough guy with a tough character. That much I sensed during our few days together. He's had a violent altercation, and he is now in the hospital in intensive care, but he will recover, I'm sure of it.

I just know he'll bounce back.

This is likely not the first violent and bloody encounter Filippov has had in his life.

"Let's wait, Joe. Give it time. We owe it to both of them. When Aleksandr recovers, we'll get them back here to California and finish this thing with our partners, our brothers."

"OK," he responds. "Let's wait." He repeats what I have told him in a calm voice, his face soon returning to normal as he sits up in his office chair.

"I am going back to Miller's office. He tells me the Title III package is soon going to be sent to Washington. Let's hope things don't get bogged down there. I'll talk to Miller about what's happened. He needs to know."

My thoughts then shift to my source, to Ms. Nazari.

Is she next? Is she in danger? The Shagirian brothers received a threat that they will be shot in the head if they talk. Filippov is in the hospital, and thugs have threatened Melnik.

There was bound to be violence, and now it's arrived. In a strange way, its arrival even feels like a relief to me. The long expected and unwelcome visitor finally showed up.

Why should any of us be surprised, given the stakes?

Diamonds, valuable artwork, precious and rare metals, they have high monetary value, no different from drugs like cocaine and heroin. The drug trafficking world is a violent and unpredictable place, driven by lust, greed, and power. Why should the world of stolen gems be any different? No matter. It's still "game on, Dr. Watson."

And now, there is blood.

# Chapter 33

I decide it is time to send Nazari back to the Shagirian brothers for a face-to-face meeting. Blood has been spilled, and things look to be unraveling, but she still has access to the players, direct access. This time, she finally manages to record an interview.

Afterwards, we review the tape together.

"Annie, I'm not sure what to make of this," I remark after listening to the recording. "The Shagirians were venting to you and sound angry. I suppose it's greed. But seriously, they already received millions from Kozlenok. If they invest it right, they'll never have to work again, and no more selling flowers on the streets of San Francisco, that's for sure. I'm not sure what their next move might be, though. Maybe they're going through a sort of separation anxiety, and they'll eventually move on. I just don't know."

"I don't think they will walk away," Nazari responds. "Yes, they are angry. They behave like spoiled children, and Kozlenok really spoiled them. They had a taste of the good life, they were on top of the world for a while. I don't like them, I really don't. But I know I need to continue to deal with them. I do it for you."

She delivers those last few words with a hypnotic gaze.

I look away for an instant to break the spell, coming close to telling her to stop doing that to me but deciding against it. Such a comment could only empower her and show weakness from my side. I am not about to give her such power over me.

"Yeah, they had their time in the sun, I suppose. But I'm not sure what they're talking about, this line of credit from Bank of America."

On the tape, David refers to using Golden ADA assets, diamonds and gold as collateral for a line of credit for the Russian government, some five hundred million.

He laments to her that he can't close the deal with the bank, something that all sounds so absurd. Is this part of the coverup plan of Kozlenok, to justify the transfer of stones and valuables from Russia to Golden ADA? I make a mental note to mention this to Filippov when he returns to California, assuming he recovers from his injuries and can travel again.

"And Annie, they were pretty open, complaining to you about Art Roggenbuck and Simon Lemke. They sure don't like them, huh? It sounds like they blame them in a way, for them getting kicked to the curb."

She just nods, wide eyed.

"Annie, you did a good job during this meeting. Nice work," I tell her.

This is the first time I have ever praised her work. She smiles.

"When the time is right, maybe in a week, I would like you to see Nina. I need you to follow up with what she told you during your previous meeting. If she is planning on leaving Andrey, and has designs on staying in the U.S., we might consider talking to her."

I float the idea but immediately regret my words. It somehow feels inappropriate or too sensitive to share investigative strategy with someone like Nazari.

It could backfire. She is a confidential source, not a trusted law enforcement colleague. She has her own agenda and motives, even if she is cooperating and working closely with me. I remind myself to keep a separation between us. I am working with her alone.

This attractive, manipulative and somewhat mysterious woman could turn on me instantly. I must always be mindful and aware of that possibility and act accordingly.

A few weeks pass before we hear from the legal attaché office in Moscow that Filippov is out of the hospital. Not surprisingly, he is still in the game. When I hear he and Melnik are eager to return to California, in a couple of weeks, I am not surprised by that either. I did sense Filippov was tough. The incident landing him in intensive care has just proved it. But it doesn't mean he's safe from further harm, or from being assassinated.

Whenever someone spills blood, there is always more. I only hope it isn't Filippov's or Melnik's blood, or my source's blood, for that matter.

As soon as I receive word that Filippov and Melnik are on their way back to San Francisco, I feel a sense of relief along with more than a frisson of trepidation.

Since they were last in California, we have accumulated more documents and financial records which need to be shared with them.

From their side, we hear they are bringing new documents with them, connected to the investigation. The first day of our meeting consists mostly of document review.

Filippov pulls me aside and shows me a detailed listing of addresses and businesses.

"Look at this," he says. "It is only a partial list of businesses and properties purchased by Golden ADA. They have diversified and expanded their business into many areas. Their ambitions have no bounds," he tells me in Russian. "I am now working with a prosecutor. His name is Lazar Aslanbekov. He is helping me to get the contracts between Golden ADA and ROSKOMDRAGMET declassified. It is important to help us prove our case."

"Declassified?" I ask.

I hadn't expected to hear this, but it makes sense.

The power elites hide their true intentions behind a cloak of authority, a clever ruse, and no doubt done successfully during Soviet times. But the times are indeed changing in this new Russia. It remains to be seen if Filippov and his prosecutor can remove that veil of secrecy. I can only hope they'll succeed in doing so.

"Yes," he affirms. "They did this to hide their true intentions and actions, and they will claim they carried out everything in the interests of the state. They will argue that these documents are state secrets that cannot be disclosed, never. Pretty clever, huh?"

"Yeah. Clever. But do you think you'll get these documents declassified? In our country, this is difficult to do. A judge will rule on this? How does it work?"

It sounds tricky and insurmountable, and I'm finding it difficult to believe MVD investigators in Russia can uncover "state secrets" and that high-ranking Russian officials can be prosecuted and held accountable in a trial court. It might just be a first.

I am nearly certain this never occurred during Soviet times. Power was in the hands of a select few, the Soviet elite, or nomenklatura as they were sometimes called.

If the judges and prosecutors didn't follow orders, they would be sent to the gulag. It was all a Potemkin village, a choreographed facade. The rule of law was a mere fiction.

When convenient, the law could apply to the masses but certainly was not for those holding the true reins of power and authority in that suppressive and authoritative state.

As we end our first day together, I pull Doherty aside.

Now, it's just him, me, and our Russian interpreter, Nick, translating the more technical documents, many of which are a bit beyond my Russian language abilities.

"Joe, what about getting Aleksandr and Vasily out of San Francisco for a couple of days? Down to my area, to Monterey?" I suggest.

Doherty agrees.

***

We drive Filippov and Melnik to the Monterey Peninsula, easily finding a nice quiet hotel in the area as it's off season. Filippov and Melnik seem to soak up the experience. Appreciating an escape from the big city for a couple of days.

We have access to the Bureau's local office so we can continue working and discussing case strategy, exploring the possibility of Doherty and me traveling to Russia to conduct joint work on the case.

In the back of our minds, the Title III affidavit is looming large. We don't mention the Title III to Filippov, or that we are waiting on the judge to issue the order so we can intercept the telephone calls of Golden ADA and the identified subjects, including Andrey Kozlenok. By law, only those with a "need to know" and allowed by the issuing judge have access to the powerful investigative tool, the Title III court-authorized electronic intercepts.

I hope the Title III will illuminate the full network of co-conspirators, helping to prosecute them for their crimes, but it is no guarantee.

It is late afternoon when Doherty asks me for a restaurant recommendation for dinner.

He knows I live in Monterey and am far more familiar with the area than he is.

"What about Carmel?" I ask.

Carmel is a small and scenic coastal town near the famous Pebble Beach Golf Course. It was an artist hamlet years ago, with several Hollywood stars in residence, including Bing Crosby, Doris Day, and former Carmel mayor, the actor and director Clint Eastwood.

Day and Eastwood both owned businesses in the small village, where the homes did not have numbered street addresses for mail delivery, only the names of streets and residents.

"I know a nice Italian place, quaint and cozy. I have never eaten there, but whenever I walk by with my wife and kids, it's always full and looks so inviting. There are only a handful of tables inside, but we could try it. What do you think? Not sure if they like Italian food, but who doesn't, right?"

As soon as I open the door to La Trattoria de Napoli, I feel as though I have just walked into someone's home. This is the real deal.

The intoxicating aroma of freshly baked bread, pasta, bubbling tomato sauce, garlic, and basil takes me back to my Italian friend's kitchen growing up in New York, and to my mother's kitchen when she would make spaghetti and meatballs for special occasions.

Yes, this is the place. The waiter, sharply dressed in a white shirt and black tie, immediately finds a corner table for us. The music playing is pure Frank Sinatra.

I quickly survey the small restaurant with its crisp, clean white linen tablecloths, flickering candles, and baskets of freshly cut Italian bread everywhere.

On the wall, I catch several photographs, not of Italy, but of what look to be city scenes of Hoboken, New Jersey with its unmistakable attached townhome style brownstones, and dramatic views of the New York City skyline in the background.

I excuse myself from the table to inspect the photographs, mostly black and white photos from the 1930-1940s era, not unlike the ones from my grandfather's era as a NYPD detective.

There are also several photos of Sinatra from his youth. It occurs to me these aren't stock or commercially available images I am looking at. These are family photos, personal and one of a kind. I sit back down at the table, and we order.

Filippov and Melnik seem relaxed and happy to be out for the evening with us.

It is also good to see them again after so many weeks, and after their hellish ordeal when they returned to Moscow following their first trip to California.

I only can hope they will survive this case, and we'll all live to see it through, together, to a successful prosecution. I have no clue what awaits us tomorrow, or the next day, or the next, but I let the troubling thoughts fade, immersing myself in good company.

The restaurant is near capacity, with couples, a few families with children, and the five of us. There are fewer than thirty patrons in the cozy setting, including our table.

I look around the restaurant to see what others have ordered. The food looks simple, but I can tell it is of high quality. It feels as though we're in Italy, perhaps at someone's nona's home for Sunday afternoon homemade pasta. This is home cooking at its finest, using nothing but fresh and simple ingredients. The combination of the Sinatra music playing in the background, and the array of Hoboken photos affixed on the wall, sparks my curiosity.

I ask the waiter if the owner's available this evening as I would like to speak with him. The waiter gives me a look of concern as he figures I am intending to lodge a complaint against him, or the food, or the service. Melnik understands English fairly well, and he gives me the same look. I tell him in Russian that it's OK, all good.

Less than two minutes after speaking with the waiter, the owner approaches our table. I like the guy immediately. He doesn't seem at all concerned, nor does he appear defensive, given that he surely anticipates I have asked to speak with him to complain about his food or staff. He doesn't have an attitude either.

There is nothing arrogant about this guy. He feels genuine to me.

His accent is immediately familiar, but more northern New Jersey than New York City. Having grown up in New York, I can tell the difference. It is subtle, but it's there.

"You are from Hoboken?" I ask.

"Yeah. Yeah, that's right, Hoboken. You know Hoboken?"

"Sure. Been there a few times. But I have never been to your restaurant. You have a fantastic location here in downtown Carmel. You're a long way from New Jersey."

"So are you," he says in a joking manner.

He must detect my slight New York City accent from growing up there.

"Yeah, well, I used to study at DLI over in Monterey, the language school. I don't want to take your time as I see you're busy, but I can't help but ask, do you know Sinatra?"

"Yeah, sure. Our families in Hoboken were close at one time. We had a falling out years ago, but I keep the photos on the wall and play Sinatra music sometimes. My patrons love it, the combination of the Sinatra music and the food. Guess it goes together. Right?"

"It does. Your food is great, by the way. My colleagues and I love it. They are from Russia, but Joe, Nick and I, well …" I pause, motioning by hand to each of them at the table.

"We're from the FBI. Our Russian friends here, Aleksandr and Vasily, they are investigators from the Russian police. They are our partners."

It is the first and only time in all my years in the Bureau that I identify myself as an FBI agent in a social setting, a restaurant no less, to a total stranger.

To this day, I am not sure why I did it.

"Wow. You are here working on a case?" he asks.

"Yes. And this is their first time in Carmel, and here we are, in your restaurant. They've never had Italian food before, nor Italian wine. They certainly seem to love your cooking and your place," I add. The owner pulls up a chair and sits with us. We chat for a while about Italian food, New York City, Hoboken, and about Russia, and the Bureau.

The owner introduces himself as Julian Carrico, originally from Hoboken.

He asks me if we are in a rush. I tell him we are in no rush, not this evening.

We are taking a break from our hectic schedule.

A half hour later, most of the patrons have already left. The place is now empty except for us, the owner, his chef, a couple of waiters, and some staff.

The owner gets up from the chair, walks over to the front door, and places the "closed" sign in the window. He tells us the open wine bottles are all complimentary, from him to us.

Nearly a dozen stand opened and spread out on the wooden counter.

I fill our glasses from one of them, a rich Chianti from Tuscany. Melnik raises his glass first. "To us, to the hunters," he says. We clink glasses. Melnik, keeping his glass raised, continues his toast as he explains what he means by the term, "hunters."

"We are investigators, all of us, but in the purest sense, hunters, out to catch our prey, the criminals. They give chase and we track them, following closely. To catch them, we need to be strong, attentive, sometimes brave, and at all times, fair and just. We will catch our prey if our motives are pure. We will catch them at a time and place of our choosing, not theirs."

To me, Melnik's toast is revealing, genuine, and true.

His words are profound and give me pause. I am taken aback by this junior officer and his turn of phrase. I second the toast, raising my glass.

"Yes, Vasily, to all of us, to the hunters," I tell him in the now nearly empty restaurant.

There is no one else, only the hunters. The chase is on. It is far from over.

I turn toward Nick and Doherty. "This guy, Julian Carrico, the owner, he represents America this evening, our country." They both only look at me, perplexed.

"He doesn't know us. Completely clueless about the case, he does not know what we are working on with our Russian colleagues. He knows virtually nothing about any of us at this table tonight. Despite this, he has welcomed us to his restaurant, his now closed restaurant, as his guests. In a way, he not only represents the best of our country, but he also represents the citizens of it, welcoming and accepting our Russian colleagues here, Aleksandr and Vasily."

For the next two hours as we sit together in Carrico's restaurant, his now closed restaurant, he doesn't probe us about our work. He is no doubt curious, but respectful of our privacy. For Filippov and Melnik, it will be the most unforgettable and enjoyable evening they have ever experienced in the United States, made possible by the gracious and welcoming Carrico, La Trattoria de Napoli's owner from Hoboken, New Jersey.

The next day, we continue our work together.

Filippov and Melnik show us a handful of documents they have brought from Russia. There are copies of incorporation papers, financial statements, contracts, and witness statements. It is overwhelming and will take time to review and analyze everything. I make a mental note to give Sharon a heads up about the documents coming her way.

I ask Filippov about his ballpark estimate of the amount removed, or looted, to date. He tells me they don't yet have an accurate accounting, but his best guess is somewhere between 150 to 400 million dollars, maybe more, an enormous sum.

The case involves more than diamonds, he explains. The conspirators have access to precious metals, gold, artwork, and much more. Filippov also tells us they were prepared to steal not just millions, but billions if no one stepped up to stop them.

From the proceeds of selling the diamonds and gold alone, Filippov has identified several properties in Europe and Russia, and the names of acquired businesses involved in the manufacturing and distribution of pharmaceuticals, aircraft, and consumer goods.

It will be a difficult, costly, and time-consuming undertaking to trace and recover the converted proceeds from the large-scale thefts.

My head spins at the prospect of undertaking such work. I push the thought out of my mind for the time being as Filippov stuns me with his next utterance.

"President Yeltsin and the head of ROSKOMDRAGMET, Eugeniy Bychkov, go way back to Sverdlovsk, and they are still close friends."

"What does this mean, Aleksandr? For the case," I ask.

Filippov has just confirmed what Nazari and Katerina earlier told me.

As if this news isn't enough, Yeltsin is up for reelection, and his most serious opponent is a communist hardliner. It doesn't take a political affairs expert to realize the stakes are incredibly high, not only for the future of Russia and its people, but also for the investigation, and for Filippov and Melnik. If Yeltsin orders the MVD to close their investigation, that will be the end, at least from the Russian side.

The U.S. investigation will continue, but without the cooperation of the Russian MVD.

Filippov and Melnik could both be in even more danger than they presently are, armed with so much potentially damaging and compromising information.

Information that Yeltsin's opponent would be more than eager to have.

"I am an investigator, nothing more. I am ordered to investigate, and that is what I do. If I am ordered to stop, I stop. I will have no choice," Filippov says. He shrugs, accepting reality.

He doesn't want to comment more on the hypersensitive topic.

It is enough for me. He has shared it with me and Doherty. Now it is up to me and Doherty, and our task force, to help move the case forward, efficiently and thoroughly.

Our task force can speculate and theorize all day long about the different scenarios that can unfold in Russia, but it really doesn't matter. We need to continue to do our jobs, to collect evidence, and to identify all the players, at least those operating in the United States. More importantly, we need to share everything with Filippov and Melnik in a timely manner to help them build and strengthen their case. Perhaps, in this way, it will make it less likely Yeltsin will order the case closed, to shut things down on the Russian side.

But it is Russia, after all, and it is impossible for me to truly understand and appreciate what is going on behind the veiled curtain.

I am an American FBI agent, working in California, operating in a world very different from the one with which Filippov and Melnik have to contend, and in which they survive.

"Dennis," Filippov turns and addresses me. "I would like you to arrange something for me, if it is possible."

"Sure, Aleksandr. What is it?"

"I would like to testify while I am here. To testify in your Federal Grand Jury. I would like to go on the record with them and to share the results of my investigation, so far at least, with the jurors. Do you think you could arrange that?"

I am speechless. Once again, Filippov surprises me. Doherty and I step away to discuss the implications of Filippov testifying and what it could mean for the case.

"Give me a few hours, Aleksandr. I will call Terry Miller and see if we can arrange it. He will have to support this, and we can't be inside the room with you. The Federal Grand Jury meets in secrecy. It will be the panel of jurors, a court authorized interpreter, and AUSA Miller. How does that sound?"

He nods affirmatively.

I step outside of the room to call Miller.

"Terry, I have a favor to ask. Actually, I think it's a promising idea. Not sure if you've ever done anything like this, but here's the proposal," I tell him.

I relay to him what Filippov has asked about testifying to a Federal Grand Jury and laying out his investigation. Miller is supportive and immediately checks on the date and time when the jurors will be in session.

"Can you get here first thing tomorrow? It's the only window. Hey, I don't know if this has ever happened before, a Russian police officer testifying at a Federal Grand Jury in northern California. We may be the first … Well, Filippov may be. Cool, huh?" Miller adds.

Next morning, I drive Filippov to the courthouse in San Francisco.

He looks relaxed, telling me he is well prepared as he turns to enter the courtroom where the jurors are already sitting.

Miller steps out of the room to greet us. "You'll do great, Aleksandr, I'm sure."

Filippov takes his folder full of papers, and the door closes behind him. The thought crosses my mind he may want to memorialize the work that he, Melnik, and his MVD colleagues have already done, if the powers that be decide to close their case.

Or, if the unthinkable were to occur, someone assassinated them. I push the dark thought out of my head, happy to see Filippov and Miller emerge from the room after over two hours.

"His performance was exceptional. Filippov answered all the questions from the jurors. Wish you could have been there, but it's a closed session, as you know. That's our law, the rule of law. But I don't have to explain that to you, do I?" Miller tells me, laughing.

I take Miller's remark as an indirect reference to that time when the Vice President wanted information about our case, and the law, our rule of law, stopped him cold; truth to power, the rule of law to power. I only nod in agreement.

Filippov and Melnik leave for Moscow the next day. Just before Filippov boards his flight from SFO, I remember to ask him about this line of credit tale David Shagirian mentioned during the meeting with Nazari. Filippov tells me he's heard something vague about Golden ADA seeking the line of credit purportedly on behalf of the Russian government, but he doesn't have details to confirm the rumor.

He comments, "Stuff like this is classified. State secrets, as you'd imagine. I hope Aslanbekov can eventually convince a judge to declassify these documents. Only then will we know the full story."

I tell him we'll stay in close contact when he's back in Russia, and if I learn anything more from my side, I will let him know, using the number code we have devised.

Shortly after Filippov's return to Russia, his superiors promote and place him in charge of his own MVD "untouchable" squad, with several of his investigators fully dedicated to working the case in Moscow. There are individuals and witnesses there who still need to be identified and interviewed. Millions from the Russian treasury have already been looted and remain mostly unaccounted for, having either vanished into numbered Swiss bank accounts, or been secretly converted by corrupt Russian officials to their personal benefit.

It will take a lot of time and effort for Filippov and his squad of untouchables to identify all the stolen, now hidden, and converted assets. A part of me wants to reach out to Katerina in Moscow and ask her about this "line of credit" story to get her take on it, but I decide against it. It could unnecessarily put her in harm's way if she were to probe.

Filippov stands a better chance of uncovering the truth behind this line of credit scheme, if only he and Aslanbekov can somehow gain access to those "secret" documents. It strikes me as a desperate, weak, and pathetic attempt by the conspirators, claiming they were only helping their country to survive the chaotic economic transition, and that their intention was to use the looted treasures as collateral for a sizable bank loan to benefit their country.

In early 1995, Kozlenok abruptly resigns and steps down from his CEO position, no longer managing the day-to-day business of Golden ADA. His reckless spending has finally caught up with him and his company. Either someone in Moscow orders him to step down, or he himself sees the writing on the wall, deciding it is time to go.

No matter, there will not be a second act for Andrey Kozlenok. He has become a liability to the company, and to those around him. In his place, Art Roggenbuck and Simon Lemke step in to fill the leadership vacuum.

Roggenbuck, appointed as CEO of Golden ADA, works to rein in the spending and boasts that his mission is to bring the company back from the brink of collapse.

He travels to Moscow with Lemke, promising the Russian government that Golden ADA will repay everything owed to the Committee, as long as the flow of diamonds continues unabated. It is pure fantasy and naiveté. They are both out of their depth. The company is too far gone to salvage. It will never again receive diamonds, rough or polished, from Russia.

Despite the dire situation, the two Americans hold their own press conference in Russia to announce their noble intentions and mission to save the company.

They give their word to repay everything owed to the Russian government, once the flow of diamonds resumes. Their words fall on deaf ears in Moscow.

In San Francisco, it takes another month for the final approval of Title III.

It is too late. The intercepted conversations offer little insight into what has transpired or is transpiring inside Golden ADA. The flow of diamonds from Russia to the Golden ADA vaults has stopped entirely, and the conspiracy is fast unraveling.

Yet, there are thousands of carats' worth of rough stones already stored away in the company's Brannan Street vaults that need to be cut, polished, and eventually, sold.

However, the company has largely committed the proceeds of those future sales to repay the Russian government and address the mounting corporate tax debt resulting from Kozlenok's wild and unchecked spending.

With Kozlenok now in the shadows and the Shagirian brothers gone, damage control efforts led by a group of corrupt Russian officials, out to save themselves, are at full throttle.

Filippov and his squad are closing in, and fast.

The tables have dramatically turned, and the clock is now ticking, against the conspirators.

This turn of events is dramatic, from the dark period when Filippov was hospitalized after a severe beating, and Melnik received threats and was told to stop the investigation, or else.

# Chapter 34

While Filippov's investigation in Russia continues, there is still plenty of work ahead, both in Russia and in the United States. The conspirators, powerful figures in Russia, will not quietly walk away or admit their guilt, returning what they have stolen.

It will never be that easy.

In the United States, with Kozlenok in the shadows, and the Shagirian brothers gone, the pace of investigation slows. It is a stark contrast to the days when Kozlenok's boundless ambition was driving the company, and the diamonds were freely flowing out of the Russian storage vaults into the greedy hands of Kozlenok and the Shagirian brothers.

The complicated chess match is far from over, but the nature of the game is evolving.

It is only a matter of time before one conspirator steps forward to cooperate. The clock is ticking for all of them, not only in Russia, but in California as well.

Perhaps not as loudly, but it is ticking.

I am in my office in San José, working on an unrelated case, when my telephone rings on an unremarkable day in early September 1995.

The FBI's San Francisco Office Special Agent on duty is calling.

"Cos, there is an individual here, named Ashot Shagirian. He has just walked into the reception area, unannounced, telling me he's been threatened and wants the FBI to protect him. I've checked his name in our system, and your name, and Doherty's, popped up. You have him listed as a subject. What would you like me to do, or to tell him?"

I stand up and close my office door, stunned.

This new twist is not entirely unexpected, but it is surprising to me when it finally happens. I immediately call Joe Doherty to let him know Ashot Shagirian is now sitting in the FBI San Francisco office's reception area, and he has told the Special Agent on duty that he has been threatened and wants protection from the Bureau.

Protection from what or whom, I can only guess.

There is no reason for me to suspect Ashot is aware of our ongoing investigation or that his sudden and unexpected appearance in the Bureau's office is at all related to it.

We need to get to him, quickly.

He can simply walk out, change his mind and disappear on us.

His presence may be connected to Kozlenok's alleged threat that the brothers will end up with a bullet in each of their heads, but we cannot confirm it until we talk to Ashot Shagirian.

I tell the agent on duty to ask our visitor to sit tight, and agents will soon be there to speak with him. "If it looks like he's going to leave, do whatever you can to convince him to stay."

I jump into my Bureau car and race to San Francisco to meet up with Doherty.

We need to conduct the interview as though we know nothing about Ashot and the other players at Golden ADA.

We escort Shagirian to a secure interview room. He speaks perfect English, appears well educated, and is wearing a coat and tie. He comes across as a sophisticated, and well-mannered person, not rude or arrogant in any sense.

As soon as he speaks about the threat, he trembles.

He has the look of a person under extreme stress.

He explains to us that he and his brother, David, have been running a company in San Francisco involved in diamond cutting and distribution, called Golden ADA. That was until they were forced to relinquish their ownership interests several months ago.

We only nod as I take notes.

"We were working with an individual from Russia named Andrey Kozlenok, our partner. My brother and I had a falling out with Andrey, and he bought out our interests in the company. We both decided it was better to let him do that than to litigate the dispute in court. After all, we have families to support. Litigation would be costly and take a lot of time.

"We have no current affiliation with the company, although we established the firm several years ago and led its day-to-day operations, along with Andrey. There has been a recent change in ownership, and an individual from India, Rajiv Gossain, who bought Kozlenok's shares, is now running the company."

Shagirian, at first trembling when he spoke with us, has finally calmed down. We remain in a passive, listening mode, allowing him to continue to speak. He explains the company is not in a stable financial position because of mismanagement by Kozlenok and others.

"So, tell us about this threat. We will need the details if you expect us to take action to protect you," Doherty tells him.

"Take your time, Ashot, and you can speak in Russian to me, if you prefer," I add. I don't want him to freeze up on us or suddenly leave.

He has come to our office of his own free will.

"Gossain threatened me and my brother a few days ago. He'd asked us both, David and me, to meet with him in his office. I showed up alone, figuring he wanted general background stuff or information about our clients since we'd run the company for so long.

"That wasn't the reason; he said we owe the company many millions, and he wants it back. That we are personally on the hook for it, and the Russians want it. Forty-five million dollars. If we didn't comply, he threatened to have my brother David kidnapped and beheaded. He was very direct and blunt, a real thug. I know the Russians put him in charge."

"Ashot, have you spoken with him since?" Doherty asks.

"No. I spoke only with my brother, and we agreed I should go to the FBI for our protection."

"Good. So, when Gossain threatened you, was there anyone else present?" I ask.

"Yes. His head of security was there, a guy named Shane Sullivan. I have known Shane for a while. He is a high-ranking police officer with the San Francisco Police Department."

"Oh? And what did Mr. Sullivan say while Gossain was saying these things? Making these threats," I ask him.

"Nothing. He just sat there. I don't remember him saying anything, and I don't understand why he would just sit there, speechless and motionless."

"Did Gossain explain why or how you owe forty-five million? You mention they bought out your ownership interest when you left the company, right?"

"Well, we received five million dollars as part of the buyout. Our attorneys described it to us as a 'golden parachute.' Two and a half million each, to relinquish our ownership shares in Golden ADA," Shagirian explains. He slowly takes a sip of water and continues.

"Gossain claims we embezzled millions from the company. This isn't true. I don't doubt he intends to carry out his threat against me and my brother."

"Ashot, we can't just go out and arrest Gossain based on what you are telling us. I don't doubt what you are saying is true. But to prove this, we will need more. Would you and your brother be willing to work with us? To possibly record conversations with Gossain and others at the company?" Doherty steps in to ask.

"Yes, and we will be there to guide you, and to help insure your safety and the safety of your families. But Ashot, we have little time. Gossain expects a response from you, and we have to take his threats seriously. Who knows what he intends to do next?" I add.

"OK. Let me talk to my brother and get back to you," he says calmly.

It is understandable he wants to discuss the matter with his brother.

It is a big step for both of them.

There'll be no turning back if they decide to work with us.

He likely understands that recording conversations, potentially incriminating ones against an individual like Gossain, who could be a Russian proxy or from the Russian underworld, is a serious, life-altering decision.

The witness protection program could move them to a place far from their homes in California. Shagirian has lived in the U.S. long enough to understand the implications of such cooperation with law enforcement. Yet, he must feel genuinely threatened by Gossain, enough to make him voluntarily appear at the FBI office in San Francisco, seeking protection.

We decide not to reveal anything about our investigation to him.

He could later use the information as leverage for his own personal benefit, to help extract himself and his brother from their precarious dilemma.

For me, things seem to come full circle.

Shagirian's assertion that none other than Shane Sullivan, a sworn police officer, was sitting there passively in the room while the threats were being leveled at Shagirian by Rajiv Gossain is disturbing and repulsive to my core. I reflect on that lunch with Sullivan many months earlier. Yes, Sullivan is in deep, possibly in over his head.

As Shagirian leaves the office, he promises he will inform us of his decision as soon as he can. But first, he needs to speak with his brother, and his family.

It is a big step, this potentially life-changing decision.

"Ashot, whatever you do, do not discuss this with anyone. No one, Ashot. Not with your attorney or friends. No one can know you are talking to us. It can backfire on you, and put you, your brother, and your families in grave danger. You understand, right?"

I convey the warning to him in a serious and blunt manner. Whether he appreciates the gravity of what I tell him is difficult to judge.

"I'll get back to you as soon as I can. I understand fully. Thank you for meeting me."

With that, we shake hands and he walks to the elevator, leaving the protection of our office.

"Joe, what's your take? Will he work with us? He's in a mess for sure. This is a coin toss. He may decide to negotiate on his own with Gossain and return some of the money.

"He doesn't know we're already aware it's not the first time someone at Golden ADA is threatening him and his brother with violence. After all, the 'golden parachute' buyout happened only after the alleged bullet to the head threat by Kozlenok.

"Interesting that Ashot Shagirian skips over the details surrounding their departure from the company. He says nothing to us about 'a bullet in the head.' But I get it. In some respects, that bullet in the head threat is even more serious than the Gossain threat. Kozlenok told the brothers they were never to disclose anything about their work at Golden ADA, never.

"Yet, here is Ashot, seeking the protection of the FBI. He and his brother are in quite the pickle, aren't they?"

Doherty says, "Yeah. A pickle of their making. I agree; it's a coin toss as far as Ashot and David working with us. Either way, we'll know in a couple of days. Let's hope Gossain doesn't kidnap them or have one killed in the interim. We'll have to get out there and track down the Shagirians if we don't hear tomorrow. The risk of harm's too high. You agree?"

"Yeah. You're right. Well, we still have to give them space to decide. Regardless, the clock is ticking for both of them, and perhaps for my old friend, Shane Sullivan. Full circle, Joe, full circle."

# Chapter 35

"Are you sitting down?" Terry Miller says as I pick up the telephone in my office.

"Huh? What now, Terry?" I ask. I can only imagine what he's about to tell me.

"Ashot's attorney called me this morning. Apparently, he met with you and Doherty yesterday at the San Francisco office. Is that right?"

"Yeah. I was about to call you this morning to discuss it. I suppose I should have called last night to give you the heads up. He claims Rajiv Gossain, the new owner of Golden ADA, threatened him. We're waiting for him to reach out to us today with his decision about cooperating and working with us," I explain to Miller.

"I'm sure you told him to keep quiet and not discuss this with anyone. Apparently, as soon as he left your office, he ran over to his attorney, and that has now set off bells and whistles all over the place. Can you and Rich Marino get up here, fast, so we can figure out a game plan, how to deal with this? It's a bit of a mess. Hey, shit happens, right?"

By his tone, Miller doesn't seem upset, just anxious, which is understandable given the unexpected turn of events.

"I'm on it, Terry. I'll reach out to Marino. Doherty's dealing with unrelated things for most of today. I'll let him know. Marino and I will get to your office as soon as we can."

I hang up and reach out to Marino. We arrive at Miller's office in less one hour.

"So, guys." Miller pauses and takes a breath. "The cat is out of the bag. Ashot couldn't keep his mouth shut after meeting with you and Doherty yesterday. Apparently, others at Golden ADA know, according to Ashot's attorney. I have compiled a list of persons you should interview, today." Miller hands me and Marino a lengthy list of names.

"Terry, are you kidding us? You want us to talk to people like Art Roggenbuck, Simon Lemke, and Shane Sullivan? I don't get it."

"We need to lock in everyone's story. When you interview them, focus on what they know about the alleged extortionate threat to the Shagirian brothers. This way, if we wind up in court and they testify, it will be more difficult for them to later contradict their previous statements to you."

"OK. I get it. So, we go out there, try to talk to as many people as will speak with us, and focus on the circumstances of the alleged threat, right?" I ask.

"Yep. Exactly. Look, some may tell you to take a hike, and not be willing to talk. Others may reveal more about what has been going on over there at Golden ADA. You never know how this will play out. You guys will have your work cut out today. With these interviews, I am sure you will have an interesting day."

Miller is right. The extensive list of interviewees means we will need to hit the road and start immediately.

I turn to Marino as we jump into his vehicle. "Rich, I have a proposal for you. How about I take the lead in the interviews today, and you take the notes?"

"Really? So, I will write up the report as well?"

"Rich, it will make things easier for us in the long run. Believe me, it won't be the last time we have to do something like this. The next time, I will take the notes, draft the report, and you can take the lead in conducting the interviews. How does that sound?"

"OK. I agree. Well, you're going to do a lot of talking today, and I'm going to do a lot of writing," he says, and laughs. "Let's get started. I suppose we need to start with Ashot's attorney and go from there. Let's see who lawyers up and who won't speak to us. Ashot just couldn't keep his mouth shut. Disappointing, but I'm not surprised."

By midafternoon, we've already interviewed five or six individuals from Miller's list. We save the more interesting players from Golden ADA for the later part of the day.

Art Roggenbuck, Simon Lemke, and Shane Sullivan are the last ones we are planning to speak with. We find Roggenbuck alone in his office. "Art Roggenbuck, Private Investigator," the brass plaque reads on the entry door. It is a modest office suite with similar type businesses on the same floor of the rundown office building.

As soon as I step into Roggenbuck's office, it feels as though I have traveled back in time to another era, to the offices of none other than Jake Gittes, PI, the main character in the Roman Polanski classic film, "Chinatown."

Roggenbuck is no Jake Gittes, judging by physical appearance at least.

I am taken back to my newspaper delivery days. The Artful Dodger character from the movie Oliver Twist was what we all called him in those days, the grossly overweight newspaper representative who would visit us weekly to collect the fees paid by the customers on our routes. We never called him Art or Arty.

To us, he was the Artful Dodger until someone came up with a better nickname.

Art Roggenbuck had spent his last year in Golden ADA as CEO until Gossain bought the company from Kozlenok and had him removed.

By all rights, he should at least be an interesting character to sit down and talk to.

"Gentlemen, good to make your acquaintance. How can I assist you? Please take a seat."

His tone is welcoming, unassuming, and disarming.

I am not swayed. He is a clever, sly fox, no doubt about it.

"We are hoping you can give us information concerning the Shagirians and these recent threats."

I deliberately keep the question open ended and vague. Roggenbuck may try to portray himself to us as an easygoing, back-slapping, good old boy, but he is anything but.

In reality, he is an astute, politically connected and savvy operator, having previously managed San Francisco Mayor Jordan's campaign. It is not his first rodeo, not by a long shot.

"Yeah, I heard something about Gossain threatening Shagirian. Actually, Shagirian called me about it. Told him he should go talk to the FBI if he's genuinely concerned. I really don't know this Gossain guy. As soon as he arrived at Golden ADA, he kicked me to the curb."

With a few carefully chosen words, Roggenbuck has distanced himself from the company, from Shagirian, and, importantly, from any criminal or civil liability exposure.

Marino and I decided beforehand not to ask Roggenbuck about Golden ADA unless he opens the door first. He says nothing about his time at the company, nothing about Golden ADA, and nothing about his previous boss, Andrey Kozlenok.

Does he suspect we're already familiar with Golden ADA, and have been investigating the company and its players? Possibly. It is difficult for me to judge.

At the end of the interview, we exchange business cards. Marino and I depart his office on good terms. The door is open for further contact as Roggenbuck isn't about to leave San Francisco soon. It is his home city, and home base. It's possible we'll cross paths again with this Artful Dodger before our chess match ends.

"Well, shall we? It's about time to call on our former California State Senator," I tell Marino. "This ought to be interesting. At least I hope so."

I ask Marino to stop a few blocks away so we can talk before heading to Lemke.

"Rich, How do we want to play this? The guy was general counsel for Golden ADA until recently. Heck, he was in Moscow with Roggenbuck not long ago, lobbying the Russian government to keep on bankrolling Golden ADA, with diamonds. But he is, or was, an elected official, and he's still a politician, and 'of counsel' at that high-powered law firm."

"Let's just get in there and do this. We may learn something, you never know. I'll follow your lead. I'm most eager to hear what nickname you'll come up with for Simon, after the 'Artful Dodger.' Please don't disappoint me," he says with a heavy sigh. "OK. Game on," Marino says as he steps out of the vehicle and closes the door.

"Hey, that's my line!"

"Oh, I meant 'game time,' not 'game on.' Sorry."

The secretary guides us to the immense corner office of Simon Lemke, no doubt the largest in the firm. It is the most ornate law office I have ever set foot in, beyond anything I have ever seen, even while summer clerking during my law school days with some of the most prestigious firms in New York and Philadelphia.

There he is, Simon Lemke, sitting comfortably behind the massive mahogany desk.

I already sense where he wants us to sit.

He is going to remain seated behind his desk while we talk to him. I spot a coffee table and furniture in another corner; that would be an acceptable seating arrangement, offering us far greater comfort and putting us all on the same level.

But no. For sure, he will want us to sit in those two uncomfortable looking chairs while he remains safe, fortified behind his protective barrier, the desk.

The thought crosses my mind to just walk out. We will gain nothing, learn nothing.

Lemke has known of our impending visit for the entire day, plenty of time for him to rehearse and to prepare for our arrival and for our questions.

But we have to check the box regardless.

We have no choice but to talk to him, to at least exchange business cards. It is too late to regroup or change our approach. But I do not intend for Marino and me to sit in those two ridiculous chairs, with Lemke calling the shots from behind his desk.

His office and entire persona tell me he is a power broker and well connected. That is the message he wants to convey. He doesn't stand or step away from his desk to greet us.

This former State Senator is in charge, not us. He could pick up the phone and call my boss, Rick Webb, or perhaps Director Freeh, in Washington.

But I cannot allow him to exploit the power dynamics of the room, and of his standing. It doesn't matter to me who he can call or to whom he is connected.

I'm going to conduct this interview on my terms and not accept the power dynamics even though we're on his turf, inside his imposing space.

To shift the power dynamics, I need to act, and quickly.

On his wall, I notice an array of impressive paintings and a series of photographs, immediately shifting gears and commenting on the display, surveying the impressive array.

I remain on my feet, standing my ground. Rich Marino stands close to me, giving me a look, a bit perplexed, but we've worked with one another for some time.

I have to assume he understands what I'm doing, that I need to pull Lemke away from behind his desk, away from his protective shield, to shift the power dynamics in the room.

Finally, Lemke slowly stands and walks over to us. We shake hands, and the conversation begins. For the next several minutes, I ask about the individuals depicted in the photographs. The photos are a virtual who's who of local, state, and national political movers and shakers.

Lemke appears to relax, seeming to enjoy the unexpected casual back-and-forth discussion. He tells us about the photos, along with each of the individuals depicted.

I deliberately avoid mentioning the alleged threats, nor do I make any reference to Ashot or his brother David. I decide not to ask probing questions about Golden ADA, or about Lemke's previous affiliation with the company.

Yet, I have now taken control of the interview on my terms, and in my way.

Whether Lemke is processing what I am doing, it does not matter to me.

What matters is not revealing anything of any substance to him.

If he thinks Marino and I are not very astute investigators, so be it. To pose any question regarding the issue at hand, the alleged threat and what he knows or doesn't know, is to reveal something. And I do not want to reveal anything to this former Golden ADA general counsel, and former state senator. There is absolutely nothing to gain. I would be moving the chess piece and taking my hand off of it. No, I will not touch that piece, not today at least.

We exchange business cards after nearly twenty minutes of casual conversation, all while standing. I make one vague reference to Lemke's work as general counsel for Golden ADA in the past. He doesn't bite or react to my comment.

I will not open the door a second time for him.

As far as I can tell, he takes the two of us as nothing more than knuckle-dragging Feds, nowhere near the level of his elite society world, not by a long shot.

We depart his office on good terms, and he tells us his door is always open if we would like to speak with him in the future.

Once outside, Marino turns to me, shaking his head.

"Yep. He thinks you are dumb, and I am dumber."

"Rich, that's just the way it has to be sometimes. We would get nothing out of that interview. He would have stayed barricaded behind his desk if I hadn't done what I did. He would never tell us anything of value or relevance. But we had to meet him. So, it's done, over. Granted, we got nothing from him, but he got nothing from us either. Thanks for going along with it. Guess you know me better than I realize.

"Rich, we did our jobs, held our egos in check. We surprised him and put him off balance. I don't think he expected us to behave the way we did. Let him wonder about our intentions and interview methods all he wants. But he's too arrogant to give it a second thought, believe me. If we ever talk to this former state senator again, the next time, it will be on our terms, not his. Mission accomplished, Rich. Enough for today. Let's go home."

"Hey. What about his nickname? You promised," Marino says jokingly.

"San Simeon, the castle-like residence of the publisher and politician William Randolph Hearst. Fitting, huh?"

"OK, I suppose. But I prefer 'rhyming Simon,' just has a better ring to it. No matter, 'San Simeon' will have to suffice, for now," Marino says.

There is one more interview yet to be conducted.

SFPD Lt. Shane Sullivan awaits.

But tomorrow.

# Chapter 36

"It's your AUSA," is all Miller says as I pick up my phone. He sounds as if he is in a good mood this early morning.

"Oh, my AUSA? What's up? Another attorney has contacted you today?" I ask jokingly.

"Actually, yes. This time, it's the attorney for Shane Sullivan. I guess Shane heard you and Marino were running around the city yesterday interviewing Golden ADA staff, and he probably feels left out. Who knows, maybe he's wondering why you haven't spoken with him yet, or perhaps he's looking forward to it," he adds with a bit of sarcasm.

"Yeah, we also didn't speak with—and won't be speaking with—Rajiv Gossain, since he's a potential subject of the investigation. Sullivan knows the drill. Subjects are the last to be interviewed, if ever. They are indicted and then arrested."

"Yep. Well, what about you and Joe Doherty getting out there and talking to him? He's already lawyered up, so his attorney will be in the room with you. I told his attorney we have no present plans to indict Sullivan. We don't, right?" Miller asks.

"I wish I could say yes, but no, Terry, no current plans."

I later meet up with Doherty to discuss our strategy when we interview Sullivan. I sit in the chair next to Doherty's desk.

"Ashot told us Sullivan was in the room when the threats were being made by Gossain, and Sullivan just sat there. The bottom line for us is to convince Sullivan to cooperate fully. Look, he survived the transition from Kozlenok to Roggenbuck, and now to Gossain. He has seen a lot; we don't know the extent. You know how I feel about him, but if he wants to cooperate, he's going to have to wire up. It's that simple. I think that possibility is remote, don't you, Joe? A high-ranking SFPD official wiring up against whom? Gossain?

"Perhaps others at Golden ADA? Once Shane Sullivan sees me, it will dawn on him I've been investigating Golden ADA for a long time. Well, it should dawn on him. There will be a lot of thoughts racing through his head, that's for sure."

"So, we listen to what he has to say, and avoid revealing anything about our case, and what we know, right?" Doherty asks.

"Yep. I don't think we'll need to say much. Sullivan will talk a lot, it's his nature. Remember what I told you about the lunch we had together a couple of years back? Believe me, he is going to talk. It may be a lot of self-serving nonsense. Granted, he already knows what he'll say and feels safe to admit to. He's had plenty of time to prepare. We don't have direct evidence against him as far as his criminal involvement in the extortion, these threats.

"But if he's more involved than we realize, he may be worried we've already caught him talking on a Title III, or on a recording somehow. The other factor possibly weighing heavily on his mind may relate to the other conspirators. He may suspect one or more individuals involved have already stepped forward and are cooperating with us."

"Well, let's get on with it. He'll come to the office late this afternoon with his attorney. I already reserved a room for us. It's showtime!" Doherty says with a grin.

In that moment, he reminds me of none other than Chuck Barris, the creator and wacky host of TV's outrageous 1970s "The Gong Show."

I start the conversation as soon as the introductions are over. Sullivan seems to recognize me from our one prior engagement, but I am not certain. He and his attorney sit across the table from Doherty and me.

"We're talking to many people these days, as you probably have heard."

I want to put Sullivan off balance immediately and let his thoughts wander about who may already be cooperating with us. We go through the routine background questions to include his current position ... positions.

Doherty then steps in. "Shane, just for the record, you are here voluntarily, you are not under arrest, and you can leave at any time. We will not give you Miranda warnings, since you are not in custody. You understand, correct?"

"Yes. I got it, understood," Sullivan says and nods. He seems agitated, a bit wired, and I glimpse his leg moving up and down rapidly. He is doing his best not to reveal tension and anxiety, but his body, his leg, is giving it all away. The nervous tic doesn't stop.

Doherty continues, "You've worked at Golden ADA for a long time, Shane."

"Yes, but I'm only responsible for security, protecting the employees and the company's assets." He does not specifically mention diamonds.

"How about threats? Threats made to employees, staff, and former staff, is that part of your job responsibilities to deal with things like that? You're still a sworn police officer at SFPD, right?" I decide to push his buttons. "What can you tell us, from your long experience there, about your dealings with threats like that?"

I am waiting for his attorney to step in and object, but he doesn't.

Sullivan moves both legs, so rapidly that the nervous tic has now travelled up through his torso, to his arms. Soon, his entire body is vibrating and shaking. The tic beginning with one leg has spread. It is surreal to sit across from a senior and experienced law enforcement officer who appears unable to control or quieten his body.

Doherty and I exchange a quick glance. Do we comment on what's happening, or let it go, for now? I decide to remain silent about what I'm observing.

Doherty does the same and says nothing. I find myself speechless and can't help but stare at Sullivan, now literally buzzing in place as he sits there in the chair, facing us.

The flashback hits me hard, out of nowhere, right in the middle of this interview. I feel myself zoning out but can't suppress or control it. I now see Uncle John, the corrupt detective, where Sullivan is sitting and shaking uncontrollably. My aunt is crying, and so are my cousins. My uncle has just shot himself with his service revolver. He is dead.

The circumstances leading to death by his service weapon are murky and unclear.

In the next instant, I am transported back to the classroom in law school. In front of my class is former NYPD detective Robert Leuci, the one and only "Prince of the City."

He tells our small group of third-year law students about his amazing journey from his days as a corrupt narcotics detective to his undercover cooperation with the U.S. Attorney's Office. The case results in the arrest and prosecution of judges, attorneys, and NYPD officers.

AUSA Rudy Giuliani, now Mayor of New York City, starts the investigation when he convinces Leuci to work with him and the FBI.

Leuci is as tight as a drum as he speaks with us. He is also shaking.

This is a guy on the razor's edge. He asks us if we have ever heard of him, and if any of us have read the book, "Prince of the City" or have heard about the soon-to-be-released motion picture of the same name, with Treat Williams in the lead role.

Doherty kicks my foot under the table to bring me back.

He gives me a look. It is now my turn to speak.

Surprisingly, Sullivan agrees to wear a wire and secretly record conversations with Rajiv Gossain about the alleged extortionate threats made against the Shagirian brothers.

We agree I will meet Sullivan alone this evening, to outfit him with the concealable device, and to send him into the meeting. Sullivan signs the consent forms to wear the device and record the conversation. He soon departs with his attorney.

"Hey, you sort of zoned out on me for a few minutes in there. Are you OK?" Doherty asks.

"Yeah, I'm fine. Well, that was interesting, and surprising, huh?"

I have never before outfitted a "nagra," the Bureau term used for the concealable recording device on the body of a sworn police detective. This will be a first for me.

I have mixed feelings about it. To wire up someone I have strong suspicions is himself corrupt does not sit well, but this may be the first step in what could be the start of a long journey with SFPD Lt. Sullivan. Or it could be a one-time event, depending on the outcome of the meeting. No matter, it is game on for tonight.

"Shane, you need to take off your jacket, and your shirt," I tell him in the now empty, but secure, FBI parking lot. I unwrap the rigging for the nagra device and anchor it around his torso with the microphones on his chest. "Don't worry, Shane, I've done this many times, and neither the device nor the microphones will move or emit any sound. But let's test everything to be sure, and for you to feel comfortable."

We test the equipment, and it works perfectly.

The quality of the recording from a nagra is usually superb and clear.

I hope this will be no exception.

Sullivan appears far more relaxed this evening than he was during the afternoon interview. I figure he may have had a few drinks or taken something to calm down.

I need him to be relaxed for his dinner meeting with Gossain. Gossain likely knows the Shagirian brothers are cooperating with the FBI and may be guarded when speaking with Sullivan. I don't know the dynamics between them but I am soon to find out.

We agree to meet afterwards in the same secure and deserted Bureau parking lot. I tell Sullivan to take his time and not rush through the meeting.

"If Gossain wants to talk, let him talk," I tell Sullivan. "Don't interrupt and don't be pushy with him. I know you've conducted many interviews as a detective, so you probably don't need me to explain stuff like this to you."

I feel as though I am briefing a new and untested confidential source. In a way, he is, although he is a high-ranking law enforcement officer in SFPD.

The tricky part is that he may be corrupt and compromised too. During our afternoon meeting, he admitted nothing, and claimed he was not in the room when Gossain was allegedly threatening Ashot Shagirian. I suspect otherwise but have no way of proving it. He soon departs in his vehicle, heading for the meeting with Gossain at the restaurant.

I wait for him in the parking lot, and in less than three hours, he is back. He removes his jacket and shirt, and I detach the device from his torso. "

How'd it go?" I ask.

"I think it went fine. Gossain was mostly relaxed, but a bit edgy with me at times. You'll have to listen to the tape. I don't recall any direct admissions about the threats, but it was a free-flowing and lengthy conversation."

Sullivan's take on the meeting does not surprise me at all. He was no doubt keyed up for the meeting, and perhaps more focused on protecting his own hide than trying to elicit incriminating statements from Gossain concerning the alleged threat.

I listen carefully to the entire recording the next day at my office. Unfortunately, there are no admissions from Gossain, not even a hint. Sullivan did not turn off the recording device during the meeting, that much I can tell, but it doesn't mean he didn't somehow signal Gossain that he was being recorded. The thought lingers in my mind.

The bottom line for me is that Shagirian's panic attack after Doherty and I met him, running to his attorney's office, and his attorney then disclosing the news to others, closes the door on any possibility of obtaining incriminating evidence against Gossain and others.

As I sit quietly in my office chair, pondering my next move, a thought suddenly emerges. Perhaps Ashot and his brother David are more astute than Doherty and I give them credit for.

Ashot's disclosures to his attorney that he was going to work with the FBI could have had precisely the effect he and his brother wanted all along. After all, Gossain and Kozlenok are now on notice of the Bureau's involvement, and that they themselves could now be targets of a serious criminal investigation. Is that enough incentive for them to back down and not carry out their deadly threats against the Shagirian brothers?

Are the Shagirian brothers that calculating? Could this be reason enough to deter Gossain and Kozlenok from taking any action to harm them? Possibly. Either way, the Shagirian brothers are taking an enormous risk with their own safety and security.

After listening to the tape again with Doherty, we both reach the conclusion Sullivan's usefulness as a potential cooperating source or witness is limited, at best.

It will be Sullivan's first and only time that I wire him up for such a meeting.

Shane Sullivan will never become a Prince of the City like former NYPD narcotics detective Bob Leuci. That much is certain to me.

# Chapter 37

"Annie, you are sure he's gone?" I ask, after Nazari calls for a meeting. "It's not just a business trip or something like that?"

"No. Nina tells me Andrey is gone, really gone. He's somewhere in Mexico, maybe Costa Rica. Even she doesn't know. After Gossain threatened David and Ashot, Andrey freaked out. Apparently, he is convinced the FBI will arrest him."

"Annie, that's not true. I don't know why he would think that unless he's getting paranoid and panicking. How is Nina taking this?"

"She's pretty calm. She tells me she would like to talk to the FBI herself. I've never told her I've been working with you, but I've told her I know some people in law enforcement who could arrange such a meeting."

"If she were to come in to talk, we can't make her any promises. Not for immunity, not for permanent residency, nothing like that. That said, let me give it a bit of thought. With Andrey out of Golden ADA, it might be OK for me to meet with her and see what she has to say.

"I'll get back to you, and Annie, please don't forget to never reveal to anyone about working with me and with the Bureau. Promise?"

"Yes. I would never do that."

I reach out to Doherty about Nina.

We conclude there isn't much downside to talking with her.

"Let's do it. When can she come into the office? We can show her copies of cancelled checks from Andrey's account made payable to his girlfriend to 'motive' her cooperation," Doherty says, only half joking.

"Yep, a woman scorned. OK. I'll see when she's available, and get back to you," I tell Doherty.

Two days later, Nina Kozlenok and Annie Nazari come to the office together.

Doherty and I are there to greet them.

Nina shows poise and calmness. She is sharply dressed in a business suit. She and Annie Nazari would be a dynamic and lethal pair if they were to team up together to do business or something nefarious, it strikes me.

Doherty and I run through standard background questions for Nina and gradually shift to a more focused line of inquiry to gauge her knowledge of the day-to-day operations of Golden ADA, in the days when her husband, Andrey, was running the company.

"Andrey kept a lot of things from me. He used to ask me for advice on some matters, but there were a lot of things he never shared with me. He liked to have me around whenever we had client or customer gatherings to help promote business, that sort of thing."

I want to believe everything she is telling me, and in the male-dominated business world, it is a believable story. However, my gut tells me there is more here than meets the eye. When Annie Nazari first met Nina at that gala, she described Nina in considerable detail, as a sharp woman, capable of doing far more than Andrey was allowing her.

Is Nina ambitious, and the real brains behind the entire operation, whispering in Andrey's ear, telling him what businesses to buy, what investments to make, who to trust, and who not to trust? Perhaps even putting a bug in his ear that he should leave the United States?

Highly educated, she is, or was, one of the elites of Russian society.

She speaks four or five languages fluently. So, she can try to portray herself as an innocent victim but the reality is likely something else entirely.

Doherty and I need to be careful not to reveal more than we should to such a person, to the charming wife of Andrey Kozlenok. Even if their marriage is strained, it may be nothing more than a calculated illusion, all created for our consumption.

No doubt we are still in a chess match, and Nina may be a chess master in her own right. No matter. I can't help but like her. There is something that seems genuine and nice about this woman. But it could be part of her charm campaign, nothing more.

We end the meeting on good terms as we present our business cards to her. At the very least, we have now established a direct line of communication with Nina, the wife of Andrey Kozlenok, all thanks to Ms. Annie Nazari.

Does Nina know where all the skeletons are hidden, or where missing assets—diamonds and other valuables—have been stashed away? That remains to be seen. Doherty and I decide not to push the issue. She isn't going anywhere, according to Annie Nazari at least.

While our analysis of all the subpoenaed documents isn't yet complete, there is no smoking gun showing that Nina is, in fact, inside of the conspiracy.

But our analysis is far from complete.

Aleksandr Filippov and his MVD squad of untouchables is also still out there, compiling their evidence, and uncovering more and more.

The clock for Nina may be ticking. We just don't hear it, not yet.

When my phone rings several days later, it is none other than Andrey Kozlenok on the other end. I am not surprised.

Nina has likely given him my telephone number, which I expected her to do.

"Andrey, thanks for reaching out to me. I understand you aren't in California right now. When are you returning? We need to talk," I tell him in Russian.

He answers me in perfect English. "I don't know. I am developing new businesses at the moment, in Mexico, and will soon leave for Central America. There are wonderful opportunities here."

"I can imagine, Andrey. But listen to me in case we get disconnected. Andrey, you haven't been indicted. We have no plans to arrest you. You need to return to California as soon as possible. Your family is here. We can sit down and talk this through once you are back."

"I hear what you are saying, but it is a very difficult and stressful situation for me as you can imagine. I have done nothing wrong. In fact, I am the actual victim. Many others all around have duped me, forcing me to do things I didn't want to do. I had to hand over my company, and now it is in the hands of that Rajiv Gossain. I had no choice.

"They have taken virtually everything from me, leaving me with nothing. Do you understand how difficult things are for me right now?"

He does not sound desperate to me. Nor does he seem panicked. He sounds genuine, but even on the run, he is a master manipulator, portraying himself as a victim. It takes everything for me not to laugh aloud.

Andrey Kozlenok is anything but a victim. A self-promoting fraudster, conman, perhaps, but he is no victim. He seems to have drunk his own Kool-Aid.

"Andrey, if they arrest you and take you back to Russia for trial, your fate will be out of my hands. You are better off returning to the United States. You must realize this. There is nowhere for you to hide, Andrey. You may be a victim as you say, but you are a marked man. They will find you no matter where you go, and no matter where you try to hide.

"Don't play games with them, Andrey. This is no chess match where you can outmaneuver or out strategize your opponents. Think about it and call me back whenever you like. Anytime, day or night, but soon. I am here, waiting for you."

I shift my closing words back into Russian to emphasize my point.

The line goes dead. It is the first and last time I will ever speak with Andrey Kozlenok.

# Chapter 38

"Here, look at this," Sharon says as she hands me a document.

"What is this? A vacancy notice for the assistant legal attaché position in Moscow? Really? Is Bob Backus leaving already?" I ask.

"Appears so. Don told me to give this to you before he left work today."

"What do you think, Sharon? Shall I?"

"Apply? Of course. This odyssey, my brave Odysseus, is slowly but surely coming to its end. But other adventures await you, just over the horizon, far to the east, across the vast ocean separating the new world from the old."

"You're quite dramatic today, and you've been reading the Iliad. Good for you. I will apply, and if it is my destiny, so be it. No man or woman born, coward or brave, can shun his destiny."

I look at the vacancy notice. "I don't know what my chances are of being selected, but I'll put my name in. Why not? But keep it between us for now. OK?"

"Yes, definitely. Well, there's still plenty of work awaiting us here. What's the latest with the Title III?"

"Not a lot of activity, unfortunately. With Andrey Kozlenok in the wind, the Shagirian brothers gone, and Rajiv Gossain in charge, things have changed dramatically and slowed. I think most of the real action is in Moscow, with Aleksandr Filippov and his team in the middle of the whirlwind. I just hope they're being careful."

An eerie quiet ensues for the next several weeks.

Filippov calls to tell me they are close to charging several high-ranking officials for abuse of official position, bribery, and other crimes. I tell him Kozlenok has fled, and it doesn't appear likely he'll return to the United States soon.

The quiet breaks in a sudden, dramatic manner, like some mysterious ghost wave smashing into the bow of a ship. Something like that.

Doherty calls me, so furious he can barely speak. "I can't believe they, well, he, Miller, did this. The IRS raided Brannan Street this morning. They are seizing the premises, carting away stuff. It's a mess. The case is a mess."

"I didn't know, Joe. But I'm not surprised. There've been rumblings about the huge unpaid tax bill for them, which is nearly seventy million. Let me call Miller and sort this out."

Miller explains he only got a heads up from the IRS Civil Division of their intention to seize the premises the day before.

"It's outside of my control. The IRS Civil Division has the power to seize assets for nonpayment of business taxes. It's done. Heck, looks like Gossain had already started liquidating the company's assets. If the IRS had waited much longer, there would have been nothing left, nothing," Miller tells me.

"Terry, FYI, Doherty is incensed because nobody informed him."

"Heck, no one told me either. That's the IRS for you. Their civil division doesn't always coordinate with their own criminal division.

"Hey, on the good news side, the Shagirian brothers are facing serious criminal tax evasion charges. I've already spoken to their attorney. They may submit to a proffer arrangement. It will allow them to tell us their side of the story, with their receiving qualified immunity. You game for talking to them? You and Marino? They are moving to Florida, near Tampa, I understand."

"Sure. But what about Brannan Street? Are IRS examiners there now?"

Miller says, "Yep. They're seizing automobiles, diamond cutting and polishing equipment, paintings, artwork, rough and cut diamonds ... They've already attached liens to bank accounts, and on businesses of Golden ADA, Shako Real Estate, Shako Air, among their many other subsidiaries. Boy, those guys were on top of the world. It's pretty much over for them now. What a fall, what a fall." Miller repeats the phrase as his voice trails off.

"Terry, things are far from over. I am heading over to Brannan Street. I've never been inside of that building, you know. 999 Brannan Street; who can forget such a number? Turn it upside down, and it's the sign of the devil. Fitting, huh?"

I show my FBI credentials to the IRS inspectors guarding the entrance and I am waved into the headquarters building of Golden ADA, a massive structure and operation.

I walk through several offices to find the diamond cutting rooms, full of specialized equipment. I open a few drawers, seeing diamonds everywhere.

There are loose diamonds inside of drawers, on tables, affixed to the cutting and polishing machines. Rough and polished stones of all shapes and sizes, everywhere.

I can only assume and hope hidden cameras are in place to prevent unauthorized personnel from simply walking out the door with precious stones stuffed inside their pockets.

At that moment, I realize I am neither enamored nor impressed with the shiny little stones. In fact, I conclude I don't like diamonds, feeling no connection, no attachment, and no attraction to these small, cold, and inanimate objects.

I slowly walk up several flights of stairs to the executive office wing.

The photos hanging on the executive wing's walls freeze me in my tracks. I stand there alone and stare. There are photos of Andrey, David, Ashot, Nina, the "Artful Dodger" Roggenbuck, and "San Simeon" Lemke. There are also photographs of Andrey, David, and Ashot posing with U.S. Vice President Al

Gore, and with First Lady Hillary Clinton, along with other political figures of some notoriety, federal, state, and local.

Kyrisha, "roof," the word springs into my mind. It's all about having that special "roof," for protection, and to project an image of power and influence.

It seems like most of the photos were taken at political fund-raising events.

Standing in front of the photo of Andrey, I gaze at his image. "It's check, Andrey. Your 'kyrisha' has collapsed. When you needed them most, your so-called friends abandoned you. Your money didn't buy the influence, power, and protection you thought it would," I whisper as I continue to study the photographs.

There is no one else. I am alone in the executive wing.

"It's your move, Andrey. It's 'check' and soon, it will be 'checkmate.' The clock is ticking for you, my dear Andrey. You are nearly out of time."

The end is near, I can feel it. But it isn't checkmate, not yet. I walk out of the building into brilliant sunshine and reach for my sunglasses. The San Francisco morning fog has finally lifted, for now. The IRS later confirms it is the largest civil seizure—some $70 million in business assets—in the history of their northern California regional office.

***

"So, how do you want to play this play, this next act?" Rich Marino says as he turns toward me, cramped in the middle seat on the full flight bound for Tampa.

"How? I will take the notes and write up the report. As agreed, remember?"

"I thought you had forgotten. I don't mind either way."

"No, Rich. My turn, and my promise. We never broke promises where I grew up, never."

For the next two days, Marino and I sit in the spacious home of the Shagirians and conduct the agreed upon proffer interviews.

We start with David. He takes us back to the beginning, to 1991, and to that first meeting with Andrey Kozlenok. His story starts in a mystical world, the theater.

It's fitting. The theater, after all, is the place where all disbelief is suspended.

Grigor Azarian had been a producer in a Moscow theater, becoming acquainted with Kozlenok because of his own theater interest.

Azarian had already been a friend of the Shagirian family for several years.

Azarian eventually moved to California and in late 1991, he reached out to David and told him he was bringing some "interesting Russian people" which included Andrey Kozlenok, to meet him and his brother Ashot.

David was working as a handyman in the San Francisco area, while his brother Ashot had settled in Los Angeles. David spent several days with the three Russian visitors who said they were working for a joint venture known as Sovkuwait-Engineering.

Kozlenok boasted he was one of the first real businessmen in all of Russia, and he was working on many government type projects, including "a big fight with the Diamond Cartel De Beers."

David asked Kozlenok, "Who is De Beers?"

Kozlenok explained some problems experienced by the Russian government with De Beers, relating to the distribution of Russian diamonds through De Beers' channels.

Russia was losing billions of dollars a year, Kozlenok reported.

Kozlenok eventually asked if David and his brother Ashot were interested in participating in a secret project to open a diamond business in the United States, as he claimed to know the family's background in Armenia. He told them he felt he could trust them, and was confident they would eventually learn the diamond business.

David and his brother Ashot later travelled to Moscow, where Kozlenok took them on a tour of several government facilities, including gold leaf and jewelry manufacturing plants.

They brought their family jewelry with them to Moscow and handed it over to Kozlenok. Kozlenok accepted the jewelry as the downpayment for a 40-percent interest in their new venture, to be called Golden ADA, the initials of their first names. Since he was the only U.S. citizen among the three, they designated David the president of the company.

In early 1993, the Shagirians met Eugeniy Bychkov, Chairman of the Russian Committee of Precious Gems and Metals—ROSKOMDRAGMET.

Golden ADA was renting office space in the prestigious Transamerica Pyramid building in downtown San Francisco.

Bychkov informed them his committee would be sending them diamonds, gold, and jewelry items to sell on a consignment basis, of sorts. He also told them the money earned could be invested in various ventures and in Russian companies.

Bychkov mentioned De Beers, telling them it was a bad organization and they needed to be careful. Bychkov told them he was a "best friend" of Russia President Boris Yeltsin, as they had worked together for a time in the city of Sverdlovsk, now known as Yekaterinburg.

David's proffer interview takes nearly two full days.

He also tells us, in exacting detail, about the brothers' roles in dealing with the shipments of gold coins, valuables, and diamonds, rough and polished.

I find David's story concerning the Russian gold coins to Golden ADA, and what the company ultimately does with them, to be disturbing.

As David explains to us, the gold coins unexpectedly arrived at the Golden ADA vaults directly from Russia, individually wrapped in nearly eighty wooden crates.

The pristine coins had never been in circulation and were all impressed with the image of the last Russian Tsar, Tsar Nikolai II. Kozlenok directed David and Ashot to melt down the coins into gold bullion to finance the different projects on which they were working.

A cousin of the Shagirians, employed at Golden ADA, found a company in Los Angeles, Elite Imperial Metals, willing to melt down the coins into bullion.

They produced enough documentation to convince Emerson Steele, the owner of Elite Imperial Metals, that the coins had not been stolen or unlawfully acquired.

The cousin made several trips in a U-Haul van, transporting the coins to the company in Los Angeles. Eventually, they sold the gold bullion and Kozlenok allegedly took several of the gold bars to Russia to pay off corrupt officials and ensure the continuing flow of Russian diamonds into the vaults of Golden ADA.

David claims to have no information about the missing Fabergé bejeweled egg.

He heard rumors, he asserts, that Andrey acquired such an egg but David never laid eyes on the mysterious object. I make a mental note to follow up with Filippov and Melnik.

The priceless egg needs to be found as it belongs to the people of Russia, and on display in a museum, not in the greedy hands of someone like Andrey Kozlenok.

Months prior, I overheard conversations during the Title III intercepts concerning so-named "window-cut" diamonds. I had never heard the term used to describe a polished stone before; I had known diamonds were being cut and polished into a variety of shapes, which included pear, oval, round, and princess cut. Window cut was something new.

I ask David if he knows anything about window-cut diamonds.

He explains this special cut allows experts to peer inside of the rough stone to value and understand with what sort of diamond they are dealing, almost a biopsy for diamonds.

They also do it, he reports, to comply with the Russia De Beers contract, which allows only 5 percent of Russian diamond production to be shipped overseas for processing.

However, another 10-15 percent may be sent overseas if such stones are already in the process of being polished.

The window cut enables them to comply with this technical requirement, according to David. The mystery is solved, my curiosity about the mysterious window cut satisfied.

David speaks extensively about the circumstances of the brothers' eventual falling out with Kozlenok, and with Bychkov.

The details, provided by David, and later by his brother Ashot, closely track what Annie Nazari reported to me months before, including the threat of a bullet in their heads if the Shagirians ever disclose anything about their activities during their time at Golden ADA.

As we finally end the long interview on the second day, David tells us he has something for me, something he has been holding for a long time. It is my FBI business card.

I ask him how he has come into possession of it.

He tells me SFPD Lt. Shane Sullivan, the head of security at the time for Golden ADA, gave it to him after we met in that North Beach Italian restaurant a few years prior.

According to David, when Sullivan handed him my business card, he also told him the FBI was interested in Golden ADA's activities, and he wanted to make sure Dave and Ashot Shagirian were aware of this.

I am disappointed but not surprised to hear the story. My gut and instinct told me that Sullivan was corrupt and couldn't be trusted. I take the business card from David's hand, and thank him for sharing the story, and for returning the card to me.

The Shagirian brothers will eventually plead guilty to federal criminal tax evasion charges in U.S. District Court. Their high-flying days with the San Francisco and Moscow elites has ended. However, the case remains far from done.

# Chapter 39

In mid-1996, I am selected for the position of Assistant Legal Attaché in Moscow. My wife and our young children accept and embrace the move to faraway Russia.

In Moscow, our son takes up ice hockey, and our daughter continues to practice ballet.

As a young American girl, she becomes the first foreigner ever admitted to the prestigious Bolshoi Theatre's Academy of Choreography.

Work-wise, the assignment is as challenging as any I will ever have with the FBI.

I am still involved in the Golden ADA case, albeit limitedly since Doherty remains in San Francisco, becoming case agent when I depart for Russia.

Doherty visits Moscow several times as there are missing diamonds and other valuables which include at least one Fabergé bejeweled egg. Assets still need to be identified and seized, not only in the United States, but also elsewhere, in Europe and in Russia.

Filippov and his team meet with me periodically, as they are busy completing their preparations for the eventual criminal trials of the primary culprits, including Bychkov and a Minister of Finance among other high-ranking Russian government officials.

Kozlenok is still in the wind.

He and his family fled first to Mexico, then to Costa Rica, and onward to Belgium. The most recent intelligence is that they may be living somewhere in Greece, under aliases.

One Moscow summer evening, Doherty and I have an invite to an INTERPOL reception at a new building they have recently acquired. As I step into the lavish palatial estate near the Russian Ministry of Foreign Affairs, I am stunned by its opulence and splendor.

I ask our INTERPOL hosts how they acquired such an impressive building for their exclusive use. They tell me it once belonged to a notorious organized crime group, recently dismantled. When I return to our offices at the U.S. Embassy the next morning, I ask Doherty to look at his list, the list he compiled of Golden ADA real estate holdings and purchases around the globe. Sure enough, on the list is that very building.

Full circle. The world is indeed "tight" as the Russian expression goes.

A few weeks later, as Doherty's temporary assignment at the legal attaché office is ending, I drive him to a meeting with

Lazar Aslanbekov, the Russian lead prosecutor for the Golden ADA case. He is also handling other unrelated matters.

It is summer 1997 when we arrive at Aslanbekov's office to discuss the routine and unrelated matter. Doherty has asked me to accompany him so he can discuss the issue with the prosecutor without the help of an interpreter. Just moments after we arrive in Aslanbekov's office, his telephone rings. I ask him, in Russian, if he would like us to step outside and wait until he finishes his call. He motions for us to remain.

I hear his side of the conversation as he speaks.

"You got him now? Good," Aslanbekov says to the other party on the line.

My curiosity is now stoked. Got who? I wonder.

The conversation is brief. Aslanbekov hangs up the phone.

Before he can say another word, I ask, "Lazar, were you just talking to Aleksandr?"

"Da, yes," he responds.

"And who exactly does Aleksandr have in custody?" I then ask.

"Andrey. Andrey Kozlenok. Aleksandr is in Athens. He has taken custody of Kozlenok. They are about to board the flight to Moscow."

Russia and Greece agree to use a nineteenth century treaty between the two countries, dating from the time of the Russian Imperial Empire and the Kingdom of Greece, as the legal basis for extraditing Kozlenok from Greece to Russia to stand trial. In late 1999, Andrey Kozlenok and other conspirators face trial in a

Moscow courtroom, and the court convicts them all for crimes including abuse of power, bribery, corruption, and grand theft.

However, before President Boris Nikolaevich Yeltsin leaves office, he will grant pardons to many individuals, to include most of the Golden ADA conspirators.

Kozlenok will serve out his three-year sentence in prison and then quietly vanish to parts unknown. Bychkov will eventually return to the diamond business.

There are still missing and unaccounted-for assets and diamonds.

Filippov and his team continue their work to identify and recover those valuable items, with the continuing help of the FBI.

In U.S. District Court in San Francisco, the Russian government brings a civil lawsuit against Golden ADA to recover some of the converted assets and missing diamonds.

In the years to follow, there are several suspicious deaths related to the Golden ADA matter, to include Rajiv Gossain.

To this day, his death, and that of several others, remain unsolved, shrouded in mystery.

# Chapter 40

My family and I travel back to the United States for several weeks of R&R later that summer. The Bureau tells me to stop in at FBIHQ en route, so of course, I do so.

While there, I am told I need to submit to a polygraph before I can return to Russia. They fail to give me any reason for it. I can only suspect my work in the Golden ADA investigation is related to this, perhaps as a payback from the C-I side of the Bureau for outmaneuvering and outplaying them. Perhaps they are still holding onto their grudge.

But this is nothing more than speculation on my part. Other players and agencies were involved too; these also had their differences and issues with me.

I pass the polygraph test and duly head to Monterey for a brief check up on our home. But first, I decide to swing by the Bureau's San José office for a quick and unofficial stop.

There, I find Sharon Austin busy working at her desk; she is happy to see me, standing up from her chair to unlock her file cabinet, pulling out a large, sealed envelope.

"It's for you. Don told me to give this to you. He's on vacation but somehow knew you would swing by the office," she says as she hands me the envelope.

"Huh? What is this, Sharon?"

The full-sized official-looking envelope has what looks to be an abbreviation of some sort, OSI, printed in large lettering, and has my name filled in as addressee.

"What is OSI? I have never seen this abbreviation before. It's another agency or what?"

"You don't know anything, do you? How are you managing in Russia without me? Sit down and let me enlighten you. Like old times, huh, when you first asked me about the diamond trade. Are you ready?"

"Ready for what? No matter. Go ahead, enlighten me."

"OSI is the abbreviation for the Office of Special Investigations, a special unit in the Criminal Division of the United States Department of Justice. OSI came into being because of the efforts of a congresswoman from New York, Elizabeth Holtzman.

"She discovered the US government had a list of over fifty alleged Nazi war criminals living in the United States and was doing nothing about them. They created OSI with the mission of tracking down these Nazi murderers and ensuring they faced justice.

"Well, amazingly, to this day, the executive branch has not yet opened its files on Nazi war criminals, but this may soon change. Ironically—and please pay close attention to me—Russia, yes Russia, has already opened its archives.

"Several Eastern European countries have also done the same. Here's my research report, prepared for you. Read it carefully," she says as she hands me the folder.

"Hang on, Sharon. Let me open this envelope and see what this is all about."

I tear open the sealed envelope to find yet another sealed envelope inside.

"It's a lead to investigate. Addressed to me. Huh?"

"What is it they want you to do?" she asks.

"Find and interview some suspected Nazis," I tell her.

I stopped by the San José office only as a courtesy; instead, I am now being handed a document directing me to find and interview suspected Nazi war criminals.

"Well, Sharon, wish me luck. Hey, this Congresswoman from New York, Elizabeth Holtzman, she's the real deal, huh?"

"Yep. Just don't let her down. Now get back to Russia."

Sharon locks the file cabinet and prepares to head home for the evening. "Fair winds and following seas, Odysseus."

"I see you are still reading Homer. That's good. The Gods will favor you. Farewell for now, Sharon."

We say our last goodbyes in the Bureau's parking lot as I jump into my rented vehicle and head south to Monterey. There, I hope to catch up with my sister before heading to Moscow.

"You don't know anything, do you?" stays in my head as I drive south to Monterey.

Sharon is right. Nazi war criminals are still out there, all right. They need to be found and brought to justice. That much I now know.

Melnik was also right, that memorable evening at the Italian restaurant in Carmel, when he raised his glass, telling us we were hunters.

He and Filippov would have found my latest OSI assignment, to hunt down suspected Nazi war criminals, intriguing. They'd willingly have joined me in the quest if they could.

My sister flew into Monterey a few days earlier from Florida.

With our house unoccupied, and my family visiting relatives in New York during the summer school break, I tell her she can stay as long as she likes.

I update her on things as we walk to the beach to begin our run.

"There's lots to catch up on, isn't there? The serial killer's still out there somewhere in the shadows. But please, Jen, no more trips to Kansas City without me. Things are quiet there for now, but he'll strike again, I know. But let's not talk about such dark things," I say. "And what about that LAX woman? It would be interesting if you ran into your double while you're here, wouldn't it? I'd love to be a witness to that encounter."

"And so would I, so would I," is all she says.

I add, "And I've been thinking about our uncle Bill lately, and those UFOs; they are also out there, somewhere. Sometimes, I find I'm tempted to dig around the Bureau's archived case files. I know I'll find something. But, how about you? You still see apparitions?"

"Not every day, but I still see them occasionally. Sometimes, I don't actually see them, I just feel them, and sometimes, they just appear. They look and talk like normal, everyday people, like my encounter with the elderly couple at Cranberry Lake. And what about you?"

"Not very often. Sometimes, I can feel a presence, just like that time in Carmel. I stopped briefly in a shop when I was there with our Russian colleagues. The feeling was strong. I asked the owner of the store if his place had otherworldly guests. He looked at me as if I was from another world myself but then whispered that the shop has a presence of sorts, so he thinks. I can take you there sometime and you can see for yourself.

"Anyway, I still have flashbacks that come over me, often without warning. Something usually triggers them. My last one was intense and hit me in the middle of an interview with a corrupt detective. I sort of spaced out for a minute or two."

"Oh? Well, I get that. You and our brother were closer to Uncle John than I was. Sad, huh? I haven't seen our cousins since our uncle killed himself. I don't know what's become of them since."

"Are you still doing your research, working on your thesis, and digging up our grandfather's old cases?" I ask.

"Of course. It's important to understand the past. It's always with us, you know. Even the past we aren't yet aware of is there, influencing and guiding us in ways we can't understand or imagine. Not yet."

"Well, Jen, you've got your soccer ball, and I've got my rugby ball. Let's toss and kick these things around, then go for a run. The beach is usually quiet this time of day, just before sunset. You'll see."

We each launch our balls high into the air and give chase.

We finish the run near the beach parking lot.

My sister heads back to the house.

I have told her I'll stay just a few minutes longer to kick the rugby ball around in the sand.

Earlier, I noticed an athletic looking blonde woman running in the opposite direction, giving us a once over.

Something felt odd. My sister didn't notice her, or at least she didn't let on if she did.

The same woman now also appears to be finishing her run and heading to the parking lot. I walk through the parking area, taking the shortcut back to the house.

As she opens the driver's side door to her late model BMW roadster, she turns toward me and asks, "Well, was it worth it?"

"Huh? The run. Yes, of course. It always is," I answer her politely.

"No, your case, Special Agent Cosgrove, your case,"

Her accent is distinct and odd but feels strangely familiar. It suddenly hits me. The accent is Afrikaans. She is from the Republic of South Africa.

This woman has the same unmistakable accent I've heard before on the rugby pitch. I have experienced playing alongside ruggers with their distinct accents from across the globe, Kiwis, Pacific Islanders, English, Scots, Welsh, Aussies, Irish, and Afrikaners.

"You follow the Springboks from South Africa?" I ask her as I spiral my rugby ball high into the air.

"Of course," she answers. "And you?"

"Me? Definitely not. The New Zealand All Blacks are the only team for me, always have been. Well, since I first picked up a rugby ball, such a long time ago."

She removes her sunglasses, revealing her eyes are crystal blue, nearly translucent.

"So, was it worth it?" she repeats.

I give her a closer look. Yes, it's the same woman who was sitting alone at the restaurant bar that day, a few years back, when Rich Marino and I were meeting with Dmitri from the San Francisco Russian Consulate. She was so striking in appearance, I never forgot her.

"Of course, it was worth it. Of course. Taking on the corrupt, the empowered, those who think they are above the law and can't be touched. It's what I do, what we do in the Bureau, what we are sworn to do, for our country, and our people."

She looks at me and says nothing.

I turn away for a fleeting moment, tossing the rugby ball again high into the air, catching it, and turning back to face her.

"And as far as your diamonds, your precious stones, I hear they are manufacturing synthetic ones. You can barely tell the difference. What will you do then?"

She laughs.

"We'll see about that! The customers, and you American consumers, you will always prefer genuine diamonds, the real ones, don't you think?"

Before I can respond, she enters her vehicle and rolls down the driver's window. I am standing there, thinking I need to grab her license plate number before she speeds off.

"Well, I'm off. Good day, Special Agent Cosgrove. Oh," she says, and pauses. "Good hunting." She closes the window and speeds out of the parking lot in a cloud.

She's gone.

"Dos-vee-dan-ee-ye de-vou-ch-ka," I shout back at her vehicle as she speeds away.

The sun is setting.

I need to get off this beach.

A sneak peek of the next book

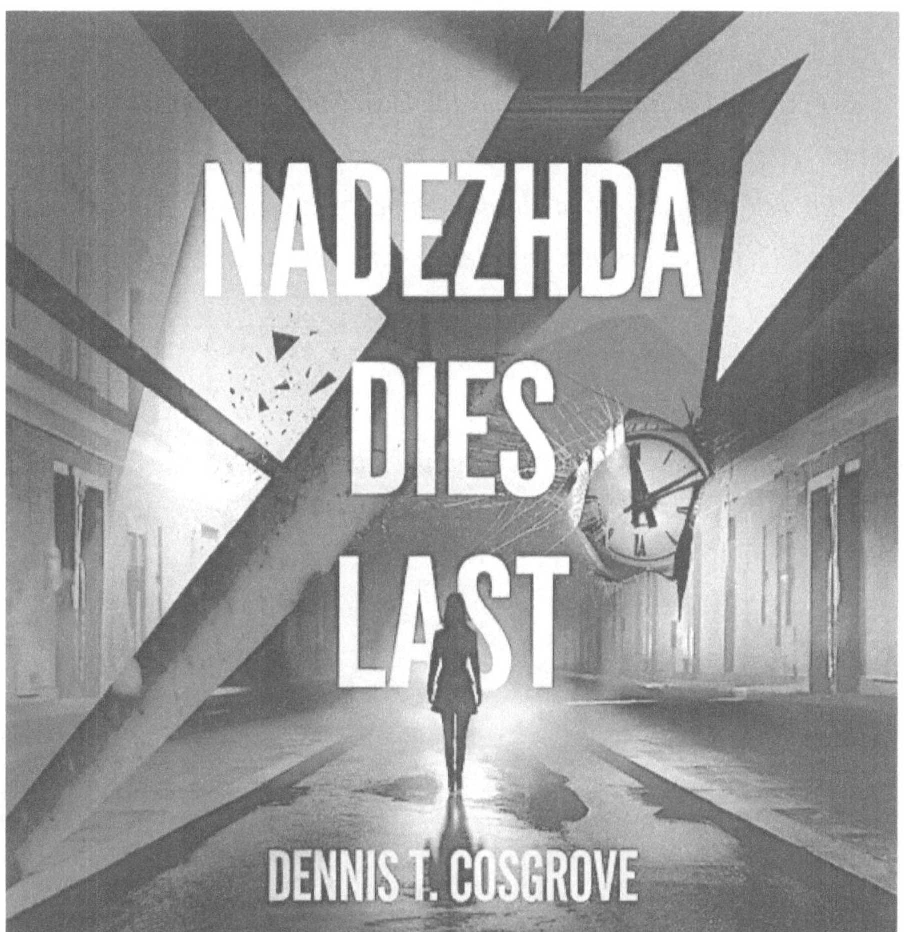

NADEZHDA
DIES
LAST
DENNIS T. COSGROVE

*Abruptly pulled from his post at the U.S. Embassy in Moscow and sent to Athens, Greece, on an urgent mission, an FBI Special Agent finds himself thrust into a deadly game of deception. A Russian supermodel has been brutally murdered—and her friend is missing.*

*The clock is ticking.*

*Can he find the missing girl and stop a killer in his tracks?*

# Chapter 1



"What did you get your mother for her last birthday?"

"Sharon, it's you?" I ask the familiar voice on the call, surprised she's even contacting me just days after saying goodbye in the San José FBI parking lot.

"Well, in 1931, the daughter of Marjorie Merriweather Post, Eleanor Barzin, gave her mother a Fabergé egg for her birthday. Now, that's quite a gift," she says.

"Yeah. I can't top that. Heck, I can't remember what I got my mother for any birthday but it wasn't a Fabergé egg, that's for sure. Where's this going, though, Sharon? Very enlightening, but I'm with my sister; we're in the car heading to Carmel for dinner. But I'm intrigued, naturally. You know me. And you've been doing more research on Fabergé, and on our mysterious and missing egg, so it seems."

"A lot of research, Odysseus, a lot. You think your odyssey is over, Special Agent Cosgrove? I think it's only begun. It would never be that easy. But you knew that all along, didn't you?"

"I'm sure going to miss you in Moscow, Sharon. A few days ago, during a courtesy visit to your office, you gave me that OSI lead. I sense you're far from done with me. Maybe toying with me a bit, perhaps?"

"Nope. I'm sending you more background on those eggs. You can pull up my full report once you're in Bureau space."

"But this isn't the real reason you're calling, is it?"

"Oh, I see you haven't forgotten the basic rules of the art of the interview, have you?"

She laughs.

"I'm not the sharpest investigator as you well know, but I have to give you credit. You've got my full attention, skipping the 'how are you doing' stuff, just like my sister here. She never bothers with the 'hi' and 'how are you doing' formalities either. You'll have to meet her someday. So, what's up? Why are you calling?"

"Yeah. You've got me there. Don called last night, told me to reach out to you. You need to go back to Washington. He didn't say why, just to tell you to get back there. He didn't sound upset or anything, but you know Don Pierce. He'll not show his hand, not to me anyway."

"OK. I was planning on leaving Monterey in a few days' time to fly to New York to meet up with family, so we can all return to Moscow together. Now, it seems I'm heading back to Washington. Regardless of the reason, can you tell me who I'm expected to meet?"

"Don said to call him as soon as you arrive, and he'll explain everything."

"Got it. Well, Sharon, since you've now revealed the actual reason for reaching out, give me the abbreviated version of your report on Fabergé eggs, and this Ms. Marjorie Merriweather Post and her daughter. My sister here's into this sort of thing, and it's not classified or law enforcement sensitive, so go ahead ... We might as well talk it through."

"OK, well, the Fabergé bejeweled egg gifted by Eleanor Barzin to her mother is known as the Catherine the Great egg, and it's on display at the Hillwood Estate Museum in Washington, along with many other items from the House of Fabergé."

"OK, so? I need to go there and steal it, photograph it, or what?"

"I'd have thought it was obvious," she says, chuckling. "You can hardly go looking for a missing Fabergé egg without having seen one up close, can you?" She leaves a timely pause for effect. "Oh, and while you're there, find the curator of the collection, introduce yourself, and let her or him educate you about this stuff, and about Ms. Post and her former husband, Joseph E. Davies. Now, Davies was the third husband of Ms. Post, heir to the Post cereal—General Mills—family fortune. While the two of them were working and living in Moscow in the 1930s, Stalin's regime was busy selling off the treasures of the Romanov family and former Russian aristocrats for hard currency. Davies and Post just happened to be there at the opportune time, buying everything they could get their hands on in the pre-war days, to include items from the House of Fabergé. And that included the bejeweled eggs, of course."

"And do I mention searching for the missing egg? Like you say, I'm not even sure what it looks like. But you know who told me she once glimpsed it? Heck, a part of me believes she's got her hands on that egg. Perhaps Nina gave it to her to hold for a while. Anything's possible."

"Dennis, we can talk about that another time. Just so you don't sound like a complete moron if you talk to the curator, based on my research, there are two prime candidates for the egg that Andrey Kozlenok likely has, or had: the 1909 Alexander III Commemorative egg, and the 1903 Royal Danish egg. As far as photos of them, well, that's another story but I've sent you detail in my report that you should find useful."

"Thanks, Sharon. We'll be talking again soon, I have a feeling … So many questions and issues remaining unresolved. Not sure where all of this is heading … the OSI lead you 'gifted' me, the missing Fabergé egg, and now this unexpected stop in Washington. But that's for another day. So, au revoir—or dos-vee-dan-i-ye—for now. The Romanovs spoke mostly French amongst themselves, you know."

I hang up the phone and look at my sister sitting in the car, looking straight out the windshield. I've seen that expression on her face before.

"OK, Jen. What's up? You heard most of that call. You look like you want to say something. What? It's my life, Jen. I'm just along for the ride," I tell her.

"Hmm. Give me a minute. I'm processing all of this. So, Sharon calls you out of the blue and tells you that you need to go to Washington, then gives you a briefing about that missing Fabergé egg. I have a feeling your life's about to get way more complicated, Dennis.

"Well, let's leave that all aside for now. Take me to that shop where you felt the presence of that poltergeist or whatever it was. Then we can have dinner at that Italian restaurant your Russian friends liked so much."

"Sure. Promise me one thing when we walk into that shop. Don't suddenly fall into some sort of hypnotic trance or start speaking in tongues," I tell her, only half joking.

"Yeah, I promise," she remarks. "Funny thing is that this will be the first time we're 'operational' together, taking on an otherworldly entity. Seems only fitting in a way, don't you think? Will be an excellent test for us as a team, right?"

I open the door to the quaint shop, full of an assortment of sundries ranging from pocket watches to knives and kitchen utensils. Some items look new, and some appear older and used, perhaps gained from an estate sale. We've barely set foot in the shop when an item—a wine bottle opener with some sort of emblem—tumbles off a shelf onto the floor a few feet in front of us. My sister and I exchanges glances as I stoop to pick it up. The emblem is a double-headed eagle, the symbol from the days of the Russian Imperial Empire. I shake my head.

The sound of the item falling is probably what brings out the owner from behind the counter, peering around before his brows rise and his eyes light up. He seems to recognize me from my prior visit, the time when I asked him about his 'otherworldly' guest.

He takes the opener from my hand, returning it to its proper place on the shelf.

"He's letting us know he's here, and he's happy you're back," he tells me. "At least, I think he's happy. If he wasn't, you'd be picking up one of those knives, not this unique wine key bottle opener. Perhaps it's meant for you to buy?"

I want to chuckle; is he really hopeful of a sale? It would be rude to laugh if so.

"I'll take it," says Jennifer to my surprise, stepping forward and taking the opener back off the display shelf. "I could use one of these, and this one looks like it has a history. Besides, how can I not buy it when it comes with a rather unique recommendation?"

"For you, mademoiselle, it's yours for free," the owner tells her.

So, he wasn't angling for a sale after all.

My sister smiles, then leans forward, kissing the owner on both cheeks.

"Yeah, my brother told me about your mysterious friend, but you've no reason to be concerned. He's a harmless fellow, just wants to be acknowledged and appreciated sometimes."

"Yes? You think so?" the owner asks her.

"Absolutely. Merci, cher ami," she tells him in perfect French.

He's captivated, kissing her hand.

"OK, sis. Let's go. You can visit with your friends another time. I'm starving, and our table's waiting."

Julian Carrico, owner of La Trattoria de Napoli, greets us at the door. He nods to me and gives me that look, signaling that he remembers me from many months prior when I was at his restaurant one night with my Russian law enforcement partners.

At least that is how I process it.

He brings the menu over to our table once we settle in, describing the evening's specials.

"Good to see you back here so soon," he says, looking at my sister. His remark confuses me because he's blatantly addressing his words to her, not me.

She has never been to his restaurant before, has she?

Unless, of course, she's decided not to reveal it to me. For whatever reason, I can't imagine.

"You must mean my brother, Dennis, right? He recommended your restaurant to me and here I am, but I haven't been here before," she says.

"No? Sorry," he responds, searching for words to extract himself from a possibly embarrassing assumption.

I step in to bail him out. "Julian, I was here months ago with my Russian law enforcement partners. That night, you closed the restaurant for us."

"Oh, yes. I remember. How are they? Are they back in Russia?"

"Yes. Busier than ever. They really enjoyed your restaurant. Thank you for being such a wonderful host that evening. They all told me they'd never forget that night. This is my sister, Jennifer; she loves Italian food, so I just had to bring her. I only returned to Monterey a few days ago. I'm working in Russia these days."

"Interesting. I guess I'm just getting old, but there was a young lady here a few days ago who looked just like you, Ms. Jennifer."

"Oh, yes? And did you talk to her at all? I know you have many customers, and it's impossible to recall every meeting, I suppose," she asks, and instantly, I see where my sister is going with this conversation. She's probing for information, likely suspecting that the young lady was none other than our mysterious 'friend' the LAX woman, the one who told me she lives in the Monterey area with her husband, studying at the language school. I almost want to mention all this to Julian, to free him from his state of embarrassment at the mix-up.

But I don't, staying quiet. Sometimes, things are too peculiar to describe.

Anyway, he can't be that mortified by it since soon, he mentions it again himself.

"You know something? I am pretty good with accents. In fact, I picked up your brother's accent, and remember telling him he was no stranger to the New York area if you know what I mean. But your accent, well, your voice, it's also not much different from that young lady I mistook you for. Well, no matter, I am probably imagining things. You know how it is when we get older ..." He ponders on it, then promptly defends his position again as if unable to let it go. "Honestly, I am good with accents. Might have something to do with being in the restaurant business and having clients from all around the world."

"Well, Julian, where was she from based on her accent?" Jennifer asks.

"Hard to say. Maybe Washington? I seem to recall her asking me about our local seafood and mentioning Maryland crabs. She also named a couple of restaurants in the Washington D.C. area. I think she was with an older gentleman that evening. Much older, so it could have been a relative or a business associate. But I don't probe, you know; it's none of my business. The customers, they deserve their privacy …"

And with this, he is pondering yet again, a quizzical look taking over his slightly distant expression. "But I noticed her jewelry. Her necklace, it looked Greek or Byzantine. Diamonds and sapphire, set in gold, really exquisite. Anyway, don't listen to me, rambling on! Enjoy your dinner. The waiter will come over and take your order. No rush tonight. We don't care about turning over tables, unlike many restaurants in the States. The table is yours for the evening."

With that, he smiles and wanders away with a slight wave of the hand, soon gone.

I turn to my sister, knowing exactly what she must be thinking, able to read her like a book.

"Jen, don't go there. Please don't. Let's just enjoy the evening," I tell her, anticipating she won't let this go. She told me many weeks ago that the LAX woman was no fluke, not a chance encounter. Now with this new and unexpected information from Julian Carrico, she is going to head down the rabbit hole again, losing herself in its tunnels. There will be no stopping her.

"You're the one who brought me here, don't forget that. And you want me to what, just forget it? Seriously? Aren't you wondering what's going on? I thought you were an investigator?"

"I am. So, the girl may have lied to me at LAX about her husband in the army. But so what? I can't blame her. Just because I showed her my FBI credentials doesn't mean she's going to spill her guts about her whole life and everything she's doing in Monterey, right?"

"Stop. Let's back up. You spot her at LAX, thinking she's me. Then you hear her speak. Then you approach her and talk with her. She vanishes when you land at the airport in Monterey, and now she has surfaced right here in little old Carmel, at this restaurant with an older gentleman, wearing an exquisite necklace—no, an unforgettable necklace! Well, for Julian, that is.

"And, oh, it just happens to be at the very same restaurant where you dined with your Russian partners. And you're telling me you're not even wondering or curious about what is going on here? Hmm." She pauses as she looks at the menu. "How is the veal?"

"What? You didn't just ask me about the veal, did you?"

"Yeah, so what? You have something against veal?"

I shrug, moving back to the awkward topic at hand.

"Never mind, long story. So, are we supposed to drop everything and start searching the Monterey peninsula for this mysterious woman? And if we find her, what then? Am I supposed to arrest her for bearing a resemblance to you?"

"We already know her taste in restaurants. Let's call her LAX, OK? And LAX probably enjoys shopping, window shopping, checking out the local jewelry stores and specialty boutiques.

I'm going to be here for a few more days, anyway, so it's an easy decision.

"I'll walk around the downtown area and check out the upscale jewelry stores and boutiques. Perhaps she bought the necklace locally, and if so, a jeweler could recognize her, well, me. They might even think I'm her, then I'll use my 'gifts' to get them to tell me everything they remember. Heck, I may even get a name! They're salespeople after all, and if they think I'm there to buy something else for my exquisite collection … Plus, with a name, we might figure out who she is. If I spot her on the street, I won't approach her, only follow her to her car, home, whatever. Unless she approaches me instead, of course."

Jen never even stops for a breath, leaving me unable to interrupt her lengthy monologue.

She seems to have it all planned out in her head.

What she's just suggested—that the stranger may well approach her—is certainly a possibility; after all, which of us would not stop and speak to a stranger if they happen to be identical to us? It would be far more peculiar to walk on by, saying nothing.

But something tells me it's all a bad—no, a terrible—idea of Jen's.

And I need to stop her before she does something regrettable.

"Please don't do this, Jennifer. I think this is pure coincidence, a fluke, nothing more. It's a strange one, that's for sure. But it doesn't mean there's something nefarious going on with this LAX woman. I know I'll not succeed in changing your mind, and you're going to do whatever you think is right but be careful, okay? Odds are there's nothing here, but if by some remote chance you're on to something, things could take a dramatic turn.

"Remember, I'm heading for Washington tomorrow, then flying back to Russia."

"Yes, I know that," she says with a shrug as if she can't possibly imagine needing me.

"But I won't be able to help you, Jen," I reiterate with greater emphasis.

Whether she wants my help or not, I'm determined not to leave her in a potentially dangerous situation. "Before I leave, let me give you contact information for my old bureau friend, Paul Campo, and for my friend, Monterey County Sheriff Deputy Vance Stevens. Tell them you're my sister, and you need help. They'll respond, that much I can guarantee. Well, I hope it isn't necessary but these few days back here in California have brought a lot more drama than I expected, what with my 'OSI' lead, the developments in the search for the missing Fabergé egg, that South African woman on the beach—no, I actually didn't tell you about that one—the poltergeist in the shop, and now this LAX woman! I don't think I can take much more, frankly. So, let's just relax, try to have a nice quiet dinner, and enjoy the Frank Sinatra music."

I raise my glass of chilled vodka. "To us, the hunters."

Jen gives me a puzzled look.

"Yeah, to the hunters, why not?" she says as we clink glasses. "What is with that music, by the way, and those photos of Frank Sinatra?"

"No. Don't ask. Leave that alone. Please."

"OK, just curious. But what? You don't like Frank Sinatra or Hoboken? That Julian fellow sounds like he's from that part of the world."

"Yep. But not tonight. Your brother needs some downtime. OK?"

"Sure thing, brother. I'll give you a break, I promise … For tonight."

# Chapter 2

My mobile phone rings as soon as I enter my hotel room in Pentagon City. I've been here often; it's close to the Metro, but sufficiently distant from both the District and FBI headquarters. "You're here, right?" the voice asks. I take a second or two before realizing it's Don Pierce, my former boss from the San José Organized Crime and Drug Squad.

"Yeah. So, you've got a tracker on me or what?"

"Yep. Well, Sharon sent me your flight details, and I figured you'd be at the hotel about now. Once you're settled, meet me in the lobby."

"Sure, Don." I try not to allow my mind to speculate what Don has to share with me, whether it's good or bad. I just need to accept it and deal with it.

He's sitting in a quiet corner of the lobby, with his usual cup of black coffee.

He starts as soon as I sit down. "Well, you're probably wondering why I asked you to return to Washington, but it's not that simple. Heck, I'm not thrilled about being here. I hate that place, FBIHQ. I'd rather be windsurfing, believe me. So, here's the deal. Remember your polygraph?"

"Yes, Don. The one I passed and put behind me. That one?"

I'm trying not to be sarcastic.

"The examiner told you that you passed. Well, it's unfortunately not that simple. Apparently, your results were inconclusive; the questions around your foreign contacts gave him the most trouble. I told him you had many foreign contacts. After all, you work in Russia, so what does he expect? I don't know if they want to retest you or interview you, or what their intentions are."

"So, I'm back here for what, Don? I don't want to sound paranoid, but are the counter-intelligence folks behind this? Are they still angry about my engagement with the San Francisco Russian Consulate and my ignoring that other agency's request to be their personal spy? What is this about? If they want to pull me and my family from our assignment in Moscow, fine, pull me, or us, but this is crap, Don. You and I both know it."

"Look, Cos. Just let it play out. You need to go tomorrow morning to the Assistant Director for International Operations. I honestly don't know if this is related to the polygraph. They only told me to reach out and make sure you don't head directly back to Moscow. I asked for details, but they wouldn't give me anything. The only reason I even know about the polygraph is because I know the examiner in that unit."

"Don, I'll be there tomorrow morning, but why are you here, in Washington?" I ask. Sharon told me that Don Pierce was on leave, and the fact he's in Washington seems odd.

"It's nothing to do with you. There's another issue I'm dealing with. It's just a coincidence, so let it go. Hey, you might have to hold off on that lead I sent you from OSI."

"The Nazi war criminals, the ones I'm supposed to find and interview? It will have to wait? Seriously?" What other issue could take precedence over finding Nazi war criminals, still at loose? But with FBIHQ bureaucrats, you just never knew.

Logic and common sense didn't always apply.

"Yep. But they're not going anywhere, believe me."

"OK, Don. I understand. Some part of me thinks that these issues, hanging out there, seemingly unrelated, are in fact related. Maybe it's just creeping paranoia, something like that."

"You know I'm a man of few words, and I'm not a believer in conspiracy theories, but I'll tell you this," he says, and takes a long sip of his coffee. "We're in a different world. Who would have thought we'd ever have an office in Russia and be working with Russian law enforcement? Not me. I once told you that everyone was corrupt in Russia, and your diamond case was a waste of time. Turns out I was wrong. I don't want to tell you that you're just being paranoid about the issues floating all around, from the missing Fabergé egg to the OSI lead, and your being summoned back to FBIHQ. Just go with your gut, your instincts like you did during the Geschke kidnapping case, and it will all work out in the end. I suppose so, anyway."

"Don, you're sounding like my sister. That's a scary thought." I laugh it off.

"Hey, I have to get going, but I'm here if you ever need me. We'll stay in contact. Sharon can always get in touch if you want to reach me urgently. Later, Cos."

Pierce and I shake hands, and he exits the hotel lobby.

Remaining seated at the small corner table, I stare into my coffee cup, trying not to let my mind wander. But the truth is there's been much to ponder these last few days.

It started with the beach run with my sister, when I encountered that mysterious woman from South Africa. Then there was the LAX woman and how she resurfaced at the Carmel restaurant.

Nothing seems to have closure or resolution.

The serial killer's likely out there too, stalking his next victim in Kansas City.

It's all in the past, and a distraction in some ways, or so I often tell my sister and myself.

Jen would tell me otherwise, insisting that the past is always with us, even the past we don't know, such as our grandfather's cases from when he was an NYPD detective so many years ago.

I return to my room to change clothes.

There's still enough light to head for a run on the nearby Mount Vernon trail. While it's no beach, it will have to do for today. I need to clear my mind and reset.

Tomorrow, FBIHQ awaits.

I must accept the fates, good or bad.

# Chapter 3

"Cos, come in, take a seat," Assistant Director Ben Nolan says in response to my knock on his office door. It's not yet eight a.m., but most of the HQ staff look as though they've been here for hours. Nolan stands, closing his door. "I know you weren't expecting to be back here before heading to Moscow. Thanks for coming in. I wouldn't have asked unless it was important."

"It's OK, Ben. I can catch up on some other items while I'm here. So, what's up?"

I just hope they can resolve the issue quickly. My gut is already telling me otherwise.

"Dennis, before we start with the main reason I've brought you in today, let's get the other issue on the table," Nolan says. He pauses and takes a long breath. "I got a visit a few days ago from the counter-intelligence directorate, this recently appointed Deputy Assistant Director Tiffany Ames. She got her hands on a copy of your polygraph results and was waving it in my face, claiming your results were inconclusive, and they need to resolve some 'issues' before you step back inside Russia. I pushed back on that idea, told her I needed you back there."

"So, Ben, she wants what from me? To resign because of inconclusive results? They're still upset about my interactions with the Russian diplomats in San Francisco. What's this about? Payback? They need to let it go. I don't like them, Ben, and I don't trust any of them, frankly. They have issues with agents like me on the criminal investigation side of the organization, dealing with Russian diplomats and foreign law enforcement. And now, I'm in Russia, dealing with their intelligence agencies as well. They feel threatened."

"Cos, I hear you, but they smell blood in the water. Your inconclusive results relate to your contacts with foreign nationals. I told them—well, this Tiffany Ames—that you're in regular contact with foreign nationals. What do they expect when you live and work in Russia?"

"Ben, they can retest me if they want. So, now this is going to hang over my head indefinitely? Well, it's their move. They can object to my returning there, or step aside and let me get back to doing my job."

Nolan reaches into his desk drawer and pulls out an envelope.

"It's for you," he says. "Before you read the contents, let me give you some background. Ames brought this over to me; she tells me the Director's office gave it to them for their review before passing it on to my office, International Operations."

"Yes? And what does this have to do with me?"

"I'm getting there. Patience, Cos. She practically threw the envelope at me, telling me that 'your boy' had been mentioned in the Director's office when the higher-ups were trying to figure out how to handle this one. She called it a 'gift' for me and my department, then stormed out in a huff. You see how my life is here? You better stay out in the field, far away from this place."

I say, "I wouldn't last a day at headquarters. Beware of Greeks bearing gifts."

It just sounds right, given the circumstances. The C-I side of the Bureau notifying Nolan that they had a 'gift' for him … they're up to something, and whatever's in that envelope is no gift.

"Yeah. Funny you mention the Greeks. Well, go ahead, open it up, give it a read. It's from the Director's office, passed through the C-I folks, and now it's yours. Take your time."

I slowly open the envelope and pull out the documents, immediately noticing Russian printed text, several pages of it, followed by what looks to be the English translation.

There are also some official-looking documents in Greek, or at least they appear to be in Greek, and what looks to be some sort of autopsy report with a sketch diagram of a body, perhaps a female. I flip back to the Russian documents.

On closer inspection, they look to be from the Russian embassy in Washington.

The attached cover page is from the Director's office.

The note is brief, but to the point, so I read it aloud.

"Contact senior MVD representative at the Russian Embassy in Athens. FBI to assist MVD to resolve. IOS to support as needed. NTK. Signed, Director."

'NTK' was the Director's personal touch, meaning 'need to know.' The investigation would remain confidential. If you knew about it, you had better have a good reason.

"Ben, what does this have to do with me? I'm in Moscow. This lead, well, my first read on it, looks to have something to do with Greece, not Russia. There's a Legal Attaché office in Athens that's more than capable of dealing with this stuff, right?"

"It's not that simple. Believe me, if I could keep you out of it, I would. The documents in that envelope don't reveal everything. The Director's chief of staff called me; he told me to give you the lead, and you would have the Director's support, but keep everything on the down low.

"Reading between the lines, I think the Director liked how you dealt with the diamond case in San Francisco. Your star is rising, but you can crash and burn in a flash in this organization, as you well know."

"So, what's next? This is a murder investigation? I see the autopsy report. Well, the victim was killed. And her friend, missing or kidnapped."

"Take the file, head over to Athens. The Legal Attaché office knows you're coming and will support you. Believe me, they won't mind you being there. They've already got plenty on their plate to deal with, unrelated to this. They're a regional office and cover several countries. You can read the file on your way across the pond. You've been to Greece before?"

"Yeah, many years ago, as a midshipman. No doubt a lot has changed since those days. I recall Greece was emerging from a period of martial law and practically no one spoke English. Anyway, despite all that, I liked the place back then. So much history, amazing food, and the Greeks were mostly friendly, with just a few exceptions."

"Cos, I don't want to put more pressure on you than you may already feel, but this assignment, straight from the Director, is a priority. It's also time sensitive and it's your only assignment for now. Resolve it as soon as you can. If you need anything, I'm here. Good luck."

I stand up to shake hands with Nolan.

He's got a lot on his mind; I see it in his eyes. Whether he's holding back from revealing more, I can't say, but there's no point in pressing him. I will review the file on the plane ride over to Athens. But first things first, I'll make a quick stop at the Hillwood Estate Museum, and have a look at that genuine, one-of-a-kind Fabergé egg, the Catherine the Great egg.

***

"We're closing in fifteen minutes," says the young woman behind the ticket counter at the Hillwood Estate Museum.

"It's OK. I just want to take a walk through your collection of Fabergé pieces. Is that section open?" I ask. She looks as though she wants to close up for the day.

"Yes. But you have very little time," she says, handing me the ticket. "Here you go. It's complimentary for today. I wouldn't normally do this, so just don't tell anyone. Our secret."

"Thanks. I'm good at keeping secrets, believe me. You can count on it," I tell her.

She laughs.

I'm the only visitor left in the Fabergé room which is filled with an assortment of astonishingly beautiful pieces. But only one item interests me, the Catherine the Great egg.

It's a piece so unique and valuable that it must have its own display case, I figure. And there it is—the case is labeled—but it also isn't.

I have come all the way to the museum in this quiet suburban setting in a tree-lined street in the District of Columbia, and the piece I need to see, as Sharon has told me, isn't here.

I am left standing forlornly, looking at the empty case, contemplating what to do.

"You look disappointed. If you'd come a few minutes earlier, it would've still been there. We store it away in the evening, you see. It's our most valuable piece, as you might appreciate," the voice informs me. I turn to face the woman with the intriguing accent.

She sounds Germanic, but softer, perhaps influenced by other factors—by living abroad, speaking English, and perhaps other languages. It's difficult to say.

"I'm the curator," she goes on to say. "Normally, the staff are responsible for tidying up the place before closing, but we've been understaffed for the last few days, so I've stepped in. I don't mind; it's a privilege to handle such exquisite masterpieces."

"I came here specifically to see your Catherine the Great egg," I tell her.

"Oh? I suppose you're disappointed. Sorry. Can you come back tomorrow?" she asks.

"Unfortunately, I can't. I'm flying out first thing in the morning, and don't know when I will return. It's OK. I understand a thing or two about security," I say, and pause. "Well, there are some who would disagree with that statement, but no matter. I'll try when I return."

"Why did you come so late, just before we close? You're not with anyone else, are you? Well, it doesn't appear so," she says, scanning the room.

A part of me wants to blurt out that I'm an FBI agent, searching for a missing Fabergé egg, and my sole reason for visiting is to see an actual egg up close, to acquaint myself with its fine details so I can spot a real one.

I know nothing about this woman, the one with the intriguing accent I can't quite identify.

She looks like a curator, everything about her physical appearance conveying it, from well-coiffed hair, the lab coat which fits perfectly, down to her plain but practical flat leather shoes.

I extend my hand to introduce myself. Why not? She's the curator, and it might be useful to know someone with an expertise on Fabergé eggs.

"Actually, I'm here on business in a way. Dennis Cosgrove, from the Bureau, the FBI. Nice to meet you," I tell her, figuring, so what if she knows who I am, and that I've come to see their Fabergé egg just minutes before closing time. Nothing to lose, is there?

"Dr. Hedwig Kiesler, the curator here. You can call me Heddy."

"Let me show you my credentials," I tell her as I reach into my jacket pocket.

"Why? I believe you. Follow me," she says as she opens the door to what looks to be a storeroom. "Wait here and I will bring it back out."

In a few minutes, the curator returns with a small wooden box. She places it on the worktable and carefully opens it. There it is, the Catherine the Great egg. It's smaller than I imagined, but its detail is far greater. A person could spend hours gazing at the piece, it's that intricate.

The stock photo that I once saw doesn't come close to revealing its unique artistry.

This is no ordinary work of art. I am stunned, and left speechless, staring at the piece.

"Yes. This is the normal reaction when people first see this extraordinary piece, this piece of history. Quite normal. Does this satisfy your curiosity? Look, I need to lock up. Here's my card in case you need anything in the future. There are missing eggs out there. They are not all accounted for, but you already know that, don't you? It's why you've come, isn't it?"

## About the Author

Dennis T. Cosgrove, as his daughter tells it, lives in 1974—a time and place he's never quite left. His debut novel, *The Diamond Game*, offers an immersive journey through the perspective of a child, a teen, and an FBI Special Agent during the chaotic end of the Cold War. He weaves together his personal and professional life to create a compelling and authentic narrative. His next novel, *Nadezhda Dies Last*, will release soon. You can email him at: dennistcosgrovereaders@gmail.com.